THE PRINCE'S WAR

(THE EMPIRE'S CORPS—BOOK XIX)

CHRISTOPHER G. NUTTALL

The characters and events portrayed in this book are fictitious. Any similarity to real persons, living or dead, is coincidental and not intended by the author.

Text copyright © 2021 Christopher G. Nuttall

All rights reserved.

Printed in the United States of America.

ISBN: 9798466369144
Independently published

No part of this book may be reproduced, or stored in a retrieval system, or transmitted in any form or by any means, electronic, mechanical, photocopying, recording, or other-wise, without express written permission of the publisher.

Cover By Tan Ho Sim
https://www.artstation.com/alientan

PROLOGUE II

EARTH, TEN YEARS BEFORE EARTHFALL

SARAH WILDE AWOKE, in pain and darkness.

It wasn't the first time she'd awoken in a strange place, head throbbing as she tried to recollect what she'd done the previous evening. The sorority motto was practically "one evening in heaven, the next morning in hell" and she knew from bitter experience, after a year at Imperial University, that it was more than technically accurate. She and her peers had consumed vast amounts of everything from alcohol to mood-altering drugs in pursuit of mindless hedonism, all the while doing as little actual studying as they could get away with. It wasn't as if the professors cared. Sarah had heard, from one of the more radical student activists, that the staff preferred students to be zonked out of their minds. It kept them from considering how little they actually *learnt* at the university.

She kept her eyes closed as she quietly assessed the situation. She was lying on a hard stone floor…a relief, given how many times she'd woken up in a stranger's bed. The air stank…she didn't want to think about what it might be. Her clothes were rumpled, but in place. Her body was aching. Her wrists…a flash of alarm shot through her as she realised something cold and hard was wrapped around her wrists. Her hands were firmly bound behind her back…she heard someone moan, the sound far too close for comfort. Her eyes snapped open and she looked around in panic. She was in a cage, surrounded by cold metal bars. And she wasn't alone.

Her memory returned in a flash. There'd been a protest march. She'd gone because it was the popular thing to do, not out of any real conviction. She didn't understand the issues, nor did she care. She'd joined the marchers and then...her memories were scattered, so badly jumbled she wasn't even sure they were in the right order. There'd been bangs and crashes and flashes of light so painful she'd thought she'd been blinded and then...and then nothing, until she'd woken in a cell. Her heart sank as she looked from face to face. She didn't recognise anyone within eyeshot, but they were all clearly in the same boat. They'd all been arrested.

Sarah swallowed, hard. It wouldn't be *that* bad, she told herself. The cops would realise they'd made a mistake soon enough. She'd heard stories of being arrested, stories told by activists, that made it sound like a grand adventure. She heard someone being sick behind her, coughing and spitting to keep from choking on their own vomit. An adventure? She promised herself that she'd never go to another protest march as long as she lived. The activists could find someone else to march in their protests.

Someone catcalled. She looked up and through the bars. There was another cage on the far side of a walkway, crammed with male prisoners. They looked savage...she shuddered helplessly, trying not to draw attention. The bars didn't seem solid any longer. She lowered her head, wishing for water...wishing it was just a nightmare, wishing she could wake up in her own bed. She heard banging and crashing in the distance and forced herself to look, just in time to see two uniformed women marching towards them. They were banging their truncheons on the bars, waking the prisoners from their slumber. Sarah groaned in pain as the noise grew louder. She wanted—needed—them to stop.

The women stopped in front of the cage and peered at the prisoners. "You," the leader said, jabbing a finger at a girl in a tattered pink dress. "On your feet."

The girl shook her head. "I want my lawyer."

"Hah." The guards laughed. "She wants a lawyer."

Sarah opened her mouth to protest, but it was too late. The lead guard pointed a flashlight-like device at the protesting girl. Her entire body jerked, twisting unnaturally. She screamed in pain, then collapsed in a heap. Sarah stared in horror, unable to understand what had happened. It was…it was unthinkable. It was beyond her imagination. It was…

The guard pointed at her. "You. On your feet."

Sarah forced herself to stand, despite her fear. The guard beckoned her forward, through the cage door, then shoved her down the corridor. Sarah tried to keep track of their movements, as they frogmarched her through a string of unmarked corridors and elevators that went up and down at random, but rapidly lost her bearings. It occurred to her she was being marched in circles, just to confuse her, although it seemed pointless. The building was just too big. She wondered just where they were. She hadn't seen any large police station within the university sector, not on any of the public maps. But she'd also been told there was a great deal that was never put on the terminals.

They shoved her into a small room and pushed her onto a stool, then stepped back. Sarah looked up and saw a man sitting behind a desk, his eyes on a terminal in front of him. He looked bored and harassed, his face suggesting he no longer gave a damn about his job or *anything*. She shivered, despite herself. She'd seen that expression before, on the maintenance staff who kept the university running. They seemed to loathe the students they served with a white-hot passion. She had always wondered why they didn't look for better jobs.

The man spoke in a bored monotone. "You have been convicted of public disorderliness, taking part in an unlicensed political rally and various other charges. Your appeal has been filed, reviewed and rejected. The original conviction stands. You have been sentenced to involuntary transportation."

Sarah blinked. It was hard to follow his words, but…"I…I want a lawyer."

"You have already been convicted," the man said. His tone didn't change. "You were caught in the performance of illegal activity. The state-appointed lawyer made a valiant attempt to defend you and your comrades, but the evidence was damning. The appeal was unsuccessful. You have been sentenced to...."

"I...." Sarah swallowed, hard. "It was...you can't do this!"

"You were caught in the performance of illegal activity," the man repeated. "You have been convicted."

Sarah stared at him in shock. It...she'd heard rumours, sure, about what happened to people who stepped too far out of line, but she'd never taken them seriously. No one she knew *really* believed them. The police were a joke. It was....

The man didn't wait for her to speak. "Your contract has been sold to the New Doncaster Development Corporation. You will be transported to New Doncaster shortly, once the remainder of the involuntary transportees have been processed. You may make a choice. As a young and presumably fertile woman, you may marry a farmer on the planet and assist him in developing his territory. If you agree to this, the corporation will forgive the debt you owe them. If you...."

Sarah found her voice. "I don't owe them anything!"

"They bought out your contract," the man said. "They own you."

"You can't own a person!" Sarah tried not to raise her voice, but it was hard. "Slavery was banned under the constitution...."

"You're a convicted criminal," the man said. "You have to pay your debt to society. The corporation has bought your contract and is offering you the chance to repay them...."

"By marrying a man I've never met and...." Sarah found it hard to put her thoughts into words. "It's barbaric! My parents...."

"Are no longer part of the issue," the man said. For the first time, she heard a hint of exasperation. "The corporation *owns* you. You can repay your debt, in the manner they suggest, and the slate will be wiped clean. Or you will find yourself on contract duty when you reach the planet, which could be anything from working in the fields to slaving in a brothel. You would be well-advised to accept their terms and strive to make it work. This is the one chance you'll get."

Sarah shook her head. "I'm not a slave!"

"The corporation owns you," the man repeated. "Maybe you are not *legally* a slave. The fact remains they can treat you as one until you repay their debt. Choose."

"I can't...." Sarah tried to protest. "I don't know...."

"Choose," the man repeated. "I have no more time."

Sarah pinched herself. Nothing happened. It was...it was a nightmare. She'd only gone to a protest march! It wasn't as if she'd done something *really* wrong. And yet...she recalled hearing, somewhere, that Earth was so overpopulated that the sentence for just about *anything* was deportation, unless one had a good lawyer. She wanted to demand her rights, as a free citizen, but...tears prickled in her eyes as she realised she wasn't a free citizen any longer. She was property. She'd been sold to the highest bidder. Her family would never see her again. Would they ever know what had happened to her? Would they try to come looking? Or would they simply wind up arrested and deported themselves? Or....

Cold anger burnt through her as she gathered herself. She'd survive, she vowed. She'd build a new life for herself...no, she'd make the corporation regret it had ever enslaved her. She'd make it pay, even if it cost her everything. She'd make it pay.

"Very well," she said. She needed to play dumb, for a while, until she knew what was really going on. And then she'd find a way to take advantage. "I'll do as the corporation says."

And then, her thoughts added silently, *I'll make them pay.*

CHAPTER ONE

MARINE BOOT CAMP, MERLIN

THE WOODS WERE DARK, oppressive.

Roland, once Prince Roland of Earth and now Recruit Roland Windsor of the 7th Training Regiment, kept his head down as the squad picked their way through the trees. Visibility was terrifyingly variable, streams of light broken by pools of shadow that made a mockery of his enhanced eyes. The trees were large enough to conceal infantrymen below, their branches easily big enough to host a sniper or two. He swept his eyes from side to side, all too aware the enemy could be lurking anywhere. The mission *had* to be completed successfully. He wanted—*needed*—to progress. He couldn't go to the Slaughterhouse until he convinced his instructors that he could become a full-fledged Marine.

Take it seriously, he told himself, sharply. *You don't want to get into shit because you were woolgathering when you needed to watch for trouble.*

He inched around a tree, then darted to the next. The mission was relatively simple, they'd been told, but the simplest things were often the most complex. The training company—broken down into squads—had to make its way through the forest, flushing out the enemy positions before they could rally and counterattack. Roland was tempted to wonder if they'd been sent on a wild goose chase—he'd heard shooting, yet hadn't seen the enemy—but he knew better. The fact the enemy *hadn't* greeted them with a hail of fire was almost certainly a bad sign. They were probably dug in somewhere further into the forest, waiting for the recruits to stumble into their trap. Roland cursed under his breath as he paused, listening carefully for the slightest hint of movement. It was hard to be sure. The local wildlife was just too loud. A drunkard could pass unnoticed against the din.

Goddamned insects, he thought. He wasn't sure who'd thought to introduce the tiny bugs to the training ground, but it was a stroke of evil genius. The chattering bugs provided all the sonic cover a hidden enemy force could want. *If only we could get rid of them.*

Recruit Walsh stepped up beside him, her face pale. Roland glanced at her, then held up a hand to signify she should remain behind as the rest of the squad advanced. They were dangerously spread out, and he was tempted to suggest they closed up, but he knew it would be asking for trouble. Their uniforms were supposed to make it hard for the enemy to detect them, yet hard wasn't the same as impossible. A single drone, orbiting so far above them even *his* enhanced eyes couldn't see it, would be enough to call fire down on their heads, if they slipped up and showed themselves. Better to remain spread out until they knew where their targets were. He nodded to the others, then resumed the advance. If he drew fire himself....

Nothing happened. The treeline remained quiet. Roland frowned. He wouldn't be *happy* if someone hit him—the instructors would be very sarcastic, even if he hadn't fucked up—but the rest of the squad could unleash hell on their opponents. It would be better to know the worst at once, rather than remain in ignorance of the enemy positions. The training ground was huge, easily large enough for an entire army to remain hidden if it wished. Roland kept his eyes open as the squad moved up to join him, but there was nothing. It was all too easy to believe they were completely alone.

Or we're lost, which puts us on track for promotion to lieutenant and a court-martial, he thought, with a flicker of amusement. He'd no idea why so many Marines seemed to believe their lieutenants couldn't read maps—his first exercise in map-reading had been a disaster, yet he'd gotten better at it with practice—but it didn't matter. *There's no way we can simply march out of the training ground and get hopelessly lost.*

The squad continued to advance, pushing through the trees and avoiding the handful of half-baked trails within the woods. Roland couldn't tell if they'd been made by animals or humans, although they'd been taught to stay off the paths as much as possible. A *smart* enemy would have their mortars already zeroed on the path, ready to unleash hell the moment their targets came into view. Unless…sweat continued to trickle down his back as the trees opened suddenly, revealing a grassy valley with a farmhouse and a pair of barns at the bottom. It looked deserted, but that was meaningless. The enemy could be using it as a base. They had to clear it before they continued the advance.

He glanced at the rest of the squad, then led the way forward at a run. Their uniforms were designed to provide a certain amount of concealment, but he'd been cautioned not to rely on it. The human eye was attracted to movement, even if it couldn't make out what was actually *moving*. Roland had heard cautionary tales of defenders who'd been so keyed up they'd fired at shadows. He'd thought the stories were absurd until he'd been on guard duty himself. It had worn him down so much he'd nearly fired on a friendly convoy. And *that* would have landed him in real trouble. Better to get into attack range before the enemy had time to react to their presence.

Roland reached the side of the farmhouse, unhooked a flashbang from his belt and hurled it through the window, looking away as the grenade detonated. The flashbangs weren't lethal, at least under normal circumstances, but anyone caught in the blast would be too busy projectile vomiting or trying not to collapse to worry about the intruders. He counted to five, then allowed Walsh to heft him up and *through* the window. He landed neatly, weapon raised and ready. The room was deserted. There weren't even any tripwires that might be linked to IEDs or other surprises. He frowned as the rest of the squad joined him, then carefully led the way through the rest of the house. It looked oddly clean for a building in the middle of a training ground. That worried him, although he wasn't sure why. The corps was known for its attention to detail. The instructors would have gone to some trouble to make sure the building *looked* as though it had been abandoned in a hurry.

"Search the barns," he ordered, as they completed their sweep and hurried outside. "Quickly."

His heart pounded as they glided through the rest of the farm. The farmhouse was nice and rustic, but it might also be a trap. They hadn't had *time* to thoroughly search it. He checked his threat detector and saw nothing, but it wasn't reassuring. There was an ongoing war between the techs who designed early warning and detection technology and the insurgents who tried to come up with ways to fool it. It was quite possible they'd missed something. The instructors were ruthlessly pessimistic. If there was even a slightest chance someone would be hit, they'd be hit. There was no room for the luck of the draw on the training ground.

Hard training, easy mission, Roland quoted, silently. *Easy training, get the shit kicked out of you on a real mission.*

Recruit Singh caught his eye. "It's clear, sir."

Roland nodded, turning his eyes towards the far side of the valley. *Anything* could be hidden within the trees, anything at all. He was tempted to call in and ask for support, perhaps even an update from the drones, but he knew it would be pointless. They'd been cautioned not to risk any sort of contact until they encountered the enemy, just in case. His superiors would not be amused if he risked contact just because he needed his hand held. They'd be very sarcastic.

He scowled as the squad prepared to resume the advance. His fellow recruits didn't know him as anything other than Roland Windsor, a young recruit keen to be the best of the best, but his instructors knew who he'd been, only a few short months ago. Roland didn't blame them, not really, for having their doubts about him. He looked back at himself when he'd been the Childe Roland, Heir to the Imperial Throne of Earth, and cringed.

He'd been a spoilt little brat, a mindless pleasure-seeker who'd drunk and drugged himself constantly just to stave off boredom...he shuddered when he remembered everything he'd done, to people who didn't dare say *no*. He'd been trapped in a gilded cage and he hadn't even *known* it, not then. He'd been a puppet who couldn't even see the strings!

His eyes swept the distant hills, although his thoughts were elsewhere. Specialist Belinda Lawson, a Marine Pathfinder, had saved his life and soul. She'd swept into his palace and transformed his life, knocking some sense into his head...too late to save the planet, perhaps, but not too late to make a man out of him. Shame swept over him as he remembered how he'd tried to get her into bed, as if she'd be interested in an overweight princeling. And she was dead...or worse. His superiors—his new superiors -hadn't been entirely clear on what had happened, but he feared the worst. She would have come to see him, wouldn't she? He wanted to believe she would have.

Perhaps you were just another assignment to her, his thoughts pointed out. *You were surrounded by people who were paid to keep you happy and dumb, people who didn't give a shit about you. She might not have given a shit about you either.*

He tensed, suddenly, as he heard rotor blades in the distance. A helicopter swept low over the hills, heading straight towards them. Roland swore as he saw the weapon pods hanging under its stubby wings; anti-tank rockets and heavy machine guns that would punch through his body armour as though it wasn't even there. The training brief hadn't mentioned helicopters...not directly, at least. The instructors had a habit of throwing unpleasant surprises into the mix, just to make sure the recruits knew their intelligence, no matter how much the spooks vouched for it, couldn't be taken for granted.

"Take cover," he shouted. "Hurry!"

The sound grew louder as he hurled himself into a ditch, near the farmhouse. His mind raced as he saw Walsh take up position near the treeline. The farmhouse might have been a trap after all, although not in the way he'd thought. There could be someone on the hillside with a low-tech telescope, linked to a simple telephone line...he sucked in his breath. His instructors had warned him, time and time again, that just because something was outdated didn't mean it was useless. A pre-space telescope and telephone wire would be pretty much impossible to detect unless the Marines got lucky.

He stayed still as the helicopter thundered over the valley, rotors chopping through the air. Insurgents had learnt to fear the ugly aircraft a long time ago, all too aware the pilots could rain down death on them from overhead in relative safety. It took a great deal of luck to take down a helicopter without MANPADs or other heavy weapons, luck the umpires wouldn't grant in a training exercise. Roland gritted his teeth, hoping the helicopter pilot would assume they'd gotten into the treeline before the aircraft got into position. Between the camouflage and the local wildlife confusing the craft's sensors, they might just get lucky.

They know we can't have gotten that far away, he thought. It didn't *look* as though the helicopter was carrying a squad of troops, but appearances could be misleading. The aircraft was big enough to carry six or seven men in addition to the pilot and gunners, if they didn't mind getting very friendly. Roland himself had been crammed into tiny aircraft with his peers several times, during the last few months. *And they might think they have us pinned down....*

The helicopter fired a machine gun burst into the trees. Roland frowned, unsure what the gunner had seen. None of the shells had gone anywhere near the recruits, not unless he'd misjudged where the other two had hidden. Perhaps they'd seen a fox or something move and fired on instinct or...perhaps they were just trying to intimidate the recruits. It might work out for them. Roland didn't dare move, which meant they'd be pinned down right until the exercise ended or they were caught by the bad guys and humiliated...he peered towards the treeline, wondering if there was already a line of enemy troops moving towards them. It wasn't as if *they* had to worry about being seen.

Book One: The Empire's Corps
Book Two: No Worse Enemy
Book Three: When The Bough Breaks
Book Four: Semper Fi
Book Five: The Outcast
Book Six: To The Shores
Book Seven: Reality Check
Book Eight: Retreat Hell
Book Nine: The Thin Blue Line
Book Ten: Never Surrender
Book Eleven: First To Fight
Book Twelve: They Shall Not Pass
Book Thirteen: Culture Shock
Book Fourteen: Wolf's Bane
Book Fifteen: Cry Wolf
Book Sixteen: Favour The Bold
Book Seventeen: Knife Edge
Book Eighteen: The Halls of Montezuma
Book Nineteen: The Prince's War
http://www.chrishanger.net
http://chrishanger.wordpress.com/
http://www.facebook.com/ChristopherGNuttall
ALL COMMENTS WELCOME!

CONTENTS

HISTORIAN'S NOTE vii
PROLOGUE I ix
PROLOGUE II xiii

Chapter One 1
Chapter Two 10
Chapter Three 19
Chapter Four 28
Chapter Five 37
Chapter Six 46
Chapter Seven 55
Chapter Eight 64
Chapter Nine 73
Chapter Ten 82
Chapter Eleven 91
Chapter Twelve 100
Chapter Thirteen 109
Chapter Fourteen 118
Chapter Fifteen 127
Chapter Sixteen 136
Chapter Seventeen 145
Chapter Eighteen 154
Chapter Nineteen 163
Chapter Twenty 172
Chapter Twenty-One 181
Chapter Twenty-Two 190
Chapter Twenty-Three 199
Chapter Twenty-Four 208
Chapter Twenty-Five 217

Chapter Twenty-Six	226
Chapter Twenty-Seven	235
Chapter Twenty-Eight	244
Chapter Twenty-Nine	253
Chapter Thirty	262
Chapter Thirty-One	271
Chapter Thirty-Two	280
Chapter Thirty-Three	289
Chapter Thirty-Four	298
Chapter Thirty-Five	307
Chapter Thirty-Six	316
Chapter Thirty-Seven	325
Chapter Thirty-Eight	334
Chapter Thirty-Nine	343
Chapter Forty	352
AFTERWORD	359
APPENDIX	365
HOW TO FOLLOW	371

HISTORIAN'S NOTE

The Prince's War is written to be as self-contained as possible, but refers to events within *When the Bough Breaks* (*The Empire's Corps III*) which are summarised in the prologue. It takes place roughly a year after *When the Bough Breaks* and a month after *The Halls of Montezuma*.

CGN.

PROLOGUE I

FROM: *An Unbiased History of the Imperial Royal Family*. Professor Leo Caesius. Avalon. 206PE.

IT IS EXTREMELY DIFFICULT TO TRACE the history of the Imperial Royal Family—as it became known—past the final stages of the disintegration and the early days of the Unification Wars. Part of this, of course, is an inevitable result of the wars and their attendant devastation; a great many records were lost and/or deliberately destroyed during the fighting. Certain factions, particularly during the opening stages of the conflict, believed that it would be better to erase the past so the human race could stride forward into a brave new future, and therefore set out to capture or destroy as many records as possible. Others simply ignored the danger of historical erasure, and revisionism, until it was too late.

But a far more significant problem was caused by the newborn Imperial Household's determination to legitimatise its position. There were no shortage of academics willing to take thirty pieces of silver—or, more practically, lands and titles—in exchange for creating largely or entirely fictional genealogies for their patrons to use as propaganda. The results were quite remarkable. The First Emperor was hailed as the direct descendent of such figures as Alexander the Great, Augustus Caesar, Elizabeth Tudor and many others, ranging from Albert Einstein to George Washington and Joe Buckley. Links were drawn between him and nearly *every* figure of consequence, to a truly absurd degree. He was not only the sole heir to every kingdom on Old Earth, but also lands that simply never existed, including little known fictional kingdoms such as Gondor, Narnia and Wakanda.

This had two unfortunate—and entirely predictable—effects on academic enquiry. An unwary student, more intent on getting a good grade rather than actually *think* about the material in front of him, might not notice the inconsistencies and frank impossibilities, such as a marriage between Queen Elizabeth Tudor of England (1533-1603, PSE) and Shaka Zulu (1787-1828, PSE), a marriage that would have been unlikely even if the two *hadn't* lived and died nearly two hundred years apart. A more perceptive student, on the other hand, might realise there were just too many discrepancies to be accidental and come to the conclusion that the whole field was irredeemably damaged beyond repair. Such students would either leave of their own accord or, if they alienated their academic supervisors, would be pushed out or simply sidelined. The Imperial University's administrators knew very well there were fields of enquiry that could not be touched, not without angering their patrons. What was the life of one student compared to the whole university?

Perversely, the truth is better than the fairy tale. The First Emperor—whose name was largely stricken from the records, to be replaced by a decidedly impersonal title—was a high-ranking military officer during the early years of the disintegration. Realising the endless wars were futile—his autobiography makes no mention of the burning ambition that was a mark of his career—he convinced a number of his fellows to mount a coup, seized control of the government and then embarked upon a series of increasingly sophisticated military campaigns to bring the rest of the settled worlds under his control. He was more than *just* a naval officer, it must be noted; his skill at convincing former opponents to join him, or at the very least not to oppose him, was quite remarkable. When he took the title of Emperor, he rewarded his followers by making them Grand

Senators. They in turn rewrote history to make it appear they had *always* been part of the rightful ruling class.

Whatever else can be said about the First Emperor, he did his work well. By the time his son succeeded to the Imperial Throne, the empire was on a solid footing and could easily survive a handful of weak or clumsy rulers. There was enough of a balance of power, the ruling class felt, to ensure both a degree of stability *and* a certain amount of social mobility. It should have endured forever.

It did not.

It took years—centuries—for decay to start to take hold, but it did. A trio of weak emperors allowed the Grand Senate to take more and more power for itself, then—worse—failed to play the different factions within the senate to right the balance of power. Social mobility slowed to a crawl, successive emperors losing much of their influence as they were increasingly dominated by the aristocracy. Many lost themselves in mindless hedonism, whiling away the hours with wine, women, song and pleasures forbidden even to the aristocracy. The handful who tried to reclaim their birthright were swiftly slapped down by the new rulers of empire. Emperor Darren II was assassinated—it was blamed on terrorists, but the act was clearly ordered by the aristocracy—and Empress Lyudmila was held prisoner by her unwanted husband, then murdered when she produced an heir.

By the time the Empire entered its final days, the Imperial Throne was occupied—to all intents and purposes—by Prince Roland, known to the public as the Childe Roland. He was officially declared a great moral and spiritual leader, but the reality was somewhat different. Prince Roland—the Grand Senate hadn't been able to decide on when he should be formally crowned—was, by the time he entered his teenage years, a useless layabout. The only good thing that could be said about him, it should be noted, was that he'd not fallen as far into depravity as some of his ancestors. It was generally believed that it was just a matter of time.

The Commandant of the Terran Marine Corps, in a desperate bid to turn the situation around, made use of the Corps's long-held power to appoint bodyguards to the Imperial Household and assigned Specialist Belinda Lawson to take care of the prince and, hopefully, make a man out of him. She was rather more successful than one might expect, knocking some sense into the nearly adult prince, but it was already too late. Earth collapsed into chaos and it was all Belinda could do, along with the prince, to escape. The Empire died and, as far as anyone outside the Corps knew at the time, Prince Roland died with it. In reality, he was transferred to a Marine Corps starship.

This was, as far as the Corps was concerned, an awkward position. Roland *was* the legal ruler of the known galaxy. However, practically speaking, he ruled nothing. The Empire was dead and gone. The Corps could not recover even the Core Worlds, already blighted by civil war, let alone the rest of the settled worlds. Roland was an Emperor without an Empire; an unfinished young man who might be an asset but might equally become a burden. And that left the Corps with a serious problem.

What—exactly—were they going to do with Prince Roland?

He frowned. He could hit the helicopter with a rifle-launched grenade, if he could get up and take aim before the craft blew him to atoms. But... he didn't have time. Roland knew, without false modesty, that he was one of the fastest gunners in the training company and even *he* didn't have enough time to take out the helicopter, not unless something happened to divert its attention. His mind churned. He needed a diversion. If he did nothing, they were screwed.

A plan occurred to him. He put it into action before he could think better of it. He signalled Walsh, instructing her to send a microburst message to their superiors. The messages were supposed to be undetectable and untraceable, but he knew the helicopter would have the very latest in detection gear, manned by people who knew precisely what to look for. The aircraft rotated rapidly, bringing its machine guns to bear on Walsh. Roland didn't hesitate. He rolled over, slotted the grenade into place and fired it at the helicopter. It went through the gunner's hatch and detonated inside. A moment later, the helicopter rose into the sky and vanished.

Got you, Roland thought. The boot camp was supposed to be realistic, but even *his* instructors drew the line at using *real* bullets and grenades. The helicopter was officially dead now and would remain so until the exercise terminated. *You'll be buying the drinks when we finally get some leave....*

He tried not to feel guilty as he stumbled to his feet and looked at Walsh. She wasn't dead, of course, but her training suit had locked up. She would remain immobile until the exercise ended or, depending on timing, the umpires collected her and put her on the sidelines. She'd be hopping mad afterwards, Roland reflected as the other two joined him. He promised himself he'd make it up to her, if he could. He would almost sooner have preferred to be 'killed' himself. At least he would have volunteered to serve as a human sacrifice.

There was no time to discuss it, he told himself, firmly. *She'll understand.*

He gritted his teeth as they resumed their march through the trees. He'd been told, when he'd been a child, that it was his duty to look after the empire as a whole, rather than the individual people within it. He hadn't realised, until much later, that it was a form of manipulation, that one could justify almost anything by insisting it was for the good of the empire. What was a single life compared to the uncountable trillions who made up the empire as a whole? It was nothing more than a number, perhaps even a rounding error. It was hard to argue that a single life mattered....

And yet, Walsh was a friend. He knew her. He knew she'd had hopes and dreams of her own before Earthfall. He knew she wanted to be a Marine, that she'd joined the training company in hopes of making it to the Slaughterhouse. She was a living breathing person, a friend and a rival, a comrade and an enemy...no, never an *enemy*. They might have been on opposing teams, from time to time, but they weren't *enemies*. He respected her and the rest of the company in a way he'd never respected anyone, back when he'd been the Childe Roland. And she was going to be mad at him in the aftermath of the exercise. She was probably going to punch him in the face.

Which is no more than you deserve, his thoughts mocked. If someone had done that to him, without his permission, he would have been livid. *Belinda would probably have kicked you in the nuts. It was bad enough when you tried to cop a feel....*

He pushed that thought out of his mind and forced himself to keep going, heading towards the enemy position. Time was running out. They had to flush the enemy out before the umpires called a halt, before...he wondered if he'd be ordered to retake the training section again. He'd done some sections of boot camp twice now, at the whim of his superiors. Roland wasn't sure if they were testing his patience, if they thought he'd tell them he wanted to quit if they didn't let him complete boot camp and advance to the Slaughterhouse, or if they just wanted to be sure he knew everything he needed before it was too late. The Slaughterhouse was the final test, as far as the corps were concerned. And he was damned if he was failing. He owed it to Belinda to succeed.

Singh made a gesture as he peered around a tree. *Enemy in sight.*

Roland nodded, pushing his thoughts and doubts aside. They'd located the enemy lines. It was time to make war. He'd worry about the rest afterwards…

…And yet, as he braced himself for the advance, he couldn't help wondering if he *really* had what it took to become a Marine.

CHAPTER TWO

BARAKA ISLAND, NEW DONCASTER

"THEY'RE LATE," Steve Rowe whispered.

Sarah Wilde shook her head as she pulled the cloak tighter around her hair, concealing as much as she could. They were over twenty miles from the nearest official settlement, well away from anyone who had any interest in reporting their presence, but there was no point in taking chances. She'd learnt her lessons well, in the ten years she'd spent on New Doncaster. They'd been paid in blood and pain and humiliation...she clenched her fist, then calmed herself. There was no point in showing her anger so openly either. Her men wouldn't be impressed.

She clasped her hands behind her back and waited, feeling sweat seeping into her shirt. The heat had once daunted her, leaving her drained and worn after an hour in the sun, but she'd grown used to it over the years. The sky was darkening rapidly, the twin moons hidden behind tropical clouds. A storm was on the way. She could feel it in the air. It was never easy to predict the weather, not on a world as bizarre as New Doncaster, but the locals knew how to read the signs. Those who didn't learn before it was too late rarely lived long.

Steve glanced towards the distant peaks. "The squad is in position."

"Good." Sarah allowed herself a tight smile. The militia had been patrolling more aggressively lately, as if the landowners had come to realise they had worse problems than a few bandits or runaway indents. She had no idea what had gotten into them—her sources hadn't been too clear on who'd issued the orders, or why—but there was nothing to be gained by worrying. "Tell them to keep a close eye on the approaches."

"Of course." Steve shot her a jaunty salute, then turned away. "I'll see to it at once."

Sarah hid her amusement as the younger man hurried into the shadows. It wasn't easy to keep the young men from starting a fight, from allowing years of bitter resentment and anger to turn to violence…a fight, she knew all too well, the rebels would lose. It had taken her years to come to grips with the local power structure, to understand how the landowners dominated the world; she'd needed months to put together a plan to take the bastards down, then longer—perhaps too long—to put the pieces in place. Steve and his comrades didn't understand the value of patience, even though they'd *seen* militiamen—and the regular troops—crashing through the jungles and swarming the islands to get at rebels and runaways. It wouldn't be long, she feared, before they jumped with or without her. They wanted to be free while they were young enough to enjoy it.

Something moved in the darkening sky. Sarah sucked in her breath as a dark shape materialised from the clouds, dropping rapidly towards them. The orbital satellite network was a joke, and the weather patterns made it hard to track even a full-sized shuttle passing through the atmosphere, but it was still possible *someone* had caught a sniff of the shuttle as it dropped out of orbit. Or that there was a spy, somewhere within her organisation. Sarah had done everything in her power to keep the information compartmentalised—she'd isolated or killed a handful of chatterboxes, even though they'd probably been innocent—but she was uncomfortably aware word might have spread further than she'd like. The loudmouths and agitators weren't the problem. The real problem was the spy who kept his mouth shut, then reported back to his masters. She couldn't keep *everyone* in lockdown or all hell would break loose.

The shuttle descended smoothly, barely slowing until it was only a few short metres above the treeline. Sarah held up her flashlight, blinking it on and off to tell the shuttle precisely where to land. She hadn't given them precise coordinates, not when the spacers couldn't be trusted. Some of them hated and feared the landowners as much as the plantation workers, debtors and townies; some were only in it for the money. She felt a wave of envy, mingled with resentment. If she'd been sent to the spacers instead, who knew what she might have made of herself?

She put the thought aside as the shuttle landed neatly on the ground, hatches snapping open a moment later. Sarah heard thunder in the distance as she motioned to the coolies, then hurried forward. The coolies were too much like the debtor labour gangs for her peace of mind—she'd once spent a few hours looking up where the word came from, then shuddered—but there was no choice. There were few paths in the jungle. The rebels couldn't have driven trucks to the landing zone even if it wouldn't have drawn unfriendly attention.

A spacer, face already shining with sweat, met her at the hatch. "Everything's here."

Sarah nodded. There was no time for anything else, not even basic politeness. The shuttle had to be unloaded quickly, the coolies carrying the boxes deeper into the jungle before it was too late. If the militia caught a shuttle on the ground…it would be bad. The spacers prided themselves on not bending the knee to the landowners, but they weren't meant to get involved in planetary affairs. It would cause a major incident if the shuttle *did* get caught. The landowners would insist on more supervision of the high orbitals…if nothing else, the more independent-minded spacers might decline to continue supplying weapons to the rebels. They'd be embarrassed as hell. Their peers would be pissed for bringing more planetary control and regulation into their lives. And they might leave the system once and for all.

She hefted a box, then carried it out of the shuttle. Her subordinates were already dividing up the goods, directing the coolies to carry them to the hidden bases with the ease of long practice. Sarah allowed herself another smile. The rebels weren't entirely democratic—they couldn't afford to take a vote in the middle of a war—but she'd made sure everyone took a turn at being the boss, partly to see who had real potential and partly to ensure everyone remembered they were all in it together. The last thing they needed was a split between upper and lower rebels. The landowners would take full advantage of a crack in the ranks.

"We'll see you in a week," the spacer said. His shipsuit looked drenched, as if he'd gone swimming without bothering to undress first. Sarah understood. The heat had caught her by surprise too, the moment she'd been marched out of the shuttle. "Good luck."

Sarah nodded and turned away, slinging the box over her shoulder. It was uncomfortable as hell, but bearable. Besides, it was important that she was seen to be doing her fair share of the work. Too many of the older rebels still saw her as an upstart...she'd loathed it at the time, but she understood now. They'd never been sure how much they could trust a newcomer. She had the same problem now.

Steve hurried up to her, his face grim. "We have incoming, from the north!"

"Shit!" Sarah forced herself to think. The northern trail was wide enough to take armoured cars, but they'd have heard them coming a long time before they came into view. "How many?"

"Looks like a platoon, perhaps two," Steve told her. "No heavy weapons."

Sarah bit down on a curse. Men on foot could make it to the landing zone before the shuttle took off, before the rebels had a chance to get into the jungle and vanish. It was unusually brave of the local militia to come so far from the plantations...she wondered, suddenly, if they were facing regular troops rather than the militiamen. It wasn't impossible, but unlikely. The regulars normally drove around in armoured cars, rather than advancing on foot. But if they'd caught a sniff of the shuttle....

"Tell the guards to engage them, at a distance," she ordered. "Keep them back."

Steve frowned. "We could take them."

"No." Sarah shook her head. Steve was right, in the short term. They *could* wipe out the enemy platoon. In the long term...they'd draw too much attention too quickly. "Give the order. Slow them down long enough for us to escape."

"Understood," Steve said. "I'll see you back home."

Sarah nodded and turned away, motioning for the remainder of the coolies to pick up speed as the shuttle crew prepped for departure. The thunderstorm was growing closer now. It wouldn't be long before the rain started, reducing visibility to almost nothing. The rebels and the militia might be within bare metres of each other, neither side aware the other was there until the skies started to clear. It had happened, time and time again....

And just pray Steve does as he's told, she thought, as she joined the retreat. *We don't want to alert the landowners until we're ready to put a knife in their backs.*

• • •

Lieutenant Richard Collier had decided, after only a few short hours, that he hated Baraka Island. The air was hot and humid, the insects seemed to love the taste of human blood and, worst of all, the militia thought they were the best of the best, swanning around in uniforms so ostentatious that he was surprised they weren't all dead from heatstroke. Their leader, Captain Tarquin Ludlow, was so keen to make a name for himself that he'd even insisted on going out on a night patrol, despite the complete lack of air cover and armoured cars. Richard scowled at the upper-class twit, seriously wondering what would happen if he *accidentally* put a bullet in the young man's back. Richard had faced enough runaways, bandits and outright rebels to *know* the militiamen were dangerously exposed.

He kept his face under control as the platoon advanced up the trail. Ludlow was brave enough, he supposed, but there was a difference between bravery and sheer, pig-headed stupidity. The militiamen were trained to fight in defence of their homes, and landowner plantations; they weren't experienced enough to face the rebels deep within the jungle. It would be nice to bring home a few scalps—Ludlow had openly promised to put heads on display to discourage other rebels—but Richard hoped they made it through the patrol without encountering the enemy. Ludlow seemed bound and determined to bring the rebels down on their heads.

Which would make sense, if we had supporting elements in place, Richard told himself. He'd forced himself to study tactics throughout the ages when he'd been promoted, all too aware a townie officer had to be twice as good as any landholder if he wanted to see promotion again. *But we don't....*

Thunder rumbled, in the distance. Richard glanced at the sky. Lightning was flashing within the clouds. It was going to rain...they'd have to find shelter, somewhere, and hope for the best. The roads were going to turn to mud, once the rain began. He'd been in convoys that had been stopped by the roads suddenly turning into swamps. The ever-present sound of buzzing insects grew louder, just as a dark shape appeared above the treeline and kept rising. Richard blinked. A shuttle? It couldn't be a legitimate landing. The ATC system was a joke, but the militia would have been told if someone had requested permission to land in the backcountry. And why the fuck would anyone so much as *want* to land so far from the plantations? Smugglers. It *had* to be smugglers, delivering arms to the rebels.

"Move faster," Ludlow bellowed. "We have to catch them before they scatter!"

Richard glared at his back. "Don't charge into their fire," he snapped. Their window of opportunity was closing rapidly, if it hadn't already closed, but running forward like mad fools would only get them killed. "We need to...."

"Shut up," Ludlow snapped. He raised his voice. "Follow me!"

The militiamen picked up speed, hurrying up the road. Richard cursed under his breath. The rebels wouldn't have picked the landing zone unless they were entirely sure they could cover the shuttle long enough for it to escape. And it already *had*. The rebels could either linger long enough to give the militiamen a bloody nose or simply vanish further into the jungle, relying on the weather to shield them long enough to make a clean break. Richard hoped Ludlow wouldn't try to keep up the pursuit. It would be folly. The militiamen would wind up in deep shit....

Gunshots rang out, directly ahead. Richard saw Ludlow fall, like a sack of potatoes. Richard hit the ground a second later, screaming for the rest of the militiamen to take cover. A handful were gunned down before they even realised they were under attack, the remainder crawling back as fast as they could. Richard cursed Ludlow and his superiors as savagely as he could, even as he lifted his assault rifle and emptied a clip towards the rebel positions. It was wasteful—and he was sure he hadn't hit anyone—but it might force the rebels to keep their heads down for a few seconds. The militiamen were right in the open. It was just a matter of time before they were wiped out.

"Get back," he shouted. "Stay low and get back!"

He bellowed orders as loudly as he could, grimly aware the rebels could already be closing on his location. If they swept in from the east and west as well as the north, the militiamen would be captured and slaughtered before they could make it out of the trap. Bullets whipped through the air, the rebels pouring fire into their position. Richard saw a couple of his men raise their rifles and return fire, trying to force the enemy to keep their distance. He doubted it would be effective. The rebels had too much of an edge.

His hand dropped to his radio. The piece of shit—it was made locally; he'd heard the contract had been given to the landowner who'd offered the largest bribe—crackled loudly, but little else. There was certainly no reply when he tried to call for help. Between the planet's atmosphere and their location, miles from anywhere of importance, it was unlikely there would be any help coming before it was far too late. Ludlow might not even have bothered to clear his patrol with his militia superiors, let alone the army command. No one would know they were in trouble until they were reported missing the following day. His lips quirked as he reloaded, taking aim towards the enemy positions. For all he knew, they might be logged as AWOL. His superiors might never know what had *really* happened to the patrol.

"You three, keep firing towards them," he ordered, gesturing to three militiamen who looked slightly more composed than the rest. "Everyone else, keep inching back."

He forced himself to think. They were a long way beyond the wire, but...if they could break contact, they could get out of the trap before the rebels killed them. Perhaps. The rebels had to know the patrol was isolated, perhaps even alone. There would have been far too much disturbance if the entire militia, and the regulars, had started to advance north. The rebels couldn't possibly have missed them. A blind man would have noticed....

Thunder rumbled, again. Rain started to fail, the first few drops giving way to a torrent that threatened to sweep away the ground underneath. Richard allowed himself a moment of relief, then ordered the platoon to slip away. The rebels seemed to have the same idea, breaking contact and heading north. Richard shook his head as the firing came to an end. The bastards had good reason to feel pleased with themselves. They'd given the militia a bloody nose—and they'd killed an officer, as well as a bunch of volunteers—and they hadn't lost a single man. Richard tried to tell himself they'd killed a few rebels, but he couldn't force himself to believe it. The odds suggested the rebel force was completely unharmed.

And they were getting something from the shuttle, he thought, numbly. *What?*

He put the thought out of his mind as they kept walking, slipping and sliding as the ground started to turn into a swamp. There was no time to go back for Ludlow's body, no time to recover any of the dead...hell, some of them might only be wounded, doomed to die alone before dawn. He felt sick, even though he knew there was no choice. The patrol had been cut to ribbons. The remaining men were in no state to recover the bodies. He needed to report back...

His heart sank. His superiors would probably blame him for the disaster. Ludlow was dead. He was in no state to answer charges of gross incompetence. And even if he'd survived...Richard wondered, suddenly, if Ludlow had *known* something was going to happen. It defied belief they'd just *coincidentally* stumbled onto a smuggler landing. Ludlow was—had been—smart enough to pay for information and yet dumb enough not to share it with his superiors, not when he thought he could use it to make a name for himself. Hell, he might just have been lured into a trap.

A surge of hatred overcame him. *And if that fool had been a little more careful, he might not have gotten himself killed.*

CHAPTER THREE

MARINE COMMAND BASE, SAFEHOUSE

MAJOR-GENERAL JEREMY DAMIANI, Commandant of the Terran Marine Corps, stood at the armoured viewport and peered into the storm. Safehouse was not, and never would be, safe for unprotected humans. The snow looked pretty, the white flakes promising a winter wonderland that would keep a child occupied for days, but it was poisonous. A young child who sought to play in the snow, without a spacesuit, would be dead before their parents could yank them to safety. The morbid thought persisted, even though he knew he had many other things to worry about. The corps had won battles on Hameau and Onge, at the cost of revealing their survival as a fighting force to the remains of the empire. He knew there would be consequences. He just didn't know what form those consequences would take.

He sighed, feeling his age. It had been a year since Earthfall, a year since all hell had broken loose, a year since…he didn't want to *think* about how many untold billions had died in the last twelve months. The number was beyond calculation. Earth was dead. Many Core Worlds had been devastated, perhaps even destroyed; hundreds of thousands of smaller settlements, asteroid habitats and starships had been lost, either dropping completely out of what remained of the civilised galaxy or—worse—running out of supplies and dying, alone and unmourned, in the night. The spooks insisted that the galaxy was starting to calm down, that newer governments—some democratic, some dictatorial—were starting to re-establish order. It felt like a sick joke. So many had died that the galaxy would never return to normal.

The storm seemed to blow stronger, poisonous snow brushing against the viewport. Jeremy had never been blind to the empire's flaws, but he was all too aware that the order it had tried to maintain—sometimes at gunpoint- had been far superior to the chaos that had replaced it. The idealists spoke of democracy, while the would-be rulers insisted people were divided into masters and slaves; the truth, Jeremy knew, was that the vast majority of people wanted security, stability and a guarantee the rules would not change on a whim. The Empire had brought order, of a sort. It had tried—at least in theory—to impose a framework on the settled galaxy. And now that framework was gone. He thought, wistfully, of the seeds the corps had planted along the edge of explored and settled space. It was tempting to believe they'd survived and prospered, that they were raising new hope thousands of light years from the remnants of the jaded and cynical empire. He feared he would never know.

His intercom bleeped. "Sir, Colonel Anders and Doctor Williamsburg have arrived."

Jeremy let out a breath. "Send them in," he ordered, as he turned away from the windows. "And then hold all my calls unless they're Priority One."

"Aye, Sir."

The hatch opened. Jeremy nodded to the newcomers, directing them to seats. He wasn't sure how long they'd be talking, let alone what sort of resolution they could make. The matter was an odd one. Part of him was tempted to bury it, to let the matter rest in peace along with Earth itself. And yet, he couldn't help feeling as though they should be able to make something of it. He sighed, inwardly, as he poured the coffee, a sign that they were to talk freely. Being indecisive wasn't one of his normal traits. But then, there was a difference between dealing with volleys of incoming fire and political headaches that might plague his successors long after he was gone. They might curse him in the future, if he made the wrong choice now.

He placed the mugs on the table, then sat himself. "It's good to see you again," he said, truthfully. "I take it Merlin hasn't caused any real problems?"

"No, sir," Anders said. "The planetary government hasn't raised any objections to us continuing to operate the boot camp, as long as we stick with the pre-Earthfall agreements. I have a feeling that may change, as the government gets used to no longer receiving orders from Earth, but right now no one wants to rock the boat."

"It will certainly change if we turn the facility into a full Slaughterhouse," Jeremy predicted, taking a sip of his coffee. "And right now we desperately need one."

"Yes, sir," Anders said. "Frankly, I doubt Merlin will accept any proposal to actually upgrade the facilities. Even if they did, it would be a headache for us. I would prefer to set up a new Slaughterhouse on an uninhabited world, rather than someplace with a local government and red-light district."

"True," Jeremy agreed. "But that's not why we're here."

He took a breath, then leaned forward. "How is Prince Roland coping with Boot Camp?"

Anders frowned. "With your permission, sir, I'll allow the doctor to give you the medical report."

Doctor Williamsburg nodded, curtly. "Physically, the prince is in the top tenth percentile of the entire human race. His family bloodline received all the latest enhancements over the years, resulting in everything from perfect eyesight and hearing to an immune system that is capable of handling almost every disease known to man, save perhaps for a handful of genetically engineered biological weapons. His enhancements are so advanced, sir, that the combination of proper food and hard work caused him to slim down, then build up his muscles at astonishing speed. Frankly, if I hadn't read both his own testimony and Specialist Lawson's reports, I wouldn't have thought he was ever a drunkard or a drug addict. His enhanced body flushed most of the toxins out before they could do permanent damage."

Jeremy quirked an eyebrow. "You didn't believe the reports?"

"The prince was drinking from a very early age, if he is to be believed, as well as taking all sort of drugs, ranging from purified bliss-out to solid-rock," Doctor Williamsburg said. "If a normal person had abused his body like that, he would be dead within weeks. The caretakers were certainly not trying to actually take *care* of him. They practically gave him whatever he wanted, when he wanted it. The simple fact he *did* put weight on is testament to just how badly he pushed the enhancements to the limit. Enhancements or no enhancements, if he'd continued down that route I think he would still have killed himself within two to three years."

"I see." Jeremy shook his head. He'd known the Grand Senate had a vested interest in keeping the prince fat, happy and dumb, but it still shocked him just how badly they'd allowed the young man to get out of shape. It wasn't as if they'd *had* to let him turn into a slug. "And now?"

"Physically, he's fine," Doctor Williamsburg said. He pulled a terminal from his belt and placed it on the table. "I did a complete assessment before we left, as per orders. Under normal circumstances, sir, I wouldn't hesitate to recommend he be sent on to the Slaughterhouse. Mentally...."

He paused. "I've conducted a handful of psychological interviews with the prince over the past year. He is undoubtedly smart. Many of his problems stemmed from ignorance and inexperience and they can both be corrected. He's also deeply ashamed of the...*person*...he was, to the point he's determined to make something of himself by joining the corps and climbing all the way to the top. And he is also determined to make Specialist Lawson proud of him. He hasn't said so, in so many words, but he has something of a crush on her."

Jeremy frowned. "And do you think we should *let* him begin advanced training?"

"I have my doubts, to be honest," Doctor Williamsburg admitted. "Most of the time, he's the perfect recruit. He does learn from experience and he's never made the same mistake twice. And yet, there are worrying hints of...*brittleness*, if not entitlement, buried within his psyche. He might make it through enhanced training, or he might not."

Anders cleared his throat. "He also shows worrying hints of ruthlessness, sir," he added. "In a previous training exercise, he used one of his comrades to lure an enemy helicopter out of position so he could hit it with a grenade. It worked, to be fair, but it came at a price. And he doesn't mingle *that* well with his teammates. He isn't a slacker or a barracks-room lawyer or any other flavour of asshole. There's no suggestion he doesn't carry his weight and more. He hasn't had his behaviour *corrected* by his instructors and his comrades."

He made a face. "On paper, he's pretty close to perfect. In reality... maybe not so much."

Jeremy sipped his coffee. "What do you suggest we *do* with him?"

"I doubt Boot Camp can make him better," Anders said. "He's already retaken two of the four training cycles, passing with flying colours. We're reaching the limits of what we can reasonably teach him, or when we can reasonably hold him back. He needs to either go on to advanced training or be shunted aside into the auxiliaries. I doubt he'll quit."

"He won't," Doctor Williamsburg said. "He's not a quitter."

Jeremy nodded, appreciating the irony. The corps didn't kick someone out of basic training unless they committed one of the cardinal sins, breaking the rules that were read out to new recruits until they could recite them in their sleep. A man who was too stubborn to quit might become a good Marine, if he overcame the hurdles and made it through the entire training course; a man who did quit was discharged as soon as possible, just to ensure he didn't infect the rest of the recruits. It was traditional that a recruit had to make that decision on his own. Jeremy understood the value of tradition, but there had been times—during his stint at Boot Camp—that he'd thought it was a mistake. There'd been some recruits who really should have been removed before they quit of their own accord.

And if we did tell him he couldn't continue, he mused, *it would raise the issue of precisely what we should do with the prince.*

Jeremy's lips twitched in cold amusement. Legally, Prince Roland was the ruler of the entire galaxy. Practically speaking, hardly anyone who'd survived the past year would recognise the claim. The newly independent planets, star systems and sectors wouldn't place themselves under the rule of the Imperial Family again, let alone the deeply corrupt and self-serving Grand Senate. And...Prince Roland hadn't done a good job of winning hearts and minds when he'd been younger. The Childe Roland had been a useless lump of flesh, a spoilt brat who made all other spoilt brats looked sweet, charming and innocent by comparison. It was unlikely, to say the least, that the galaxy would decide a year of military training would turn a bratty youth into a grown man. They'd be far more likely to assume the training had just made him worse.

He considered the options, briefly. It wouldn't be *hard* to hide Roland. He could go into deep cover, perhaps on a colony ship heading out past the Rim, or simply change his name and take up residence on a black colony. And yet, that would mean depriving the corps of what little advantage could be gleaned from possessing the legitimate heir to the throne. Jeremy was too experienced a Marine to believe it would be a war-winning advantage, but it sat ill with him to simply discard something before he was sure it wasn't worth keeping it under his control. And yet...he felt a flicker of irritation. Prince Roland was a *person*, one that had grown up considerably even before Earthfall. He wasn't a tool Jeremy could use however he liked.

You might feel that way, his thoughts mocked. *But far too many others will try to either kill the poor bastard or use him.*

"Your last report made it clear he has nearly passed the fourth training quarter," Jeremy said, to Anders. The younger man knew the prince far better than his superior. The chances were good he had at least *some* idea of how the corps should proceed. "What do you propose?"

Anders met his eyes. "We were recently tapped to put together a training mission for New Doncaster," he said. "They need to expand their army rapidly and begged for help, which was eventually forwarded to us. I earmarked a handful of training staff to be sent at the end of the current training quarter. I'd hate to see them go, but...."

He shrugged. "I'd like to put Prince Roland in command of the detachment."

Jeremy said nothing for a long moment. "A brevet promotion?"

"He's already qualified as an auxiliary, on the command track," Anders said. "It wouldn't be the first time we've rotated a promising young officer through a detached command, just to give them some experience *and* see if they want to make the role permanent. The training staff would understand. We can ask them to keep a close eye on him too."

Jeremy nodded. Technically, the training staff were low ranked; practically, they were senior and experienced enough that only a fool would discount their opinions. Anders hadn't told his staff about the prince's true identity, and he wouldn't even if the prince was sent to New Doncaster, but he'd make it clear they were to evaluate his officer potential as well as his chances of getting through advanced training. And if the prince turned into an arrogant ass who refused to listen to his NCOs...at least it would happen somewhere relatively safe.

"It might work," he said. "We would have to take care of him, though."

"We're sending a company of Marines to bolster the locals until their forces are ready to take the field," Anders said. "They can take care of the prince."

"That wouldn't give him room to flourish," Jeremy said. "Or make a complete ass of himself."

"No," Doctor Williamsburg agreed. "The prince holds qualified Marines in high regard."

Anders frowned. "And we cannot attach a qualified Marine to his staff without raising eyebrows," he said. "Someone will smell a rat."

"No," Jeremy agreed.

His mind raced. No mere auxiliary could be allowed to outrank a full-fledged Marine, not without a very good reason. A starship captain could issue orders to the Marines on his ship, but...he shook his head. There was no way to finagle the arrangement without tipping off the more experienced men that there was *something* special about Prince Roland. It was just possible someone might figure out the truth. In hindsight, perhaps they should have insisted Roland change his name when he entered Boot Camp. Roland was hardly an uncommon name—there were dozens of people with the same name in the military—but Roland *Windsor* was in the right age bracket. If he was being treated as a hot potato, with rights and privileges not normally offered to anyone....

And if he thinks we're appointing a babysitter, he'll rebel, Jeremy thought, crossly. It was what he would have done, when he'd been a young man. He'd given his old babysitter a very hard time indeed. Roland was ten years older than the young Jeremy, but perhaps—if the reports were accurate—not much more mature. *We need to protect him without making it obvious what we're doing.*

He looked at Anders. "When do you intend to return to Merlin?"

"Tomorrow, unless you want me to stay longer," Anders said. "I want to be back there for the end of the training quarter, then detach the training staff as per orders."

"Roland can be attached to the training staff as their CO," Jeremy said. "Make sure someone on the staff knows they have the authority to override him, if he fucks up spectacularly. This is a chance for him to prove himself, but not at the cost of a dozen lives. Make sure they know it. I'll give the matter of his protection some thought."

"Yes, sir," Anders said. "What about Specialist Lawson? He already respects her."

"He has a crush on her," Doctor Williamsburg said, again. "Frankly, I wouldn't expect them to develop anything resembling a healthy partnership. The relationship is just too tangled."

"It isn't as if they were ever lovers," Anders said, curtly. "They're professionals. They can deal."

"Specialist Lawson is currently unavailable," Jeremy told them. Technically, Belinda Lawson should have been placed on long-term leave, with a quiet understanding she didn't have to come back if she didn't feel up to it. She'd been through utter hell even before she'd been assigned to the prince. Practically...she was on detached duty, carrying out a mission well above their pay grade. They didn't need to know anything beyond the fact she was unavailable. "I have something else in mind."

He finished his coffee and stood. "It is possible we're wasting our time with the prince," he said. "It's also possible he could be the key to everything."

"He needs more seasoning before he can be the key to anything," Doctor Williamsburg said, softly. He tapped the terminal, meaningfully. "Right now, I worry about him."

"We all do," Jeremy said. He wondered, coldly, if it would be better just to advise the prince to move to a distant colony and keep his head down. His instincts told him the prince would be useful, though the more practical side of his mind insisted on pointing out that the prince was effectively powerless. "But the needs of the empire, or what's left of it, outweigh the needs of any one man."

CHAPTER FOUR

MARINE BOOT CAMP, MERLIN

ROLAND FELT...ODDLY OUT OF SORTS.

It wasn't something that sat well. The training company had completed its final set of tests, from military exercises to exams that tested their knowledge and their ability to think under pressure. He'd slept for hours afterwards, when they'd been ordered to leave the old barracks and move to the transient barracks near the spaceport, then found himself at something of a loose end. They were technically graduates, ready to move on to the Slaughterhouse—or whatever had replaced it—but they were in limbo. He didn't like it. He preferred to know what was going to happen next.

He stepped into the firing range, signed for a pallet of ammunition and started to practice his shooting. The rest of the company had headed to the local town, to celebrate their success before they were sent out, but he'd chosen not to accompany them. He'd been to the town once and...he simply hadn't felt comfortable. It wasn't something he could put into words, just a sense that the environment was slightly out of kilter. Besides, it wasn't as though he could let himself relax into wine, women and song. He had strict orders to keep his true identity to himself. And his comrades couldn't be allowed to suspect he was keeping something from them.

The rifle twitched in his hand as he moved from target to target. Roland watched the holograms come and go, seemingly at random. The programmers delighted in having the enemy troops materialise in impossible places, as if he was playing an arcade game rather than training for war. He supposed it made a certain kind of sense—training was designed to push them to the limits, in hopes war itself would be easy—but it still struck him as odd. He pushed the thought out of his mind as a little girl in pigtails wandered in and out of his vision, his rifle tracking her before she vanished again. He breathed a sigh of relief. He knew terrorists liked using women and children to carry bombs, but he didn't want to think about the implications. He certainly didn't want to have to shoot an unwilling bomber, particularly a child, if it could be avoided. And yet, the practical part of his mind pointed out, the poor kid was probably doomed anyway.

He sat back and clicked the safety as the simulation came to an end. His score appeared in front of him, calculated with absurd precision. One hundred possible targets, ninety-three hit; ten civilians, none hit. He breathed a sigh of relief. They might have graduated, they might have been told they'd be marching boldly into the unknown future, but he was sure the instructors would have told him off for shooting a holographic civilian. It might even have been classed as a war crime. And there was no way to keep the enemy from turning the child they'd forced to carry a bomb into a martyr for the cause.

"Good shooting," a voice said, from behind him. "The colonel would like to see you in his office."

Roland blinked as he spun around. He'd been so wrapped up in his own thoughts he hadn't noticed Sergeant Flint, coming up behind him. The sergeant would probably have said a few sharp things about his lack of situational awareness, under other circumstances. Roland nodded, returned the unspent ammunition to the trays and inspected his rifle before slinging the weapon back over his shoulder. It had taken him months to get used to the idea of carrying the rifle everywhere, even in the shower. The instructors would have bawled him out—or worse—if he'd left it behind. Who knew when one might be attacked without warning?

"Understood, Sergeant," he said. "I'll report to him at once."

He frowned, inwardly, as he started to walk towards the cluster of administrative buildings to the north of the camp. The base had always felt, to him, as though the staff were on the verge of packing up and departing at a moment's notice, even though it had been in place for several decades. Roland didn't pretend to understand precisely why the local government had authorised the Marines to set up shop some distance from the capital, but he didn't need to know the specifics to understand the base might turn the entire planet into a target. The corps had enemies. One of them had turned the Slaughterhouse into radioactive rubble. Who knew what they'd do to Merlin if they thought the corps was moving operations there permanently?

The colonel's secretary nodded curtly, then jabbed a finger at an open door. Roland nodded back politely—it always paid to be polite to the staff, Belinda had told him—and stepped through the door. Colonel Anders was sitting beside his desk, studying a paper report. Roland guessed it was something secret. Computer terminals were wonderful, and the corps had the best WebHeads in the known galaxy, but it was impossible to be sure they were entirely secure. Anyone who wanted to read a paper report would have to break into the colonel's office first. It wouldn't be easy for anyone, even a fully trained Marine.

Roland straightened as the colonel looked up at him. "Recruit Graduate Windsor, reporting as ordered."

"At ease." Colonel Anders gestured to the door, then the coffee pot. "Shut the door, pour yourself a drink and sit down."

"Yes, sir."

Roland did as he was told, an uncomfortable frisson of unease shooting through him. It wasn't hard to notice *he* hadn't been called in for career counselling, not yet. Unless...he frowned inwardly, unsure why the colonel would deal with him personally. Did the colonel even know who he was?

It wasn't clear. He'd been told never to discuss it with anyone unless they broached the topic first. He made a mental note to watch his tongue carefully, just in case he said the wrong thing. He'd spent enough time in the barracks to know the recruits were always under observation.

"Your stats are very good, in most places," Colonel Anders said. His face was artfully bland, his voice calm and controlled. "You do, however, have some curious issues we want you to tackle before proceeding to advanced training. Or do you wish to proceed sideways to the regular formations or auxiliaries?"

"No, sir," Roland said. He'd almost sooner have been hauled up in front of the camp's CO for a bollocking. It couldn't have been worse than this. "I want to continue to the Slaughterhouse."

The colonel's lips twitched. "Right now, that would be nothing more than a thoroughly unpleasant way to die," he said. "But I take your meaning."

He leaned forward, resting his elbows on his desk. "We feel you need more seasoning before you proceed onwards. And we are prepared to offer it to you, if you are prepared to make use of it."

Roland didn't hesitate. "I am."

"We shall see." Anders smiled, openly. "Have you ever heard of New Doncaster?"

"No, sir," Roland said.

It wasn't quite true. He vaguely recalled hearing *something* about the planet, back when he'd been living in the Summer Palace, but he hadn't paid any attention. It had been something he'd had to sign, in his position as heir to the throne…it wasn't as if he'd bothered to think about it enough to realise he wasn't being given a choice. He'd signed the papers and then gone back to whatever he'd been doing. And…he kept the memory to himself. Better to let the colonel think he was completely ignorant than assume he knew more than he really did.

"You'll be given the full reports, if you accept the posting, but the short version of the story is that the planet is dangerously unstable," Anders informed him. "The local power structure was unsteady even before Earthfall and we think it unlikely any of the moderate factions will be able to establish order, let alone assist the planet in transitioning to a more stable power structure. If the government loses control, the best the planet can possibly hope for is a brief civil war followed by either a fascist or a communist state. From the point of view of the average citizen, there will be very little to choose between them.

"The government has requested the corps provide both a sizable force to stiffen their militia and a training mission to expand their regular army into a force capable of imposing order long enough to make a more orderly transition. We simply don't have the numbers to do more than provide a very minimal force to stiffen their forces, but we can and will provide a training mission. We'd like you to take command of the detachment."

Roland blinked. "Me?"

"You." Anders met his eyes evenly. "Your orders are to establish a training post, start churning out soldiers who are able to face the rebels on even terms and eventually become training officers themselves. Ideally, you should be able to avoid being drawn into the fighting yourself, but—under the circumstances—we're not expecting you to refrain from engaging the enemy if you feel it necessary. We doubt the rebels will let you train a few thousand soldiers without making *some* attempt to stop you."

"No, sir," Roland agreed. He forced himself to think. "Why me?"

"Because you have promise," Anders said. "And, at the same time, that promise needs to be tempered and shaped by actual experience. This deployment is a very low priority for us—if not for them—but it does offer a chance for you to get that experience and prepare yourself for the next stage of training. I have it on good authority"—he smiled, briefly—"that command experience at this stage of your career will look very good on your resume."

Roland said nothing for a long moment. It sounded good—command experience was hardly something to sneer at, not if he gained it before starting advanced training—and yet he was sure he wasn't being told *something*. New Doncaster didn't *sound* very important, in the grand scheme of things. The corps couldn't be everywhere. It might be better to let the locals fight it out, then dicker with whoever came out on top. And yet… if the corps stood aside, it would have no influence over the final victors.

A thought struck him. "How important is New Doncaster?"

Anders gave him an approving look. "The planet itself provides a considerable amount of raw materials that are difficult, if not impossible, to produce elsewhere, along with much of the foodstuffs for the star system. The remainder of the planets and asteroids within the system are very loosely under the planet's control, at least on paper, but practically speaking they are effectively independent. There's a very real chance they'll make that independence official if the planet collapses into civil war, or simply ally themselves with warlords, secessionists or flat-out pirates. The planet's atmosphere is unusual, as you'll see in the survey reports, but even a pirate ship would have no trouble dropping KEWs on the cities and towns. And, right there and then, another set of warlords would be born."

"With support from the industrialised asteroids," Roland said. "It might be tricky to deal with them."

"Quite." Anders tapped the desk. "We want a fairly stable planetary government that is capable of taking the cork out of the bottle and letting some of the pressure escape before the whole bottle explodes. There are factions on the surface that might be reasonable, if they feel they can risk offering compromises without having the offer be seen as a sign of weakness. A strong and reliable army is the first step towards putting the planet on a more stable basis."

Roland said nothing for a long moment. "The only training I've done was back when I was assisting with the first-quarters," he said. He didn't want to think about being a first-quarter recruit himself. He'd been told the recruits went through Boot Camp to get the inevitable mistakes out of their systems, but he'd made so many he was sure he'd set a new record. "And all I really did was show them how to take a punch."

"You don't have to do the training yourself," Anders informed him. "You merely have to command the training detachment."

"Yes, sir." Roland wasn't convinced. If all they wanted the CO to do was sit in his office and play with himself, they didn't need *him*. They didn't need anyone. "Sir...permission to speak freely?"

"Of course." Anders sounded vaguely amused. "You do know you have to ask questions, if you wish to be enlightened?"

Roland didn't rise to the bait. "Sir, you don't need me to command the detachment," he said, carefully. "Or am I missing something?"

"You don't need to train the new recruits," Anders agreed. "But do you think you're just going to sit around doing nothing?"

"No, sir," Roland said.

"Quite right," Anders agreed. "You'll be handling the negotiations with the local military establishment. You'll be arranging for a training camp, you'll be organising recruitment and planning for newcomers to start proceeding along their career tracks; you'll be a barrier between your men, who will want to get on with the jobs they're trained to do, and local officials who'll want to get in their way. Your job is not to train the new recruits. Your job is to make it possible for the training staff to do their jobs."

He smiled. "And you'll find, quite quickly, that the devil is often in the details."

Roland supposed that made a little more sense. The concept of running interference was hardly unknown. Hell, he understood how to stall and delay as well as study the official and unofficial power structures to determine what was really going on. Belinda had made him study, back on Earth. He'd dared to hope he'd make something of himself before the final collapse had begun, forcing them to flee. Once he got there....

"I see, sir," he said. "I'll do my best."

"Good." Anders reached for his terminal and tapped a command. "Your orders will be in your inbox, along with your brevet promotion to Auxiliary Captain. I suggest you remember this promotion will not be permanent, even if you decide you want to transfer to the auxiliaries permanently. Your work will be reviewed, so you'd better be prepared to justify your decisions."

Roland swallowed. "Yes, sir."

"Don't take it too personally," Anders said. "A great many decisions are scrutinised, no matter who makes them. There's always *someone* who thinks he can do better than the man on the spot."

He paused. "You'll meet the training staff this evening, then board the freighter tomorrow for transport to New Doncaster. I suggest you and your aide spend the remainder of the afternoon studying the intelligence reports, then putting together a list of resources you wish to draw from our stockpiles here. There's no guarantee we'll be able to ship anything to New Doncaster after your arrival, so you may find yourself thrown back on the planet's resources."

"Yes, sir," Roland said, then stopped. "My aide?"

Anders keyed his terminal. The door opened. Roland glanced behind him, then stood as an auxiliary officer—a lieutenant—stepped into the room. She was…frumpy, he noted; she dressed as if she was trying very hard to vanish into the shadows. Her red hair was tied up in a bun, her uniform hung loosely, as if it had been tailored for someone bigger and fatter. It was hard to take her seriously. She might have cleaned up nicely, he decided, if she'd let her hair down, donned something a little tighter in all the right places and put on a little makeup, but…she didn't even *begin* to have Belinda's presence. Roland was almost disappointed.

"Roland Windsor, please allow me to introduce Marine Auxiliary Lieutenant Rachel Green," Anders said. "She'll be your aide for the duration of the deployment. I suggest you make sure she stays by your side as much as possible. You will not be able to rely on anyone else outside the corps once you land on New Doncaster."

And she wouldn't have reached that rank unless she was actually very good at her job, Roland thought. What *was* Rachel's job? She was clearly no fighter. She'd know the basics, perhaps, but…even that was hard to believe. Administrative assistant? Someone who knew how to navigate the files might be very helpful. Or…or what? *They wouldn't have assigned her to the deployment unless they felt she'd be useful.*

"It's a pleasure to meet you," he said, holding out a hand. Rachel took it and shook it lightly. "I'm sure we'll get along fine."

"I have some files for you to review," Rachel told him. Her voice was businesslike. "I've also taken the liberty of booking an office for our use."

"Make sure you review *all* the files," Anders said. Roland's attention snapped back to his superior. "And good luck, Captain Windsor."

Roland nodded, hiding his feelings as best as possible. If he screwed up...his career was doomed. He might as well stay on New Doncaster. God alone knew what the corps would do with him if he couldn't complete even a single assignment....

I'll just have to make it work, he thought. He had the feeling the assignment was going to be far more complicated than he'd been told, but... he told himself, firmly, he wasn't going to fuck up. *Whatever it takes, I'll make it work.*

CHAPTER FIVE

KINGSLAND, NEW DONCASTER

LIEUTENANT RICHARD COLLIER stood on the deck and watched, keeping his thoughts to himself, as the crew steered the boat towards the giant harbour. The entrance was half-hidden by a number of larger ships, ranging from paddle steamers to giant freighters that bound the islands together into a single political entity; smaller ships, from tiny rowboats to mid-sized sailing and motorboats, buzzed around them, too small to have to worry about the tides. He gritted his teeth as a small aircraft roared overhead, rattling through the air as it vanished into the distance. It would have been easier for his superiors to order him to get onto an island-hopper and fly from Baraka to Kingsland. He couldn't help feeling that the orders to take a small boat instead had come from people who were half-hoping he'd go AWOL somewhere along the way.

He gritted his teeth as the boat made its way past a pair of giant freighters, their hulls covered with rust, and into the mouth of the harbour itself. He'd been tempted. God knew he'd been tempted. It would have been easy to jump ship at some point and vanish into the countryside, or sign on an independent freighter and simply never bother to look back. He doubted anyone would care enough to try to track him down—and, even if they did, good crewmen were so hard to find that it was unlikely any of the captains would betray him. If push came to shove, they might even tell the searchers he'd fallen overboard one dark night. But he owed it to the men who'd died to tell the truth, even if it cost him everything. It wasn't as if he'd been likely to rise any further anyway.

The wind shifted, blowing the stench of dead and rotting fish across his nostrils. He grimaced in disgust. The harbour wasn't the cleanest place in the world. The dockyard workers were forbidden to unionise, or do anything that might improve their lot, and so they did as little as possible. Richard had heard suggestions that underground activity was steadily increasing, with work slowdowns and lost or destroyed machinery and tools putting a damper on harbour activities. The wiser MPs argued for at least *some* concessions, but the dockyard owners kept blocking them. They owned the docks, as well as the worker contracts. They weren't going to give them up for anything.

Richard hefted his knapsack as the boat slid alongside the pier, the crew hooting and hollering in anticipation of a night on the town. The captain would start signing wage chits shortly, sending the crew to the harbour bank before they headed out to get drunk, chase girls and pick fights. Richard almost envied them. He would have liked to get drunk himself. Instead...he winced, inwardly, as he spotted the official car waiting at the top of the pier. They were desperate to hear his testimony, after forcing him to spend days in transit. He stepped aside, took a moment to steady his legs, then started to walk to the car. The driver greeted him with a salute. Richard wondered if that meant good news, then shook his head. The driver didn't know anything about him. He might have been a great deal less respectful if he'd known Richard was *en route* to a formal inquiry, if not a court-martial.

He sat in the rear of the car and watched, grimly, as the vehicle picked its way through the giant harbour and out onto the streets. There were more police and militiamen in evidence, a number searching passing pedestrians while others looked around as if they expected to be attacked at any moment. The prostitutes who normally lined up outside the gates, looking for sailors with money and a desire for female companionship, were gone. Richard doubted they'd gone very far. The red-light district—a warren of bars, brothels and everything else a sailor might need when he returned from the sea—would steer the sailors towards the waiting girls. Richard shuddered, inwardly. He'd met a couple of the women during training. They were indents who hadn't known what they were getting into—or what was getting into them—when they signed their contracts. The vast majority would probably give it up in a flash if they were given better options.

The car picked up speed as it left the red-light district behind, passing through a military checkpoint and heading onto the motorway to First Landing. Richard leaned back in his chair as the countryside rolled by, trying to meditate as best as possible. There'd be no rest when he reached the capital. He'd be lucky if they pointed him to a washroom before putting him in front of the board. He wondered, idly, if his superiors really *had* hoped he'd quietly get lost during the voyage home. It would certainly have helped them sweep the whole disaster under the carpet.

He sat up as they passed another military checkpoint, then entered the capital itself. The outer districts were little better than makeshift shacks and hovels, a grim reminder of the economic slowdown that had swept over the planet shortly before Earthfall. The transient barracks had overflowed months ago, leaving far too many people on the streets. Richard was surprised they hadn't been sent out to the islands yet, perhaps drafted into indent or debtor work gangs. As it was, the districts were steadily turning into a powder keg, dominated by criminals and underground factions. It was just a matter of time before something blew.

They passed yet another checkpoint, then entered the heart of the city. The buildings here were stone, the old, prefabricated structures removed and repurposed long ago, but they bore the marks of constant rainfall and high temperatures. Richard had heard rumours the buildings were literally melting, but he didn't believe it. Not really. New Doncaster's government wasn't known for efficiency—the landowners dominated the government and intended to do so for the rest of time—but even the weak government should be able to take care of its property. The truth was probably a little more mundane. He didn't care what it was.

He took a breath as the car stopped in front of Government House. That he'd been called *here*, rather than the military headquarters or the local militia garrison, boded ill. And yet...he clambered out, the heat billowing around as soon as he stepped out of the air conditioning, and nodded to a young woman in a simple shirt and skirt. She was pretty enough, he noted, but if she was working at Government House she was probably way out of his league. The landowners didn't like the idea of their daughters actually doing more than marrying well and perpetuating the dynasty, but even they had to admit their daughters were more trustworthy than townies or debtors. Richard knew, all too well, that the landowners were right to be paranoid. They had far too many enemies.

Government House was, thankfully, air conditioned. His escort showed him to a washroom, waited patiently as he splashed water on his face and adjusted his uniform, then took him to a small conference room. Richard felt his heart sink as he stepped inside. There were five men sitting behind a table, studying him with grim eyes. He recognised the Prime Minister and General Falk, the highest-ranking uniformed officer on the planet, but the others were strangers. And yet, one of them looked oddly familiar.

He winced, inwardly, as he snapped a perfect salute. If the PM himself was in attendance....

General Falk nodded, curtly. "Lieutenant Richard Collier," he said. "State, for the record, precisely what happened during your recent engagement with the enemy."

Richard wanted to stand at ease, but he didn't quite dare. "Sir," he said. "Captain Ludlow led a patrol consisting of two platoons of militiamen, thirty-seven men in total, into the backwaters of Baraka Island. The stated objective of the mission was to give the militiamen a chance to operate beyond the wire, without any real danger of encountering something we couldn't handle. As night was falling, with us isolated from the nearest fortified position, we spotted a shuttle taking off and returning to orbit. We believed it was a smuggler landing in the outback and hastened towards the landing zone, in hopes of catching the groundside party before they had time to scatter.

"We ran into an ambush. The enemy force caught us, picking off Captain Ludlow as well as most of the vanguard. The largely untried militiamen started to panic, adding to the chaos. A number were shot in the back as they attempted to run. It was clear to me that remaining where we were was suicidal, so I organised a fighting retreat. The enemy pressed us until the rain started, at which point they broke contact and retreated into the backcountry. I took the remnants of the patrol back to the nearest base, where we made contact with our superiors and reported the incident."

He took a breath. "The following day, an armoured patrol linked up with us and we returned to the battleground. We found nothing. There was no trace of any bodies, either ours or theirs. We were unable to determine what was landed, or where it was taken. We swept through the area, with aircraft and artillery on call as well as armoured cars, but the enemy declined to show themselves. The local militia HQ ordered us to return behind the wire before nightfall, which is what we did. At that point, I received orders to make my way back to Kingsland. I handed the remnants of army detachment over to the next officer in line, then did as I was told."

"My son *died* on your watch," the oddly familiar person snapped. "What were you thinking?"

Richard cursed, silently. The man had to be Captain Ludlow's father. Damn it. The family was so well connected that they could force the PM to take a personal hand or risk losing his post when the next election cycle began. He wondered, again, if he should have jumped ship somewhere during the voyage home. The PM wasn't likely to stand in Lord Ludlow's way if he wanted Richard hung, drawn and quartered. General Falk wouldn't muster anything more than a token protest. He knew which side his bread was buttered on.

"We had no reason to believe we would encounter a sizable enemy force," Richard said, although he had his doubts about that. Captain Ludlow might have heard *something* and decided to tackle the issue himself, rather than referring the matter to his superiors. Or the shuttle might have been bait in a trap. "Your son was caught by surprise. He died well...."

"But he died, when you were there," Lord Ludlow said. "Why didn't you stop him?"

Richard almost laughed. Even if Captain Ludlow and himself had been social equals—and they weren't, not by a long way—he'd still been outranked. There were times when a junior could offer blunt advice to a senior, but never in front of the enlisted men. Captain Ludlow would have ignored him if he'd tried to suggest a more careful approach to the landing site. He might not even have been wrong. The longer the militia took to get there, the longer the enemy would have to scatter and break contact without a fight.

"He was my commanding officer," Richard said, finally. "I couldn't override his decision."

"The fact remains, a patrol was largely destroyed on your watch," General Falk said. "Why didn't you retreat at once? Or try to charge the enemy positions?"

"The enemy positions were concealed within the foliage and probably quite well dug-in," Richard said. If it *had* been a planned ambush, the enemy had carried it out perfectly. "If we had charged their positions, we would have been slaughtered. I ordered a retreat as soon as I managed to assert control over the remnants of the patrol, who were panicking under enemy fire. It was not easy to get them falling back in an orderly pattern, laying down fire to keep the enemy from chasing us down. The rain saved our bacon."

He sighed, inwardly, as the argument ran around and around the table. The fix was definitely in. Captain Ludlow wouldn't be blamed for the disaster, even though it had been largely his fault and he wasn't around to complain. The army would give him a posthumous medal and cover up the whole affair, ensuring that neither the army nor the militia learnt anything from the ambush. He wondered, bitterly, if he'd be put in front of a formal court-martial or simply dishonourably discharged from the army, despite the years he'd spent working his way up the ranks. It wasn't as if anyone would stand up for him. He had no connections worth a damn.

"This is what you get for letting townies join the army," Lord Ludlow insisted, curtly. "He should have stopped my son from being killed."

Richard cleared his throat. "My Lord, what would you have had me do?"

Lord Ludlow glared. Richard didn't blame him for being angry over his son's death—Captain Ludlow had planned to do a term in the regular, then switch to the militia until he inherited his father's land and titles—but there were limits. Captain Ludlow had never realised there was no peace beyond the line, not on the plantation islands. He'd given the enemy— bandits or rebels, no one seemed to know—a clear shot at him. They'd taken it. And he hadn't lived to learn from his mistake.

He forced himself to wait, listening to the argument as it went on and on. Lord Ludlow wanted him shot—or, at the very least, dismissed from the service in disgrace. The two strangers seemed more concerned about the implications of the disaster, arguing that the army should deploy more troops to Baraka before all hell broke loose; Richard suspected, privately, that there just weren't enough regulars to make a difference. The landowners were reluctant to recruit townies, like him, and flatly refused to recruit debtors and indents. And yet...without more manpower, there was little hope of securing even the *major* islands.

The PM tapped the table, then nodded to General Falk. Richard straightened, bracing himself for the worst. They'd had four days to argue over what to do before he'd arrived, four days to read the reports from militia officers who hadn't been anywhere near the engagement as well as the report Richard himself had submitted. The politics had probably been smoothed out well before he'd realised what awaited him. They wanted a scapegoat. Richard—a townie in an army dominated by landowners—was practically tailor-made for the role.

"Lieutenant Richard Collier," General Falk said. "Your conduct during the engagement has been assessed and found wanting. You failed to inform your superior of an obvious trap, resulting in his death; you failed to rally your men in time to counterattack; you gave the order to retreat too late, resulting in the deaths of several more militiamen. It was sheer good luck that your failures did not result in the destruction of the entire formation."

Richard gritted his teeth in frustration but said nothing.

"These charges merit a general court-martial," General Falk continued. "However, given your previous service record, it has been decided that you will be summarily withdrawn from front-line combat duties and assigned to the interstellar training program as a liaison officer. If you perform well in that role, your career will be reassessed and—hopefully—you will be permitted to return to the front lines. We trust that meets with your approval?"

Richard felt his cheeks redden in humiliation. The fix was definitely in. His court-martial would be a formality, and probably held well away from anyone who might blow the whistle, but it would still require an open discussion of how Captain Ludlow's mistakes had contributed to his death. Richard would go down, but he'd have the satisfaction of taking the Ludlow family's reputation down too. Assigning him to a training post would keep him out of the way, perhaps even keep him from saying the wrong thing to the wrong person. And just what *was* an interstellar training program anyway? The Empire was gone.

He forced himself to think. He was tempted, very tempted, to tell them to take the transfer and stick it somewhere the sun didn't shine. Who knew? If they tried to court-martial him, he could hire a good lawyer and make it hard for them to pin anything on him. Except…he shuddered. The landowners had so much influence he probably didn't have a hope in hell of getting a fair trial. General Falk wouldn't have dumped on him so badly if he hadn't been dumped on himself by his superiors. The political firestorm would sweep over his career, and his family, and every hope of political reform. There was no hope at all of coming out ahead. He doubted he'd be able to do more than dent their reputation.

"Yes, sir," he said, finally. "Might I ask who I'll be working with?"

"The Terran Marine Corps," General Falk said. "They've finally agreed to send a unit to stiffen our lines."

Richard nodded, keeping his thoughts to himself. The Marines were supposed to be good, the best of the best, but he'd heard that before. Captain Ludlow had been an up-and-coming young man, a credit to the service, or so Richard had been told. And the young man had walked right into a trap and been killed before he had a chance to realise his mistake.

"Dismissed," the PM said. "And we wish you the best in your new posting."

"Yes, sir," Richard said, stiffly. "I'll do my best to make the planet proud."

CHAPTER SIX

MARINE BOOT CAMP, MERLIN

"THIS PLANET IS HEADING FOR TROUBLE," Roland said, after an hour spent reading through the reports. "There's no way to get around it."

He frowned as he surveyed the stack of paper files. The official government reports from New Doncaster were mindlessly optimistic, to the point it was hard to take them seriously. They seemed to believe that everything would go exactly the way they wanted, as if nothing whatsoever could or would go wrong. It was like looking at a gambler who'd busted out repeatedly and yet continued to insist he'd hit it right *next* time. The more practical reports from the spooks, and a handful of traders passing through the system, made it clear the planet was on the verge of civil war. There were just too many fault lines and too few people willing to admit something needed to be done.

"Yes, sir," Rachel said. Her voice was flat, emotionless. She'd proved she knew her way around the file system—she'd printed out hard copies, pointing out it was easier to absorb things written on paper rather than a terminal screen—but little else. She seemed willing to do whatever she was told yet unwilling to do things on her own initiative. "The best-case projection is that the explosion will take place in two years, assuming nothing is done about it."

Roland scowled. That projection struck him as mindlessly optimistic, too, although...his scowl deepened as he remembered the early post-Earthfall assessments that had been passed around the recruits. The spooks had insisted that it had been easy to predict that Earthfall was on the way, before it actually happened, but impossible to say precisely *when* it would happen. Roland understood—the chain of events that had triggered the final disaster had been hard to predict—but it was still irritating. He would have preferred a world that exactly followed the predictions.

No, you wouldn't, he told himself. The projections were horrific. New Doncaster was in for an orgy of score-settling, with vast numbers of people raped, murdered or simply enslaved. It was going to be a nightmare. *Something is going to have to be done.*

He buried himself in the files, assessing how the locals saw their government working and comparing it to how the government *actually* worked. On paper, the official government was remarkably reasonable; in practice, the system was so sewn up that the landowners—the ones on top—saw no reason to hide or cushion their dominance. Roland shuddered. He'd watched the Grand Senate tighten its grip, unaware of just how many people were coming to realise the Empire no longer worked for them. In hindsight, it was no surprise that Earthfall had been followed by a series of civil and interstellar wars. The Empire's population had taken advantage of the chaos to settle a few scores of their own.

Rachel cleared her throat. "Do you want to get something to eat before we make our way to the shuttle?"

"Please." Roland stood, brushing down his uniform, then did his best to parody a male romantic lead. "Would you care to join me for dinner in the commissary?"

Rachel smiled. It was a very tiny smile, so faint that Roland knew he would have missed it if he hadn't been looking at her, but it was very definitely a smile. He hid his own amusement as they walked down to the commissary, idly wondering what sort of fool would take a date to the Marine restaurant. The food was plentiful, and they didn't have to pay, but it was hardly a good place to take anyone. The girl would probably dump the poor fool on the spot.

The thought made him smile as they entered the hall—it was nearly empty—and collected trays of food, before sitting at a small table. He'd grown up eating only the finest foodstuffs in the empire—he dreaded to think, in hindsight, just how much food he'd wasted every month—and yet he knew he was going to miss the commissary when he left the camp for the final time. The food might be basic, but it was filling. And the company was better. The Summer Palace had been filled with servants, who had put up with everything from rudeness to sexual assault, and political figures who wanted his blessing. He wondered, idly, what had happened to the men who'd seemed to think his signature would make a difference. If they were still alive, they were probably cursing themselves for not doing something more practical with their time.

He studied Rachel thoughtfully as he chewed his food. She was polite and professional and...he was sure, deep inside, she didn't have the slightest idea who he really was. And yet, she was so professional she refused to talk about herself. Roland had been trained to show an interest in people—he could say the word *fascinating* in a hundred different tones, each one encouraging the listener to keep talking—but Rachel seemed to have been taught to keep her mouth shut. He'd barely been able to pry anything out of her. She seemed to want him to think of her as nothing more than part of the furniture. It was a very odd attitude for a Marine auxiliary.

Although you haven't met that many, he reminded himself, dryly. *And the ones you have met were all trained to assert themselves over the recruits.*

His terminal bleeped as a message arrived. He glanced at it, then shook his head. He'd filed a request for a message to be passed to Belinda, wherever she was, but it had been rejected. He hoped that was good news, but...it was hard to be sure. It wasn't as if he was a close relative. She'd been badly injured during the flight and...he'd been *told* she'd survived, that she'd resumed her duties, but he didn't *know*. It was quite possible her superiors—his superiors—had lied. Her unit had been so highly classified he hadn't even known it existed until well after he'd met her.

Rachel looked up at him. "Good news?"

"No," Roland said. He was tempted to ask her if she knew any backdoors they could use to get into the files, but that would get them both in deep shit. "But it doesn't matter."

He kept his eyes on her as she finished her dinner. It was odd. He knew he was jaded—he'd seen nothing he wanted in the brothels near the camp, the few times he'd gone on leave—but he was barely aware of her femininity. Perhaps it was because of the training—he'd never been aware of the female recruits either—but it was still odd. He wondered, suddenly, what the rules were on relationships between auxiliaries. He'd never thought to look them up. It had never crossed his mind he'd be one of them. And he supposed it should have.

You outrank her, he reminded himself, sharply. *Fucking a subordinate in your chain of command is a court-martial offense.*

Rachel's terminal bleeped. "The training detachment has assembled," she said. "They'll meet us at the shuttleport, before departure."

Roland stood. "And then we'll be on our way."

"Quite," Rachel said. "Are you looking forward to it?"

"Yes," Roland said. "And no."

He felt a yawning sensation in his stomach, despite the meal, as they returned to the transient barracks to pick up his carryall. On paper, the mission should be simplicity itself. The corps had handled hundreds of training missions over the past century, using Marines as a stopgap to keep insurgents from overrunning the local government while training troops to stabilise the situation and give the locals a stake in their own protection. In practice, the more he looked at the files, the more he wondered if they were about to be dropped in the shit. New Doncaster was important, but not *that* important. The corps might have written the planet off if they'd needed the manpower elsewhere.

"You won't be coming back," Rachel reminded him. "Is that all you've got?"

Roland nodded, curtly, as he slung the carryall over his back. He'd once had so much luggage that he—or, more accurately, his keepers—had had to hire a small army of servants to pack, transport and unpack his trunks. He'd never gone anywhere without his personal cooks, maids, tailors and cleaners. Now...he had a couple of uniforms, a small collection of underwear, a personal terminal and very little else. He'd been called bland and boring by his bunkmates for not having a porn collection. He hadn't been able to find the words to explain he considered most *porn* to be boring.

Not that we had much time for jerking off, he reflected. *There must have been something in the water.*

He felt oddly nostalgic as they made their way through the barracks, past a pair of checkpoints and down to the spaceport. The new recruits were already arriving, drill instructors shouting as they stumbled into ragged formations. It would take weeks for them to learn the basics and a number would decide they couldn't take it and quit. Roland approved, when he thought about it. If someone couldn't handle the first month of Boot Camp, better they quit rather than trying to stick it out until they passed the first quarter. There was nothing to be gained from wasting time.

Rachel kept pace with him easily as he picked up speed, jogging along the roadside. Roland was surprised. He'd had the impression she was slightly overweight, although her uniform was so baggy it was hard to be sure. He'd certainly met more than his fair share of politicians who'd had their outfits expertly tailored, just to hide their paunches. He didn't know why they didn't simply have the fat removed. It wasn't as if they couldn't afford it.

A flight of heavy shuttles flew overhead as they reached the outer gates. The guards checked their ID chips, then their orders, before letting them enter with strict instructions not to go wandering outside the designated areas. Roland nodded in understanding. The spaceport was a military base, *de facto* if not *de jure*, and anyone caught in the wrong place by the MPs would find themselves in hot water very quickly. Roland doubted anyone would cut any slack for *him*, even if they knew who he was. The spaceport came first.

He put the thought out of his mind as he led the way into the hangar. The training detachment had already requisitioned their supplies, piled up and waiting to be transferred to the shuttles. The men themselves—ten auxiliaries, all with more years in the corps than he'd had of *life*—were inspecting the supplies or reading the files, quickly listing everything else they might need. Roland hoped they'd get what they wanted before it was too late. Logistics wasn't his field—he had a feeling he would need to brush up very quickly—but even he knew there were shortages everywhere. It would be a long time before Merlin could make up much of the shortfall.

A short, stocky man caught his eye and stood to attention. "Officer on deck!"

This isn't a starship, Roland thought, with a flicker of amusement. *This is a spaceport.*

The humour faded as he surveyed his new command, leaving him feeling like an imposter. He hadn't had much time to read up on his people, to do more than memorise their names and faces, but it was clear they could handle much of the mission without any input from higher authority. They were strong and capable, perfectly able to do everything *he* could... it struck him, suddenly, that he'd been put in a position where he could sit on his ass and do nothing and still succeed. The men in front of him wouldn't hesitate to relieve him if he turned into a *real* burden. It would be embarrassing and the corps wouldn't be pleased, but it would be better than an actual disaster. The files had made it clear the planet was on the verge of outright civil war.

"For those of you who don't know me," Roland said, "I am Marine Auxiliary Captain Roland Windsor. I have been placed in command of this deployment"—he felt more like an imposter than ever—"and I intend to make it a success. I hope to have a chance to speak with each of you while we're in transit, to get to know you all a little better, but—for the moment—I want you to know you are welcome to speak freely to me. I think I know what I'm doing. You may well disagree with me."

He hesitated. Did that hit the right notes? The men in front of him had over a century of experience. Did they think him a promising young man—or a fool? He wanted to ask, and yet he didn't dare. It would show his insecurities...as if they'd expect him not to be insecure. He doubted he was fooling them. They'd trained more young recruits, from all kinds of backgrounds, than he'd had hot dinners. They knew he was making it up as he went along.

"The mission may be straightforward," he continued, "but we will proceed on the assumption it will be anything but. There are too many political factions on New Doncaster for us to expect them to be *rational*, particularly when their interests are threatened by our activities. If you have any concerns, I expect you to bring them to me. My experience is somewhat limited."

Non-existent, he corrected himself, silently. *And they know it, too.*

"We should be boarding the shuttle in four hours," he finished. "Is there anything else you need, now, that they're reluctant to provide?"

The short man—Master Sergeant (Auxiliary) Brian Wimer, according to the files—took a step forward. "Sir," he said. Somehow, he managed to make the *sir* sound real. "Our first tier of requests have all been filled. Our second tier"—he held out a datapad—"has been a little harder."

Roland took the datapad, dismissing the remainder of the group to return to their duties as he scanned the file. "Modified construction equipment? Automated diggers and builders?"

"I read the file, sir," Wimer said. "The weather on New Doncaster is terrible. The locals use quarried stone or wood to build most of their habitations, neither of which is ideally suited for us. Even laying down a training ground is going to be difficult. A small collection of automated equipment would make the difference between a defensible position and one we might have to abandon, if we come under fire."

"I see." Roland vaguely recalled reading that Wimer had been in the Construction Corps before transferring to the training unit as an auxiliary. He was surprised Wimer hadn't been sent elsewhere. The corps was short of trained manpower almost everywhere. Wimer could have written his own ticket, given his skills. "You think you can make the training base secure?"

"A combination of secure firing positions and trained defenders, sir, would make it a great deal harder for anyone to overrun the base," Wimer said. "If we had only one, we would have to abandon the position before it was overrun."

Roland nodded. He'd been taught how to attack and defend a fortified position. A small force, heavily dug in, could stand off an entire army... as long as the ammunition held out or the enemy didn't bring up heavy weapons. It was hard to believe a concrete blockhouse could be blown out of the ground, but there were smart shells and heavy bombs that could effortlessly vaporise the entire structure. He'd seen bunker-busters that could tear a complex out of a mountainside or clean nukes designed to punch holes in enemy lines, allowing the Marines to advance through the rubble. Wimer was right. If they could secure their bases, they'd be harder targets for anyone who wanted to start a civil war.

"I'll do what I can," he said. He knew better than to *promise*, not when there was no guarantee of success. "Is there anything else?"

He placed the request into the system, then spent the next few hours—Rachel constantly at his back—checking through the pallets of supplies. He'd learnt the hard way just how easy it was to miss something, for the supply officers to *forget* to provide something upon request; he'd been cautioned, time and time again, that it was harder to file complaints if one discovered something was missing in the middle of an engagement. Rachel seemed to approve, he noted, as he finished going through the boxes. If nothing else, he reflected, he knew what he had at his command. Weapons, ammunition, drones, machine tools, training supplies....

"Sir," Wimer said. "We're ready to load the shuttle."

Roland nodded, feeling a twinge of regret. He doubted he'd ever return to Merlin. Either he went on to the Slaughterhouse—or its replacement—or he died on New Doncaster. Unless he became an instructor himself. It wasn't impossible. The corps believed in rotating experienced men through the boot camps, just to ensure the training program was constantly up to date. Who knew what lessons might be lost if the ones who learnt them weren't allowed to spread the word?

"I'll give you a hand," he said. Marine officers weren't allowed to keep themselves *that* aloof from their men. It wasn't as if he had anything more important to do. "And then we'll be on our way."

CHAPTER SEVEN

BARAKA ISLAND, NEW DONCASTER

THE MORNING HEAT SEEMED to be constantly rising as Sarah Wilde slipped out of the outback and stepped onto the muddy road, making her way down towards the plantation and the town beyond. The wind constantly shifted, at times blowing the stench of alien foliage across her nostrils only to switch, moments later, to a warm sea breeze that was almost a relief. She checked that her hat was firmly in place, then brushed down her skirt as she continued to walk into the open. It was risky to expose herself now that her plans were being finalised—and she'd convinced most of the rebel factions to unite under her leadership—but there was little choice. It was easy to lose the sense of what was *really* happening if one remained in one's base, isolated from the outside world. She'd learnt that lesson the hard way.

Sweat trickled down her back as the road widened suddenly, revealing the plantation on the edge of town. The fields were lined with bushy trees that were somehow, subtly, wrong to her eyes, a grim reminder that New Doncaster wasn't a wholly human world. Sarah had never been a country girl—she'd grown up in a CityBlock where there were no parks or gardens—but even she felt oddly ill at ease when she looked at the crops. They were just *wrong*. Dark figures—indents and debtors—moved among the stalks, tapping a handful to drain the oil and transport it to their masters. Sarah didn't pretend to understand the details of the planetary economy, but she knew the basics. The oil—and many other biological products—fetched a high price on the interstellar market, providing the outsider currency that kept the landowners from having to share power with the townies, let alone the debtors and indents at the very bottom of society. It was no wonder that the planet was permanently on the verge of a giant explosion. She'd spent the last few years working to make sure the explosion actually destroyed the old order and created room for the new.

She kept moving, careful not to draw attention. Their masters insisted they only had to work until they paid off their debts, but the smarter ones quickly worked out they'd *never* pay off the debt. They'd be angry, then start plotting…some of them would flee into the backcountry, some would turn into bandits and some would start plotting bloody revenge. She hoped the latter kept their heads down until the rebellion began. An uprising now would risk alerting the landowners before it was too late. It was bad enough they'd had to engage a patrol that had gotten too close to the landing site. She feared the enemy commander had gotten a little *too* lucky. One spy somewhere in her chain of command would be enough to ruin everything.

Her heart twisted as she passed the fields and hurried to the town. It looked small and picturesque, from a distance, but the appearance hid an ugly reality. Most of the wooden buildings were built with slave labour—whatever the law said, there was no doubt the indents were little more than property—and the population lacked any real control over their own lives. Only a handful of citizens had any real autonomy—the doctors, the dentists, the trained professionals—and those careers were only open to townies and landowners. The sheer scale of the corruption had astonished her, when she'd finally realised just how deeply it was woven into the entire society. Didn't they *realise* they were running out of time?

She shook her head, allowing her eyes to wander over the distant ocean. A handful of bigger ships were resting in the waters, waiting for the tides to rise so they could enter the harbour and start unloading; dozens of smaller fishing boats darted around, splitting their time between the big island and the uncounted dozens of semi-legal settlements within the habitable zone. She sucked in her breath as she spied the clouds, forming with terrifying speed. It had scared her, once, to see how quickly the weather could change from dry to a total downpour. Now...she was used to it.

A militiaman spotted her as she walked into town and moved to block her way. "Papers, please."

Sarah sighed inwardly and dug into her pouch. The locals didn't seem to realise that simply handing out dozens of ID papers, from simple residency permits to internal passports, made it very easy for corruption to flourish. Sarah and her comrades had had little trouble finding someone in the issuing office who could be bribed, someone who'd issued them all the—perfectly valid—documents they needed to go anywhere they liked. It wasn't as if the local militia would dare get in their way. And even if they did....

She grimaced. The militia were largely time-servers. She'd gotten out of trouble more than once, in her early days, by going down on her knees and giving her would-be captor the best oral sex he'd ever had. It was astonishing how much they'd overlook in exchange for venality. Now...she wasn't so sure that would work. The militia had lost a dozen militiamen, only five days ago. They might be a little more alert. She silently assessed the man in front of her, preparing herself to draw her dagger and stab him before he could stop her. She might get away. The militia wasn't always popular amongst the townies.

"You may pass," the militiaman said, clearly disappointed her papers had checked out. She was sure he'd been hoping for a chance to angle for a bribe, either monetary or sexual. "Just remember to be back at the farm by nightfall."

Sarah bobbled a curtsey, took her papers and hurried away before he could change his mind. Her papers insisted she was a farm girl, the daughter of an independent farmer; she was, she'd been assured, too high and yet too low to draw the wrong kind of attention. There weren't many independents on Baraka and the ones who'd made it, paying off their debts to the settlement corporation, tended to have powerful connections. It was a good cover, although she was all too aware of the risks. There was a slight, but unavoidable chance she'd encounter someone who *knew* the farmer didn't have a daughter like her.

Or someone who thinks he'll get a part-share in the farm if I marry him, she thought, with a flicker of grim amusement. Her papers insisted she was nineteen, nearly nine years younger than she really was, but the average farm girl married at sixteen, as soon as she was of legal age. Sarah didn't pretend to understand it. *He might be very disappointed if he finds out the truth.*

She smiled as she made her way down the street, stepping between puddles of water from the previous rainfall. The townspeople either ignored her or nodded politely, perhaps assuming she wasn't particularly important. Sarah kept her eyes lowered demurely, but she was well practiced at taking information in without making it obvious. There were armed guards outside the bank, as well as the harbour gates. The latter looked surprisingly professional. They didn't even wolf-whistle at her as she walked past.

Troubling, she thought. *Are they bringing in reinforcements from the rest of the inhabited islands?*

The thought mocked her as she entered the alleyway, then knocked once on a plain wooden door. There was a long pause, long enough for a normal visitor to knock twice, then the door opened. Sarah allowed herself a moment of relief as she stepped into the cool air inside, closing the door before she removed her hat. The interior smelt faintly of perfume and something indefinable. It brought back memories, most unhappy ones. It also reminded her of precisely why she was fighting the war in the first place.

"Welcome back," Joyce said. "You're looking well."

"Thanks," Sarah said, as she gave the older woman a hug. "How's business?"

"It never falters." Joyce led her into the tiny sitting room. "It won't be long before the afternoon rush begins."

Sarah nodded, curtly. There was never any shortage of customers for the brothel. The sailors, the militiamen...even townspeople with no qualms about cheating on their wives...they all passed through the brothel's doors. And they talked...oh yes, they talked. Sarah had taken full advantage when she'd started to put her plan together, developing networks that stretched all the way to Kingstown and beyond. She felt a flicker of the old disgust as she took a seat and accepted a cool drink, leaning back in her chair as she sipped. She was prepared to do anything to advance her cause, but... she liked to think there were at least *some* limits.

"The girls have been busy, then," she said. "How are the newcomers?"

"Patty is too flirty to be of any real use, although she does have a knack for making customers happy," Joyce said. "Hannah and Bella are doing well. I've got them listening to what their clients say and reporting back to me. Grace"—she shuddered—"I'm afraid Grace got *the* treatment. She's nothing more than a walking corpse."

Sarah shuddered, too. She'd been threatened with being *adjusted* once or twice, when she'd been shipped to New Doncaster and put to work in the brothels. It was a far cry from the handsome farmer she'd been promised. And if Grace had been *adjusted*...she cursed under her breath. The poor girl might walk and talk and open her legs on command, but her personality was gone. Her will was gone. She followed orders, any orders. It was sickening.

Joyce seemed to sense her unease. "The militia has been in a bit of a tizzy," she said. "They lost fifty men in the outback, from what they say. Their commander got recalled to Kingstown in a hurry, leaving someone else in command. I don't know if reinforcements are on the way...."

"They didn't lose fifty men," Sarah said. They'd recovered five bodies and stripped them of everything before dumping them in the swamp. There might have been more, but she doubted it. The militia couldn't have moved fifty or more men up the road without being noticed a long time before they sprang the ambush. "They're lying again."

"Or a bunch of young twats deserted and their superiors decided it would be better to claim they'd been killed in honourable combat," Joyce said. "One of our clients was going on and on about someone who got himself killed, along with a few others."

Sarah filed it away for later consideration. The militia was very much a mixed bag, from men who wanted to look brave and heroic without actually being in any real danger to time-servers who'd been given a flat choice between service or jail. The men who wanted to genuinely face danger joined the army instead, which shipped them from trouble spot to trouble spot without giving them much, if any, time to rest and recuperate. She knew from grim experience they tended to be tougher than the militia. They certainly had more mobile firepower and air support on call.

And the person who was complaining might be worth trying to recruit, she thought. She had a number of militiamen on the payroll, from dissidents to outright traitors. *It's something to think about when we have a moment.*

"We also got a message from Kingstown," Joyce added. "It's not good news."

Sarah braced herself. She'd been expecting the hammer to fall for months now. The more she'd woven the disparate rebel factions into a single entity, the greater the chance of a single mishap—or traitor—leading to the destruction of the entire force. She was all too aware there were people, like Steve, who wanted to take action, who wanted to lash out at the landowners and their allies. And yet, if they didn't manage to crush most of the opposition in their first strike, victory would become a great deal more challenging. She thought of the facilities along the coast and shuddered. If they remained in enemy hands, the war would never be won.

"The government has concluded an agreement for the deployment of two Marine units to the planetary surface," Joyce said. "One unit will apparently secure the spaceport while stiffening the militia, the other will embark on an ambitious training program to raise new soldiers to strengthen the army."

Her lips twitched. "Stiffening the militia is *our* job."

Sarah ignored the weak joke as she forced herself to think. The army was tough. Anything that made it stronger was bad news. And yet, where were the recruits going to come *from?* She'd done her best to assess the manpower available to the landowners—a difficult task, given how much was considered classified—and even her most pessimistic calculations had suggested the landowner manpower was reaching its limits. They were reluctant to draw on townies....

They might have changed their minds about that, she thought. *If they think we'll kill most of the new recruits, they might think they won't have to pay a price for giving the townies guns and teaching them how to use them.*

It was possible, she supposed, although she had her doubts. The townies might be quieter than debtors and indents—and rebels—and they certainly had more to lose, but they also knew they were just as screwed as the rest of society. They would demand a high price before they started flocking to the recruiting stations; they'd want better political representation, perhaps even a widened franchise. They might even want some of the unsettled islands to be declared estates, then constituencies. And who knew what would happen then?

"It might be nothing more than a flash in the pan," she said. She had some allies amongst the townies, mainly younger citizens who were starting to chafe against society's rules. "Or it might be quite serious."

"The Marines are supposed to be good," Joyce warned. "Their combat record is unmatched."

Sarah smiled. "They said that about the militia, too," she pointed out. "And half the time the militiamen don't stand their ground when they don't have heavy firepower on call."

"And half the time they do," Joyce pointed out.

"Yeah." Sarah leaned back in her chair and tried to recall what little she'd heard about the Marine Corps. She'd had a lone professor who'd seemed to have a man-crush on the Marines—he'd left the university under unexplained circumstances, shortly before she'd been arrested and deported—but the remainder had been long on military-bashing and short on details she could use. "They might just be overrated."

She shook her head. "When are they due to arrive?"

"I don't know," Joyce said. "There was some suggestion they were either on the way or already here, but details were sparse. Reading between the lines, I think our Prime Minister and his cronies got the negotiations started without bothering to get approval from the MPs, then did a lot of arm-twisting to get them to agree to support the plan. It's possible the government wasn't given much of a choice. We supply products that simply can't be had anywhere else. It's possible outside powers told the government to take the Marines and clean up their mess, or else."

"Or else what?" Sarah wasn't so sure. "An invasion?"

"It's possible," Joyce said. "And if that happens it would be pretty bad for the landowners."

"True." Sarah snickered. "I guess they'd outlive their usefulness very quickly."

"Within seconds," Joyce confirmed.

Sarah smiled, then leaned forward. "Do we have any confirmation? Anything we can use to make contact with off-world allies?"

"Not as far as I know," Joyce said. "A lot of what I hear, as you know, is second or third-hand. There's just no guarantee even a majority of it is accurate. The negotiations were conducted by people who don't patronise my brothels, so...."

"They don't talk out of turn," Sarah finished. The truth would get out—it always did—but it would take time. "If we secure control of the world, quickly, would they deal with us instead?"

"I don't know," Joyce said. "There are just too many unanswered questions."

"And no way to get them answered in a hurry," Sarah said. She glanced at the clock as it chimed, once. Time was running out. She wanted to be well clear of the town before the sailors were released from the docks. "We may have to move our timetable up a little."

"It might be a good idea," Joyce agreed. "If they tighten up the sensor network in orbit, it'll certainly make life a great deal harder."

Sarah stood, brushing down her skirt. "Keep me informed," she said. "Try and cultivate someone with the access we need, perhaps someone in the militia HQ. There has to be someone who can be induced to give us more accurate information."

"Oh, there will be," Joyce said. "I know a couple who have...left themselves open to blackmail. It will be risky to make contact, but...it might work."

"Do it." Sarah pulled her hat into place. "Leave the regular message in the standard dead drop."

"Understood," Joyce said. "Do you want to meet the new girls?"

Sarah shook her head. It was better they never saw her. What they didn't know they couldn't be forced to tell. And besides...she shivered. She didn't want to remember what it had been like to work in the brothel. She knew, all too well, that she could easily have been worked until she dropped and then left to die.

But I survived, she told herself, as she took her leave. *And I'll make them pay.*

CHAPTER EIGHT

NEW DONCASTER SPACEPORT, NEW DONCASTER

ROLAND HAD BEEN CAUTIONED, more than once, that military service was ninety-nine percent boredom and one percent screaming terror, but he'd never understood how true that saying was until he'd boarded the transport and found himself forced to wait, with very little to do, until the freighter reached New Doncaster. He hadn't entirely wasted the time—he had spoken to each of his subordinates, as well as reading and rereading all the files—but it still felt as though he'd done nothing. It was a relief, when the freighter finally entered orbit, to board a shuttle for the surface. At least he was doing *something*.

He strapped himself in and listened, with half an ear, to the pilot's safety briefing. It was remarkably serious, compared to the normal quirky lectures from pilots who took their small craft into danger time and time again. New Doncaster's weather was dangerously unpredictable, the pilot warned, and they might run into a storm at any moment. Roland doubted it could be as hazardous as a drop into the teeth of enemy fire, but he checked his belt and straps carefully as the shuttle disengaged from the freighter. Rachel sat next to him, as prim and composed as ever. He still hadn't managed to draw her out of her shell.

The viewscreen came to life as the shuttle descended into the atmosphere. New Doncaster was a blue-green orb, but—as the shuttle continued its flight—the planet started to look decidedly odd. A green-blue band of life was wrapped around the equator, the northern and southern hemispheres—outside the habitable zone—half-hidden under white clouds that looked harmless, but were actually incredibly dangerous to anyone unlucky enough to be caught in the storms. It wasn't impossible to live outside the band of islands that made up the habitable zone, according to the files, but it was extremely difficult. The only people who risked it were isolationists or runaways. Everyone else kept their distance from the *de facto* border.

He gritted his teeth as the shuttle rocked, violently. He'd made a dozen parachute drops during his training, jumping from aircraft carefully designed to look as though they were going to fall apart at any moment, but this was worse. The shuttle shook again and again, unnerving him despite his appearance. He felt powerless, helpless. There was nothing he could do to save himself, if something went badly. Taking a parachute and jumping into the heart of a storm would be suicide. He wondered, grimly, if the shuttle would try to abort the landing and head back to orbit. The files had cautioned that it had happened on a regular basis.

There's no danger, he told himself, as the shaking grew even worse. The shuttle was in the grip of an angry god, intent on ripping the craft to pieces. *There's no danger....*

Rachel seemed perfectly calm, somehow, as the shuttle steadied just long enough for them to relax before the shaking started again. Roland asked himself how she could remain so calm in the face of apparent danger. It wasn't as if she was stupid. He was sure there was a sharp mind hiding behind her frumpy exterior, a degree of expertise he knew he couldn't hope to match. And yet...he resisted the urge to take her hand as the shaking grew worse and worse. It wouldn't make things any better for either of them.

The shuttle dropped, abruptly. Roland saw a cloud of *something* rushing towards them, an instant before the viewscreen blanked. The shuttle's gravity field flickered—for a horrible moment, he was *sure* the shuttle had flipped upside down—before the flight steadied once again. He didn't allow himself to relax, not this time. He'd been caught by surprise once before.

"Lady and gentleman," the pilot said, through the intercom. "We have passed through the worst of the storm and are now *en route* to Kingstown Island Spaceport."

Roland frowned as the viewscreen came back to life. Kingstown was a fairly large island, large enough—according to the files—that calling it an *island* understated the point. There was enough land surface for everything from farms to factories, from a spaceport that shipped raw materials to high orbit to a fishing industry that kept the islands fed. His unease deepened as the shuttle swept over the waters, the viewscreen focusing—briefly—on hundreds of ships in the blue waters below. They were a strange mixture, everything from simple sailing ships to metallic tramp freighters and even a large cruise liner. The files had insisted the planetary tech base was actually quite low, allowing the inhabitants to maintain it without a constant stream of supplies from the interplanetary and interstellar community. It made sense, but Roland suspected it was a political nightmare. People who knew about the existence of fusion cores and drive fields wouldn't be happy with anything lesser. Who wanted to drive a petrol car, or sail a wind-powered boat, when they could have something far more efficient? And yet, a colony world that became dependent on the outside universe was doomed. Roland had been told that hundreds had regressed, sharply, as interstellar trade fell into the shitter. New Doncaster was fortunate to have escaped that fate.

He leaned back in his seat as the spaceport came into view. It was larger than he'd expected; a handful of prefabricated hangars, a cluster of landing pads and runaways, several aircraft that looked disturbingly primitive, a pair of buildings that looked like military housing and were probably transient barracks for new colonists. A pair of air defence units were clearly in evidence, situated a little too close to the fence for his peace of mind. His heart sank as he realised just how many buildings were far too close to the fence. They provided far too much cover for anyone who wanted to sneak up on the fence and start shooting. There were no clear fields of fire outside the spaceport. Whoever had designed the installation clearly hadn't considered the possibility of it coming under attack.

And it will, Roland thought. *It's the gate to the stars.*

The shuttle came to a halt, then lowered itself to a landing pad. A *thump* ran through the craft as it touched the ground. Roland felt tired and worn, as if he'd been through a major firefight rather than a bumpy shuttle ride. It was all he could do to unstrap himself, as soon as the safety light clicked off, and force himself to stand. His uniform was damp with sweat. Rachel, beside him, looked utterly unbothered by the flight and landing. Roland eyed her thoughtfully, then hefted his knapsack and headed for the hatch. It was already hissing open. The shuttle pilot probably wanted to get back to orbit as quickly as possible.

"Captain Allen said he'd meet us at the spaceport," Rachel said, quietly. "Remember, he outranks you."

Roland nodded, curtly. He might be a captain, at least on paper, but it was nothing more than a brevet rank. Captain Michel Allen, on the other hand, was an experienced officer who'd been in the corps longer than Roland had been alive, with a string of accomplishments that made Roland feel like a fraud. He tried to tell himself that Captain Allen had been young too, once upon a time, but it was hard to believe. The man's record was just too long. The idea of Roland working with him, let alone giving orders to him, was absurd....

And you don't have the authority to give him orders, he reminded himself. *You're meant to work closely with him, not to boss him around.*

The shuttle was cool, but the heat struck him the moment he stepped through the hatch. He started to sweat, again, as he looked around the spaceport. The sunlight was a shade *too* bright, the blue sky a strange shade that felt subtly *wrong*. He saw a haze over the distant city, suggesting that visibility was going to be as variable as everything else. A pair of tiny aircraft rested near the hangar, both so small he couldn't help wondering if they were toys. It seemed impossible that they could *fly*. The shuttle wasn't the largest spacecraft in the galaxy and yet it made the aircraft look tiny.

His sense of unease grew stronger as they made their way towards the spaceport terminal. A cluster of Marines were guarding the fence, and running patrols around the hangars, but the whole arrangement looked dangerously insecure. People in local clothing - short-sleeved shirts and shorts—were everywhere, carrying boxes and goods towards the waiting shuttles without—as far as he could tell—any real vetting. He doubted Captain Allen was pleased. Why hadn't he done anything about it? His men could have taken a great many more precautions, without impeding the spaceport's staff as they went about their work. He glanced up as a pair of Raptors passed overhead, weapons pods clearly visible under their stubby wings. The Marines were making a show of force. He had a feeling that boded ill.

The terminal loomed in front of them. An older man, wearing simple BDUs, stepped outside and looked them up and down. Roland straightened automatically. Captain Allen—he'd read the man's file—bore the scars of decades in the corps, his bearing suggesting he'd been in and out of the hospital several times during the course of his career. His hair was hidden under his helmet, but Roland was sure it was cropped close to his scalp. Captain Allen looked like an officer who'd decided practicality was more important than appearance. Roland approved. He'd been cautioned that anyone who put appearance ahead of practicality was likely to get himself and far too many other people killed.

"Sir." Roland didn't salute. They were in a combat zone. "Marine Auxiliary Captain Roland Windsor, reporting."

"Glad to see you." Allen's voice was terminally unimpressed. "This way."

He led them into the terminal, past a set of empty inspection stands and into a small office. It looked strange, a combination of expensive furnishings and military-grade folding tables, chairs and terminals. A small coffeepot hummed by the wall, next to a drinks cabinet that had been carefully sealed with duct tape; the wall was covered with maps of the planet and the major islands, pinned over more elaborate decorations that were more likely to distract rather than inform. Roland guessed the office had once belonged to the spaceport manager. It had the unmistakable whiff of someone who saw his position as a chance to get rich while doing as little as possible. He wondered, idly, what had happened to the former owner.

"Sit." Allen poured them both mugs of coffee, then sat himself. "What do you make of our defences. Speak freely."

Roland hesitated, then took the plunge. "Dangerously insecure, sir."

"Correct." Allen met his eyes. "On paper, I have an entire company under my command. In practice, I have sixty-three Marines and thirty auxiliaries. Half of those are required to remain on Quick Reaction Alert at all times, when they're not flying on patrol or sweeping through suspected rebel camps. I don't have the manpower to secure the spaceport properly and, for political reasons, I am not allowed to tighten security, vet the workers or do much of anything as long as the spaceport doesn't come under direct attack. The only reason we're stationed here, Windsor, is because the local government cannot afford to lose the spaceport. It would put a real crimp in their operations."

"And cut off their income from off-world," Roland added. "I assume the rebels know that too, sir?"

"Yes." Allen indicated the map. "So far, they've made no major effort to test our defences, but we suspect that'll change shortly. They have a certain interest in keeping the spaceport intact too, as large parts of the planet's economy are dependent on a constant flow of income, but"—he shrugged—"there are limits. They'd take a hit, sure, if the spaceport went up in flames. It wouldn't be lethal, not for them. It's just a matter of time before they decide the spaceport has outlived its usefulness."

He made a face. "I won't sugar-coat a shit sandwich for you. The locals are in denial—their intelligence staff couldn't find its own asshole with both hands and a GPS terminal—but there's a constant low-level insurgency going on beyond the line. Lots of little incidents, some of which are probably spontaneous, some of which are clearly planned and carried out by larger rebel cells; a steady stream of murders, kidnappings, bombings and general harassment operations. The rebels haven't yet made the transition to a high-level insurgency, one that poses a threat to the government, but I think it won't be long now. Quite frankly, they should have taken the threat seriously a great deal sooner."

"I read the reports, sir," Roland said. "How long do we have?"

Allen snorted. "My mid-case assessment is six months to a year, unless the government wises up and starts making—and honouring—promises. A lot depends on just how many cells the rebels manage to establish over here, how many alliances they form between the different factions. Best-case, we're looking at five years, which is probably mindlessly optimistic; worst-case, it could kick off tomorrow. I think the only thing holding them back is the grim awareness that once the operational tempo gets up and running, they're going to have to take and hold territory and that will pin them in place. They won't be able to slip back into the undergrowth and vanish."

Roland took a breath. "How much support can you give me?"

"Very little," Allen said. "Like I told you, most of my force is pinned down guarding the spaceport. I can't spare more than a couple of platoons, at best, for supporting the local forces. If you don't get your forces up and running before the balloon goes up, the locals are fucked. Whatever emerges after the war, it won't be anything like the current order."

"I see." Roland wasn't sure if Allen was being realistic or defeatist. The Marines could and would hammer the insurgents, whenever they showed themselves, but they couldn't be everywhere at once. And if they took down a Raptor...Allen would lose half his deployable force in a single, terrible moment. "How *are* the locals, as a fighting force?"

"A very mixed bag," Allen said. "Their regular army is reasonably professional, certainly when compared to the militia, but it is just too small to be effective. The militia ranges from very tough and experienced bushwhackers to pretty-boy units that refuse to patrol, even inside the wire, because they'd get their uniforms mussed. Their officers are sometimes very good, with genuine leadership skills, but the majority are—at best—little more than timeservers. They also have issues with serving away from their homes and families. The regulars have been trying to deploy officers to stiffen the militia, just as we're intended to do, but the results have been decidedly mixed. The militia officers are usually high-class assholes and refuse to take orders from middle-class assholes."

"I know the type, sir," Roland said. "They'll be screaming for help when the insurgency kicks into high gear."

"By then, it will be too late," Allen said. "There was a bill proposed in their parliament, six months ago, for regular officers to outrank their militia counterparts. The MPs were outraged at the very thought and flatly refused to allow the bill to be debated, let alone voted upon and signed into law. The bottom line, as I said in my reports, is that the planet is unwilling or unable to help itself and, if it wasn't so important to the sector's economy, I would advise pulling out and letting the locals fight it out for supremacy."

Roland grimaced. "Who do you think will win?"

"Hard to say." Allen sipped his coffee. "The rebels have the better cause. They also have a great deal of support. There's a lot of resentment nearly everywhere, even here. We've picked up rumours of a new rebel leader, one who's united the cells under his banner. And we think they have some support from off-world. It isn't impossible. There's quite a few factions amongst the spacers who want to give the planetary government a black eye.

"On the other land, the government has a sizable amount of firepower—with or without us—and, if used properly, could prevent the rebels from gaining control over the core islands and, eventually, winning the war. They could promote their better officers and discharge the incompetents, allowing the former to actually *fight* without being held back; they could take action to address the inequalities in their society, the electoral system that makes it hard for anyone who isn't a landowner to make any real changes to their society. But that would require them to take a good hard look at their own world, and how their own actions are making things worse for themselves. I doubt the government can do it without being overthrown by their own people."

"Crap," Roland said.

Allen laughed. "The government liaison officer is on his way," he said. "He's a good man, but he's in the political doghouse. Hopefully, you and your team can work with him to build up the regulars before it's too late. Time is not on your side."

Rachel cleared her throat. "Sir, why is he in the doghouse?"

"He had the misfortune to survive when an upper-class twit got himself and a bunch of others killed," Allen said. "And they made sure he got the blame."

Roland's heart sank. *That* boded ill.

CHAPTER NINE

NEW DONCASTER SPACEPORT, NEW DONCASTER

IT WAS HARD, AS RICHARD DROVE the official car through the checkpoint and parked outside the spaceport terminal, not to feel a flicker of resentment. No, he corrected himself; a *lot* of resentment. He was an officer on detached duty and he should have had a driver, as well as a bodyguard, but both of those perks had been denied. He'd been cautioned, in the week since he'd been assigned to the Marines as a liaison officer, to keep his head down as much as possible. He had too many enemies in high places now, all determined to make him pay for their failings. And....

He felt a moment of wistfulness as he spotted the Marines patrolling the perimeter. They didn't have to wait for orders from superiors who didn't have the slightest idea what was going on, any more than they had to work their way through a long checklist before they called down fire on enemy positions. *Their* officers knew what they were doing and, when their subordinates had concerns, responded with neither sarcasm nor total indifference. It was hard not to feel he should have joined the Marines instead, even though it would have meant service light-years from his homeworld. The Marines didn't have so many nitwits in high places. Insisting their commanding officers worked their way up the ladder, rather than buying commissions, ensured they developed an understanding of the realities of war before it was too late. *They* wouldn't have walked straight into an obvious trap.

His heart clenched. He'd spoken to his father, and some of his friends, and they'd all agreed he needed to keep his head down. He wasn't even allowed to talk about what had happened to his former CO. He could have cautioned the other regulars about how the rebels had better weapons and tactics now, but…he wasn't even allowed to do *that*. No one wanted to hear about the ambush, let alone think about the implications. He liked to think that *someone* in the military was aware of the threat, and was considering what to do about it, but he doubted it. The landowners had spoken. The ambush had succeeded because Richard had been an incompetent failure; anyone who dared suggest otherwise would rapidly find themselves reassigned to the islands on the edge of the habitable zone.

There haven't been many incidents here, he reminded himself, crossly. *It's easy to believe there's nothing to worry about if you haven't seen the enemy at close range.*

He sighed. He'd checked the records, when he hadn't been feeling sorry for himself, and discovered the rebels hadn't been active on Kingsland. It wasn't reassuring. The rebels would *have* to take the battle to the capital island if they wanted to *win* and the lack of enemy activity suggested they were planning something. There hadn't even been much labour agitation over the past six months. It was quiet. Too quiet. Richard was grimly certain it was just a matter of time before something exploded.

And then we'll have no time to recover, he thought. *They'll hit us so hard we'll lose the war in the first blow.*

He looked up, then climbed out of the car as two people came into view. One was a young man, so handsome he could have stepped right off a recruiting poster; Richard loathed him on sight. Short dark hair, dark eyes, a strong chin, muscles on his muscles…the bastard had either had genetic enhancements spliced into his bloodline or he'd spent an awful lot of time having cosmetic surgery. Richard was *sure* all the young women wanted him. The young woman behind him was…Richard frowned, unsure if he was seeing things. She looked…odd, wearing an ill-fitting uniform that didn't, he noted, impede her movements in any way. Sloppy, without actually being such; he wondered, suddenly, if she wanted to be underestimated. She looked like a woman on the plantations, someone who'd wear a very loose dress to hide her figure. And yet, she was a Marine. Perhaps. He wasn't entirely sure what a Marine auxiliary *was*. The briefing notes had been so vague he'd been unable to make head or tail of them.

"Welcome to New Doncaster," he said. He was *damned* if he'd call the newcomer *sir*, not until he proved himself. "I'm Lieutenant Richard Collier, Regular Army."

"Captain Roland Windsor, Marine Auxiliaries," the newcomer said. His accent was odd, a strange mixture of upper and lower class. "Thank you for meeting us."

Richard nodded, curtly, as the woman introduced herself too. Roland was a Windsor? There was a family with that name amongst the landowners, although—as far as he knew—none of their members had left the planet and joined the Marines. The only one he'd met had been an excellent sniper, although—like the rest of the landowners—reluctant to follow orders from a townie. He dismissed the thought in a moment of irritation. The odds of Roland Windsor being related to *the* Windsor Family were incredibly low. It wasn't as if they had a monopoly on the name.

He opened the car doors. "I have orders to show you the training grounds, then I am at your disposal."

"Thank you." Roland sat carefully, in a manner that would allow him to draw his pistol in an instant. "I understand you recently encountered the rebels?"

"Yes." Richard bit off a response that would probably get him marched in front of a court-martial board. Again. "It's all in my report."

"It wasn't forwarded to me," Roland said. "And I would like to hear it from you."

Richard sat in the driver's seat and turned the key in the ignition. He wasn't surprised the report hadn't been sent to the newcomers, even though they needed to know what they were up against. The brief report of Captain Tarquin Ludlow's death had been long on praise for the dead man and short on actual detail, to the point no one who knew *anything* about the military could believe a word of it. There'd certainly been no attempt to examine the lessons of the brief, yet violent encounter. They weren't even trying to examine the mistakes they'd insisted *he'd* made. And now the newcomers were asking him.

He guided the car through the gates and onto the road. "Are you asking on or off the record?"

"Off," Roland said. "A great deal gets left out of the official reports."

Richard said nothing for a long moment. It was hard to be sure, but he had the impression Roland had seen very little—if any—active service. Marine training was supposed to be good, the best of the best, but—outside bad flicks—drill instructors didn't *really* torture, maim and kill their recruits. There were limits to how far they could go, particularly with live ammunition. Roland might have aced training exercises while never having been in any real danger. A bullet—a real bullet—cracking through the air could easily ruin someone's day.

"Off the record, then," he said. Roland had asked, after all. It would be rude not to answer. "What happened was a goddamned nightmare."

He went through the whole story, starting with Captain Tarquin Ludlow being assigned as the unit's CO and ending with his recall back to Kingstown. Roland listened, asking a handful of questions that ranged from practical to pointless. Richard wasn't sure if Roland was trying to cover all the bases, get a solid read on Richard himself or doing something that only made sense to an inexperienced Marine. He understood questions about rebel weapons and tactics, but the politics of landowner militiamen?

The car glided down the road, circumventing the capital until it finally reached a checkpoint outside the garrison. Richard stopped by the armed guards, allowed them to inspect his papers, then drove into the garrison itself. Memories rose in his mind as the skies started to darken. He'd done his basic training here, when he'd been young and foolish. He wondered, idly, how many of his peers had survived. The government might not be interested in acknowledging it, but there *was* a war on. The loss rate was terrifying.

He parked the car, then climbed outside and opened the doors. The air felt hot and humid, a clear sign a thunderstorm was on the way. Roland looked around with interest, his face under tight control. Richard tried to see the training ground through his eyes and winced, inwardly, at just how primitive it must seem. The prefabricated barracks were watertight, and the training ground itself was solid concrete, but the remainder of the facilities were sorely lacking. His superiors had had to fight for every clip of ammunition, filling in reams of paperwork every time they wanted to hold a training exercise. It wasn't a surprise that most of the regulars were terrible shots. They wanted to do better, of course, but they just couldn't get the ammunition. The budget wasn't there.

Rachel caught his eye. "Where is everyone?"

"There are two training garrisons," Richard told her. He wasn't sure what she really was, if indeed she was anything beyond an aide, but he wasn't going to be rude. "Right now, the current training class are exercising in the second garrison"—he waved a hand towards the distant hills—"somewhere over there. This garrison is largely empty right now."

"Really?" Roland sounded concerned. "How many men can you train at any one time?"

"In theory, a thousand," Richard said. It was hard to keep the bitterness from his voice. "In practice, considerably fewer."

"How so?" Roland didn't look at him, choosing instead to survey the rows of prefabricated barracks. "You need a steady stream of replacements."

Richard hesitated. He knew the answer. *Everyone* knew the answer. But telling the truth to outsiders might get him in trouble. *More* trouble. And who knew what would happen then?

Roland seemed to read his mind. "Whatever you tell us will not be repeated."

"I've heard that before," Richard said. Oddly, he almost believed Roland. The young man—Richard thought Roland was a year or two younger than he was—had an air of cool certainty that made it hard to doubt Roland. It was probably an act, but..."Do you really want the truth?"

"Yes."

Richard took a breath. "First, the bosses are reluctant to recruit from the lower classes," he said. "They were reluctant to accept *me*, when I volunteered, and my family is not in debt. And second, the training cadre is often parcelled out to the combat zone. Too many of them get killed, or worse, before they can be rotated back again or new ones prepped to take over. Does that answer your question?"

"I see." Roland said nothing for a long moment. "We did bring a handful of new training staff with us. We should be able to start recruiting and training on a far larger scale."

Good luck with that, Richard thought, sardonically. There weren't enough landowners to fill the training slots, even if they wanted to be infantry, and they remained reluctant to recruit townies. Taking debtors and indents...the nasty part of his mind wanted to suggest they tried to propose just that, in hopes half his superiors would have heart attacks the moment they got the message. *The problem isn't a shortage of warm bodies, the problem is that they don't want to use the warm bodies they've got.*

"We'll also need to expand the facilities," Roland continued. A low rumble split the air. "What is that?"

"Thunder," Richard said. He was surprised Roland didn't recognise it, although...if the stories about humanity's dead homeworld were true, most natives had lived in warrens far beneath the surface. They might not even have seen the sky, not until it finally fell. "We'd better get into cover."

He led the way into the nearest barracks and stayed by the door, watching as they looked around the building. It wasn't bad, just very basic. The recruits had cleaned it from top to bottom before boarding their buses, leaving it as good as new. Richard remembered his first days in the barracks and winced. It hadn't been easy, not when he'd been away from home for the first time. Others had had it worse. They'd never so much as shared a room with anyone, not even their siblings, before joining the army. They'd had to get used to it in a hurry.

Lightning flashed. The rain started to fall. Richard crossed his arms over his chest and watched the raindrops splashing on the training ground, his heart sinking as visibility dropped to almost nothing. There were guards at the gates, and a handful of regular patrols around the fence, but the training camp was almost undefended. The rebels hadn't attacked yet, but it was just a matter of time. The only upside, as far as he could tell, was that there was nothing irreplaceable within the base. They could repair any damage quickly, if the base remained in their hands.

Roland joined him after he'd finished inspecting the bunks. "Just how close *are* we to the capital?"

"Not far," Richard told him. He had happy memories of scrambling over the wire and sneaking out for a night on the town, then sneaking back into the base before sunrise. It had cost him badly—he shuddered to think of going through morning exercises with a hangover—but it had been worth it. There hadn't been much to do in the barracks after lights out, beyond sleep. "We used to sneak out every so often for fun and games."

"Really." Roland sounded disapproving. "That'll have to change."

Richard felt a hot flash of anger. "Do you think you can just *say* something and make it happen?"

"No." Roland looked, just for a second, as if Richard had struck a nerve. "This training centre is far too close to the city. We'll need to establish a more permanent base somewhere a little further away."

"And how do you intend to do that?" Richard gave him a sardonic look. "Do you think it'll be easy buying the land and turning it into a base?"

"No," Roland said. "But there are *lots* of uninhabited islands, are there not? One of them could become a training base."

"Sure," Richard agreed. "If you can convince the owner to sell."

Roland shrugged, his eyes on the rain. "There's never any shortage of problems to solve," he said. "And none of them will be solved if you don't try."

"Trite," Richard said. "Is that what they teach you in the Marine Corps?"

"It makes a change from fifty-nine ways to kill someone with both hands tied behind your back," Roland said. It was hard to tell if he was joking or making a threat. "It's easy to point out problems. It's harder to solve them."

He met Richard's eyes. "What do *you* see as our biggest problem?"

"You're here to assist us in expanding our regulars, right?" Richard looked back at him, evenly. "The problem is, most of our issues are not ones you can solve. The recruiting pool is pretty small, the number of people willing to join for shit pay, shittier officers and the chance to wind up being shot at by even shittier rebels is even smaller. You're coming in from somewhere on the far side of the universe, convinced you can fix our problems. You don't even know what those problems *are*."

"Then help me to figure them out," Roland said. His voice was so calm Richard *knew* it was an act. "We can solve the problems together."

"I don't think you can." Richard turned away, staring into the rain. It was growing hotter, despite the downpour. "There is no way you can solve one set of problems without solving them all and the people you'd need to convince to help you…they won't help you, because they'll be cutting their own throats. I don't think you have a hope in hell of accomplishing anything before time runs out, when everyone on the wrong side—and everyone caught in the middle—gets it in the neck."

He shook his head as the downpour finally started to trickle to a halt. His family would be caught in the middle, when the shit really hit the fan. They'd be blamed for being townies or for contributing to the army or even trying to play a political role, in hopes the world could be changed before it was too late. Whoever won, they'd lose. He wondered if they shouldn't try to leave, to purchase shuttle and starship tickets and depart before it was too late…he shook his head. He knew his family wouldn't leave. New Doncaster was their world. And if they did go, they'd have to leave everything they'd built behind.

"We have to try," Roland said. He sounded optimistic. Mindlessly so. He could leave at any moment, if he wished. He didn't know what it was like to be trapped, to be locked in a cage with bars that were hard to see, yet very definitely there. "And we can work together to do it."

"We shall see." Richard shook his head. "There are just too many problems to overcome."

"Problems can be solved," Rachel said.

Richard tried not to jump. He'd almost forgotten she was there.

"It's just a matter of taking the big problems and breaking them down into smaller problems, then solving them one by one," Rachel added.

"Sure," Richard said. "And what if the problems are too big to break down?"

Roland grinned. "There's no such thing," he said. "Just ask the drill instructors."

CHAPTER TEN

KINGSTOWN TRAINING BASE, NEW DONCASTER

ROLAND FOUND IT HARD, despite his confident words, not to feel disheartened as the downpour finally came to an end. Richard was clearly an experienced officer with a working brain, but he had a chip on his shoulder big enough to make working with him a trial…at least, Roland reflected, until he proved himself in the other man's eyes. And if Richard had been the only problem, it would have been relatively easy to solve. But he was only the tip of the iceberg.

He felt his heart sink as he stared around the makeshift training base. It was large enough to double or triple the number of recruits passing through the gates—if indeed they could be found and recruited—but the facilities were very limited. His team would have to set up imported equipment, which would make it harder to establish a more isolated training base somewhere well away from the city. He found it hard to believe the base had been set up so close to the city in any case, close enough a recruit could easily go AWOL every night and return the following morning before anyone counted heads. Roland doubted it would be possible in a Marine barracks, but who knew? The Slaughterhouse had been kept isolated for a very good reason.

Rachel followed him as he made one last sweep around the barracks, picking his way through puddles of water that were already starting to dry in the heat, then turned and headed back to the car. It was a very primitive machine, the sort of fuel-burning rattletrap that would have been flatly banned on Earth, but Roland had a feeling it was top of the planet's very limited line. The roads were a strange mixture of tarmac, so smooth was sure they'd been laid during the early years, and rough and ready tracks that were poorly—if at all—maintained. The more he looked around the base, the more he was sure it would need to be replaced as quickly as possible. And yet, he was uneasily aware they were running out of time.

"Failure isn't an option," he muttered. "Is it?"

He scowled. His superiors weren't stupid. They'd know that some situations were beyond salvation. And yet, if he failed to do everything in his power to retrieve the situation before it passed the tipping point, his career would come to a sudden end. He'd never be trusted with anything resembling an independent command again, even if he made it through the replacement Slaughterhouse. It was much more likely he'd be transferred permanently to the auxiliaries or advised to find a nice little colony world and step out of history. The thought could not be borne.

His eyes lingered on Richard as he started the car. The older man—he was probably in his mid-twenties, making him around five years older than Roland—would have to be turned into an ally. Somehow. Roland was all too familiar with people picking and choosing their words around him, but less so at turning them into friends and allies. Belinda would have done it easily, he was sure. She'd certainly had no trouble turning the palace staff into her allies. He didn't have the slightest idea where to begin. In theory, he'd been in sole command of his palace, with the power to grant whatever rewards and punishments he liked. In practice, he'd learnt—very quickly, when he'd grown a little more aware of his surroundings—that his authority had been very limited indeed. He could promise Richard the world, only to discover that Richard's superiors had other ideas.

He leaned back in his seat as Richard guided the car into the city, studying the surroundings with keen interest. The outskirts seemed dominated by a network of prefabricated buildings, shacks and hovels; a handful of industrial buildings, set a little further into the city, surrounded by houses and apartment blocks that looked more than a little unsteady. The streets were slightly slanted, allowing water to run into the gutters and flow down to the rivers. He had the strangest feeling that the city—barely a town, by Earth's standards—was actually *melting*. The residents would have to work hard to keep their city from being worn down by the rain.

"It isn't that much of a problem," Richard said, when Roland asked. "The stone and metal buildings are relatively immune to rain. The wooden ones have been treated to keep them from decaying. It's the smaller homes that are in real danger. They keep planning to replace them, but it never happens."

Roland frowned. "Why not?"

Richard said nothing as he steered the car onto the road leading to the spaceport. "Several reasons," he said. "A number of colonists arrived just after Earthfall and discovered, too late, that the farms and suchlike they'd been promised simply didn't exist. Some got shipped out to the other islands, but the majority remained here. And then refugees started flocking here when the rebels started becoming more active…in short, the government doesn't want to do much of anything about them. I think they're hoping the refugees will eventually become debtors and added to the labour pool."

"Ouch," Roland said. He studied the shacks as they drove past. Men, their eyes dead and listless, stood everywhere. Half-naked children ran around in droves, shouting and screaming as they tried to find some entertainment in the ruins of civilisation. There were no teenage girls and few older women…Roland knew, from his training, that that was often a very bad sign. "I thought you didn't get many colonists."

"It's complicated." Richard shook his head. "We—the landowners—purchased a hell of a lot of debtors and indents, just to put them to work in the fields. Independent colonists weren't so welcome. Many were simply turned down when they tried to apply. This time…a bunch of colony ships were redirected here, we don't know by who. We didn't want them, but we couldn't tell them to go away either."

Roland frowned as they turned into the spaceport and passed through the gates. He was going to have to find a way to get Richard to unwind completely, perhaps by plying him with alcohol. Or...he briefly considered a handful of other options, before drawing a blank. He couldn't bribe the man and he couldn't offer a promotion consummate with his abilities. Chip on his shoulder or not, the man clearly knew what he was doing. And to be blamed for his superior's stupidity....

It happened to me too, Roland thought. He'd looked himself up in the databanks once, while he'd been in transit. It was astonishing how many of the documents he'd signed without reading had had real-world implications, how many people had suffered because—they'd thought—of the Childe Roland's whims. *They cursed me, unaware I was little more than a prisoner in a gilded cage.*

"I need to speak to my people," he said, once they'd passed through the checkpoint and parked in front of the terminal. "Where will you be staying?"

"I am at your disposal," Richard said. Only a very sensitive ear could have picked up the irritation in his tone. "Where would you like me to stay?"

Roland chose to ignore the irritation. "Stay here. If we have to remain at the spaceport for longer than a few hours, you can sleep in the transient barracks if you don't want to go home."

He sighed, inwardly, as he clambered out of the car. He'd always had the impression that military deployments were planned out so carefully that nothing, not even a single bullet, was forgotten. The real world, as he'd discovered during his training, was nowhere near so obliging. A smart deployment plan would assume, right from the start, that there would be glitches, that some matters would proceed slowly and others at terrifying speed...he wondered, suddenly, if they even had transports to take their supplies to the training base. It wasn't as if they'd been allowed to take a small fleet of trucks with them. He'd assumed they'd find transport on New Doncaster.

One thing at a time, he told himself.

He made his way back into the terminal, Rachel at his heels, and checked the secure datanet. His team had already landed, their supplies placed into one of the hangars until they could be moved to their final destination. Roland gritted his teeth, unsure how to proceed. Take over the training base, as unsuitable as it was, and do the best they could? Or try to set up a new training base somewhere else? He briefly considered using the spaceport, then dismissed the idea before it had time to flower. The spaceport was still too close to the city for his peace of mind.

His heart sank as they made their way towards the hangar. There were stevedores everywhere, moving so fast that it was impossible, even for the Marines, to check and recheck their IDs and workloads before they went in and out of the hangars. Some buildings were more heavily guarded, but…he shook his head as he reached the entrance, passed the guard and stepped inside. The hangar was huge, so huge that their supplies barely filled a fraction of it. His team was checking the manifests, talking in low voices as they ran down the lists. They straightened to attention as Roland cleared his throat. He felt like a fraud, again, as he looked at them.

"I have inspected the local training base," he said, and ran through a list of his observations. "The base does have the basics, but it is too close to the city for comfort and the facilities are very primitive. We would need to install most of our supplies just to *begin* to bring it up to acceptable standards. Should we go ahead and do it?"

"Sir, we are not training Marines." Brian Wimer smiled, humourlessly. "The locals may want us to set up at least a basic facility near their city. We can work on establishing a more isolated base later, when we have time to do so."

Roland frowned. "Wouldn't that let the recruits bunk off whenever they felt like it?"

"We would secure the fences," Wimer assured him. "The point is… we're not trying to train Marines. Or a special unit. We're trying to train basic infantrymen, local infantrymen. Better they do it imperfectly, as they say, rather than us doing it perfectly. There's no point in trying to do everything by the book if the book doesn't fit the scene."

"They'll probably complain about us taking over the base," Sergeant Gillis added. "But we can deal with that another time."

Roland nodded. "We just need to arrange transport to the base, then we can move the supplies," he said. "And then we can start recruiting."

He frowned as he checked the supplies, comparing the crates in front of him to the manifest he'd downloaded from the freighter. The supplies would run out, eventually. They'd have to arrange to obtain more from local sources...he made a mental note to assign Richard to supervise the process, at least partly to keep someone more corrupt from stealing the money and supplying the recruits with junk. He'd also have to see about getting them some heavier weapons and armour, perhaps even aircraft. There were hundreds of battle-tested designs in the mission's datacores. If the locals could produce them, they would.

"Speak to Captain Allen or his staff," he ordered Rachel. "See what they can give us in the way of transport."

Rachel nodded, curtly. "Yes, sir."

Roland rubbed his forehead. The heat and the stress were starting to get to him. His body would adapt to the heat—his genetic enhancements would see to it—but he wasn't sure how he'd cope with the stress. The mission had barely begun, and he was already running into problems. It would be a great deal easier if he could find someone to give him orders, but he knew that wasn't going to happen. And there was no way he could lose himself in the fiddly little details either.

Shaking his head, he went to find Richard. The local officer would be able to make some calls, perhaps arrange for an escort for the supply trucks. The rebels probably knew the Marines—and their training mission—had landed. There were so many people coming in and out of the spaceport that Roland felt uncomfortably naked. Very few of them were vetted and, reading between the lines, he was reasonably sure the vetting process itself was unreliable. If Allen had had the manpower, he'd have banished the locals a long time ago.

And instead, he's pinned in place, Roland thought. He understood what it was like to be pinned down by incoming fire, but Allen's men were held in place by political and military considerations rather than enemy activity. Perhaps *that* was why the rebels had refrained from poking the bear. Allen and his men were largely immaterial to the struggle as long as the rebels stayed out of their gunsights. *It isn't an easy place to be.*

• • •

"On your feet," the supervisor snapped. "We've got a job!"

Bryce Ambrose jumped to his feet, trying to look eager. The supervisor was an asshole with a mouth that, in a fairer society, was just crying for a punch in the face. It wasn't as if he was important, although he regularly bragged of his brother's uncle's father's connections to someone the loader gang had never known existed, but it wouldn't do not to pretend to be eager. A man in his position, a man without any place in society, could not afford to lose his job. It would mean going back on the streets on a world that showed little mercy for the homeless, or worse, accepting permanent servitude on one of the plantations. And it would also make him useless to the rebel alliance.

The supervisor kept barking orders, as if he thought himself an army sergeant or a prison warden, although Bryce was sure the asshole's only experience with such men came from bad stories and worse flicks. They lined up and marched out to the hangar, passing a cluster of Marines who studied them carefully. Bryce felt a flicker of envy as they walked past, wishing—not for the first time—that *he* commanded such respect. No one would mess with him if *he'd* served on Han, or Corpus, or one of the hundreds of other worlds the corps had seen action. And yet, there was no point in wishing for something he couldn't have. The corps didn't have a recruiting station on New Doncaster. They'd never been allowed to open one.

He pushed his resentment aside and kept his eyes open as the supervisor barked more orders. The Marines seemed to find him amusing. They were real hard men, not…overpaid fools who thought they were more important than they were. There were ten Marines within eyeshot, weapons clearly visible, who kept their eyes on the crates as if they contained a fortune in gold and silver. Bryce hoped for a chance to get a look inside, as they hefted them up and carried them to the trucks, but they were all carefully sealed. He amused himself by gauging the weight and trying to guess the contents, although it was hard to be sure of anything. He'd leave his guesswork out of the report when he went to the brothel at the end of the day. His superiors would not be amused if he told them something that was later found to be untrue.

The Marines kept an eye on the workers, even after the crates were loaded onto the trucks. Bryce had considered trying to pocket a terminal, in hopes it could be decrypted by a rebel hacker, but the Marines were just too close. He wasn't surprised, when the trucks were finally on their way, to be ordered to pass through a security checkpoint for a quick pat-down before they were allowed to leave. The bonus—in cash—was a pleasant surprise, as was the supervisor being held back for 'consultations'. The supervisor wouldn't have a chance to demand a share for himself, not before the workers had spent their bonuses in the bars and brothels. It almost made him feel guilty, as he made his way back to the city. But not guilty enough to refrain from passing his report to his superiors.

"Room 101," he said, as he entered the brothel. "Please."

The doorman pointed him to the half-hidden door, sending him up a flight of rickety staircases that opened into a concealed bedroom. Bryce regretted not having a chance to look for a girl himself, even though he knew his duty was more important than anything else. The woman sitting on the bed was pretty enough, with a hint of something exotic in her face, but she wasn't a whore. Her clothes concealed everything, while her eyes were hard and cold. Bryce shivered, despite himself. He'd met enough whores who hated men so much he was sure they'd eventually snap and murder a customer. And yet this woman chilled him to the bone.

"Report," she ordered.

"There's at least ten more Marines, who landed approximately fifty-seven crates of supplies," Bryce told her. He ran through everything he'd seen, finishing with a summary of his private conclusions. "They're clearly up to something."

"Quite probably," the woman said. "And they were careful not to let you leave unsearched?"

"They searched us all," Bryce confirmed. He had the feeling he wasn't telling her anything new. It didn't bother him. He'd be surprised if he was the only spy within the spaceport. "They were very careful."

"Interesting," the woman told him. "Keep an eye on them for the moment. We'll decide what to do soon enough."

CHAPTER ELEVEN

GOVERNMENT HOUSE, NEW DONCASTER

"I'VE BEEN...ASKED...TO GIVE YOU A MESSAGE," Richard said. "The Prime Minister would like to meet you in person."

Roland said nothing for a long moment. The message was polite, but he knew perfectly well it wasn't a request. Of course it wasn't. Richard might be trying to soften the blow or the PM might be trying to be diplomatic, on the assumption that Roland was more than a cog in the machine, but it didn't matter. The PM wanted to see him and that was all there was to it.

He sighed, inwardly, as he surveyed the training ground. Wimer and his men had taken over, converting the primitive barracks and facilities into something more suited to train raw recruits without any actual danger. They'd done so well, on their own, that Roland felt rather superfluous. He'd spent a few days walking around the wire, and through the countryside until he reached the ring road around the city, in a bid to get a feel for the terrain, but little else. He'd once heard of an officer who'd stayed in his office and died there, and no one had even noticed until months later. He was starting to understand how and why it had happened.

"I suppose we shouldn't keep the PM waiting," Roland said. He heard a rumble from the sky and looked up. The clouds were gathering, again.

The rain was a greater impediment to military operations, he'd been told, than enemy fire. "Shall we go?"

Richard nodded, curtly, and led the way towards the official car. Roland followed, studying Richard's back. The older man hadn't warmed up to him, although—when pressed—he'd become a valuable assistant as well as source of local knowledge. Rachel hurried over to join them, her expression somehow managing to look reproving without being too noticeable. Roland tried not to roll his eyes. It wasn't as if he'd been planning to dump her on a strange world. He'd be okay if she wasn't permanently glued to his side.

But it might be wise to have a witness when you meet the PM, the more practical side of his mind pointed out. *You're not going to record everything you do in there.*

The car roared to life and drove out through the gates. Roland had put some effort into making the defences a little stronger, from cutting down trees to provide clear fields of fire to raising the fence and establishing more regular patrols. He was uncomfortably aware that his improvements were minimal, compared to what was required, but there was little more he could do right now. Captain Allen couldn't spare the manpower to reinforce the training base and the local military was reluctant to assign a permanent force to his command. It was political, apparently. Roland snorted in disgust. In war, the simplest things were often the hardest.

He leaned forward as they drove into the centre of the city. The buildings were solid stone, designed and built in a fashion that had been out of date centuries ago. They passed a set of statues and through a pair of gates, before coming to a halt in front of Government House. It was impressive, although there was something slightly skewed about the design. The builders had taken a very basic design and scaled it up, as well as making a handful of minor alterations. He had to smile as he saw water dripping off the roof and splashing into a tiny moat, where it was channelled back to the river and down to the sea. Government House, at least, did not look as if it was on the verge of melting into a pile of sand and dust.

Richard parked under an awning and turned off the engine. "Good luck."

Roland opened his mouth to ask what he meant, but bit off the question as a young woman walked up to the car and opened the door. She wore a business outfit that was carefully tailored to display her figure without showing any skin, something that would have impressed Roland a great deal more if he hadn't grown up in the Summer Palace. It was seductive and yet...there was a certain amount of plausible deniability. He put the thought aside for later consideration as he clambered out of the car and stood. The young woman smiled at him. She was, part of his mind noted, quite pretty.

"Welcome to Government House, sir," she said. "I'm Elaine, Administrative Assistant to the Prime Minister. If you'll walk this way...."

I can't walk that way, Roland thought, as she led them into the building, her hips swaying in a natural seductive rhythm. It was an old joke, but it still made him smile. *And I'm not going to underestimate you, either.*

He kept the thought to himself as he looked around. Government House was elegant, the floors and stairs made of solid marble and the walls lined with portraits of great figures from the past. He started, slightly, as he saw a portrait of his father on one wall, the plaque underneath identifying him as ROLAND XXXI. The artist had clearly never seen the long-dead emperor—he'd died when Roland had been seven—in real life. He'd made the man look more handsome than he'd ever been and dressed him in an outfit he'd never worn. Probably. It had been tradition for an emperor never to wear the same outfit twice. Roland had never given it any thought until he'd joined the corps and realised just how wasteful it had been. He dreaded to think how much of his household budget had been spent on clothes.

Elaine kept walking, passing through a pair of outer offices before stopping in front of a simple black door and knocking. There was a pause, just long enough for Roland to wonder if the PM was making a power play, before the door opened. Roland stepped inside. The office was smaller than he'd expected, not much bigger than an officer's quarters on a MEU, but—like the rest of the building—strikingly elegant. The desk, chairs and bookshelves were all made of mahogany, resting on a carpeted floor. A large chandelier provided light; a window looked over the city beyond the walls. Roland hoped the glass was reinforced and tinted. A sniper in the right place could put a bullet through the PM's head. Hell, a man with the right sort of sensor could probably read the PM's lips.

He tried not to smile at the thought. *That would be dreadfully misleading....*

"Captain Windsor," Elaine said. "Please allow me to present Lord William Oakley, Prime Minister of New Doncaster."

The PM stood and held out a hand. Roland shook it as he studied the man. The PM looked to be in his early sixties—tall and thin, with short grey hair and a face that looked distinctly fatherly—but Roland was all too aware that looks could be deceiving. The man was studying him back, with just the same level of interest. His smile might be warm and welcoming, but there was a definite hint of cold-blooded calculation in his eyes. Roland refused to lower his guard. A man who clambered up the ladder into a position of power could not be underestimated. He wasn't quite sure how the PM had become PM—the files had been a little vague on that point—but he would be more interested in maintaining his own power than improving his world. The Grand Senate had had the same problem. And now the Grand Senate was dead.

"Welcome to New Doncaster," Lord William said. He gestured to a chair, then nodded to Elaine. "How are you finding our lovely world?"

"Wet," Roland said, more to test the waters than anything else. It would be interesting and informative to see the PM's reaction. "The reports didn't do the rainfall justice."

The PM smiled. "It's hard to explain to offworlders, particularly those from Earth," he said. "Half of them refuse to believe in the rain, even when it's splashing down and soaking their clothes; half of them think the rain is extremely dangerous and refuse to go out in the downpour. Hard to blame them, of course, but still...."

He shrugged, elaborately.

Roland nodded thoughtfully. There'd been so much gunk in Earth's atmosphere, even before Earthfall, that the rain had been dangerous. Not that most citizens had ever *seen* the rain. It was, at best, something that happened on other planets. Or, perhaps, as mythical as the unicorn, the dodo, and a political leader who actually gave a damn about his people.

Elaine returned, with a small tray of food and drink, a china teapot placed next to a cake stand laden with sweet things. Roland would have been more impressed if he hadn't seen bigger and better displays in the Summer Palace, although he did have to admit the cakes looked healthier than the cream treats he'd eaten as a young boy. Elaine poured three cups of tea, then vanished as silently as she'd come. Rachel accepted a cup, but didn't sit. The PM paid no attention to her. Roland guessed he thought Rachel was part of the furniture. She was so quiet that it was easy to forget she was there if one didn't pay close attention.

The PM sipped his tea, chatting about nothing. Roland felt a flash of irritation—God knew he'd had thousands of pointless conversations, before Belinda had come into his life—but forced it down before it showed on his face. The process wasn't entirely pointless. They were building a rapport, laying the groundwork for later, and more productive, discussions. And yet, it frustrated him. He'd spent enough time in the corps that he'd learnt to love discussions that went straight to the point and orders that were too clear to be easily misunderstood.

"The situation is unstable, to say the least," the PM said. His tone didn't change, but Roland picked up on the shift in mood anyway. "Can you give us a far greater commitment from the corps?"

Roland kept his face expressionless, somehow. There was no way in hell he could offer the planet *any* commitment, certainly not one that bound the entire corps. It was so far above his pay grade it might as well have been in the next star system, seven light years away. And the PM should know that…probably. Marine officers had a great deal of autonomy, when it came to dickering with the host government, but there were limits. Captain Allen couldn't make any agreement either. How could he?

"I believe the corps is severely over-stretched right now," he said, carefully. He didn't know any details, beyond the unclassified updates that had been downloaded onto the freighter's datacores. "We are attempting to stabilise multiple planets at once, putting a far greater strain on our resources than we anticipated. It may be impossible to reinforce the company already deployed here, let alone deploy a second company. The manpower simply doesn't exist."

The PM studied him for a long cold moment. "We are, dare I say, an important world," he said. "Surely that earns us far more consideration from the corps."

Roland kept his face under tight control. New Doncaster *was* important, true, but not *that* important. The interstellar shipping networks, and the governments that were steadily replacing the empire, would probably be quite happy to either take the planet for themselves or simply negotiate with whoever won the impending civil war. The corps might prefer to stabilise the planet, but it was starting to look as though there was no point in propping up a government that would collapse the moment the Marines were withdrawn. Roland had studied a number of case histories during transit. They'd all agreed that failing to produce a government that could actually govern, when outside troops were pulled out, was pretty much identical to accepting eventual defeat.

"I am not a diplomat," he said, finally. It wasn't true—he did have some training in diplomacy—but there was no point in trying to be polite. "May I speak bluntly?"

"You may," the PM said.

"The corps can only make a commitment to you if you make a commitment to the corps," Roland said. "More practically, if you make a commitment to yourself. My orders are to establish a training centre and churn out enough soldiers to stabilise the situation, but your local policies are making it difficult. It suggests to us, very strongly, that you are—at best—refusing to take your situation seriously. There's no point in us throwing you a lifejacket if you refuse to put it on."

The PM stiffened. "There are limits to what we can do."

"There are limits to what *we* can do, too," Roland countered. "The corps has a vested interest in seeing this planet stabilised. But it is also aware of the danger of wasting time and resources, which are in very short supply these days, in trying to fix problems that cannot be fixed. We can and we will provide support, but it is very dependent on you taking steps to fix your own problems. If you are reluctant to do so, and you make my task impossible, the corps will pull me out and leave you to deal with your problems alone."

He waited, wondering what the PM would say. He'd crossed a line—several lines—even though he'd had permission to speak bluntly. It was the kind of rudeness that would be remembered, even though every word of it was true. Being true would only make it worse. The PM wouldn't be able to come up with a rational reason to dismiss Roland's words....

"There are limits to what we can do," the PM repeated. "What would you *have* us do?"

Roland took a breath. "We have two immediate problems. The first is that we need to set up a better training base, somewhere a little more isolated. An island, perhaps one belonging to your family, would be ideal."

"I'll discuss it with my family," the PM said. "And the second problem?"

"We have a training team, but we need recruits to train," Roland said. "The recruiting program, as far as I can tell, is very low-key. You have recruits rushing to the offices at the rate of one a week, if not a year. You need to offer better salaries and, more importantly, recruit from all levels of society. Right now, you just aren't tapping your manpower resources very effectively."

The PM's voice hardened. "There are...*issues*...with recruiting soldiers from outside the upper classes."

"There are also *issues* when you lose a war," Roland pointed out, dryly. "You have a class of people who are in long-term, if not permanent, debt.

Right now, that's a major cause of resentment and the rebels are using it to recruit insurgents. You can offer to pay the debts, or simply write them off, if the debtor serves in the army for five years or so. And, when they leave, they'll have a nest egg they can use to set up business or buy land of their own. You'll have laid the seeds of an economic boom."

Which might not be entirely in the interests of the landowning class, he added, silently. *But neither is losing a war.*

The PM smiled. "Do you know how many problems I'd have trying to get such provisions through parliament?"

"Not as many problems as you'll have if you lose the war," Roland said. He wanted to hammer the point, time and time again. "And even a constant low-level insurgency is going to drain your resources until you simply run out or outside powers intervene. You are reaching the point, Prime Minister, when the rebels can take the offensive openly. Even if you survive their opening blows, you'll still find it very hard to retake lost territory and salvage the situation if you don't have a sizable military force on call."

He paused, allowing his words to sink in. "People generally try to join the winning side. If it becomes apparent, at least on the surface, that you are going to lose, it will set off a tidal wave of defections as people hurry to join the rebels while they still have something to offer in exchange for their lives. Once that happens, the end will come very quickly. I submit to you, Prime Minister, that you must not let the war reach that stage or it will be the end."

"I'll discuss it with my party supporters," the Prime Minister said, slowly. "But tell me…what guarantee can you offer that the new soldiers won't turn into a threat themselves?"

Roland bit off the sharp response that came to mind. It wouldn't be remotely helpful. "If you treat them well, and reward them for their service, and generally don't try to screw them, the vast majority will be happy to let bygones be bygones. People don't revolt if they see things getting better. They revolt when they think there *is* a chance to make things better and the people in charge are just getting in their way. You have the choice between managing a process that will allow people to climb the ladder or watching, helplessly, as they start chopping the ladder down. Which choice do you think offers you the greatest chance for survival?"

The PM studied him coldly. "And if you're wrong?"

"It's up to you," Roland said. "Save yourself, by doing what you can now, or accept eventual defeat by doing nothing. The choice is yours."

"I shall discuss it with my supporters," the PM said. "And we will see what they say."

"Tell them to hurry," Roland advised. "Time is not on your side."

CHAPTER TWELVE

KINGSTOWN TRAINING BASE, NEW DONCASTER

RICHARD WOULD NOT HAVE BELIEVED, if someone had told him, that the government could actually do something *quickly*. He'd thought, when he'd driven Captain "Call Me Roland"—Windsor to Government House, that the younger man's optimism would be crushed in short order. The landowners were so conservative that it was a minor miracle they'd agreed to use horses and carts, let alone cars, trucks and armoured vehicles. The thought of them listening to any suggestions from a mere offworlder, let alone actually putting them into practice, was thoroughly absurd. And yet...they'd actually *agreed*. He'd pinched himself when he'd read the message from Government House. The training program would be expanded, to the point they would be recruiting from debtors as well as townies and landowners. It was quite astonishing.

He scowled as he found the weasel words at the bottom of the official authorisation. They could recruit from the independent debtors, if they wished, but not from the ones whose contracts—and debts—were owned by various landowners. Somehow, he wasn't surprised. The independent labour pool was composed of unskilled workers, rather than ones with skills their owners—*de facto* if not *de jure*—wanted to keep. That was going to cause problems in the future, if he was any judge. It wouldn't be *that* hard for a debtor to find forged papers and vanish into the army. Hell, he might even find a way to help them.

Roland looked pleased as he scanned the document, either ignoring the weasel words or simply misunderstanding them. Richard would have liked to make fun of him for the latter, but he'd made the mistake himself. It was easy for the landowners to hire lawyers to draft contracts only they could understand, contracts that seemed to say one thing and really meant another. One could think one was refusing permission for something, only to discover—too late—that one had *granted* it. Richard hated to rain on Roland's parade, if only because Roland genuinely *had* made progress, but it had to be done. Roland had to understand his victory wasn't as complete as he might have thought.

"They haven't given you as much as you think," Richard said, flatly. "And you have to understand the limits they've set."

"Really." Roland met his eyes. It was hard to be sure, but Richard had a theory Roland had never seen any *real* action. "What have they done?"

Richard took a breath. The truth wasn't written in any file. On paper, the planetary system looked perfect, perhaps a little *too* perfect. The reality, as countless colonists had discovered over the years, was a little different. And it was about to threaten everything Roland had done.

"There are people who went into debt to emigrate from Earth to New Doncaster," Richard explained. That much, at least, was in the files. "The first type of debtor owes his debt to the government or the settlement corporation, which is pretty much the same thing. The vast majority of them started out as unskilled workers, who either found themselves semi-permanent positions on the farms and plantations—sometimes on the waters—or joined the worker pool and moved from job to job without ever quite making enough to pay off their debts. The second type owes his debt direct to the smaller companies or landowners; they're generally skilled workers, treated a little better than their unskilled counterparts, but rarely allowed to buy themselves out of debt. They're the ones you will need, as you expand the army, but they're also the ones you're not allowed to recruit."

Roland grimaced. "The government is refusing to pay their debts?"

"I don't think they can, even if they wanted to try," Richard said. He'd crunched the numbers himself, when he'd realised how the system worked. "It isn't just repaying the debt, with interest, they owe. It is somehow compensating their employer for their future earnings as well as everything else."

"Fuck." Roland glared at the paper. "And it'll just make matters worse."

"In the long-term, yes," Rachel said. "In the short term, you have to survive long enough to actually *have* a long-term."

Richard hid his amusement with an effort. He wasn't sure what Rachel *was*, but he was sure she was more than *just* a secretary. God knew she didn't dress or act like the secretaries he'd met, ones who'd clearly been hired for their looks rather than their common sense. He didn't think *Roland* had picked up on it, although he and Rachel had to have been working together for the last few months. Half the time, Roland seemed to forget that Rachel even existed. It was a rather odd relationship.

"Point taken," Roland said. He looked at Richard. "Where do we start recruiting?"

"Unskilled workers are generally hired on a weekly basis," Richard said. He had to force himself to remember. He was a townie. He'd never had to search for short-term employment. "They go to the Labour Market, where they are recruited and told to report for work on Monday. Every one of them goes to the market, even if they think whoever is employing them now will continue to employ them. They'd hate to miss out on a better job somewhere else."

He paused. "There may be trouble with the staff, if you try to recruit there," he added. "They get commissions from employers and you'll be making their lives harder."

"They'll just have to deal with it," Roland said. "Tell me, does the constant insecurity help keep wages down?"

Richard smiled, sardonically. "However did you guess?"

"Get the car," Roland said. He stood, brushing down his uniform.

"We'll go to the market and get sorted out, then...do whatever we have to do to recruit more men."

"You might want more bodyguards, too," Richard cautioned. He didn't blame Roland for wanting to get on with it, but they had to do a *little* planning. He racked his brain for ideas they could use, when the time came to try to convince young men to join the army. "And you're going to have to start printing out leaflets for prospective recruits. Paper promises mean a great deal more to them."

"I'll speak to Captain Allen, ask if we can borrow a handful of his men for a close-protection detail," Roland said. He sounded oddly hesitant, as if he was reluctant to bother the older man. "And you can help me discuss possible wording in the car."

Richard shook his head, torn between amusement and irritation, as they climbed into the car and drove back to the city. Roland had hundreds of ideas, most of which—Richard wasn't surprised to note—weren't practical. Richard was starting to wonder if Roland came from aristocratic stock—it *was* possible he was a very distant relative of the Windsors—although Marine training had clearly knocked some of the arrogance out of him. He had plenty of ideas, but he seemed quite happy to listen to criticism and advice that made his ideas better. Probably not officer material, the cynical side of Richard's mind insisted. He had often thought that officer training included a mandatory lobotomy.

Clearly, they forgot to remove your brain when they promoted you, his thoughts whispered, nastily. *What a terrible oversight.*

He put the thought out of his mind as they drove up to the Job Market and parked outside the door. It was heaving, as always; long lines of debtors queuing up in a desperate attempt to find work for the week that would pay enough to meet their living costs and leave them with something they could put towards their debts. The air stank of quiet desperation and hopelessness. The men—and a handful of women—weren't stupid. They knew that only a handful of them would ever clear their debts, let alone create new lives for themselves. Even the security guards, arms crossed over their chests as they stood by the door, looked grim. They were as replaceable as the men who passed under their watchful eyes.

"This way," he said, as he held up his ID to the guards. They barely glanced at it. "You'll see when you get inside."

The converted warehouse opened up in front of him as they made their way through the doors. A handful of stalls, manned by representatives from the big labour combines; a cluster of shifty-looking men handing out papers for jobs that were, almost certainly, more or less off the books. Richard groaned, inwardly, as he spotted the booths right at the back. They promised to repay all debts, in exchange for a lifetime of service in the plantations or the mines. The offer might look good, on paper, but it was little better than a death sentence. The debtors would be lucky to last long enough to retire and, even if they did, they'd find themselves rapidly discarded or simply thrown into the ocean to drown. It was a hellish nightmare, one he'd learnt to hate. There were times, in all honesty, that he understood precisely why the rebels wanted change.

Roland's lips thinned as he looked around, then stepped towards a young woman with very old eyes. "Who's in charge here?"

The woman flinched, as if he'd hit her. "That would be Mr. Bates, sir," she said. "Would you like me to take you to him?"

"Yes, please," Roland said.

Richard followed, silently noting how Roland slipped the young woman a tip. He hoped no one else had seen it. There were too many places that expected tips to be shared—or, more accurately, handed over to the bosses—for him to be sanguine about the woman keeping the money. He'd once had to pretend to get very close, too close, to a waitress just to slip a coin into her pocket without being noticed. There'd been no other way to do it. He knew too much about how his father had struggled, in his early life, to just leave without giving the poor woman a tip....

He'd expected Mr. Bates to be fat and ugly and generally unpleasant and that was exactly what he was. The man looked as if he'd never gone hungry, not even for a day; his stomach looked as if it was constantly on the verge of bursting out of his shirt and breaking his belt. He scowled as he saw Roland, his eyes shifting to Richard long enough to dismiss him as unimportant. He didn't pay any attention to Rachel at all.

"I'm a very busy man," he said. The glare he shot the young woman was telling. Her flinch was worse. "What do you want?"

"I am going to open a recruiting station in this building," Roland said. The sheer assurance in his voice was staggering. "You are not going to get in my way, *are* you?"

Bates stared at him. "I make the decisions here and...."

Roland produced the orders from the government and laid them on the table. "I have permission from the Prime Minister himself to recruit however I see fit," he said. He grinned, savagely, as he repeated his question. "You are not going to get in my way, *are* you?"

"I...." Bates stared at the documents, with their official seal, then looked away without reading them properly. "I...I...I'm sure we can come to some arrangement."

He wants a bribe, Richard thought. *Cross his palm with silver or he'd do everything in his power to keep us from recruiting a single man.*

Roland's smile grew wider. "I'm sure we can come to some arrangement, too," he said. "You let us get on with it, without interference, and we won't beat the shit out of you and throw whatever's left into prison."

Bates blanched. Richard was torn between amusement and disgust. Bates wouldn't stay long in prison, for the very simple reason that prisoners were normally reclassified as indents and sent to work camps on distant islands. Bates wouldn't last a week on the farms or in the mines, even if he didn't run into someone who remembered him from the market. He'd probably made an impression on everyone who'd passed through the building, everyone who'd had to bend the knee in hopes of getting a better job that might just pay more than a pittance. Richard rather hoped Bates would try Roland. He had a feeling Roland wasn't bluffing.

"I...." Bates swallowed, noticeably. "I can clear you one of the booths at the back...."

"You'll put us at the front, where everyone can see," Roland said. He'd probably noticed that hardly anyone went anywhere near the rear booths. "And you'll make damn sure that *everyone* sees us. Or do I have to arrest you and work with your replacement?"

Bates sagged. "I'll see to it," he said. "But I don't promise recruits."

"Let us take care of that," Roland said. He nodded to the young woman who'd led them to the office. "She'll work with us, at least until the booth is underway. You don't have a problem with that, do you?"

"No," Bates said. It was a lie. Richard could *tell* he'd intended to take his feelings out on the poor woman as soon as the visitors left. He knew the type far too well. "I'm sure she'll do a good job."

And we'll have to take her out of here, when we're done, Richard thought. *I'm sure we can find a place for her somewhere else.*

• • •

Bryce Ambrose tried not to groan too obviously as he rounded the corner and saw the line outside the converted warehouse. He'd spent too long last night in the bars, drinking himself senseless before making his way back to the flophouse and collapsing into his bunk. Two of his bunkmates had woken him, a few hours later, when they'd gotten into a fight over something stupid. Bryce had gone back to sleep when they'd both been hurled onto the streets, but he hadn't slept well. He'd decided, as he ate a ration bar for breakfast, that he should have spent his bonus on whores instead.

He joined the back of the line and forced himself to wait patiently as it inched forward. He was late. All the *good* jobs for the following week would already be filled. He cursed under his breath, again, for drinking himself stupid. He could have gotten up a great deal earlier and joined the line before the doors opened, then get himself a better job before doing *something* with his weekend. Perhaps he could find something that paid a little better. The debt in his ledger wasn't getting any bigger, but it wasn't getting any smaller either. He would have liked to pay it off, or as much as possible, before he got too old to work. He had no idea what he'd do if he couldn't keep himself afloat.

A buzz of excitement greeted him as he finally stepped through the doors—the security guards were their usual grumpy selves, but for once they didn't insist on searching him—and saw a crowd gathered around a booth. He blinked in surprise as he saw a uniformed man—a Marine—standing by the booth, two more standing behind it and handing out pamphlets that were passed from person to person. Bryce took one, out of reflex rather than anything else, and glanced down. It was an invitation to join the army. He started to pass it on, then stopped himself. The paper promised that anyone who joined, and served a full term, would have their debts cancelled. Bryce swallowed, hard. He was in his mid-twenties, all too aware it would be at least a decade—at best—before he could pay off his debt. The thought of having it washed away, when he was young enough to enjoy it, was very tempting.

And yet, you've been reporting to the rebels, his conscience reminded him. *What would they say if they knew you were seriously considering joining the army?*

He forced himself to read the entire paper, his thoughts spinning as the words sank into his mind. There was no guarantee the rebels would *win.* He wanted to believe they would, and that they'd bring a new and better world, but it was impossible to be sure. And besides…they'd want a source in the army, wouldn't they? He doubted he was the only rebel spy—informant, more practically—in the labour gangs, let alone the only one who'd been given the army's offer. His thoughts ran in circles. If he joined up, he might come out ahead no matter who won.

The Marine's voice was quiet, but it seemed to echo through the air. "Take the leaflets and think about it," he said. "Discuss your decision with your friends and families. If you wish to sign up, report to the training base on Monday morning. Bring the supplies on the leaflet and nothing else. If you don't want to sign up, just pass the leaflet on to someone who might."

Bryce made up his mind. He'd sign up. It would please everyone, including the rebels. He'd be in place to spy on the Marines, and the new recruits, and—if nothing happened—at least his debt would be repaid. And then...he read the leaflet again. Five years, followed by freedom. The cynic in him wondered if it would be that easy; the more optimistic side insisted he simply couldn't lose. Whatever happened, he'd come out ahead.

Unless you die on active service, his thoughts mocked him. *But staying in the worker gangs isn't really safe either, is it?*

CHAPTER THIRTEEN

FIRST LANDING, NEW DONCASTER

"WELCOME TO BASIC TRAINING," Wimer said. "I am Master Sergeant (Auxiliary) Brian Wimer. I am the senior Drill Instructor, charged with supervising your training. With me is...."

Roland watched, from a distance, as Wimer made the speech all Marine recruits heard, for the first time, when they entered Boot Camp. There were few, if any, differences between the speech he'd heard and the one being given to the newcomers, although—now—he had the training to understand some of what he was being told. There'd been hidden meanings within the words that had completely passed over him a year or so ago.

His eyes swept over the new recruits. They were a diverse lot, in everything from skin colour to gender, although they all had the same experience of living and working on New Doncaster. Roland had seriously considered insisting they only recruited young men, for fear of what might happen when young men and women trained together, but he'd been unsure just how many recruits they'd have. In hindsight, he probably shouldn't have worried about it. The offer they'd made was so good he should have anticipated a deluge of recruits. They'd have several thousand men on the books by the time the week came to an end.

And very few of them will quit, Roland thought. The corps allowed recruits to quit at any moment and hundreds did, but the corps didn't normally offer such a huge incentive to keep men in the ranks. *They'll be too determined to get their debts paid to back out when the going gets tough.*

He frowned as he spotted an older man, right on the outer edge of acceptable recruit standards. Too old, really...he frowned, reminding himself that the medical facilities he'd used during his own training simply didn't exist on New Doncaster. A Marine who was trapped in a damaged body could have the body repaired, if he had the determination to make it, but there was no way they could offer the same service here. Even something as basic as correcting a person's eyesight or hearing might be beyond them. Roland made a mental note to look into it. They'd have to start training the recruits in battlefield medicine, as well as everything else, but there was no way they could make doctors of them. The medical teams would have to be expanded, too.

"Make a note," he said to Rachel. "We need to recruit more doctors and nurses as well as soldiers."

"Yes, sir." Rachel scribbled a line in her notebook. "It might be worth asking what, if anything, the spaceborn community can produce for us."

"Good thinking." Roland was pleased to see Rachel starting to come out of her shell. She rarely commented, but when she did her advice was always good. "They might be able to churn out a few autodocs for us."

He gritted his teeth. He'd been told that medical facilities on new colony worlds were sometimes primitive—their doctors weren't called *sawbones* for a joke—but he hadn't believed it. And besides, New Doncaster wasn't *that* far from the Core. Surely, the locals could have afforded a bigger and better medical section. It was in their interests, in the long run, to keep their people healthy. Sick and dying men didn't pay taxes, or pay off their debts.

The recruits kept going, working through the formations in a ragged bunch. They looked unsightly, to Roland's eyes, but the raw material was there. He'd probably looked worse when *he'd* reported for training, shortly after his body had recovered from the punishment he'd inflicted on it. He'd needed weeks to get comfortable in his own body again. It still horrified him to realise how close he'd come to a fatal overdose.

He turned away, heading back to his office. Wimer had been polite, but firm. He and his subordinates could handle the basic training, leaving Roland to do...something. Roland suspected his nickname would be Captain Dunsel by the end of the week. A man who did nothing, yet claimed all the credit...he snorted. He couldn't even do *that*. The local newspapers might be fooled, but his superiors would know better. They'd think poorly of him for trying to claim the credit and worse, he was sure, for telling them such an obvious lie. There was no way they'd believe he'd trained the men by himself.

"I got the updates from the factories," Rachel said, as he closed the door behind them. The fan on the desk hummed loudly, caught in a losing battle with the humidity. "They can churn out basic weapons and supplies for us. Vehicles will take a little longer, but it can be done...."

Roland listened, rubbing his forehead. Logistics were important—he *knew* they were—but he just didn't *want* to deal with them. He wanted to be out there, seeing what was going on in the city and getting a feel for the place. Rachel wouldn't approve, he was sure, but he could leave her to handle the logistics while he gathered intelligence. He tapped his terminal, sending a message to Richard. He had to be feeling as useless as Roland did, perhaps worse. They could go out on the town together.

The door opened. Richard entered, carrying a pair of civilian outfits. "Once you get changed," he said, "we'll be ready to go."

Rachel frowned. "Go where?"

"I need to study the city before all hell breaks loose," Roland said. "Richard is going to show me around."

"In disguise," Rachel said, coldly. "I need to come with you."

"I need *you* to handle the logistics." Roland hastily changed into the inexpertly-sewn shirt and trousers. They felt rough against his skin, the patchwork suggesting they'd passed through several owners before

Richard had given them to him, but they'd suffice. He stuck his wallet, service pistol and terminal onto his belt, hidden beneath the oversized shirt. "I'll be back before you know it."

Rachel's eyes narrowed. "I *strongly* advise you to either stay here or let me accompany you," she said. "The city is not safe."

"I'll be fine," Roland said. It was hard to hide his irritation. "You deal with the paperwork. That's an order."

He led the way out of the office before Rachel could object again, then looked at Richard. "What now?"

"We walk." Richard gave him a faint smile as they headed to the gatehouse. "I hope you're ready."

Roland resisted the urge to point out that forced marches had been part of his training as they made their way through the gatehouse, then onto the road leading down to the city. It looked muddier, now that so many trees had been chopped down, but he had no trouble picking his way through the puddles as the road widened suddenly. A handful of people—they looked no different than he did—were also heading to the city. Roland couldn't help thinking it wasn't very secure. The day labourers could be carrying *anything* on their backs.

"The ring road makes the formal edge of the city," Richard commented, as they crossed a bridge. "Technically, the city's authority stops here. Practically, things are a little more confused. The city has more influence than you might expect."

"It is the capital," Roland said. "Right?"

"Right," Richard agreed. "But most of the landowners don't live anywhere near the city."

The wind shifted, blowing the stench of too many unwashed humans into Roland's face. He grimaced, then tried to hide it as they walked through the slums. Eyes, many unfriendly, followed them, although he saw no real threats. The children held out their hands to beg for money—his heart twisted as he saw a little girl, her eyes pleading—but he shook his head. He'd been told, more than once, that giving money to beggars only made things worse. He understood the logic. But, looking the kids in the eye, it was hard not to open his wallet and give them everything. Only the grim awareness that their parents would probably take the money for themselves kept him from giving in.

Richard kept up a quiet, running commentary as they kept moving, never lingering in one place. The slums were populated by colonists and debtors who'd simply given up and settled in the morass, refusing to move to the islands or do something—anything—to turn their lives around. They preferred to live in their own filth...here and there, there were puddles of something Roland was sure wasn't water. He saw trickles of liquid heading down to the sea and shuddered. He'd thought he'd seen horrors, during training, but he was starting to understand he was wrong.

A thought struck him. "Where are the men?"

"Many of them are labourers or criminals," Richard said. "Others... they just stay out of sight. They're afraid of getting picked up and sent to the islands."

Roland kept walking, but the sense of unease refused to fade as they moved into a more prosperous part of town. The apartments were occupied by debtors, Richard explained, but none of them actually *owned* their homes. The sense of bitter resentment was almost a physical presence, hanging in the air like a cloud of poisonous smoke. He had the sense they were being followed, as they passed a row of stone apartments so identical it looked as if they'd been stamped out one by one, but he saw nothing when he looked behind him. The kids darted away, as if they'd learnt to fear strangers as enemies. Roland had the awful feeling they might be right.

They crossed a road and stepped into an even more prosperous area, a middle-class enclave amongst the slums. The sudden change was jarring. Roland found it hard to understand how the estate survived, let alone prospered. The people looked better dressed, yet...there was something fearful in the way they looked at the intruders, something that suggested they, too, were permanently on the verge of losing everything. Roland saw a middle-aged woman eying them suspiciously, one hand resting on something in her pocket. A gun? Or a communicator? Roland knew the type. The moment they saw something out of place, they called the police and demanded they set it right. They were hated and yet feared by their neighbours.

He frowned as he saw a poster, advising him to vote for an MP. The picture was too faded for him to make out the name, let alone the features. He wondered, idly, if elections would change anything. The files insisted the planet was a democracy, but he'd seen more than enough evidence to prove it was nothing of the sort. He made a mental note to insist the files get checked and edited, to bring them more in line with reality. His lips curved into a thin smile. The planet would have a problem attracting more colonists if it was honest about what awaited them.

The streets grew darker, again, as they made their way back towards the outskirts. The apartments got larger, small shops on the ground floor overshadowed by towering tenements that didn't look safe. There were more beggars on the streets, begging for loose change; the street corners were crowded with prostitutes in revealing clothes, offering everything from oral to anal sex to anyone willing to pay. Roland had seen enough, over the years, to know there were few limits to human depravity—he'd experimented with many of them himself—but the poor women looked ill. They were all skin and bones, their clothes practically drooping from their frames....

Richard steered him away from them. "They've probably been kicked out of the brothels," he muttered. "They'll be found dead in the streets, sooner or later."

"Fuck." Roland was appalled. "Is there nothing we can do for them?"

"No." Richard looked furious. "No one gives much of a damn about them."

The bitterness in his voice grew stronger. "They were probably promised they'd be married to a handsome farmer, or some crap like that," he said. "That was a common lie, when they were trying to recruit more girls from Earth. The poor bitches didn't really have a choice, from what I heard.

When they got here…it turned out they were going to the brothels instead. Some of them even thought they could lie on their backs with their legs open and work off their debt within a few weeks. And they were wrong. They were worked to death, then kicked out to die."

Roland winced. He knew the empire had had its darker moments, but the truth—the complete truth—had always been kept from him. It hadn't been good or evil, although it had done great good and great evil. The women he'd seen had been caught in the gears, mashed to a pulp and then tossed out to die, to be replaced by others…he shook his head. Earth was dead now. There'd be no replacements, not from the homeworld. He wondered, idly, what that would do to New Doncaster, when it dawned on them there wouldn't be any new colonists.

"Look at that," Richard said. He pointed towards a wall. Someone had spray-painted WILD on the brick, covering a mural that had clearly been painted in happier times. "What do you make of it?"

Roland frowned. "I don't know."

"Nor do we." Richard sounded grim. "There's a rumour—there *was* a rumour, as it was debunked—that there's a new rebel leader called Wild. It was never anything more than a rumour, but there were some rumblings about a young aristocrat going mad and joining the rebels. His name was Wild and the two stories got merged together."

"How wild." Roland grinned at his own joke. "Was it actually true?"

"I don't know." Richard frowned. "I doubt it. The story was debunked quite harshly, and there were stern warnings and punishments for anyone who gave it any credence, but it wasn't quite up to their normal standards. My personal feeling is that it was just a rumour, one that was more embarrassing than anything else. But I could be wrong and…."

He broke off. "It's quiet, isn't it?"

Roland looked around. The prostitutes were gone. The beggars were either hurrying away or pressing themselves against the walls, as if they were desperate not to be noticed. A thrill of alarm ran through him, one hand dropping to his belt as he glanced from side to side. The situation was going bad, even though they couldn't see any threats. He glanced at Richard, then led the way down the street. He'd memorised a couple of maps. If they kept walking north, they'd reach the ring road and all they'd have to do was follow it until they reached the base camp again.

He tensed as four figures stepped out of the alleyway to block his path. He sensed, more than heard, at least two more behind him. They carried knives rather than guns—local gun control was supposed to be strict, with firearms forbidden to anyone other than landowners—but he had a nasty feeling they'd be on him before he could draw his gun. He tensed, bracing himself for the coming fight. They were badly outnumbered. Hell, he didn't know if Richard had any unarmed combat training. Two or three Marines could hammer the street thugs without breaking a sweat, but he was effectively alone. Perhaps it would be better to run. He hated the idea of running from a fight, but it would be practical. God knew what would happen if he killed one or more of them.

The leader sneered at him. "Who the fuck are you?"

Roland tried to think of a story that wouldn't start a fight, but drew a blank. The thugs probably ruled this part of the city, pimping prostitutes, running drugs and beating up anyone who didn't pay protection. They were effectively outside the law...hell, the government might quietly approve of them oppressing people who might otherwise challenge the government's oppression. He could tell the thugs they were recruiting officers, but even that wouldn't go down very well....

Something moved, in the alleyway behind the thugs. Roland barely had a second to see a humanoid figure before it threw a brick at the thug's head, striking him hard enough to send his body crashing to the street. The thugs turned, just in time to see a second brick come flying at them. They cursed and scrambled for cover, drawing their knives. Roland didn't hesitate. He swung around, punched the closest thug in the throat and ran for his life. Behind him, Richard followed. He heard shouting and cursing as the thugs tried to decide who to follow, the two men they'd stopped in the streets or the stranger who'd practically killed their leader. Roland had no time to wonder who'd come to their aid or why. Right now, all that mattered was getting out of the city before they drew attention from the local police or the rest of the criminal element.

Rachel met them when they finally stumbled back into camp. "I signed your name to a bunch of documents you didn't bother to read," she said, crossly. Her arms were folded under her breasts, as if she were a mother confronting her naughty children. "What have you been doing?"

Roland looked at Richard, then started to laugh. "It's a long story," he said. He forced himself to calm down. "But the city is very much a powder keg. It's just a matter of time before it explodes. I guess the other cities are much the same."

"No," Richard said. "The other cities are worse."

CHAPTER FOURTEEN

FIRST LANDING, NEW DONCASTER

"THANK YOU FOR COMING," General Falk said. "I appreciate that the Marines keep you very busy."

I wasn't aware I had a choice, Richard thought, coldly. The orders had been surprisingly explicit. He'd been expecting something to happen since the brief skirmish with the street thugs and yet, there hadn't been a peep from anyone. *You called and I came.*

It was hard to keep the resentment off his face. He found it hard to admit, even to himself, but he was starting to *like* Roland. The Marine had a driving energy Richard admired, combined with a willingness to turn the world on its head to get what he wanted. He hadn't slowed down, even after the first official complaint from the labour markets and job centres; he'd merely pointed out, sardonically, that anyone who wanted to hire workers in a workers' market should be prepared to pay a great deal more. Richard suspected the sudden boom in wages wouldn't last—there were limits to how many men could join the army, let alone remain on active service—but it made him more optimistic about the future. The landowners would have problems putting that particular demon back in the bottle.

"They can spare me for a few hours," Richard said. His work was a mixture of intensive activity and long periods of boredom, sorting out recruiting mingled with reading intelligence reports and manuals that dated all the way back to the pre-space era. "What can I do for you?"

He kept his hands firmly clasped behind his back as he surveyed the triad. The PM seemed content to let General Falk take the lead, while Lord Ludlow appeared constantly on the verge of exploding. The hostile gaze he'd directed at Richard, when he'd been shown into the conference room, was a grim reminder the aristocrat still blamed Richard for the death of his son. Richard had no doubt it wouldn't have made a difference, if he hadn't survived the patrol or deserted on the way back to Kingstown. One of the other survivors would have been turned into the scapegoat and left to carry the can.

"You have worked closely with Captain Windsor," the PM said. "What do you make of him?"

Richard was unsettled by the question. Roland was—technically—a superior officer from another military branch. Asking him to comment on Roland—everything from his character to his tactical skills—was a severe breach of military discipline, even though there were few other ways to learn about the newcomer. The PM had met Roland once, as far as Richard knew; the others hadn't so much as laid eyes on him. Richard was no expert, but he had a feeling the landowners were sharply divided on the issue. They'd sooner have a Marine regiment sort out the rebels for them than risk creating an army that might easily turn against them.

And a Marine regiment is not going to materialise, Richard told himself, firmly. *We have to make do with what we have.*

He took a breath. "Captain Windsor is a superlative organiser," he said. "He has handled the task of organising training and recruitment efforts, as well as contacting local factories and industrial nodes to outfit the growing army. He has also shown the sense to leave his training officers in charge of the program, instead of trying to handle the training himself. There have been some bumps along the way, some issues that weren't sorted before they turned into headaches, but overall he's done very well.

He has fixated on the goal of creating a new and expanded army and I believe he will succeed."

General Falk's eyes narrowed. He hadn't missed the subtle implication in Richard's words. There were too many regular and militia officers who preferred to micromanage, rather than allowing their subordinates to get on with their work in peace. Roland, at least, didn't have that problem. He had complete trust in his staff. Richard envied him for that, even if there was a very real chance Roland would *still* get the blame if things went pear-shaped. Richard's former commanding officers had been more worried about the juniors behind them than the enemy in front. And some of them, he conceded privately, had had reason to worry.

"He's a pushy bastard, isn't he?" Lord Ludlow snorted, rudely. "Do you know how many complaints I've had from the labour exchange?"

Richard shook his head. He hadn't known Lord Ludlow was involved with the city's labour exchange, although it shouldn't have surprised him. Lord Ludlow's plantations hired a great deal of seasonal labour, paying as little as they could get away with for two short months and nothing at all for the rest of the year. Roland stamping into the exchange and demanding priority, waving his authorisation from the PM like a club, had probably sent the managers he'd bullied screaming to *their* managers. In hindsight, it was surprising it had taken so long for word to reach their ultimate superior. But then, Lord Ludlow had been known to shoot the messenger. Or at least fire him.

"He doesn't have the right to march in, demand we let him set up a recruiting station and snatch the best labourers for himself," Lord Ludlow continued. "And he certainly does *not* have the right to push my people around."

"He does have authority to recruit from our populace," General Falk pointed out, mildly. "We gave it to him ourselves. And he doesn't have time to be *gentle*."

Or the money to pay bribes, Richard thought. He wasn't sure how much Marines were paid, or how much of a budget Roland had been given by his superiors, but whatever he had would run out very quickly if he had to keep greasing the wheels. *Better to frighten the managers into submission than pay bribes when they won't even stay bribed.*

"His army could easily turn into a threat," Lord Ludlow said. "He's already arranging for more armoured cars and light aircraft, even basic tanks! What's to stop him from marching on the city and demanding our surrender?"

The PM looked at Richard. "Do we have to fear a coup?"

"Not from him," Richard said. He'd never had the sense Roland wanted power, certainly not *that* kind of power. "He is determined to carry out his orders, to build an army and stabilise a crumbling situation. I don't think he intends to turn on us."

The PM exchanged a glance with Lord Ludlow. Richard wasn't sure he wanted to know what they were thinking. The army they needed was a two-edged sword. Men with military experience wouldn't let themselves be pushed around, when the war came to an end. They might easily demand a greater share of the power, perhaps even a complete reform of the landowning system. And yet, what would happen without the army. It had been suspiciously quiet lately. Richard—and Roland—knew what *that* meant. Someone, somewhere, was plotting something.

"As a person," the PM said, "what's your impression of him?"

Richard found it hard to answer. He didn't have a solid impression as much as he had a flurry of contradictory impressions, each a tiny fragment of the whole. Roland, on the surface, was just another officer, even if he wore Marine BDUs rather than regular green and brown. And yet, Richard had the impression still waters ran very deep. Roland was of aristocratic stock—he certainly had the entitlement down pat—but he didn't act like Tarquin Ludlow. He listened to his subordinates and took their concerns into account, even when he didn't agree with them.

"He's a strange person," Richard said, finally. "He is fixated, as I said, on getting the job done. He has no qualms about smashing his way through any barriers in his way. He has little interest, as far as I can tell, in either personal advancement or local politics. And yet…I think that speaks of a background amongst the rich and powerful. Is he a relative of *our* Windsors?"

Lord Ludlow looked as if he'd bitten into a lemon. "If he is, we have been unable to find the connection," he said. "*Roland* is not exactly an uncommon name. It became fashionable amongst the aristocracy, after the Childe Roland was born. Our Roland is certainly old enough to have been one of them. He can't be more than a few months younger than the Imperial Heir."

Who is probably dead now, Richard thought. He'd heard the stories. Earth had been hammered into lifelessness. The entire planet was nothing more than a graveyard. *Poor bastard.*

He put the thought aside. "It's hard to be sure of anything. He's very good at projecting a mask to watching eyes, to the point it is difficult to know what he's thinking even when he's wearing his emotions on his sleeve. Or appearing to do so. If he has any weaknesses, any lusts, I haven't seen evidence of them. I think—and I could be wrong about this—that he simply doesn't care about our opinions. He wants validation from his superiors, from people who cannot be forced to give him anything, not from us."

"I see." The PM met his eyes. "Who is actually in command? Windsor or Allen?"

"It isn't clear to me," Richard said. "In some ways, they appear to be operating independently. But I think Roland would defer to Captain Allen if push came to shove. The Marines respect experience and Captain Allen is a very experienced officer."

Lord Ludlow snorted. "And Roland Windsor?"

"I don't know," Richard said. "But my feeling is that Roland has very limited experience."

"Which may explain why he keeps stepping on toes," the PM mused. He glanced at Lord Ludlow, then looked back at Richard. "Thank you for your time, Lieutenant. Keep us informed of how things proceed. If you do well, you will be promoted when the assignment comes to an end."

Richard saluted, keeping his face under tight control as he turned away. He wasn't blind to what the PM was *really* saying. It was a bribe, plain and simple. If he kept an eye on Roland, if he reported anything even remotely worrying to his superiors, he would be rewarded after. A promotion...he'd be the highest-ranked townie in the army. And yet, the thought of betraying Roland cost him a pang. Roland was a very definite improvement on his previous commanding officers. At the very least, he was taking the war seriously. Richard didn't want to betray him. He wanted....

Perhaps it's time to level with him, to explain how politics actually work, he thought, as he walked out of the building. The skies were overcast, clouds pregnant with rain. *And let him know, before it's too late, that he has enemies in high places.*

...

It was not, technically, Sarah's first visit to First Landing—she'd been driven through the city when she'd arrived on the planet—but it was the only time she'd been able to walk the streets and look around. She wasn't impressed. The capital city was more *solid* than most cities and towns on New Doncaster, at least the ones she'd seen, but the locals didn't seem to know there was a war on. She'd gone to some trouble to make sure she had papers permitting her to be in the city, papers that should have had police and militiamen waving her on hurriedly, but no one had asked to see them since she'd landed at Kingsport and made her way north. Kingstown Island was so insecure she was tempted to believe she could simply walk into Government House with a handful of men and win the war in a single blow.

Which would be a good way to get yourself killed, she thought, as she passed a handful of shops. *Government House isn't really the centre of government.*

She kept her eyes open as she skirted the edge of the government sector—there were a number of soldiers and policemen in evidence, along with others concealed out of sight—and made her way down to the brothel. A line of new recruits had formed outside the doors, moving slowly forward as they waited to take full advantage of their leave. They didn't hoot or holler as she passed, something that bothered her even though she knew she should be relieved. They hadn't spent long in training, but it was clearly already having an impact. They certainly *looked* a lot more orderly than the militiamen she'd fought as she'd united the rebel factions into a single force.

The guard at the side entrance nodded to her, then opened the door. Sarah walked up the stairs and into a tiny bedroom, then keyed a terminal as her guest was shown into the chamber. The sound of two youngsters making love pervaded the air. Sarah was sure they were faking it—her own stint in a brothel had convinced her it was more important to get the client off rather than enjoy herself—but it didn't matter. She couldn't afford to have anyone thinking there was something *off* about this meeting. If people started to wonder, the entire spy ring would collapse in short order.

"Welcome," she said. "We look forward to hearing your report."

Recruit Bryce Ambrose nodded, curtly. He'd had the bright idea of signing up to the new army, without bothering to consult his immediate superiors until it was too late for them to say no. Sarah wasn't sure what she felt about that, not yet. Bryce Ambrose wasn't—hadn't been—the only spy amongst the spaceport workers, and she knew it wasn't easy to direct people who felt themselves to be freelancers rather than servants, but she wished he'd consulted with his superiors. They'd worried, at the time, if he'd chosen to abandon their cause. If the landowners wised up and started treating townies and debtors fairly, rather than kicking their backsides at every opportunity, they might drain the swamp that allowed the rebels to operate freely. It would only take one turncoat to reveal the spy ring to the worst possible people.

"Basic training is hard, but rewarding." Bryce Ambrose stood like a military officer giving a report. "We spent the first two weeks learning to follow orders and getting into shape, then spent time drilling in military tactics and suchlike before they allowed us to use training guns on exercises. It seems to be paying off. They haven't let us use real guns yet, but that'll be happening soon."

Sarah frowned, studying Bryce Ambrose closely. He was a walking slab of muscle, the kind of man—she admitted, to herself if no one else - that she would have regarded as dumb and depraved when she'd lived on Earth. If she'd seen him coming along the street, she would have crossed the road to avoid him. And yet, she knew—now—that such men were very far from stupid. She'd learnt the hard way that an intellectual was often worse than useless on a colony world. Bryce Ambrose might not be smart, by earthly standards, but he was streetwise. He was a rebel because he'd known there was no way to pay off his debt, let alone make something of himself. Would that change, as the new recruits turned into a new army? Sarah hoped not. It would be disastrous if the new army became a very real threat to her manpower.

She listened, asking a handful of questions, as Bryce Ambrose told her about his training. She'd interrogated a number of deserters, during the fighting on other islands, and they'd told very different stories. Sarah feared that boded ill. The Marines were treating their recruits with a certain degree of respect, something the landowners never offered. They might win loyalty, instead of fear. And yet, would it be enough to overcome the resentments that lingered within the general population?

"You've done well," she said. He straightened at her praise. He had no idea who she was—he'd been told she was a messenger, rather than a rebel leader—but her praise still meant something. "When do you think you'll be able to leave the camp next?"

Bryce Ambrose hesitated. "Not for a while," he said. "A couple of recruits tried to make it over the fence and wound up on punishment duties for a week. I can quit at any moment—several recruits have—but I wouldn't be able to go back afterwards. I think it will be at least a month before I get another two days of leave."

"Stay where you are, for the moment," Sarah said. "Keep your eyes open and commit everything you see to memory. Don't write anything down, not where it could be found; don't do anything, anything at all, that might suggest you're anything other than a perfectly normal recruit. When you get leave next, come here and make a report."

She keyed her terminal. A hidden door opened, revealing the madam. Bryce Ambrose would be taken to another room, where he'd be serviced—on the house—and then sent back to camp with a spring in his step. Sarah herself would slip back into the town, then head back to the port. There was a safehouse there. She'd have all the time she needed to get back to the real base before anyone realised who she was.

They're doing better than we expected, she thought, as she headed for the staircase. No one would see her leave. *And that means we might need to move the timetable forward and strike before it's too late.*

CHAPTER FIFTEEN

OAKLEY ESTATE, NEW DONCASTER

ROLAND LEANED FORWARD WITH INTEREST as the tilt-rotor flew over the island and headed straight towards the landing pad at the rear of the estate. He'd seen pictures of the mansion—he'd been surprised to discover they were quite hard to find—but they didn't do the giant building justice. It was an elegant complex, a blocky marble palace out of a historical romance surrounded by stables, fields and—right at the edge of the estate—tiny homes for the staff. He grimaced as the pilot pulled the craft into a hover, then started to descend towards the pad. The Oakley Estate was a giant island in its own right, completely off-limits to anyone who didn't have permission to land. It was easy to see how the landowners had become so detached from the world around them. They spent most of their time isolated from the remainder of their people.

Just like you, Roland's thoughts mocked him. *You grew up in the Summer Palace, remember? You spent all of your time with people who kept telling you that you were wonderful until you came to believe them.*

He glanced at Rachel as the aircraft touched down. The invitation hadn't specifically included her—it had told Roland to come alone without ever *quite* making it explicit—but he'd decided to bring her anyway. He'd been told it was just a social gathering, with no real importance, but he'd attended enough social functions on Earth to know it was almost certainly more than *just* a dinner and drinking session. The landowners would be striking deals, hammering out the details before presenting them to the planetary parliament for the rubber stamp. Roland wasn't blind to the implications of *him* being invited. The PM—and his supporters—wanted to see him in a less formal setting.

"Keep your eyes peeled," he muttered, as the hatch clicked open. "This could get interesting."

A butler—dressed in a formal outfit that had gone out of fashion hundreds of years ago—bowed politely. "Captain," he said. He paid no attention to Rachel. "His Lordship is waiting in the vestibule."

Roland smoothed down his civilian suit, then nodded and allowed the older man to lead them into the building. Rachel followed, as if she was glued to him. Roland wondered, idly, just how much attention she'd draw. She'd chosen to wear a dress that was as outdated as the butler's uniform, one that concealed far more than it revealed. He couldn't help thinking she'd either be a hit or a wallflower. Rachel would probably prefer to be a wallflower. She didn't seem remotely comfortable in public.

He put the thought out of his mind as they stepped into the vestibule. It was strikingly bright, the glass ceiling directing the warm sunlight into the chamber and sweeping the shadows away. The PM stood in the centre of the room, with a young blonde woman—she couldn't be older than twenty, although it was hard to be sure—standing just behind. Roland found it hard not to stare. Her blue dress was tight in places, enough to suggest she wasn't wearing underwear, and yet revealed very little bare skin. Roland had seen enough nudity to last him a lifetime—he was ashamed to remember how many young women he'd seen—but he had to admit there was something alluring about the newcomer. And yet....

The PM held out a hand. "Welcome to Oakley Manor, Captain."

"Thank you," Roland said. He shook the PM's hand firmly. "It was a surprise to be invited."

"Nonsense." The PM's smile looked genuine, but Roland had his doubts. "You are going to be working closely with us for many years to come. It would be good to meet in a more informal session, without the pressures of the uniform."

He stepped to one side, indicating the girl. "This is my daughter, Sandra," he said. "You and she have something in common. You're both graduates of Imperial University."

"A pleasure," Roland said. He allowed himself a slight smile. Sandra was clearly older than she looked, if she'd attended the university. "I can't say I recall meeting you."

Sandra's smile grew wider. "Me neither," she said, as she took his hand. "But at least we have *one* thing in common."

Roland allowed her to lead him through the door, as if Rachel wasn't even there. They had much less in common than Sandra knew. His file—the one that had been forwarded to the planetary government, with all the interesting bits carefully scrubbed out—claimed he'd been to Imperial University, in a bid to explain his accent, but it simply wasn't true. His tutors had attended upon him at the palace, rather than forcing him to attend the university in person. In hindsight, he suspected that had made him easier to control. How was he supposed to question what he was being told if he didn't have any outside sources of information?

"I took military history," he said. It was almost true. He'd studied it extensively during his training. "What did you study?"

"Politics, mainly," Sandra said. "It was a shame we never met."

Roland shrugged. Imperial University had been staggeringly huge, before Earthfall. The odds of them even passing on the streets were extremely low. Millions of students had passed through its gates, embracing the university lifestyle of drink, drugs and sex…sometimes, when they'd run out of other things to do, they'd even *studied*. Roland had been told that the university specialised in turning brains to mush, something he hadn't believed until he'd realised just how carefully his education had been shaped to keep him from thinking. Sandra looked smart, but there was a difference between intellectual understanding of politics and real-life experience. He wondered, idly, if she was allowed to practice now that she'd returned home. New Doncaster was hardly a textbook case of female liberation.

He listened to her chatter with half an ear as he looked around the dance floor. The band was playing an old tune, the dancers swaying in time to the music. Tables had been placed against the far wall, laden with food and drink. Roland felt a hot flash of anger at just how much food was going to be wasted, then forced it down. There was no time to get angry. He had to be on the alert.

"You've been on our world for months," Sandra said. "What do you think of it?"

"You have a beautiful world," Roland said. "I could get to like it."

Sandra smiled, then pulled him onto the dance floor. Roland felt his heart start to race as they slipped into a slow dance, her body so close to his that she brushed against him constantly. No one seemed to notice, or care. She seemed to come closer with each passing footstep, until her breasts were practically pushing into his chest...he took a breath, trying to calm himself. She was trying to seduce him. Of *course* she was. It was a little more subtle than the women he recalled from his teenage years, the ones who'd thought seducing him was the key to a better life, but he was sure of it. There was a cool deliberation to her movements that proved her intentions beyond a shadow of a doubt. Belinda was the only other person who'd inflamed him so much and *she* hadn't meant to do it.

He felt himself stiffen. He was suddenly sure she'd be receptive, if he suggested they find a room. The mansion was so large he was sure there'd be somewhere to go...he wondered, suddenly, if her father had put her up to it. She wouldn't be so daring in public if she didn't have her father's approval, would she? Roland had heard all the stories about university students and yet...she was a long way from the dead university. It had been blasted down to bedrock, along with the rest of the planet. The disaster was so great it was beyond his comprehension. He couldn't grasp how many people had died. They were just…numbers.

"I don't understand local politics," he said. It wasn't entirely true, but it would be interesting to see what kind of slant Sandra put on it. Besides, talking about something boring would help him keep his libido under control. "Tell me about it."

Sandra pulled him towards the wall, then poured them both drinks. "Look around," she said, as she passed him a glass. "All the movers and shakers are here."

Roland sipped the drink, silently grateful for his enhanced tolerance, as Sandra pointed out names and faces. Some he already knew—Richard had told him about Lord Ludlow—but others were strangers. Lords and ladies, MPs and wealthy merchants…Roland wasn't sure he followed the politics as well as he'd thought. The political system was clearly designed to conceal how it worked, rather than having everything in the open. That was almost certainly a bad sign. Secrecy often became habit-forming.

He allowed her to keep talking, noting how she'd switched tactics to make a good impression. She *was* clever. A young woman in her position would normally assume her good looks and wealth, or the promise of it, would be enough to attract anyone she wanted. If, of course, her parents *let* her set her cap at anyone. Sandra had little to look forward to beyond a political marriage. Roland's eyes swept the room. There was a surprising number of older men with younger women, not all of whom looked happy. It wasn't uncommon—the Grand Senate had done the same thing—but back on Earth the women had had a great deal more freedom. No one had cared what they did, as long as the bloodlines remained pure. He doubted it was as easy on New Doncaster.

And me listening to her is probably a good thing, he thought. *It might be harder for her to get someone to take her seriously.*

"Father needs to keep his MPs behind him or they'll push him out of power," Sandra finished. The explanation made a certain amount of sense, although he was sure he was missing something. "And then there'd be a struggle over who'd be the next PM."

Roland nodded, keeping his thoughts to himself as more and more lords and ladies—and their hangers-on—came up to exchange a few words with him, presumably gauging him for themselves. A handful were hostile, although they managed to hide it well; several of the women, including one old enough to be his mother, looked him up and down with frank interest. Roland suspected it was a deliberate attempt to discomfit him, rather than anything *real*. It had hit the spot. He barely remembered his mother. She'd died when he'd been very young.

"They all want to know what you can do," Sandra said. "And what your intentions are."

"My intentions?" Roland allowed her to lead him out into the grounds. "My intentions are to do my duty, nothing else."

Sandra smiled at him. "How long do you think you'll be here?"

"I don't know," Roland said. "I wasn't given a schedule."

"Then let me show you around," Sandra said. "I can show you the world."

Roland was tempted to ask if that was true. He couldn't imagine Sandra escorting him through the slums, let alone the penal colonies and the islands caught in the middle of a growing insurgency. He would be surprised if Sandra took him somewhere, anywhere, off the estate island itself. Her father would hesitate to let her travel to First Landing, let alone anywhere else. There was too great a risk of her being kidnapped or simply assassinated.

"It would be nice to see more of the world," he said. "Can you show me around the grounds?"

Sandra smiled and led him through a garden that managed to look both carefully maintained and unkempt. The trees rose around them, blocking his view of the manor. Sandra kept talking, pointing out berries and fruits that were safe to eat and cautioning him of the dangers of eating some of the others. Roland felt an odd little chill as he saw plants from Earth contrasting sharply with New Doncaster's native vegetation. It was rare for alien plants to survive their first encounter with the far tougher wildlife from the homeworld…he shivered, despite himself. The plants looked normal and yet they were subtly *wrong*.

"I used to play here when I was a little girl," Sandra said, as they reached a path leading down to a rocky beach. Great waves splashed against the rocks, droplets of water flying through the air. "I clambered for hours, day after day...."

Roland looked at her. There was an odd little smile—the first truly genuine smile she'd shown—playing over her face. He felt a twinge of envy, despite everything. He'd grown up in a world of luxury, yet he'd never been allowed to just be a kid. There'd never been any danger, not even the *pretence* of danger. He looked at the sailing ships in the distance, the tiny little craft that bobbed on the waves, and wished—not for the first time—that he'd been allowed to do something so carefree. His attendants—his jailors—had wrapped him in cotton wool. And who knew what else they'd denied him?

Belinda knocked some sense into me, he thought, numbly. *But I should never have been allowed to grow up like that....*

Sandra squeezed his hand. "Penny for your thoughts?"

"I never had anything like this, when I was a child," Roland said. He was tempted to throw caution to the winds and just run down to the beach, scrambling over rocks and splashing through rock pools like a child half his age. "It was just...Earth."

"Yeah." Sandra leaned closer to him. "I never understood how you people could live in CityBlocks."

Roland grimaced. He'd bet his inheritance, which was more theoretical than actual, that Sandra had never set foot in one of the bad CityBlocks. Roland himself certainly hadn't, not until Belinda and he had been making their escape from forces who wanted to kill him. They'd been dark and dingy and utterly terrifying and yet...they hadn't been the worst of the worst. The Undercity had been a nightmare, an endless warren of tiny compartments, flickering lights and toxic waste dumps. It was hard to believe anyone could live down there.

"It wasn't as though we had a choice," he said. His cover story stated he'd grown up in a middle-class family. They'd have lived in a CityBlock. "It would have been...."

The skies rumbled. The wind shifted, a wave of darkened cloud and mist—rainfall, he realised—sweeping towards them. Sandra pulled on his arm as water droplets brushed against his skin, hurrying him towards a tiny shelter at the top of the beach. Moments later, the skies opened. Roland felt water dripping down his back as they rushed into the shelter, then turned to watch the rain as it poured from the clouds. The garden—and the manor beyond—was lost in the gloom. He couldn't believe how quickly it had changed.

Sandra leaned against him, her dress damp and her hair threatening to come loose. Roland felt his heart start to race again. He knew she'd been told to get close to him, perhaps even seduce him, yet he found it hard to care. His arms went around her, holding her close. She lifted her lips to his, kissing him lightly. Roland felt himself grow hard, once again, as the kissing grew more and more passionate. He wanted her. He wanted her as badly as he'd wanted Belinda, once upon a time. And she was warm and willing and....

Not yet, he told himself. It was hard not to undo her dress. It was hard not to...he gritted his teeth. *Not yet.*

Sandra was smiling, brightly, as the rain came to an end. Roland smiled back at her, torn between the desire to possess her and the awareness it wasn't the right time. Not yet. Besides, people might be looking for them. He had no idea where Rachel was—he'd lost track of her hours ago—but she would certainly be looking for them shortly. Or...what else could she be doing? She was hardly the type of person to let a young aristocrat lead her astray.

You mean, she's nothing like you, his thoughts mocked. *She keeps her mind on the job at all times.*

He brushed himself down, then smiled at her. Her dress looked rumpled, and he had no doubt everyone would know what they'd been doing, but she was happy. "Shall we go?"

"I know a way back that's out of the public eye," Sandra assured him. "Come with me."

Roland allowed her to lead him back through the garden, marvelling at how the plants had been turned into a small maze. Here and there, he spotted traces of other couples hidden in the undergrowth. He hoped they weren't drenched, their expensive outfits ruined, although he doubted it. Sandra paid no attention, so he did the same. It was probably an unspoken part of the afternoon.

"I'll see you later," Sandra said, giving him a final kiss as they reached a side door. "I'll call you."

Roland watched her go, then sensed—more than heard—someone behind him. "Hi, Rachel."

"Hah." Rachel stood behind him, hands resting on her hips. "You do realise that girl was trying to seduce you."

"I'd say she succeeded," Roland said. The sharp look Rachel shot him was enough to force him to reconsider his next words. "She's good company."

"And she has an agenda of her own," Rachel said, tartly. "Don't you forget it."

CHAPTER SIXTEEN

KINGSTOWN TRAINING BASE, NEW DONCASTER

ROLAND'S FIRST COMBAT EXERCISE, in which he and his training platoon had been instructed to take part in a multi-unit operation spread out over a wide area, had been so bad that calling it a clusterfuck had been almost too kind. The recruits had thought themselves ready for modern war and discovered, the hard way, that they weren't. Roland knew he'd screwed up several times and he'd not been the only one. The Drill Instructors had been scathing as they'd gone through the entire exercise, pointing out each and every mistake in detail before finishing with a warning about what would happen if they made the same mistakes on a *real* battlefield. They'd be dead several times over....

And yet, looking at what was supposed to be a training exercise for the regular army and militiamen, Roland couldn't help thinking that his old platoon, with only a couple of months of training under their belts, had done a much better job. He'd been cautioned that there was always a degree of confusion in military movements, that there would be slippage as well as logistical headaches, yet the locals had managed to do almost everything wrong. The training exercise had been a complete and total disaster, to the point his instructors would have had a collective heart attack. They were damn lucky they weren't trying the tactics in a real war. It would have gotten them all killed.

He rubbed his forehead as the reports continued to come in. *His* men—the new recruits, who'd spent the last two months training mercilessly—weren't doing too badly, but the regular army and the militiamen were clearly not used to operating in large groups, let alone thinking about their lines of communication. The officers who'd seen actual service weren't so bad, but the ones who'd stayed on the peaceful islands were making basic mistakes. They'd neglected to protect their supply trucks...Roland shook his head in disbelief. The trucks had been taken off the gameboard easily. If the engagement had been real, seventy men would be dead and enough supplies to fight a full-scale battle would have either been destroyed or fallen into enemy hands. It had been all he could do to keep himself from calling the officer in command and tearing him a new asshole. The bastard needed to be stuck somewhere the sun didn't shine before he got a lot of men killed for nothing.

Richard caught his eye. "Captain Tagger is insisting his men haven't been killed, sir."

Roland bit down—hard—on the response that came to mind. Captain Tagger had been doing fine, right up to the moment he'd made a call on an unsecured channel. The artillery had promptly dropped a ton of shells on his position and the umpires had decided the entire force had been wiped out. Roland understood the confusion—there was a disconnect between what the fool had been told and what he could see in front of him—but there was no time to worry about it. Captain Tagger and his men were officially dead. They wouldn't be allowed to come back to life until the exercise was finally over.

"Inform him that the umpires have made their decision," Roland said. He wished, not for the first time, that he'd been able to bring more training outfits. It was harder to argue the point when one's suit wouldn't allow one to do anything more than lie still and pretend to be a corpse. "And if he has any further complaints, to save them for later."

He rubbed his forehead, a headache starting to blossom behind his skull. The exercise was small—compared to the big ones on the Slaughterhouse, it was pathetic—and yet it was turning into a total mess. He'd known the regulars were too small to make a difference, and that the militiamen were a mixed bag, but...he shook his head. The raw material was there, mostly. The troops had volunteered. But their officers....

They're the only field marshals with private batons in their knapsacks, he thought. He'd had a sergeant who'd cracked that joke more than once, although it had taken Roland some time to understand it. The growing number of men who'd been declared dead bore mute testament to how many of their officers were simply not up to the task. *Half of them need to be busted down to the ranks and the other half need to be shot.*

He motioned for Richard to join him as another set of bad reports came in. An officer had ordered his men to charge an enemy position. It might have worked, in a video game, but in the real world the men had simply been slaughtered. Roland clenched his fists, wishing he could wrap them around their commander's neck. It was bad enough the bastard had sent his men on a suicide mission, but...he'd had *guns* on call. He could have battered the enemy position into a pile of rubble easily, from well outside its range. There'd been no need to order his men to do anything, beyond pinning the defenders down.

"Tell me," he said. "Are they all this bad?"

Richard hesitated. "I...."

"Tell me the truth," Roland said. "It won't go any further."

"Some officers know what they're doing," Richard said. "But they're almost always the ones on deployment, not the ones polishing their uniforms here. Sir."

"I see." Roland let out a heavy sigh. "We're going to need to start an OCS, aren't we?"

Richard frowned. "Sir?"

"An Officer Candidate School," Roland said. "Even if we have to take the well-connected, we owe it to the men to make sure they have a rough idea what they're doing."

He looked at the map as yet another set of reports came in. Two companies had been ordered to launch a joint attack—a pincer—on an enemy position. On paper, it looked good. In practice...Roland gritted his teeth. The two COs were *not* cooperating, to the point the defenders had managed to smash one attack and were trying their best to smash the other. The umpires weren't sure who was winning, but it didn't matter. Any hope of exploiting the victory—if there *was* a victory—was gone. Roland tried to tell himself that better armies had been built from worse, but...he didn't really believe it. How could he?

"Cancel the exercise," he ordered. It was against tradition—normally, exercises and mock battles were fought out well past the point any sane enemy would have surrendered or beaten a hasty retreat—but they'd reached the point where continuing would harm the men's morale for nothing. "Inform the officers I want to see them in the mess hall at"—he glanced at the clock—"1700."

"Sir," Wimer said. "They'll have to hurry."

"Let them," Roland said. "And any of them who're late will regret it."

He glared down at the map as the communications system came back online and the final set of reports started to flow into the network. There'd been a whole series of disasters, most of which would have fucked up the operation beyond repair if they'd happened for real. Roland understood, suddenly, why the Imperial Army and Navy had often declared that entire units had come back to life in the middle of an exercise, even though the umpires had ruled them dead. It was frustrating as hell to look at a map and know the units were still there...he shook his head. It would be easy to fall into the trap of overlooking the sheer scale of the disasters, to write them all off as learning experiences, but he didn't dare. The next time, they might be facing *real* enemies, with *real* bullets. And then they'd be dead.

There were some bright spots. The artillerymen had done well. Mostly. They'd had the great good luck that most of the infantry commanders hadn't marched to the sound of the guns—and the ones who had, when they'd realized how dangerous the guns were, had been slaughtered in passing. The logistics chain hadn't broken of its own accord, which was a good thing, but it had shattered when the enemy had ambushed the convoys or blown up a couple of bridges. Roland frowned as he added yet another note to his ever-growing list. The bridges were supposed to be relatively solid, but none of them could stand up to high explosives or long-range shelling. They probably needed to establish a bridging element before they found their units trapped on the wrong side of a fast-flowing river.

Richard cleared his throat. "It's 1650."

"Is it?" Roland stepped back, brushing down his tunic. He'd wanted to take the field. He'd wanted to show the recruits that he had balls. He was glad, in hindsight, he'd stayed in the command post to watch the exercise. It had taught him things he hadn't wanted to know about how well his troops were prepped for battle. He hoped to hell the rebels hadn't been watching. They'd launch an attack, as soon as they finished laughing. "I'm on my way."

Rachel fell in behind them as they left the CP and walked down to the mess hall. A bunch of stragglers were hurrying to the doors, a couple hanging back as if they were planning to be fashionably late. Roland ground his teeth. He'd told them, time and time again, to take the exercise *seriously*. It was war, not a tea party.

Sandra could probably take me to a real tea party, he thought, with a flicker of amusement. He'd plunged himself into his work, when he'd returned from Oakley Island, but Sandra had kept sending him emails that were alternatively cute, insightful and slightly disturbing. *And who knows what we could do afterwards?*

He shoved the thought out of his mind as he stepped into the building, ordering Rachel to close and lock the door behind them. Any stragglers would regret it. He'd see to it personally. He'd said 1700, and he meant it. They were at war. He stepped to the front of the giant hall, relieved the chairs and tables had been pushed against the walls. It was a shame there was no podium, but it didn't matter. He'd been in worse places.

"Well," he said. It was hard not to scream. "That was an interesting set of disasters, wasn't it?"

...

Roland's words hung in the air.

Richard tensed, one hand twitching as he suppressed the urge to draw his pistol. No one, absolutely no one, spoke to the aristocracy and their children like *that*. Roland wasn't wrong—Richard had watched the disasters occur one by one himself—but none of the officers in the room would enjoy having their faults pointed out. They'd be running to their fathers and uncles and whoever had bought them their commissions, demanding they kick Roland off-world before he hurt their feelings any further. Richard felt a flash of contempt. The officers in front of him had never been in any real danger. They'd all been stationed in safe rear areas.

But they won't remain safe for much longer, Richard thought.

Roland didn't give any of them any time to recover. "We put nearly ten thousand men into the field," he said. "We strained every sinew to assemble a formidable force: new recruits, regular soldiers, militiamen. And the vast majority of them were declared dead. The umpires are still assessing the results of the battle, but upwards of seven thousand—perhaps even eight thousand—died in the last few hours. Eight thousand men! Tell me, what's going to happen when they die for real?"

It would be bad, Richard thought. The government had done its best to cover up the insurgency—it had reported Captain Tarquin Ludlow's death, without mentioning the men who'd died under his command—but the loss of so many men would be impossible to hide. Their families would demand answers and the government would have none. *And who knows what might happen if the landowners and townies both revolt?*

"You might say that it was just an exercise," Roland continued. He spoke over a pair of officers who tried to interrupt him. "And you'd be right. None of those men died for *real*. But I told you, when I briefed you on the exercise, that you had to treat it as a *real* engagement. That is the thing you did wrong, the thing that makes all your other mistakes look like nothing. You treated the whole exercise as a demented game and your subordinates suffered for it."

He kept speaking, ignoring the rumblings from the crowd. "Some of you attacked enemy positions from the front, instead of trying to sneak around and take them in the rear. Some of you didn't pay any attention to your supply lines, which allowed the enemy to cut you off and isolate you and wait patiently for you to die or surrender. Some of you forgot you had assets under your command you could have used, some of you failed to work together even though I'd ordered you to work as a team and, worst of all, one of you even used a white flag to lure the enemy in close before opening fire. What do you think will happen if the rebels realise they cannot trust our surrenders? I'll tell you. They'll kill us on the spot instead of taking us prisoner!"

His words hung in the air. "Right. We have orders to prepare for war before the situation explodes in our face. It is just a matter of time before it does. You—all of you—have a choice. You can work hard to learn from your mistakes, and mistakes made by your comrades, and turn into the leaders your men need. A good leader can inspire his men to fight long and hard and eventually accomplish the impossible. A poor leader will eventually wind up with a knife in his back, if he doesn't get himself and his men killed first.

"If you don't want to put your heads down, admit you have a lot of work to do and get on with it, you can quit. You can leave now, hand in your resignations and go back to whatever you were doing before you joined the army. I don't care. I'd sooner have ten competent officers than a hundred idiots in uniform. If you want to stay, you'll have to put in the effort to succeed. It is not easy, but it is extremely rewarding."

He pointed a finger at the door. "There's the way out," he said. "Choose."

Richard swallowed, hard, as the gauntlet was thrown down. Pushy, Lord Ludlow had called Roland. The wretched man hadn't known the half of it. Roland was staring into the faces of nearly forty men, all entitled brats who hadn't even started to earn their commissions, and daring them to be great. Richard admired his nerve, even as he envied the fact that Roland couldn't be busted back to the ranks, dishonourably discharged or even given a severe letter of reprimand. What could the government *do* to him? Kick him off-world? It wasn't exactly a punishment. Richard tended to think of it as something of a reward.

"But, sir," Captain Tagger said. "I thought...."

"You chose to defy the umpires in the middle of an engagement, after getting your men killed because you fucked up," Roland snapped. "Are you going to learn from your mistakes, or are you going to leave?"

Richard hid his amusement. Roland was stretching his authority to breaking point, and there was no point in denying it, but he did have one huge advantage. The PM and his inner cabinet had given Roland the authority and they couldn't take it back, not without looking indecisive. The vast majority of the officers in the room had close ties to the PM's faction, and even the ones who didn't ran the risk of getting in real trouble if they quit or fucked up beyond all hope of repair. Some would probably quit anyway, once the real pain began, but who knew? The ones who remained might become good at their jobs.

We'll see, Richard thought.

Roland smiled, but there was no humour in his expression. "I'm glad you all decided to stay," he said, in a tone positively dripping with false bonhomie. "We shall start with a detailed assessment of precisely *just* what went wrong during the exercise, and precisely how your decisions turned the problems into disasters, and *then* we will decide how we're going to improve."

Richard found it hard not to laugh at their reactions as Roland explained what they were going to do. They were officers. They didn't do early morning runs and forced marches and shooting practice and...Richard had to bite his lip to keep from giggling at the thought. It was absurd and yet, Roland intended to do it. Richard wondered what Captain Ludlow would have said, if he'd been told he'd be exercising every day until he could keep up with his men. Screamed, probably. He hadn't even been fit enough to run from the enemy.

And Roland is clearly not going to allow himself to be quelled, Richard thought. He'd been worried when he'd realised Roland had been introduced to Sandra Oakley. The girl was a prize catch. Even *he* had heard speculative chatter over who she'd marry. She wouldn't have set her cap at Roland unless her father had agreed beforehand. *It might be better to introduce him to the townies before it's too late.*

CHAPTER SEVENTEEN

FIRST LANDING, NEW DONCASTER

"I HOPE THIS VISIT TO TOWN isn't going to be quite as exciting as the last one," Roland said, as they drove into the city. "I've had my fill of excitement for the week."

He sighed, trying not to feel disheartened. The aristocratic officers were...some were so thick-headed the nasty part of his mind insisted they were bulletproof, some were so reluctant to get their uniforms dirty that he'd been tempted to push them into the mud, and some were plain lazy, to the point he'd had to order them dragged out of bed. The more aggressive ones were almost worse. They charged at targets like bulls charged at red capes, with about the same results. Roland had reached a point where he was seriously considering arranging a nasty accident for some of the more dangerous officers. It would be better than relying on them in a real fight.

At least they're not plotting to take you out first, the cynical part of his mind whispered. *But they're dangerous enough even when they think they're following orders.*

He looked around thoughtfully as Richard parked near a dingy-looking tavern. The district looked deprived, but nowhere near as hopeless as the poorest regions of the city. There was a certain sense of stubborn pride in the apartment blocks, a sense that life might be bad but it wasn't completely doomed. Roland wasn't sure what gave him that impression, although it might have something to do with the clean streets and apartment exteriors. The locals still tried to keep their heads above water. It was something he'd been told was—had been—sorely lacking on Earth.

Richard grinned at him, then led the way into the tavern. The air stank of cheap beer and rang with the sound of loud music. Roland tried not to wince as it assaulted his ears. He'd never been allowed to listen to any of the popular music when he'd been a child and, even as a teenager, his tastes had been sharply circumscribed. He suspected he should be grateful. Nothing good could come from popular music extolling the virtues of rape, murder and other crimes against humanity. Even some of the crap he'd heard in the barracks, as a raw recruit, had been head and shoulders above the racket heard here.

The interior was hazy, his throat burning every time he took a breath until he got used to it. A trio of young women were dancing on the stage, stripping as they belted out yet another terrible song; the cynical side of Roland's mind suggested no one came for their singing. There weren't many customers and most of the ones in view looked halfway to drunkenness. The floor was filthy, to the point that just *looking* at it made his skin crawl. He wondered, as he followed Richard into a compartment at the rear of the tavern, if he should decontaminate himself when he returned to the garrison. Rachel would have some very sarcastic things to say if he came home stinking of booze, vomit and God alone knew what else. It had been hard enough to get away in the first place.

"This place is more or less off-limits, unless you know a guy who knows a guy," Richard said, as they sat. He waved to a waitress, who nodded and ducked behind the counter. "The police never come in here."

Roland's eyes narrowed. There were hundreds of pubs, inns and taverns within the city, dozens more just outside the spaceport. Richard could have taken him to any of them if he'd wanted nothing more than a companionable drink or two...Roland knew, even if Richard didn't, that trying to get a Marine drunk was a waste of time. There *had* to be a few more classy places they could go...he felt unwell just *looking* at the table. He didn't want to think about the layers of stuff concealing the wood. His imagination provided too many possibilities, each worse than the last.

"It's a good place to have a chat," Richard added, as the waitress approached. "And to talk freely."

"I see," Roland said, neutrally. "Who comes in here, if the police don't?"

The waitress placed two giant tankards of beer on the table, then put a pair of scramblers right next to them. Roland kept his face impassive with an effort. Scramblers weren't precisely illegal, but one needed a licence to own and use one and the commercial models tended to be jiggered so the police and intelligence agencies could listen into the supposedly secure conversation anyway. Owning two of them *was* illegal, because the randomised signal fields they produced would compensate for the backdoors within the jamming. If the tavern was being monitored...the watcher wouldn't know what they were discussing, but he'd know they were up to *something*. Roland glanced around the dingy hellhole, silently assessing the best way to get the hell out if the shit hit the fan. Captain Allen would be *pissed* if Roland wound up in jail. Roland dreaded to think what his ultimate superiors might say.

Richard lifted his tankard. "Bottoms up."

Roland nodded as he lifted his own and drank. The taste was foul. He'd never really *liked* beer—he'd only drunk it, when he was younger, because it had annoyed his minders—and not being able to get drunk made drinking pointless. He swallowed anyway, telling himself his body wouldn't have any problems handling a single drinking session. He'd just have to go to the toilet a few times until the remainder of the alcohol was flushed out.

He watched, coldly, as Richard drank. The older man—not *that* much older—had never struck him as a drunkard. Richard had far more self-control. Roland was sure Richard had known he had less room for manoeuvre than his upper-class comrades, even before he'd been stuck with the blame for the death of Captain Ludlow. Reading between the lines, Roland figured Captain Ludlow had been one of the more aggressive commanders. It was just a shame he hadn't had any sense.

Let Richard get a little alcohol into his system, he thought, curtly. *It'll make the discussion a little more open and honest.*

"You do realise you've landed in a snake pit?" Richard finished his tankard and waved for another. The waitress brought it with commendable speed. "They're hoping for you to fail."

"That's dumb of them," Roland said. "What'll happen if they lose?"

Richard snorted. "I don't think they've thought that far ahead," he said. "The smart money knows the rebels will kill the lot of them, burning their estates to the ground and destroying all hope of rebuilding the pre-war economy. But the smart money isn't worth very much these days."

He laughed, humourlessly. "You're trying to save people who don't want to be saved."

"I think they want to be saved," Roland said. "But they want to be saved on their own terms."

Richard eyed his tankard thoughtfully. "Do you think anyone, anyone at all, is going to save the landowners from their own stupidity? Now, after Earthfall?"

"No." Roland was sure of it. "There's no one who'll come to your aid."

He scowled, inwardly. New Doncaster might be important to the locals, for obvious reasons, but the planet was a minor sideshow to the Marine Corps. He was mildly surprised the corps hadn't pulled Captain Allen and his men out, then waited to see who won the war. And all the other newborn interstellar powers would be even *less* charitable. They'd see no reason to keep the landowners around. Hell, putting them against the wall or sending them into exile would win them brownie points with the rebels. It might even last long enough to let them get the entire planet into a stranglehold. And that would be the end.

"Exactly," Richard said. "And they're fucking the rest of us."

Roland leaned forward as Richard downed more beer. It was clearly having an effect, yet...Roland hoped Richard would tell him something useful before the beer conked him out. He had no idea how much alcohol was in the beer, let alone how much Richard could drink without collapsing into a sodden heap. And afterwards…Richard would wonder just how much he'd said, when he'd been under the influence. Roland felt a twinge of shame, perhaps even guilt. Richard deserved better than drinking himself into a stupor.

"The system is rigged," Richard said. He drained his tankard—again—and summoned the waitress for more. "You know how it works on paper? Everyone gets a vote, as long as they're free of debt and own some land? Right?"

"Right," Roland said. "I read the files."

Richard snickered as the waitress placed more beer in front of him. "The files don't lie, not exactly, but they leave an awful lot unmentioned. You can free yourself of debt, sure, and you can even buy some land…you know what? You're still fucked. You don't get a vote that means…that means pretty much anything."

"How so?" Roland leaned forward. "You get a vote…."

"The system is rigged," Roland repeated. He cleared his throat, clearly trying to organise his thoughts. "There are five hundred MPs in Parliament, right? Each of them represents a constituency, right? But some constituencies are more equal than others. First Landing has more townies, with votes, than Oxley Island, but how many voters do you think live on Oxley Island?"

Roland frowned. He hadn't seen *all* the island—Sandra's tour had barely scratched the surface—but he doubted the resident population was *that* high. The island could probably support a few thousand people, if push came to shove, yet…it clearly didn't. His best guess was a couple of hundred residents, most of who would be servants rather than actual landowners.

"There are nearly a million people on Kingstown, and around two hundred thousand of them have the vote," Richard continued. "They have three MPs, just three. One for Kingstown North, one for Kingstown South, one for First Landing. They have the biggest majorities in Parliament... so what? There are seventeen townie MPs in total and they're so badly outvoted in Parliament that it isn't even funny."

"I...." Roland swallowed a curse as he realised how the system worked. On paper, ensuring that only landowners could vote made a degree of sense. It kept landowners from becoming the slaves of the majority. But if one made it difficult to own land, and jiggered the system to minimise the effect of the new voters...he swore under his breath. He'd wondered why there were so few townies in the army. He understood now. "There's no easy way to change the system, is there?"

"Of course not." Richard laughed, as if Roland had told a joke. "You see, the idea was that the townies would grow more powerful and steadily merge into the landowning classes. That was the plan when they settled this world. And then they discovered that they could make a steady income through selling the planet's produce instead, which lets them sideline or simply ignore the townies. And then..." —he shook his head— "they brought in shitloads of debtors and indents and turned them into slaves and then wondered why the newcomers hated them with a passion."

He snickered. "Most of them were lied to. Some were told they'd get their own farms. A handful did, but the majority wound up on the plantations. Some poor bitches were told they'd marry farmers, that they'd spend the rest of their lives as wives and mothers. And then many of the girls were ordered into the brothels until they repaid their debts to the corporation. But the system is rigged, so they just kept getting further and further into debt until they died."

"Fuck," Roland said. It wasn't entirely a surprise. He'd been sure the system was nowhere near as perfect as the local propaganda made it sound. But the sheer scale of the problem staggered him. "And no one is trying to fix it?"

"Dad is." Richard slurped his beer, then belched. "He's an MP. MP for First Landing. Secretary of the Town League. Has a majority that would make a despot blush. So what? He can vote however the hell he likes and it won't make any difference. They don't even bother to call him for votes, because his vote doesn't matter. He used to think he could put together a coalition that would make a difference, if the landowners split into two factions, but...so far, it hasn't worked. You should talk to him."

Roland forced himself to think. Richard might have said a little more than he'd intended...or he might not be anything like as drunk as he looked. And yet...he wasn't sure if he was missing something or the landowners really *were* as incompetent as they looked. Richard was a pretty good choice for liaison officer, at least on paper, but if he had a close tie to the official opposition...he snorted, inwardly. If Richard was right, the landowners might have overlooked his family connection because it simply didn't matter. Richard's father was one MP amongst hundreds. He couldn't hope to challenge the ruling party.

And if the system is completely resistant to reform, he thought coldly, *it will eventually be destroyed.*

"That girl you're fucking?" Richard's voice was starting to slur. He nearly dropped the tankard on the table. If it was an act, it was a very good one. "She's part of the system. She'll be married off to keep everything in the family...so to speak. Most of the landowners are related, you know. They might even be related to *you*."

"I doubt it," Roland said. It was possible, he supposed, but unlikely. The Grand Senate had ruthlessly culled or exiled anyone linked to the Imperial Family. New Doncaster wasn't *that* far from Earth, certainly not far enough for the Grand Senate. "And...why did you join the army?"

As he'd hoped, the sudden shift in subject loosened Richard's tongue. "I hoped I could make a difference, back when Dad thought he could do something," Richard said. "Dad was an MP. I could get at least *some* promotion, particularly if I took on the shittier tasks. I did, too...but so what? I watched a bunch of landowners with empty skulls promoted past me and then got the blame for one of them being hit in the head."

He giggled. "His head was so empty you'd think the bullet wouldn't actually kill him. It would just pass through an empty vacuum and come out the other side."

Roland shrugged, then pushed his tankard towards Richard and fired off a handful of additional questions. Richard answered, his voice slurring more and more, his words sometimes coming out in the wrong order. Roland cursed under his breath as a clearer picture continued to emerge. The system needed to be reformed—and fast—or the townies would throw their lot in with the rebels. That would turn the strategic situation upside down in the blink of an eye. Even if only ten percent of the townies joined the rebels, they'd still have a large force on Kingstown itself. It wouldn't be a war so much as an occupation—and a victory.

And would that actually be a bad thing? Roland wasn't so sure. The townies had reason to fear the rebels, but…he shook his head. He knew what had happened, on other worlds. The rebels might not draw any distinction between landowners and townies…they might even see the townies as compliant in mistreating the debtors and indents that made up the majority of the rebel forces. *Even if the rebel leaders are smart enough to realise they need the townies, if they want to build a proper economy, the rank and file might have other ideas.*

He shuddered. He'd seen the reports from a dozen worlds. The rebel forces had looted, raped and burnt their way towards the capital city, leaving dead bodies and devastated lives in their wake. Their anger had been so great—and who could blame them?—that they'd rampaged freely, tearing apart the farms and factories they needed to rebuild. Others…had been a little more thoughtful, but—in a bid to equalise society—they'd killed the goose that laid the golden eggs. Roland supposed they'd succeeded. Everyone had been equally poor.

Richard let out an odd little sound, then fell forward. Roland yanked the tankards out of the way, an instant before Richard hit the table and collapsed into sleep. The waitress looked utterly unamused. Roland rolled his eyes, then paid for the drinks—with cash—and carried Richard back to the car. There were injector tabs that could sober someone up instantly—Roland felt sick, remembering how Belinda had used one on him—but that would be cruel. Better for Richard to sleep it off, then wake up unsure of just how much he'd said. It would give Roland a chance to decide what, if anything, he wanted to do about the new information. It would be easy to pretend he'd heard nothing if he decided *nothing* was what he wanted to do.

The planet needs to be reformed, but the local government will be very resistant to any suggestion of change, he thought, as he strapped Richard into the back of the car. *And yet, if they don't ease up somewhere, the explosion is going to destroy everything in the blink of an eye.*

He sighed, inwardly. In all honesty, he didn't have the slightest idea what to do.

CHAPTER EIGHTEEN

KINGSTOWN TRAINING BASE, NEW DONCASTER

"**DON'T LET THEM GET A SHOT AT YOU,**" Lieutenant Richard Collier bellowed. "Keep your fucking heads down!"

Recruit Bryce Ambrose felt sweat dripping down his back as the training platoon marched to the sound of the guns. He'd been told that the training suit was as light as modern tech could make it, yet it was uncomfortably heavy. He'd been assured they wouldn't be wearing the rigging in actual combat, but…he shrugged. Being tagged with a laser from a training rifle was unpleasant; being shot, the sergeants had pointed out, would be a great deal worse. Bryce supposed they had a point. They'd been given a very brief introduction to battlefield medicine that had served to highlight both the risks of soldiering *and* just how little they knew.

He frowned as he ducked low, keeping well behind the point man. The platoon had been deployed into the training ground, with orders to locate and hit the enemy without being intercepted themselves. Bryce liked to think they were learning—and he was mentally compiling a list of observations he intended to pass on to his contacts—but he was starting to wonder if they were also wasting time. The Marine sergeants knew their stuff—Bryce prayed he'd never have to face them—yet the same couldn't be said for the local officers. Some of them were good, but some were dangerously incompetent; Bryce had privately resolved that, if he had to serve under one of the latter, he'd put a bullet in the asshole's back as soon as possible. It might suit the rebels to leave an incompetent in command, but...Bryce shuddered. There was no doubt in his mind that he was starting to develop comradely feelings for the rest of the platoon. How could he even consider betraying them?

Something moved at the corner of his eye. He lifted his rifle, ready to shoot, then relaxed—slightly—as a bird flew across his vision. The training ground had—naturally—been carved from lands that had resisted the terraforming and farming programs, to the point the landowners had decided to declare them a nature reserve rather than waste more money and effort trying to cultivate the land. Bryce had learnt a great deal about surviving in the outback over the last few weeks—he knew what he could safely eat, he knew where to find water—but he still wasn't sure how he'd cope. The training was hard, and the sergeants harder still, yet it wasn't *real*. He glanced up as the skies started to darken again, cursing under his breath. The last downpour had left him sloshing around like a drunken fool.

They kept inching forward, reaching an ill-carved road and crossing one by one before resuming their passage through the jungle. Someone had used a giant crusher to cut the road through the foliage and flatten the ground beneath its treads, but they hadn't bothered to lay down tarmac or spray plant-killer or do anything else to ensure the road remained undisturbed by the forces of nature. Bryce had a feeling it wouldn't be too long before the road was gone, as if it had never been. He shrugged, uncaring. The landowners were often sloppy, because they rarely had to deal with the consequences. He looked forward to the chance to turn their sloppiness against them, to take a knife and ram it into their backs. He felt another twinge of guilt. Perhaps, when he did, he could avoid killing his comrades. He didn't want to hurt them.

The point man froze, holding up a hand. Bryce froze too, bracing himself as he heard the faint sound of engines. They'd been cautioned that modern vehicles were almost silent—the sergeants had insisted a troop of Landsharks could move up behind an enemy position without being noticed—but it was rare to encounter such vehicles, even on Kingstown. The vast majority were powered by burning hydrocarbons, rather than fusion power cells. They made enough noise to wake a dead man.

Lieutenant Collier slipped past Bryce, spoke briefly to the point man—his voice so low Bryce couldn't make out the words—and headed into the undergrowth. Bryce wasn't quite sure what to make of the younger man. Lieutenant Collier was a townie, which made him effeminate at best and an outright traitor at worst, but he was a better commander than most of the landowner kids. Some of the bastards—Bryce liked to think they really *were*—were trying, he supposed; some were just going through the motions, no doubt hoping daddy dearest would ensure they weren't sent into danger. Lieutenant Collier didn't seem to have that sort of protection, although he was tight with the Marine who appeared to be in charge. Bryce hoped that was a good sign. He just feared it wasn't.

And he looks as if he has a hangover, Bryce thought. The younger man had looked cranky when he'd taken over the platoon and the heat hadn't made him any better. *What was he doing last night?*

He tried not to feel a pang of resentment as he waited. He was sure it would be easy to get over the fence and slip into the town long enough to make his report, and then have a drink or two before heading back to the camp, but he wasn't *sure*. A number of recruits had already been caught and placed on punishment duties...he'd been told, by an older recruit, that the training officers would turn a blind eye if the recruits made it out and then back again without being caught. It sounded like a sick joke to him. If the officers didn't know you'd slipped out, how could they punish you for it? And Lieutenant Collier had gotten drunk last night....

Maybe he kept a bottle or two dozen in his bunk, Bryce thought. The recruit barracks were regularly searched, with punishment duties for anyone foolish enough to bring alcohol and porn, but maybe officers got more freedom. *Or someone could have smuggled alcohol into the camp.*

Lieutenant Collier returned, looking excited. "The enemy convoy is resting," he said. "We need to move. Now."

Bryce braced himself as the platoon hurried forward, crawling through the undergrowth until they reached an overhang and looked down. The enemy convoy was sitting on the road—he couldn't help noticing that they were poised to block traffic, if indeed there had *been* any traffic—with a handful of men relaxing, smoking or taking a moment to piss before the convoy resumed its journey. It was the perfect spot for an ambush, perhaps too perfect. A flicker of doubt shot through him. Perhaps it was a trap. Perhaps....

"Target the lead vehicles first," Lieutenant Collier ordered. His voice was cold. Perhaps he also suspected they'd been lured into a trap. The trucks below them were relatively cheap, certainly compared to shuttles and starships, but losing them would hurt. "Then aim for targets of opportunity."

And if this is a trap, we're about to spring it, Bryce thought. He glanced behind the platoon, into the undergrowth. Was someone creeping up behind them? It would be difficult to escape if they were, not without lowering themselves off the overhang and exposing themselves to enemy fire. *If this goes wrong....*

"Fire," Lieutenant Collier ordered.

Bryce squeezed the trigger. The training gun jerked in his grasp, just like a *real* gun. Bryce had fired enough shots, over the last few days, to be pretty sure the designers had got it as close to *real* as possible. A handful of enemy targets might escape, because they were hidden behind canvas that would block the laser beam even though a real bullet would get through like a hot knife through butter, but the exercise software was very good. The vehicles wouldn't be allowed to operate if the software determined they'd been damaged, perhaps destroyed. He saw a couple of men hit the ground, training suits locking them in place until the exercise came to an end. He felt a flicker of pity. The suits weren't *gentle* when they hurled their wearer to the ground. They were designed to ensure the experience was not forgotten in a hurry.

He swept the gun over the convoy as a handful of men rolled over and tried to fight back, using the trucks for cover. Good thinking on their part, but they'd been caught in the open...caught with their pants down. They hadn't realised quite where the fire was coming from, not yet...they never had a chance. A handful of grenades were hurled down, flashes of light taking yet more men out of the engagement. He tried to imagine what it would be like for real and shuddered. Burning vehicles, burning bodies, burning everything....

"Hold fire," Lieutenant Collier ordered. "Watch and wait."

Bryce did as he was told, eyes sweeping the convoy for signs of life. The smarter enemy troopers might stay very still, pretending they'd been taken out of the fight. It might work, although they'd been cautioned that anyone who pretended to surrender had damn well better hope they were captured and executed by the enemy. They'd be in hot water—scalding—when they got home. Bryce had been shocked, until the instructors pointed out that fake surrenders would rapidly lead to the enemy refusing to accept *real* surrenders. And then both sides would commit more and more atrocities until one side was completely gone.

"No one moving, sir," Recruit Tenos said. "I think we got them."

"Looks that way," Lieutenant Collier agreed. "But we'll wait a little longer."

Bryce nodded. Who knew how many enemy soldiers were playing dumb?

• • •

Richard wasn't entirely sure *just* how much he'd drank, the previous evening, but it had clearly been enough to put him out of commission for *hours*. He'd woken up in his bunk, mouth tasting so awful he'd wondered if he'd actually made the mistake of ordering food. The tavern might sell cheap beer and privacy, but even the *staff* sent out for takeout. Richard had been told their food was practically poisonous. He didn't want to find out the hard way.

He tried not to groan. He'd drunk several gallons of water, eaten a greasy breakfast and swallowed a small packet of painkillers, but he still felt wretched. The bright sunlight wasn't helping. He cursed himself, savagely, as he tried to calculate how much he'd actually had. He'd planned a companionable drink or two, not a bender. Damn it.

The enemy convoy was ruined, as planned. Richard wasn't pleased. They'd set up the exercise, at least in part, to teach the convoy CO the danger of stopping in the middle of a war zone. If the attackers had used real weapons, the convoy would be flaming ruins and the defenders would be dead. Richard shook his head and instantly regretted it. Roland might have wanted to teach the convoy officers a lesson, as well as the attacking force, but he wasn't sure how well it had worked. There was just something *fake* about the attack. He wondered, idly, how many of the soldiers had worked out the entire ambush had been stage-managed.

Probably far too many of them, he thought. *They're not stupid.*

He took one final look at the convoy, then motioned for the platoon to sneak back and vanish into the undergrowth. Roland would have an *achingly* polite conversation with the convoy CO, pointing out how his mistakes had led to total disaster. Hopefully, he'd learn better over the next few days or...Richard's heart almost stopped as something dawned on him. Just how much had he *said* last night? He'd drank so much his memories were a hazy blur, when they weren't completely blank. What had he been *thinking*?

Dumbass, he told himself. *What did you say?*

He forced himself to think, despite the pain. He'd planned to carefully broach the topic of politics. He'd intended to explain the reason the government was unlikely to reform, not without significant pressure. He'd even considered pointing out the danger of getting too close to Sandra Oakley, daughter of the Prime Minister himself. Roland was barely out of his teens. He was too young to realise that Sandra had been thrown at him. And then...and then what? Richard shuddered to think how much a pretty, young girl could influence a man when his hormones were popping like mad. Richard was all too aware that he'd made a fool of himself, where young girls were concerned....

The march back to the RV point helped to clear his head, but his memories refused to surface. He'd taken Roland to the grotty tavern because it was private—and because no one important would be seen dead there—yet…it might have been a mistake. How much had he drank? How much had he said? He would almost sooner have woken up in the waitress's bed, wearing only a sock! He would have made a fool of himself, again, but at least he wouldn't have skirted the line between rough talk and treason. Just how much had he *said*?

His thoughts twisted and turned. He might have told Roland about his father. He might have told Roland about the Town League. It wasn't a banned organisation, not like the Workers Liberation Front or the Proletarian Freedom Fighters or a bunch of others, but membership in the league could easily be used against him…he'd been careful not to take out membership or to attend their meetings too openly, just in case. And yet…he could have blown his chances of accomplishing anything. Roland probably wouldn't *report* him, but….

He sighed, inwardly, as the RV point came into view. The buses were already waiting to take the men back to the garrisons. They'd get some leave when the exercises were finally finished, before taking the field for the first time. Richard had heard muttered suggestions it was time for the new recruits to prove themselves, or else. Lord Ludlow hadn't done anything overtly, as far as Richard could tell, but he'd dropped hints time might be running out. And, even if the politics didn't change, the war wasn't going to go away. The news made the planet sound peaceful. Richard had heard enough, through the grapevine, to know the insurgency was still spluttering on.

"Hand in your weapons, then board the buses," he ordered. He knew his duty. He'd deal with the rest later. "And then we can all get back home."

• • •

"Captain Harrington needs to be fired," Roland said, studying the live feed from the drone. It wasn't perfect—the planet's weather played merry hell with even the most advanced optical sensors—but it was light years better than nothing. "He practically set up an ambush for himself."

He rubbed his forehead. Captain Harrington might have made a good...actually, Roland couldn't think of just *what* he might be some good at. He was a weaselly little man, with too many connections to be easily sacked or demoted. Roland felt his scowl deepen. The bastard was bad enough in a safe rear area, but on the front lines he'd get his men killed for nothing.

"Make a note," he said, to Rachel. "We'll assign him to a useless post on one of the aristocratic islands."

Rachel nodded, curtly. Roland allowed himself a tight smile. Captain Harrington could go boss the militia, somewhere well away from the front lines. He wouldn't get anyone killed—hell, the militia on such an island would be largely drawn from the aristocracy and their clients—and he'd be out of Roland's hair. He might not even realise he'd been sidelined. He might even see the transfer as a promotion.

Only because I can't get rid of you, Roland thought, coldly. *If I could kick you out without setting off a political firestorm, I would.*

He shook his head. "Do we have an update from Ivanovo?"

"They think they've located a rebel base, as they said," Rachel said, with heavy patience. They'd discussed it when the message had first arrived, four hours ago. "But their militia can't handle it themselves."

"And Captain Allen is unwilling to spare the men," Roland said. He frowned as he studied the map. It wasn't clear just *what* the local militia had found but it was either a rebel base or a bandit hideout. Either way, it needed to be taken out as quickly as possible. The last thing he wanted was to get dragged into a long, drawn-out insurgency. "Do we have the forces on hand to tackle it ourselves?"

"Yes, if you're willing to risk involving the locals," Rachel said. "And if they know the truth...."

Roland swore under his breath. The local militia leaked like a sieve. He would bet his entire salary that any movements they made would be reported to the rebel HQ at lightning speed. And they'd either be ready for an attack or simply abandon the base and vanish into the undergrowth. Ivanovo Island was small, but *small* was a relative term. There was enough unsettled terrain to hide an army.

"We're going to have to be careful," he said. "I'm due to visit the works tomorrow, then call in on the PM. I want to take the offensive without making it clear what I'm doing."

Rachel gave him a sharp look. "If you launch an offensive on your own authority, you'll tread on a lot of toes."

"I know," Roland said. He had half a plan already. He'd just have to sit down, work out the details, then put it into operation without giving the game away too early. "And that's why we're not going to be entirely honest about what we're doing."

CHAPTER NINETEEN

OAKLEY WORKS, NEW DONCASTER

"IT'S GOOD TO SEE YOU AGAIN, ROLAND," Sandra said. "I hoped you'd return to the island."

Roland allowed himself a smile as he climbed into her car. Sandra was driving, something that struck him as a little odd in a world where everyone who was anyone had drivers of their own. He couldn't help wondering if it was a subtle form of chaperonage or an attempt to escape it. Sandra put the car into gear effortlessly, steering the car down the road and away from the army base. Roland had to admire her skill. The car was a great deal more complex than the vehicles he'd used as a child.

He studied her, feeling a twinge of lust mingled with wariness. Sandra had swapped her dress for a simple pair of slacks and a tight shirt, her hair tied up in a neat little ponytail, but she still looked stunning. Her face looked perfect, perhaps a little too perfect. Her make-up was either very subtle or completely missing. He tried not to think about the shape of her body, revealed by her outfit. It really wasn't the time.

"The army life has clearly been good for you," Sandra said. "You look ready for anything."

"Thanks." Roland had to smile. Sandra had *no* idea. "Why did you volunteer to escort me today?"

Sandra gave him a guileless smile. "I wanted to see you again," she said. "Is that so wrong?"

"No," Roland said. "But I'm surprised your father didn't object."

"Father knows I will be playing a major role in family affairs, even after I get married," Sandra said. There was an odd wistfulness to her tone, but it was hard to be sure if it was genuine. "It's important I have a rough idea of what I'm doing, before it's too late."

Roland hid his surprise. *That* was a degree of forward thinking he hadn't expected, not from the local governing class. The landowners didn't seem to realise how much trouble they were storing up for themselves. There was a very good chance that Sandra, and whoever she eventually married, would wind up dead—or worse—if they didn't find a way to stabilise the situation. Fast.

He leaned back in his chair. "I don't pretend to understand much about local politics," he said. "Why do the landowners control everything?"

Sandra kept her eyes on the road. "We bought the settlement rights. We funded the first developmental program. We set up the planetary corporation, then invested hugely in the planet in hopes of turning it into a home as well as a source of income. The current crop of landowners, by and large, are the descendants of those who invested in the colony when it was just a dream. Why should they *not* control everything?"

Roland kept his voice light. "What about the townies? Or the debtors?"

"The townies paid their own way, or rather their ancestors did, but they didn't invest much of anything in the planetary development corporation," Sandra said. Her voice was artfully bland. Too bland. She knew they were sailing into dangerous waters. "The debtors took out loans to come here, loans that came directly from the corporation. From us. Why should they have any say in government when they haven't *invested* in the government?"

Roland winced, inwardly. He wasn't that surprised. He'd heard the argument before, time and time again. Those who paid the bills called the shots. And yet, there came a time—and New Doncaster was well past that point—when those who didn't pay got tired of being bossed around. Richard had been right about that, if nothing else. The townies were sick of being unable to control their own lives, while the debtors were increasingly aware that they'd never be able to get out of debt. And why would the landowners want it to change? A program of debt forgiveness would shift the balance of power, shattering it beyond repair.

No wonder they were so unnerved by my suggestion of trading military service for debt forgiveness, he thought. *It would be a great deal harder to screw the former soldiers if they fought for their rights and knew how to do it again.*

Sandra changed the subject as the car picked up speed, wittering about famous names who were attending her gatherings in a bid to convince him to attend as well. Roland kept his answers non-committal. He'd like to spend more time with Sandra, but not with a gaggle of young aristocrats with only one brain cell between them. The knowledge he'd been worse than *any* of them, only a couple of years ago, didn't make him feel any better. He'd been a useless waste of space. They'd be just the same.

The industrial estate came into view, guarded by a handful of militiamen who insisted on checking their fingerprints and retinas before allowing Sandra to drive into the complex and park by the front door. Sandra looked thoroughly displeased, but Roland was quietly impressed. At least they were taking security seriously. The defences wouldn't keep out a determined attack, yet they'd stop a lone gunman in his tracks. He sucked in his breath as a man in a fancy suit hurried towards them, looking ready to kiss their feet. It was going to be a long and boring presentation before they finally came to the meat of the matter.

"My Lady," the man said. He bowed deeply to Sandra. "And Colonel Windsor!"

"Captain Windsor," Roland corrected, deciding not to mention it was only a brevet rank. "I don't have much time, so please could we see the factory first?"

"Of course, of course," the man said. His expression suggested he was anything but happy about it. "It will be my pleasure."

Roland kept his thoughts to himself as they were led through a checkpoint, then shown into the factory, which was much larger than expected. The manager kept up a steady stream of commentary, decrying the limited technology on one hand and, on the other, proudly declaring that everything they made in the factory was completely free of expensive imported technology. Roland understood the real message. The factory's products might be primitive—they still used petrol and natural gas for fuel—but they could be produced, and repaired, without having to ship in spare parts and replacements from the other side of the galaxy The craftsmen were clearly a cut or two above the debtors and indents. They definitely knew what they were doing.

He kept his eyes open as they moved from room to room, watching cars, trucks and even light aircraft being put together. The manager insisted it only took a few weeks to turn a pile of raw material into a car, maybe only a few days longer for a truck or an aircraft. Roland was impressed. The aircraft might be laughable, by modern standards, but they were just what New Doncaster needed. Hell, an HVM seeker warhead might completely miss them.

And replacing the expended missile would be more expensive than replacing the downed plane, he told himself. *At some point, the enemy would simply run out of weapons.*

"My father is very pleased," Sandra said. "He's made funds available for an immediate expansion of the factories."

"But we also need more and better armoured cars, tanks and aircraft," Roland said. "How many could you produce for us in a month?"

The manager hesitated. "Assuming a steady supply of workers and raw materials," he said, possibly hedging his bets, "we could churn out approximately fifty to a hundred cars or aircraft per month. It wouldn't be easy, and it would put immense wear and tear on the equipment, but it could be done. Tanks are a little harder—the best we can do, from the designs we found in historical datacores, could be put together at a rate of twenty per week...."

His voice trailed off. Roland grimaced. The manager knew—he had to know—his audience wasn't going to like his next words.

"The basic tank design is very primitive," the manager said. "Everything from engines to armour and guns are...weak and fragile, compared to a modern tank. There is no way we can produce the sensors and armour used elsewhere, let alone the main guns. The good news is that our tanks will be easy to repair or replace. The bad news is that they'll be blown away effortlessly if they go up against a single modern tank or AFV."

"And a plasma cannon will go through an entire line of such tanks like a hot knife through butter," Roland said. It wasn't a surprise. He'd seen the plans. "But the rebels won't have any modern tanks of their own."

"No, sir," the manager said. He looked at Sandra, then back at Roland. "I must caution you that there will be limits to how much we can produce, before something breaks and we have to halt production. We can draw up contingency plans, in addition to the ones we already have, but there will be limits to those, too. Ideally, we should be able to invest in new factories while also producing newer and better vehicles, but...."

"I understand." Sandra held up a hand. "I'll discuss the matter with my father, but we should be able to get additional funding for you."

"And additional workers," Roland added. "How long does it take to train a craftsman?"

"They can master the basics very quickly," the manager said. "But it's going to be harder to get them qualified if we're putting them on the assembly line as soon as possible."

And we don't know how far we can trust them, Roland's thoughts added. *The landowners won't send their sons here; the townies and debtors may side with the rebels when the shit hits the fan.*

He allowed the manager to show them the rest of the complex, his heart sinking as he saw the number of indentured workers doing menial jobs. They'd be rebels, at least in their hearts, or he was a fool. And there were limits to how closely they could be supervised...he shook his head, wondering how many weapons were already concealed within the warren-like factory complex. They churned out weapons as well, if he recalled correctly. The ammunition was produced somewhere else, but still...he winced, inwardly, as the whistle blew. It wouldn't be that hard to smuggle bullets into the compound.

The bright sunlight on the outside was almost a relief. "Well, that was interesting," Sandra said. "Did you see what you wanted to see?"

"Yes and no," Roland said. "How many of those workers are actually trustworthy?"

Sandra blinked. "My family hired them, paid their debts...."

Roland shook his head, not trusting himself to speak as they made their way back to the car. Sandra didn't understand. How could she? The indentured workers they'd seen had no hope of rising in the world, no job prospects outside the factory...Sandra herself didn't have *that* much freedom, not compared to her male cousins, but at least she lived in luxury and had *some* possibilities for making something of herself. The car rumbled to life and passed through the checkpoint without being stopped. Roland groaned, inwardly. Sloppy.

"Father is looking forward to seeing you again," Sandra said. "Should we take the direct route? Or the scenic route?"

"The direct route," Roland said. The scenic route offered all kinds of possibilities, but he wasn't in the mood. "I can't be late for your father, or he'll file complaints with my superiors."

"He wouldn't," Sandra said. "Lord Ludlow has been filing complaints."

Roland smiled, although it wasn't funny. "So I hear."

He leaned back in his chair and forced himself to relax as the car went into the city and headed towards the government district. Lord Ludlow hadn't sent his complaints to Captain Allen or Roland would have gotten a lecture, even if it had been something along the lines of *keep up the good work*. The precise division of authority between Captain Allen and himself was a little vague, deliberately so, but Allen wouldn't hesitate to pull Roland up short if Roland really screwed up. Who knew what his ultimate superiors would think? Would they assume Allen had already dealt with the matter? Or would they order Roland to leave New Doncaster at once?

Which would be something of a relief, he thought, as the skies darkened and the downpour began again. *No matter what I do, there's going to be one hell of an explosion.*

He scowled as they parked in an underground garage, then took the executive lift directly to the PM's office. New Doncaster was hot, muggy and uncomfortable, but he was starting to like it. Some of the locals were good people, others…he glanced at Sandra, feeling a twinge of regret. He wanted her, but he was all too aware she worked for her father. The PM probably assumed Roland would think Sandra was working alone. He didn't know that Roland had grown up in the Imperial Family. Sandra was an innocent, compared to some of the people Roland had met.

"Captain Windsor." The PM greeted him with a smile that was, perhaps, a little too polished, then motioned them to a chair. "I trust the factory was satisfactory?"

"Mostly," Roland said. He was mildly surprised Sandra hadn't been dismissed and sent to powder her nose, like other aristocratic ladies, although he supposed it wasn't *that* surprising. It was a hint that her father valued her as more than just a pretty face he could marry off for best advantage. Or maybe he didn't want to make an issue of sending her away in front of Roland. "Security is an issue. The complex isn't anything like as tight as it should be, sir…."

"Please, call me William," the PM said. "At least when we're alone."

Roland nodded, curtly. "Yes, sir. The complex needs both new workers and tighter security. My impression is that the craftsmen are well-trained, and can be relied upon to be relatively loyal, but the untrained men are resentful and their resentment could easily be turned against us. I would be astonished if there wasn't already a rebel spy in the complex."

The PM stiffened. "By that logic, there might be one in your army too."

"Yes," Roland said. They'd spent a great deal of time trying to figure out who, if anyone, was reporting to the rebels, but none of their ideas had turned into anything practical. "We have taken precautions, sir."

"We'll consider what precautions we might take," the PM said. "Do you think the factory can meet your needs?"

"I think it needs to be expanded," Roland said. "It depends on just how long the war lasts, of course, but I think we'll be looking at several years—at best. We need more and better weapons before the rebels come up with counters of their own. We also need to take the offensive."

"On Ivanovo?" The PM's smile had little humour in it. "Do you think you can tackle the rebels?"

Roland cursed, mentally. The news had already leaked. The islanders had been begging for help for days now, but still...he nodded. There was no point in trying to hide their destination, when his first units marched out of the camp and headed to Kingsport to board their ships. But his plans and tactics would have to remain hidden, at least until it was too late for the enemy to stop him.

He kept his face carefully blank. "I plan to reinforce the defenders first, then start patrolling the backcountry roads," he lied, smoothly. The tactics made sense, and hopefully the news would lure the rebels into a false sense of security, but he had something else in mind. "As we bring in more men, the rebels will have to either take the offensive, which will force them to engage us on our terms, or fade further and further into the backcountry. It's an island. Eventually, they'll simply run out of places to hide."

And the plan would take months, if not years, if we ever intended to implement it at all, his thoughts added silently. *They'll know that, too.*

The PM held up a hand before Roland could start bombarding him with mil-speak. "I have every faith in your ability to handle the job," he said. "I'll give you all the support I can."

"Just ensure the local militia knows to follow orders, without delay," Roland said. "It won't make victory any easier if they don't play their role."

"Of course," the PM said. "I'll have General Falk see to it personally."

Roland nodded. It was probably the best he was going to get. They exchanged a few more minor comments, before the PM's secretary warned it was time for his next appointment. Roland didn't argue. He had the authority he needed, and he didn't want the PM to start adding conditions. It would make life very dangerous indeed.

"You're going straight into danger," Sandra said, as they returned to the garage. "Do you think you'll come back?"

"I hope so." Roland felt his blood run cold. It would be the first time he'd gone into *real* danger since he'd joined the corps. He'd done well—he knew he had—but how would he perform in a *real* battle? "I'll be very careful."

Sandra looked at him. "For luck...."

She stepped forward and kissed him, hard. Roland kissed her back, his hands roaming over her back and slipping down to stroke her bottom. She shivered, her kisses growing warmer...for a moment, he wanted to take her there and then and to hell with everything else. But he didn't have time. He needed to get back to camp, plan the deployment, and work out orders that would allow him maximum flexibility with minimal warning to the enemy. He dared not assume his orders would remain secret. They'd pass through too many untrustworthy hands.

"You come back to me," Sandra said. "You hear me?"

Roland kissed her again. "I will," he said. "I promise."

CHAPTER TWENTY

IVANOVO ISLAND, NEW DONCASTER

"IT LOOKS BEAUTIFUL, FROM UP HERE," Rachel said. If she was bothered by flying in an aircraft so fragile a strong gust of wind would knock it out of the skies, she didn't show it. "What's it like down below?"

Richard frowned. "I've never served on Ivanovo," he said. "But, from what I've heard, it's just as much as a basket-case as the other plantation islands."

He leaned forward, peering through the porthole and trying to see the island through their eyes. Ivanovo was more of a country than an island, a teardrop-shaped piece of land within a sea of endless blue. The northern side of the island was dotted with the signs of civilisation—a large and growing harbour city, plantations that stretched as far south as they could—while the southern side was a maze of jungle, mountains, dead volcanoes and cliffs that plunged down to the sea. It looked small, on the map, but Richard didn't need to visit the island to know that even the *settled* parts of the island would be hellish, if they had to fight a war. The plantations were a web of crops, small streams that brought water from the wells to the farmland and bunker-like buildings that could be easily turned into strongpoints. It was perfect for an insurgency. He was a bit surprised things hadn't gotten out of hand a great deal sooner.

And Roland thinks he can handle it, he mused. It was clear Roland had a plan—a plan he hadn't bothered to discuss with Richard or any of the other local officers. Richard wasn't sure how he felt about *that*. It was hard to blame Roland for being suspicious of the locals—Richard was sure *some* of them were on the take—but—at the same time, it was insulting beyond words. And yet...his lips quirked as the aircraft banked and headed for the airport beside the harbour. *If this goes wrong, at least no one will be able to point the finger at me.*

He kept an eye on the two Marines as the aircraft dropped rapidly, trying to gauge their reactions. Roland showed no sign of concern as he saw the landscape, even though you didn't have to be an experienced officer to know that fighting their way north was going to turn into a nightmare. Hell, the town was a warren of prefabricated buildings, stone and wooden constructions and shacks that made First Landing look nice and civilised. Richard wouldn't bet so much as a single penny against the rebels already having cells within the town. The steady stream of boats and ships coming and going at all hours was more than enough to move an army into the city.

The aircraft touched down with a bump and taxied to the hangars. Richard raised his eyebrows as he saw the cargo helicopters resting on the concrete, surrounded by a handful of private security guards. Oxley guards...he wondered, idly, what they were doing there. The PM's family didn't have any *major* interests on Ivanovo, as far as he knew. They might be resting, their pilots taking a break before they resumed their flight, or...he shrugged. It wasn't his problem. Anyone who took too close an interest in landowner affairs would come to regret it.

Roland opened the hatch and jumped down to the tarmac. Richard followed, grimacing as a wave of humid air struck his face. Ivanovo was even hotter than Baraka, something he would have sworn to be impossible. The air stank of tropical crops and human desperation...he winced as he spied a group of indents, arms and legs in shackles, being marched south to the plantations. If they were lucky, they'd break free and get into the outback before the plantation owners and overseers started looking for them. If not…they'd be worked to death or killed while trying to escape or *something*. The odds of any of them paying off their debt to society were about the same as Richard discovering he was next in line to the Imperial Throne.

A militiaman, wearing an officer's uniform that made him look like an oversized bumblebee, met them as they reached the terminal. "Captain Windsor," he said. "It is my pleasure…."

Roland cut him off. "This airport is now under military control, in line with the Prime Minister's instructions," he said. "From this moment on, no one is to enter or leave, or make any attempt to contact the outside world, without permission from myself or my staff officers. My men will be arriving shortly. They will be billeted in the hangar, where you will provide them with water and rations. You may wish to file official complaints, but you can do it after the lockdown is lifted. Any attempt to send a message ahead of time will result in summary court-martial and, at best, a permanent sentence of indenture. Do I make myself understood?"

The militiaman gaped. "Sir, I….."

"Do I make myself understood?" Roland allowed his expression to darken as he repeated his question. "Do I?"

"Yes, sir," the militiaman said. "I…I must inform you that my workers are contractors who have homes and families in the town…."

"The entire complex is going into lockdown," Roland said. "That is not up for dispute. If your workers behave themselves, they will be paid for their time; if they try to leave without permission, they will wind up in deep shit. I will not run the risk of allowing a single message to leak out before my men begin the march south. Is that clear?"

"Yes, sir." The militiaman swallowed. "I'll make it clear to the workers."

Richard hid his amusement as the officer scurried off. The uniform alone was clear proof the man had never seen action, not when it helpfully told enemy snipers who to shoot. He doubted the idiot could count past twenty without taking off his pants...and he'd be dumb enough to do it, too. Perhaps the officer hadn't been shot not because he'd stayed well clear of the front lines, but because the rebels had thought he'd be more helpful if he was left alive to make life harder for the government forces. Or maybe that was just a little too clever. The airport really *was* some distance from the front lines.

"I'm going to need you to keep an eye on him," Roland said, as they swept the airport to make sure of the terrain. The hangars were large and dry, the terminal was wooden and looked permanently on the verge of collapsing into rubble. "I don't want him sending any messages to anyone until it's too late for them to do anything about it."

Richard frowned. "With all due respect, sir, the rebels will see us coming for miles."

He shook his head. The plan made a certain degree of sense, he supposed, but it sacrificed the element of surprise. He had a nasty feeling it wasn't *that* much cleverer than standing up and walking *very slowly* towards a machine gun nest. Sweeping the plantations for rebels looked good on paper, but the terrain was so awful that all their advantages would be minimised...if, of course, the rebels didn't keep their heads down and wait for the soldiers to go away again. He'd heard a couple of officers, back before the Marines had arrived, seriously suggesting they slaughter everyone on the islands and start again. The idea had been shot down, not out of humanitarian concerns—that would have been too much to expect—but because the indents all belonged to the landowners. They didn't want their slaves slaughtered. They'd have to import new ones.

"That's not the plan." Roland lowered his voice. "I didn't dare discuss it openly, not back on Kingstown."

Richard sucked in his breath. "And you're going to tell me now?"

"Yes," Roland said. "I need you to get everything ready, here, while I check out the enemy location for myself. And you must *not* let the men know what we're doing until it is too late."

Richard snorted. "It will be easy, sir," he said. "You haven't told *me* what you're doing."

"Listen carefully," Roland said. "We cannot afford to fuck this up."

• • •

"Use the bucket, you stupid bastard!"

Bryce Ambrose tried to ignore the sound of someone being violently sick as the ship made its slow way towards her destination. The air stank of shit and piss and vomit, despite the best efforts of a labouring air conditioning system. He couldn't blame the poor man for throwing up, not when he'd empted his own stomach hours ago. The ship was supposed to be safe—they'd been *assured* it was—but she was rolling and heaving to the point he kept thinking she was about to capsize. He'd worked a few shifts on the docks, back before he'd joined the army, but he'd never gone on a boat. He wished, now, that he'd thought to do it before he'd marched onto the military transport and been ordered to wait below decks.

He gritted his teeth. He'd been told he'd passed the first set of exercises and tests, although—in a bid to keep the recruits from getting overconfident—their instructors had cautioned them that they'd barely scratched the surface. They wouldn't have been issued live ammunition, let alone been sent into combat, if the government wasn't desperate for a victory. Bryce couldn't help finding it a little ominous, even as he tried not to be sick again. The new company—two hundred men—had been isolated from the rest, given an hour to write letters and wills, then cautioned not to even *think* about trying to contact someone outside the army. A young man had gotten in trouble, real trouble, for daring to bring a pocket phone with him. He hadn't realised they'd be searched before they were loaded onto trucks and driven to the ship.

And that means I can't send a warning either, he thought. He tried to tell himself it didn't matter. The army was under constant observation. And yet, he couldn't help thinking he'd failed. He hadn't reported back to his superiors because he hadn't been able to get out without being caught. *What if they don't know we're coming?*

The thought tormented him as the boat rolled and rolled again, then bumped so hard into *something* he couldn't help thinking they'd rammed another boat. Sailors opened the hatches, then shouted for the soldiers to come out. Bryce did so gratefully, breathing deeply as soon as he was on the deck. The air was hot and humid, but at least it didn't stink of vomit and worse. His eyes opened wide as he saw the harbour, the bustling town and the green mountains in the distance. Where the hell were they?

His legs felt wobbly as they were ordered—and half-pushed—down the gangplank and onto the harbour. A pair of sergeants waited, pointing the soldiers down a clearly marked path that led through a gate into an airport. Bryce forced himself to walk faster, trying to show the keenness his instructors had demanded from their trainees. It wasn't easy. He nearly fell twice before his legs started to recover. Behind him, the rest of the company didn't sound to be in any better shape. He hoped to hell they didn't have to go straight into battle. They'd be chewed up as soon as the enemy stopped laughing.

"Into the hangars," a voice barked. "Get yourselves cleaned up, then snatch some grub and take a nap. We'll be deploying shortly."

Bryce frowned. Deploying? Deploying where? He tried to estimate their location, but drew a blank. They hadn't been on the boat for long - though it had felt like an eternity—and he hadn't seen that many maps of the habitable zone, yet…there were hundreds of possible locations within a few short hours of Kingstown. An island…he snorted, inwardly, as he marched into the hangar and grabbed a bottle of water. That narrowed it down to a few hundred possibilities.

He drank the water—they'd been cautioned to remain hydrated—then forced himself to sit and wait. The army was *all* hurry up and wait; it was important to get as much rest as possible before they went into action. He wanted to sleep, but he didn't dare. He was too busy trying to think of a way to get word to the rebels. It might not matter—the harbour was teeming with spies, or he was a complete idiot—but it felt like failure. And besides, if he didn't try to pass on a warning, his superiors might wonder if he was disloyal.

It doesn't matter, he told himself. *There's no way to get a message out.*

...

Roland had been told, time and time again, that every Marine was a rifleman first. They were all expected to meet basic standards, even the auxiliaries who weren't ever supposed to find themselves in the middle of a combat zone. And yet, he was impressed by how well Rachel had coped during the march through the plantations and deep into enemy territory. She'd held up astonishingly well. Roland wasn't sure if she was more practiced than she let on, or she was determined not to show weakness in front of him, but it didn't matter. All that mattered was that he hadn't had to leave her behind.

He breathed deeply as they made their way into the mountains. The jungle was a giant no-man's land, the trails fought over regularly by rebels, bandits, overseers, hunting parties and militiamen. It hadn't been easy to catch a ride to the outskirts of the settled zone, not without raising eyebrows, but it had been a great deal harder to make progress once they left the settlement behind. The trails were dangerous, even when they weren't booby-trapped. It would have been impossible if he hadn't been using his wristcom to navigate. The signals from the neighbouring islands were just strong enough to triangulate his position.

"There," Rachel breathed, so quietly even *his* ears barely heard the words. "Look."

Roland followed her gaze. The rebel camp was nearly invisible, blended so carefully into the surrounding foliage that—he was ashamed to admit—they might have blundered right into the enemy defences if they hadn't already had a rough idea of its location. There weren't many rebels within eyeshot, but the handful he could see had assault rifles slung over their shoulders. Clear proof, he reflected sourly, that they really *had* stumbled across a rebel camp. Bandits rarely had so many weapons.

He leaned back and forced himself to watch, noting every detail. The camp was larger than he'd realised. There was a very good chance it blurred into the caves in the mountains, perhaps linked to tunnels that led down to the waters on the far side. If that was the case…he frowned. There were so many small boats plying their trade on the waters that there was no hope of keeping smugglers from bringing in more weapons, not without doing immense damage to the planetary economy. The maps claimed the cliffs were inaccessible, that no one dared bring a boat close to the rocks for fear of being dashed against them, but Roland refused to take that for granted. He'd done enough mucking around on boats to be sure the cliffs were not as much of a barrier as the locals assumed. A team of Marines could scale them easily.

Rachel glanced at him. "The plan should work, if you're ready to bet everything on one throw of the die."

Roland winced. The concept had sounded perfect, when he'd dreamed it up. And yet…he'd spent so long putting the pieces in place, without ever openly admitting to anyone beside Rachel what he was doing, that he hadn't run a basic sanity check. The concept could be turned into reality by trained Marines. His newly minted soldiers, with less training than he'd had, might not be up to the task. It could go horribly wrong.

"We don't have a choice," he muttered, as they started to crawl back to safety. The camp was too deep within the mountains for a conventional attack to succeed. Either the rebels would make a successful defence or they'd slip back into the shadows and vanish until the army went away again. "The camp is too big. It's just a matter of time before they start a major offensive."

He gritted his teeth. The reports had been vague, when they hadn't been so clearly whitewashed, but it was clear to the naked eye that Ivanovo was bad even by the standards of New Doncaster. Rebellion was coming and, when it did, the island would be bathed in blood and fire. Roland sympathised with the rebels, more than he cared to admit, but mutual slaughter benefited no one. They had to find another way,

And we have to prove we can win victories, he mused. The rebels thought they were slowly winning, that they could just keep up the pressure until the government crumbled. And the hell of it was that they were probably right. *Why should the rebels come to the table if they can think they can win?*

The air seemed to grow hotter, incredibly, as they made their way to the vantage point. "I'm going to send the signal now," Roland said, once they were in position. His heart started to race. It was the first time he'd see real action. He was as much a combat virgin as the men under his command. "And then we'll be committed."

Rachel nodded. "Do it."

CHAPTER TWENTY-ONE

IVANOVO ISLAND, NEW DONCASTER

LIEUTENANT DAKOTA STURTZ, Terran Marine Corps, disliked New Doncaster with a passion. It wasn't just that it was yet another hellhole made worse by planetary leaders who couldn't find their asses with an entire *team* of ass-kissers, although that was a constant headache for the relative handful of Marines on the planet. It was the fact that the company was so badly understrength that the Marines could barely secure the spaceport, let alone anything else. There'd been nothing from planetary intelligence—which couldn't be relied upon to add two plus two together, let alone anything more complex—to suggest the rebels intended to attack the spaceport, but the corps knew it was just a matter of time. It wasn't easy running an insurgency. Sooner or later, you had to make a bid for power or risk losing the war. And then the company would be caught in the middle. Again.

He shook his head as he sat in the Raptor and peered at the waters below. New Doncaster looked almost *peaceful*, if one was so high it that was impossible to see the people with the naked eye. He wasn't reassured. The Raptors were supposed to be immune to local weapons, but the reports had made it clear the insurgents were receiving supplies from off-world. A single HVM would be enough to *really* ruin their day. The company wouldn't get any replacements either, if there were any to spare. Dakota had heard through the grapevine that Safehouse was considering simply pulling the Marines out and abandoning New Doncaster. The training mission wasn't anything like enough to save the planetary government from a well-deserved ass-kicking.

The console bleeped. "That's the signal," the pilot said. "Sir?"

Dakota pressed his hand against the weapons panel. The Raptor's normal weapons load had been swapped out for a pair of cruise missiles, something that awed and irritated him in equal measure. They weren't *meant* to trade shots with rebels or bandits, according to the mission briefing, but Dakota had been in the corps long enough to know missions rarely went according to plan. Sure, they were *supposed* to be far enough from their target to avoid enemy notice—they'd gone to some trouble to drop off the planetary ATC net, insofar as it existed—but something could easily go wrong. It wouldn't be *that* hard for the enemy to stick a MANPAD on a boat and go looking for targets of opportunity. The rebels didn't have an air force of their own.

Not yet, he reflected. *But it's just a matter of time.*

The console came to life. Dakota checked and rechecked the targeting coordinates, then hit the switch. The Raptor shook, violently, as the two cruise missiles launched themselves from under the wing. They looked slow, but it was just an optical illusion. They'd reach their targets hard on the heels of any warning, if indeed one was ever sent. The makeshift network of primitive radar stations and more advanced gravimetric sensors might fail to detect the missiles, let alone start sending messages higher up the chain. Dakota was appalled at the sloppiness, but he had to admit it had its advantages. The rebels would have people in the ATC network. They just wouldn't have time to pass the word to their superiors.

"Missiles away," he said. He tapped a key, sending a microburst transmission back to the spaceport as the pilot altered course sharply. If there was anyone watching, there was no point in letting them have a free shot at the aircraft. "Impact in thirty seconds."

The pilot nodded. "It sure is going to be hot for someone down there, isn't it?"

...

Richard glanced at the timer, then put the whistle to his lips and blew. There was a rustle throughout the hangar as the soldiers—some playing cards to pass the time, some trying to sleep—jumped to their feet and formed ragged lines. Richard looked them up and down, hoping and praying they had everything they needed, then led the way out of the hangar. The helicopters were lined up, waiting for them. He heard gasps behind him as it dawned on the soldiers that they weren't going to be driven to the front lines after all. Richard tried not to smile. Roland's plan was either crazy or brilliant. It would work or it would turn into a complete disaster. He honestly wasn't sure which way to bet.

He snapped orders, pointing the men to their helicopters. They'd practiced boarding and disembarking while under fire—in hindsight, Richard realised Roland had been trying to prepare the men—but this time it was real. Laughs and jokes faded away as the sheer enormity of what they were about to do dawned on them. An airborne assault was nothing to laugh at, even with experienced men. *His* troops barely had enough training to know which end of a gun they had to point at the enemy.

The clattering grew louder as he ducked into the lead helicopter and took a seat. The pilot looked unhappy—he hadn't been told what they were doing, or where they were going, until it was too late to object—but brought the rest of the helicopter's systems online without any further protests. The helicopters might have been kept well back from the front lines, Richard knew all too well, yet their pilots *did* have some experience at flying under dangerous conditions. They'd flown missions into the outback before, delivering supplies and rescuing climbers. They could adapt what they already knew to war.

Of course, the rebels may manage to recover in time to open fire, Richard thought. He glanced at his watch. The timer was ticking. The missiles were already inbound. Roland and he had debated the precise timing until they were both sick of the argument, trying to judge when best to launch the mission, but they'd had to conclude there was going to be slippage. The rebels would have eyes on the airport. They might realise the helicopters were on their way before the cruise missiles arrived. *And then they'll greet us with a hail of fire.*

The helicopter lurched into the air, then turned south. Richard braced himself. Time was running out....

...

Shit, Bryce thought. *Fuck. Damn.*

It wasn't easy to hide the sense of despair that had overcome him as they'd been marched to the helicopters and ordered to buckle up. It would have been a great deal harder if the helicopter hadn't been so loud, if the turbulence hadn't been so bad that half the platoon seemed to wish they were back on the boat. Bryce was no fool. The only reason they'd be rushed to the helicopter was so they could attack an enemy target, a *rebel* target. And he'd been swept along so quickly he hadn't had *time* to alert his superiors.

And even if you had known where you were going, he told himself, *what could you have done?*

He considered a dozen possibilities, from trying to hijack the helicopter to simply shooting his comrades in the back when the assault began, but none seemed remotely workable. He would've been shot himself had he attempted any of them, if he wasn't knocked out and taken prisoner.

He knew the government had ways of making people talk. It was why he hadn't been told any more about his contacts than he needed to know—and even that, he thought, had worried his superiors. And besides...the thought of betraying his comrades *hurt*. He didn't want to stab them in the back. It wasn't as if they were landowners. The vast majority were debtors. Like him.

"We land, we pile out, we hit hard," the sergeant said. His voice was calm, reassuring. "You see someone with a gun, shoot him. You see someone trying to surrender, accept it—but be careful. You don't want to get shot by someone faking surrender until you get into range."

Bryce gritted his teeth. He was going to be fighting alongside his enemies, while being shot at by his allies. Except they didn't *know* he was on their side. How could they? It wasn't as if he'd known where he was going, let alone what he was going to do when he got there. And…it didn't matter. They'd be firing so wildly, perhaps, that they might hit him by accident. They wouldn't have time to make sure of their targets….

His heart sank. He was trapped. There was no way out. He'd have to fight and hope his superiors would understand. And if they didn't…he was screwed.

Perhaps I should just vanish, he thought. It wouldn't be that hard to leave the camp and desert, if he didn't mind never being able to return. *But then, both sides would be hunting me.*

・・・

"Twenty seconds," Rachel said.

Roland nodded, hoping to hell nothing went wrong. The cruise missiles were supposed to be precision weapons, but he'd been warned—more than once—that even the most *precise* weapons could go off course and hit the wrong targets. Their tiny brains could guide them straight into a mountain they didn't know existed, or they could be simply spoofed and pointed in the wrong direction by enemy ECM. His instructors had pointed out, contra-intuitively, the smarter a weapon was the easier it was for an enemy who knew what he was doing to trick it. Dumb weapons were… well, *dumb*, but they were much harder to spoof.

"Ten seconds," Rachel said.

Roland covered his eyes as the last seconds ticked away. He'd expected to hear something, anything, before the missiles arrived, but there was nothing. They were outrunning the sound warning of their approach. Instead, the world went white, then red, as the warheads detonated. One slammed into the mountainside and detonated, sending shockwaves through the rock; the other detonated within the valley, unleashing a superhot firestorm that burned through the jungle, flashing the foliage to ash in the blink of an eye. Roland felt a wave of heat rush over him, saw flames spreading rapidly as the last of the chemical compound burned up. It was hard to believe the flames wouldn't grow completely out of hand, although he knew better. The jungle wouldn't burn so well once the last of the fuel was gone, even if it didn't rain. And *that* was just a matter of time.

He forced himself to sit up and peer into the remnants of the enemy camp as the helicopters came into view. The timing hadn't been perfect—ideally, he would have liked the helicopters to arrive within seconds of the missiles—but good enough. The combination of the missiles and shockwaves, earthquakes to all intents and purposes, had devastated the camp. He saw a handful of people stumbling around, a couple trying to establish a line of defence as the helicopters swept down. Behind them, the camp was crumbling into rubble. He watched, with a twinge of awe, as a giant tree crashed to the ground. The treehouse within the branches was smashed like an eggshell.

"We need to get down there," he said, scrambling to his feet. "I have to…."

"Stay here." Rachel's voice was firm. "You won't help anyone if you get yourself shot before the lines are solidly established. Richard knows what to do."

Roland gaped at her. "I have to lead from the front."

"Richard can handle that," Rachel said. "What do you think will happen if you get yourself killed down there?"

"I…."

Roland didn't want to think about it. He didn't have a formal successor. Neither Wimer nor Rachel herself had been designated his second, let alone his successor if he got himself killed in action. Captain Allen would probably appoint Wimer, if he didn't detach someone from his company to take Roland's place, but it would slow the recruiting and training program considerably. The local government and military might take advantage of the chaos to claw back some authority. And...if he died, who was the legitimate heir to the throne?

No one who'd enjoy universal backing, his thoughts reminded him. There'd never been *that* many people in line to the throne. The Grand Senate had seen to that, through careful monitoring and the occasional purge. *There might be several people, all with roughly identical claims...none of whom would have support from anything more than a tiny minority of the population.*

"Fuck," he said. He wanted to yell at her, for telling him off in the middle of a battle, but he couldn't. He knew she was right. And yet, he didn't want to stay out of the fighting. He'd sent men into battle, an engagement he knew would result in some of them returning home in body bags. He owed it to them to share the danger. But he also knew he had to remain alive. He felt like a coward. He felt..."Just...fuck!"

...

Richard hadn't been sure what to expect, as the timer reached zero. He'd never been involved in anything bigger than small-unit actions, with only a handful of platoons operating in a very small area. The idea of calling in missiles from hundreds of miles away, well outside the enemy's range, struck him as absurd, almost a fantasy. And yet, Roland had taken it for granted. Richard had to admit the idea was brilliant, even as he was unsure how well it would work in practice. The missiles might easily go astray and hit the wrong target.

There was a brilliant flash of light, followed by a fireball rising into the air. Richard braced himself an instant before the helicopter shook violently as the shockwave battered the hull like the fists of an angry god. Alarms rang, but the pilot seemed calm and composed as he guided the helicopter towards the newly created landing zone. Richard had half-expected the plan to fail, for the clearing to turn into a firestorm, but instead it was just a bed of smoking ash. He unstrapped himself as the helicopter touched down, hurrying to the rear hatch. The loadmaster was already swinging it open.

"Follow me," he shouted. "Now!"

He ran forward, sprinting through the ash straight towards the rebel base. It was larger than the intelligence reports had suggested, but the missiles and fires had done one hell of a lot of damage. A handful of defenders opened fire, bullets snapping through the air; Richard returned fire, spraying and praying to force the enemy to keep their heads down. It was wasteful, despite the extra ammunition he'd brought in his knapsack, but it served a purpose. The enemy could not be allowed to regroup. If they got a mortar up and opened fire on the helicopters, the entire engagement could turn into a defeat.

A corpse lay on the ground in front of him, so badly burnt that he could barely tell it had once been human. He tasted bile as he jumped, taking cover behind a collection of log houses that were relatively intact. The enemy was trying to set up a defence line, throwing men into the fight to slow the attackers. Richard snapped orders, directing his men to hurl grenades into the enemy shacks before thrusting on. The murder holes were very much a two-edged sword, he noted, as the enemy fire slackened rapidly. A young woman—he thought it was a woman—came out of nowhere, waving a pistol. He shot her down without a second thought. The Marines had talked of taking prisoners, and Richard understood the point, but he doubted any of the rebels would surrender. The government had flatly refused to set up a penal island for permanent exiles, let alone offer the rebels a chance to reintegrate into society. They knew the best they could hope for, if they surrendered, was interrogation and death.

He stepped over the young woman and kept moving. The enemy lines were wavering, perhaps breaking. A missile shot into the air and vanished somewhere within the clouds, followed by a hail of fire. Richard had no idea what the enemy thought they were shooting at—as far as he knew, there was nothing up there; perhaps they thought the missile would come down amidst the helicopters—but it didn't matter. The rebels were running out of time. They'd have to start retreating before it was too late. And if his men got into position, they wouldn't have a hope in hell of getting out.

The ground shook again, violently. Something had just exploded... an ammunition stockpile? Or something worse? He'd heard rumours of natural gas deposits below the mountains, although he'd thought they were just scams to encourage investment...did natural gas explode? He didn't know. Right now, he didn't have time to worry about it. Bullets still ripped through the air.

He raised his voice. "Surrender," he yelled. Roland had made it clear they were to extend the offer, even if the enemy rejected it. They needed prisoners, prisoners who could be interrogated and then granted clemency... Richard had no idea how Roland was going to swing *that*. It went against the grain to make promises he *knew* wouldn't be kept. "Surrender or die!"

There was a pause, just long enough for him to think the offer might be accepted, then the enemy resumed their fire. Richard gritted his teeth. His men had performed well, better than he'd expected, but the assault was starting to flag. They'd need to regroup, then punch through the remaining enemy defences. And then....

Then they can surrender, if they want, or die, he told himself. *And that will be the end.*

CHAPTER TWENTY-TWO

IVANOVO ISLAND, NEW DONCASTER

THEY'D COME FOR HER.

Susan Watterson kept her head down, panic yammering at the back of her mind as the sound of shooting grew closer and closer. She should have known they'd come, ever since she'd fled the plantation. Working the land had been hard enough without an overseer who expected his female workers—and the males, if the whispers had been true—to lift their skirts for him whenever he wanted. He'd tried to rape her, shortly after she'd arrived on the plantation; she'd kneed him in the balls, kicked his stomach and fled into the outback before he had a chance to recover and come after her. She had no doubt he would have killed her, after making her final hours very unpleasant. She knew she'd been lucky to find the rebels—or, rather, they'd found her—before a hunting party caught her or she starved. She hadn't hesitated to join the rebellion. And yet....

Her body refused to move. She knew she'd be raped and murdered—perhaps murdered and *then* raped—if the overseers caught her, but her legs wouldn't budge. The man she'd humiliated in front of a dozen witnesses had sworn to kill her, according to the rebels who slipped in and out of the plantations as easily as water passed through soil, but her fear kept her rooted to the spot. One moment, she'd been helping to prepare the communal meal for when the scouts returned; the next, all hell had broken loose. She wanted to run and yet she couldn't force herself to move. She couldn't even clutch the weapon on her belt. The rebels had given her a pistol and taught her how to use it. And yet....

The ground heaved. She found herself flat, without any memory of how she'd hit the floor. The shock knocked her out of her trance. She forced herself to draw the pistol, then head for the trail leading further into the jungle. The enemy—overseers or militia or even regulars—had hit them hard, but the rebels knew parts of the jungle the government's forces had never visited. They'd gotten overconfident, Susan told herself; they should have spread out a little more, perhaps restarted the cell structure that had slowly turned into something a more coherent. It wasn't going to be easy to rebuild after this disaster. She wasn't even sure there'd be enough men left to pull the cell back together before the government swept over the entire island and made further resistance impossible.

She forced herself to keep moving, joining the exodus into the jungle. The sounds behind her suggested the lines were crumbling, that the soldiers had overwhelmed the camp. She gritted her teeth as a pregnant woman ran past, eyes wide with fear. The poor bitch would be in deep shit if she was recaptured, then forced to march back to her former plantation. The overseers saw pregnant women as a burden, although debts were passed through the family tree until a particularly unlucky debtor could find himself paying off his grandparents' debts. Bullets whipped through the air behind them, slashing through trees as though they were made of paper. Susan stayed as low as she could, trying to remain unnoticed. She was a lot more capable now, after a year in the camp. She could remain alive for quite some time, if she made it out of the trap. She could live off the land until she rejoined the cell or finally got caught by a hunting party.

Someone screamed ahead. Susan barely had a second to register green-clad figures before something slammed into her chest, knocking the wind out of her. Her vision blurred. The pistol went flying. She opened her mouth, only to be struck again. Her body tumbled forward and hit the ground, a heavy weight landing on top of her and pinning her firmly in place. Strong hands caught hers and yanked them behind her back, then wrapped something cold and hard around her wrists. Panic ran through her. Was she a prisoner? Was she going to be raped on the spot? Or... she forced herself to lie still, thinking desperately as her captor wrapped another tie around her ankles. The growled command to lie still and silent was almost absurd. There was no way she could get up, let alone walk. She was a prisoner once again....

Tears prickled in her eyes as her captor stood. She was helpless and doomed and...she tried to look from side to side without moving her head. A handful of other captives lay on the ground, as bound and helpless as she was. Others were utterly unmoving...dead? She'd seen more than her fair share of dead bodies since she'd been sent into exile—workers who'd died on the plantation, bandits and rebels killed in skirmishes—but these bodies were somehow worse. It was bad enough knowing that people she'd liked had been killed...here, the camp itself had been destroyed. They'd grown careless and paid for it and...she swallowed, hard, as she realised it wasn't over. The enemy, whoever they were, had at least ten captives, perhaps more. They were going to be marched back to the plantation and executed, broken on the wheel or battered to death as a warning to anyone who might be thinking of following in their footsteps. Or...she didn't want to think about it. It would be the end of the world.

• • •

Bryce couldn't help feeling a little guilty as he surveyed the prisoners. It had been sheer luck he'd realised that the man barrelling towards him was actually a woman and, again, sheer luck that she hadn't managed to take a shot at him before he'd rammed the butt of his rifle into her chest. She'd collapsed like a bag of rocks, allowing him to secure her before she could recover and do something—anything—that might get her killed. And yet, he doubted she was in for an easy time. The Marines preached the importance of taking prisoners—they'd made it clear they wouldn't tolerate the abuse of prisoners—but the government would have other ideas. The woman lying in front of him would be lucky if she was only put in front of a wall and shot.

He gritted his teeth as he straightened and looked around. He'd been relieved, at least at first, when the platoon had been directed to the rear of the camp. He hadn't realised until too late that the enemy would flee the camp, straight into their arms. There'd been no time to slow the advance or shoot the enemy runaways before they were taken prisoner. He tried to tell himself that the captives were harmless, that they didn't know anything the Marines could use to untangle the remainder of the rebel alliance, but there was no way to be sure. Perhaps he could arrange for an accident with a live grenade, a mercy kill that would save the poor bastards from interrogation and a lingering death. But he couldn't think of a way to do it that would preserve his cover.

The last of the shooting died away, leaving the soldiers to sweep through the remains of the camp. The Marines took the lead, scanning everything with handheld sensors as they hunted for records—notebooks or datacores—before directing the soldiers to recover the bodies and bag them up for transport back to the airport. Bryce was almost relieved when his platoon was ordered to stay with the prisoners—now twenty-seven in total—and make sure they were unharmed. His mind kept racing, trying to think of something he could do, but nothing occurred to him. He didn't know enough about rebel camps outside Kingstown to be *sure* the prisoners were useless. Perhaps it would be better to stage an accident and then run for his life. Perhaps....

A sergeant clapped him on the shoulder. "There's no need to look so glum," he said. "We won!"

Bryce nodded. He'd made the mistake—once—of thinking the sergeants were low-ranking peons. They weren't very highly ranked, were they? And yet, Captain Windsor—the man who'd given a bunch of officers a verbal thrashing—often deferred to the sergeants. It hadn't taken Bryce long, after that, to realise the sergeants were incredibly experienced and perceptive and, almost certainly, the greatest threat to his cover. If they had doubts about him, it was unlikely he'd be allowed to get any further before all hell broke loose.

"I'm just feeling a little pensive," Bryce said. "It happened so *quickly*."

The sergeant nodded. "Start prepping the prisoners for the journey back to the airport," he ordered. "They'll be held there until we can find a more permanent home for then."

"Yes, Sergeant," Bryce said.

• • •

"The only thing costlier than a battle lost is a battle won," Roland muttered.

The bodies in front of him had been alive and well, only a few short hours ago. He vaguely recognised one of the dead men—he'd been commended for bravery, on the exercise grounds—but the other three were strangers. One was so badly burnt that the only reason Roland knew he was a soldier was the uniform, what little remained of it. He'd thought he'd come to terms with losing people under his command, but he'd been wrong. It felt...he shook his head. He should know their names. He should have known them before they were killed in action. And yet, he didn't. He could look them up, at any moment, but it felt cheap. Wrong.

He lifted his eyes, gaze sweeping across the ruined camp. They didn't have a proper WarCAT team—somehow, he wasn't surprised—but his subordinates were doing their best to pull what intelligence they could from the wreckage anyway. Roland doubted that the rebels would have kept very good records, if they'd bothered to keep them at all. It wasn't easy to run an insurgency without some records—the corps had defeated insurgencies that had been as bureaucratic as the Imperial Revenue Service—but a smart insurgent would have written and saved as little as possible. Roland hoped for an intelligence windfall, perhaps a complete list of insurgents, but he wasn't holding his breath. An officer who counted on luck was an officer who was going to wind up disappointed, if not dead.

"They performed well," Rachel said. "You can be proud of them."

Roland nodded. The troops had done well, despite their limited training and their true target being kept from them until it was almost too late. He hadn't dared risk telling them where they were *really* going and yet... he'd known, as he'd made the decision, that it could easily have backfired. The next raid wouldn't be anything like as successful. The rebels would probably scatter, before it was too late. Roland wondered, idly, if his enemies would eventually point to the raid and declare it a failure.

"Probably," he muttered.

Rachel blinked. "Sir?"

Roland shrugged, then stepped aside to let the medics remove the bodies. They'd be buried on Kingstown, their families told they'd died well... and that their debts had been cancelled, along with any other obligations they might have had. He told himself he'd visit the families personally, just to ensure they knew their loved ones had died well...and make sure, damn sure, that the government kept its word. The last thing he needed was the government changing its collective mind. It would be penny wise, pound *incredibly* foolish. He cursed under his breath as he realised the rebels would have a perfect opportunity to damage morale. They could lie and tell everyone that the debts hadn't been cancelled. Too many people would believe them.

He put the thought out of his mind as he walked through the remains of the encampment, Rachel right behind. The rebels had done a good job. They'd hidden an entire barracks, as well as a cluster of individual homes, under the trees, then worked their way into the mountains below. The missile had done immense damage to the caves, triggering a chain reaction that had buried the evidence below a ton of debris. Roland doubted there was any point in trying to dig into the wreckage, even if they'd had the equipment. The rebels down there, if any survived, would have to pick their way out themselves. He hoped they could make it. Death by suffocation, deep underground, wasn't a fate he'd wish on his worst enemy.

His eyes swept over the bodies as they were carried back to the helicopters. They'd be checked against the records, in hopes of linking them to runaway plantation workers or deserters, then searched and dumped in a mass grave. Roland saw no point in taking the rebel bodies back to Kingstown with the remainder of the army. The government wouldn't want them. Besides, it would be better to keep the rebels guessing about just who'd died and who'd been taken alive. They'd be wise to assume the base commander had been captured, or anyone who might know something that could lead to the next rebel base, but they wouldn't *know*. Roland allowed himself a tight smile. There might be a flurry of rebel activity that would point them to the next base, even if the prisoners revealed nothing. He wasn't hoping for a windfall from that direction, either.

"Be careful," Rachel warned, as the wind shifted and blew the stench of death into their faces. "We don't know *everything* they were doing here."

Roland glanced at her. Rachel was…odd. She seemed a perfectly normal administrative assistant and yet, she'd made it to the rebel base without a single complaint. And she'd had the nerve to keep him from risking his life, despite the risk of NJP or a court-martial. The only person he'd met who'd defied him so openly, at least to his face, had been Belinda. A thought struck him. Could Rachel *be* Belinda? He had no doubt Belinda could pose as something she wasn't, if she wished, but the build was all wrong. Belinda had been taller—and bustier, part of his mind reminded him—than Rachel. If it was a disguise, it was a far more thorough one than anything he'd seen outside bad movies. Belinda would need to have had her entire body reconstructed if she wanted to pass as Rachel.

Richard hurried up to them. "Sir," he said. "The camp is secure. The prisoners are on the lead helicopters, under guard. The wounded are already on their way back to the airport."

"Good." Roland thought fast. He hadn't spent much time considering what he'd do after the raid, fearing it might be bad luck. "Assign a platoon to escort the prisoners; they are to remain at the airport, under guard, until they can be shipped back to the spaceport. We'll pull the rest of the force out once the prisoners are safe and the helicopters return."

"Aye, sir," Richard said. "Do you want to call Kingstown and tell them what happened?"

Roland saw—very briefly—a smile touch Rachel's lips. On one hand, they'd won. They'd given the rebels a black eye they wouldn't forget. The army had proved it could fight and win and, with the aid of helicopters and cruise missiles, take the war into previously untouchable parts of the map. But, on the other hand, he'd lied to just about everyone, hiding what he intended to do until it was too late. The rebels had been confused—they certainly hadn't been waiting for him—but his allies had been confused as well. And they were probably going to be hopping mad about the lies.

"I'll call them," he said, finally. They'd probably already be hearing garbled versions of the truth. The explosions and fireballs would have been visible for hundreds of miles around. "If they call me back, you'll have command. Start thinking what you'll do if that happens."

"Aye, sir."

Roland grinned, then looked at Rachel. "On a scale of one to ten, how much trouble do you think I'm in?"

"At least fifty, and that's if they're feeling generous," Rachel said. Her mouth twisted, as if she'd bitten into something sour. "A hundred, maybe even two hundred, if they're not. Politicians don't like being lied to. They consider telling lies to be their job."

"Hah," Roland said. "Very witty."

He rolled his eyes as they walked towards the command helicopter. He'd ordered the long-range communications equipment to be physically disabled, just to be sure one of the PM's pilots didn't blow the whistle ahead of time, but it wouldn't take long to fix. And then…he'd have to think of something to tell them. The truth? Somehow, he doubted that would make them very happy. Or perhaps a series of lies so complicated no one dared call them out for fear of being made to look like a fool. Roland had a private theory that one of the reasons the Grand Senate had taken control so easily was because the laws they'd backed had been so complicated that the important sections had been buried under a mountain of bullshit, at least until it was too late to change them. And then it had been impossible to fix.

Tell them the truth, he thought, coldly. His instructors had made it clear that it was better to tell the truth, whenever possible. Lying damaged a person's character and reputation, even if the lies were told in a good cause. *And take the lumps they give you like a man.*

CHAPTER TWENTY-THREE

KINGSPORT, NEW DONCASTER

SARAH HAD BEEN WORRIED—not that she'd shown it, while she'd been lurking in the rebel-run flophouse—when the army camp had gone silent. The militia and the regular army leaked like sieves, to the point the rebels often knew more about what was going on than the men in the ranks, but the newcomers were different. They'd cut off all contact by the simple expedient of locking down the camp, arresting men caught trying to leave—even if they just wanted a drink—and declaring anyone who made it out a deserter to be arrested and exiled on sight. Sarah doubted they'd worked out *precisely* who was passing information to the rebels, but it didn't matter. They'd made sure she didn't get any advance warning of anything without capturing and killing—or turning—her spies. She'd known something was coming. The lockdown proved it. But she hadn't known *what*.

"You're sure about this?" It was hard to hide the doubt in her tone. "They smashed a camp on Ivanovo?"

"Yes," the messenger said. He was young, young enough to be daring and yet hardened enough to keep his mouth firmly shut if he felt his collar was being twisted by the police. He'd probably break under chemical interrogation or torture—everyone did, eventually—but the rest of his cell would have time to go underground before it was too late. "The reports are very clear. The army launched a helicopter offensive into the outback and came down right on top of the camp."

Sarah sucked in her breath. She hadn't expected the newcomers—much less their new recruits—to take the field so soon. It had only been a few months...she considered, briefly, that they might have been tricked, that it had been the regulars who'd carried out the assault, but it wasn't likely. She'd have had a hell of a lot more warning if the regulars had started gearing up for such an operation, if their political masters let them try. The government seemed to think they couldn't afford heavy losses. Sarah rather hoped they were right.

She listened to the report, parsing the scraps of exaggerated data for truth. Stories grew in the telling, from the winners boasting of their success to losers trying to minimise the scale of the defeat. The claim that millions of rebels had been cut down, like crops in a field, was almost certainly a wild exaggeration. The entire population of the island would be dead, if the reports were true. And yet, there were elements of truth within the tales. The newcomers had reached out and smashed the rebel camp, almost effortlessly. Sarah knew it wouldn't be enough to stop the rebels from reforming and returning to the field, but it would certainly give the government time to impose a political solution. If, of course, their own people let them.

"There's an obvious question," she said, when the report was finished. "How did they find the camp?"

"I don't know," the messenger said. "Did they get lucky?"

Sarah shook her head, curtly. Ivanovo wasn't *that* big, not compared to some of the other islands, but the odds of a military force just *happening* to land on top of a rebel base were pretty much the same as the odds of winning in a rigged gambling house. No, they'd known where they were going. How? A spy in the ranks? A military patrol that had spotted the camp, then retreated without being detected? Or watching eyes in high orbit, eyes that had spotted a camp where no camp should be? Sarah grimaced at the thought. The planet's unique weather patterns made it hard for orbital eyes to pick out details on the ground, but hard was not the same as impossible. Hell, the Marines could simply have flown a drone over the island and gotten lucky. She'd been warned that their drones were very good.

"Take a message to Albert, then go back to the docks," she ordered. "See what else you can pick up."

The man nodded, took the message and hurried off. Sarah waited until he'd closed the door behind him, then sat on the bed and forced herself to think. The camp had been attacked and taken…she wanted to believe the attackers hadn't taken prisoners, but she knew better than to assume. They had to plan for the worst. If prisoners had been taken, they'd be made to talk. Sarah had no doubt of it. A government that had no qualms about publicly brutalising indents and debtors—she'd seen men and women whipped or placed in the stocks for something as minor as answering back—wasn't going to have any hesitation in torturing prisoners for information. God knew they'd done terrible things to the handful of prisoners they *had* taken, over the last few years. Sarah liked to think herself inured to horror—she'd had a rude awakening when she'd been arrested and never went back to sleep—but even she had limits. She wouldn't order someone broken on the wheel purely to make an example of them.

She cleared her mind, allowing her eyes to wander around the flophouse room. It was cramped and dirty, the floor stained and the bed sheets smelling of things she didn't want to think about. The woman who rented out the rooms probably assumed her female customers were whores, if they had enough income to rent a small room. The majority of young women would either have to share, if they were engaged in legal activities, or simply didn't live anywhere near Kingsport. Sarah found the woman's attitude irritating, but she had to admit it had some advantages. For one thing, no one ever called the authorities. If the police showed up, they'd be greeted by a hail of stones from unemployed and unemployable young men. The rebels would have all the time they needed to grab their stuff and run.

She forced herself to think logically. The newcomers *might* have captured one of the cell's senior officers. *Might*. The officers were supposed to kill themselves, if they thought there was a chance of being taken prisoner, but Sarah knew from grim experience it was hard to work up the nerve even if one had the freedom to do it. They might have been stunned and bound before they realised they were under attack. And yet, how *had* the new soldiers gotten so close without being detected? Helicopters were loud. It should have been impossible for them to get within attack range, not without machine guns being sited to blast them out of the skies or—if it seemed impossible to smack them back—for the camp to be evacuated. She knew there were some cells that had grown overconfident...had that happened on Ivanovo? Or...or what?

She put it aside—they'd think about it when they got better intelligence—and returned her mind to the question of the prisoners. Who had been captured? What did they know? If a cell leader had been captured... they didn't know *her*, not directly, nor many of her subordinates, but they could point investigators towards fishermen and sea people who took messages from island to island. Given time, the enemy could start parsing out the network...if they had the patience. It wouldn't be easy. Sarah and her comrades had done their best to keep each link in the chain as ignorant as possible, for their own good. She liked to think the enemy would make their presence obvious, if they kept an eye on the couriers. But she was all too aware she might be wrong.

At worst, she told herself, *we lose everyone on the island itself.*

She shook her head in annoyance as she stood and reached for her raincoat. Ivanovo wasn't *that* important, not in the grand scheme of things, but she'd hoped it would continue to drain enemy resources and manpower until she launched the *real* offensive. That wasn't going to happen now. The local rebels would need time—years, perhaps—to rebuild before they could pose a threat to the landowners. She wanted to think the debtors and indents would rise in revolution, but....

The skies were already darkening as she made her way down the cramped staircase and out onto the streets. The landlady gave Sarah a knowing look as she walked past, although she said nothing. Sarah ground her teeth in frustration. The landlady was technically a landowner, with a right to vote, but it counted for nothing. The system was rigged so thoroughly she might as well be a debtor. And yet, she exploited poor and desperate people instead of trying to help them. She'd be dead, when the revolution came. Sarah intended to make sure of it personally. She kept walking, ignoring the handful of youths gathered on street corners. The young men would play a role, when all hell broke loose. She'd see to that, too.

And hopefully make something of themselves, afterwards, she thought, as the downpour began. Warm water spattered against her hood, splashing around her feet. She kept walking, ignoring the camp. *They'll at least have a chance to start afresh.*

She sighed as the streets emptied. She'd grown up on Earth. She'd been told, time and time again, that the colony worlds represented a chance for the settlers to make a new and better life for themselves, a chance to get away from the stifling atmosphere of Earth and breathe free. And yet, the local government seemed determined to recreate the worst aspects of humanity's dead homeworld. A government run by the elite for the elite, a tiny middle class so desperate to keep what it had that it couldn't spare a thought for those below its feet, a poor and helpless lower class that were, *de facto* if not *de jure*, slaves. She pulled her hood tighter around her head as she saw a trio of policemen walking by, eyes flickering as if they expected to be attacked at any moment. Kingsport wasn't a safe place to be an unaccompanied young woman.

Just like Earth, she thought. *They could have built a paradise. Instead, they built a hell.*

The tavern, resting between the harbours and the tenement blocks, was a place where fishermen and sailors went to drink and screw before they went home to their families after returning from the sea. Sarah grimaced in disgust as she stepped inside, heading to the rear of the building without bothering to remove her raincoat. The sailors were drinking heavily and chattering loudly, a handful lying on the floor eating the sawdust. Sarah heard a fight in the corner and ignored it, all too aware no one would give much of a damn about the fighters. The police never came anywhere near the tavern. Her lips twitched in cold amusement. The sailors themselves might be politically powerless, but their bosses were not. They'd pressured the police not to raid taverns or arrest drunken sailors, no matter what they did. They'd created a blind spot the rebels could—and did—abuse for their own purposes.

Unless it's a trap, Sarah thought. She stepped into the backroom and silently assessed the emergency exits. There were supposed to be at least five ways out of the building, but a police officer in command of a small army of policemen wouldn't have to be brilliant to cut most of them off. *They might be waiting for us to gather and then snatch us all.*

The door opened. Sarah's hand dropped to a gun that wasn't there—if she'd been caught with it, she'd be arrested on the spot—her heart starting to race before Albert stepped into the room. She knew almost nothing about him, even his real name, although she thought he'd probably been a sailor in his younger days. It was quite possible. Sailors trusted and respected other sailors and, even if they disagreed with them, could be relied upon not to land their fellow sailors in hot water. Sarah approved, when she thought about it. A crew didn't have to like each other, but they did have to trust and respect each other. No sailor ever betrayed his peers and got away with it.

Albert nodded to her as he closed the door. "You heard the news?"

"Yes." Sarah sat and crossed her legs. "It may be a while before we know *precisely* what happened, but we know enough."

"We didn't anticipate the Marine training program would be *that* successful," Albert said, after a moment. "How long will it take for them to put hundreds of thousands of men into uniform?"

Sarah shrugged. She'd never been in a formal military training program.

Her peers had taught her how to shoot a gun—taboo on Earth—and a great many other things, from how to feed herself in the outback to running a network of rebel cells, but much of it had been learning on the job. She hadn't realised how ill-prepared she was, despite the courses she'd been forced to take while she waited for transport, until she'd found herself on a planet that could easily kill her if she made a single dumb mistake. She simply hadn't known enough to know what a dumb mistake *was*.

"There have to be limits to how many they can train at a time," she said. "But there are plenty of people who might take them up on their offer."

She grimaced. The holding pens on Earth had provided training to involuntary and indentured immigrants, but no one—as far as she'd been able to tell—had bothered to check if anyone was learning anything. She knew people who'd been arrested and exiled, along with her, who'd treated it as yet another pointless class. They'd thought they could get the credit without even showing up, let alone learning anything. It had bit them—hard—when they'd landed on New Doncaster. One young woman hadn't lasted a week before she'd patted a poisonous snake and died when it bit her.

"It is clear we need to take them more seriously," she said. "Are we anywhere like close to being ready for Operation Wilfred?"

Albert snorted. He was one of the people who disliked the codename and he hadn't been shy about making his opinion known, but even *he* had to admit that it sounded nicely innocuous. A more purposeful codename for the operation would have attracted attention, if the government or its agents picked up on it. Besides, Wilfred was a name. It could be dropped into conversation without anyone being any the wiser.

"No," he said. "Realistically, right now, our odds of success are very low. We'd do a hell of a lot of damage, and probably frighten hell out of the bastards, but I doubt we'd actually win. We need more time."

"And time is the one thing we don't have," Sarah said. "This new commander of theirs just pulled off a stunning victory."

She cursed under her breath. The government might have owned the watches, as the saying went, but *she'd* had the time. The rebels had been gradually upping the pressure, keeping the plantations and settlements under siege while laying the groundwork for stepping out of the shadows and taking formal control of large swathes of the planet. The government had responded with overwhelming force, but it had been largely wasted. They were trying to be strong everywhere and failing miserably. And yet, that might have changed.

"He's an odd duck, by all reports," Albert said. "There's a lot of question marks about his resume, his authority and quite a few other points. He reminds me of someone who inherited his boat, and his captaincy; someone who has the entitlement to demand things he shouldn't really be allowed to demand, yet is actually competent. I wondered if he might have a more experienced tactical advisor in the background, pulling his strings, but apparently not. He launched the offensive, as far as we can tell, completely on his own."

"I suppose it is easier to ask for forgiveness, after you win, than permission beforehand," Sarah said, wryly. "The government won't be pleased."

"No," Albert agreed. "But there are limits to what they can do about it."

"Yeah." Sarah would have been amused, if it didn't mean trouble for her personally. What did one *say* to an officer, an officer who wasn't quite in your chain of command, who won a stunning victory without bothering to ask permission first? Give him a medal and a stern lecture? Quietly ignore the whole affair? Or send him home in disgrace and risk demoralising your own officers? "We need to do something about him."

"Agreed." Albert frowned. "The risk, of course, is that it might be traced back to us."

Sarah nodded, curtly. "Use an isolated cell. Cut all their contacts with the greater network. If they succeed, well and good; if they fail, they won't be able to tell their captors anything of value. In the meantime, we'll keep up the pressure. We don't want them to start thinking they can just go where they like, not now. We've gone to a lot of trouble to keep them out of certain areas."

And keep their eyes firmly fixed on the plantations, she thought. *As long as they're looking in the wrong direction, they'll miss the real danger until it is far too late.*

"We'll also speed up the preparations for Wilfred," she added. It would be risky—they'd worked hard to keep the preparations undercover, to keep the enemy from realising what they were doing—but she didn't see a choice. "Time is no longer on our side."

CHAPTER TWENTY-FOUR

FIRST LANDING, NEW DONCASTER

ROLAND HAD HALF-EXPECTED, after he landed at the spaceport and reported briefly to Captain Allen, to discover Sandra driving the car intended to take him to Government House. He'd even hoped it would be true. His hormones were bubbling over after his first successful mission, even though Rachel had kept him from hurling himself into the thick of the action. But it wasn't. The driver was a grim-faced man who barely spoke, even as he helped Roland and Rachel into the car and then drove them into the city. Roland sighed inwardly, telling himself he should be relieved. Rachel wouldn't hesitate to say sarcastic things if Roland and Sandra had started making out while she was driving.

Government House looked unchanged as they drove through the security checkpoint and into the underground garage. Roland was almost disappointed. He'd filed a report and he knew several of his officers—and the helicopter pilots—had done the same. The local news broadcasts were bland and boring, without any official statement of just what had happened and why. He'd expected everyone to be shouting and screaming, cheering the proof that the newly trained men could take the rebels on in their own territory and win. He couldn't help finding the silence ominous. He hadn't exactly gone beyond the letter of his authority, depending on how one squinted at it, but he'd quite definitely gone beyond the spirit. No one liked barrack-room lawyers at the best of times. Roland had a nasty feeling the only thing standing between him and a tongue-lashing, or worse, was the simple fact it had worked. He'd given the rebels a very bloody nose.

He glanced at Rachel as they were escorted up the elevator, then into the council chamber. It might have been better to leave her at the spaceport, or send her back to report to Wimer and his comrades. There was nothing to be gained by letting her get blasted too, if the government decided to be ungrateful. He'd been the one who came up with the plan, then put the pieces into operation without telling anyone outside the corps what he had in mind. Rachel had followed orders. It wasn't always a very good defence—there were certain orders that simply *could not* be followed—but it was in this case. She was innocent.

The PM, General Falk and Lord Ludlow sat behind a table. Roland tried not to show his irritation at the sheer pettiness of the setup. There were no chairs for the guests, nothing to indicate they were even slightly welcome... Roland had seen enough power games to be thoroughly unimpressed. He'd certainly been a lot more uncomfortable in Boot Camp. If they kicked him off-world, so what? It wouldn't be the end of the world, not for him. His career would continue, while New Doncaster went straight to hell.

"Captain Windsor," General Falk said. His voice was so bland Roland *knew* it was an act. "Please explain to us why you launched a major operation without permission."

"And why you lied to us," Lord Ludlow snapped. "We signed off on a reinforcement deployment, not a daring commando raid!"

Roland hid his amusement. Lord Ludlow probably didn't know it was the catchphrase of a fictional Marine—who was about as realistic as the Grand Senate's now-defunct annual finance report—and probably wouldn't have cared if he had. He knew Lord Ludlow's type. They were so concerned about protecting their petty authority, such as it was, that they allowed matters to get out of hand rather than let someone else try to fix it. One could save his life and he'd complain it hadn't been done properly.

"My orders were to reinforce the island's defences and wage war on the rebels, before they had a chance to cause more damage," Roland said, calmly. He kept his eyes firmly fixed on the triad. "I submit to you, sirs, that that was precisely what I did."

"You were not granted authority to commandeer a bunch of helicopters, let alone use them to take troops into enemy territory," General Falk said, curtly. "You risked everything on one throw of the die."

Roland kept his voice calm. "My authority was laid down by your government, in line with both your own protocols and the agreements signed between yourselves and the imperial government. I had the authority to take the war to the enemy, including the authority to requisition supplies and vehicles if necessary. That is precisely what I did."

"The authority was intended to cover jeeps and trucks, not helicopters," General Falk snapped. "You pushed it too far!"

"I worked under the assumption that my written orders were set in stone," Roland said, with a flicker of a smile. It was definitely a barracks room lawyer moment, but the point had to be made. "The helicopters proved to be the key to victory. They were borrowed, used, and returned to their rightful owners. Their pilots volunteered to remain in their craft, for which they were promised hazard pay. It all worked out for the best."

Lord Ludlow glared. "You did not put the operation together on a whim," he said. "The helicopters would not even have been there, if you hadn't summoned them to Ivanovo along with their ground crews and supplies. You could have discussed the operational plan with us at any moment, before you took flight to Ivanovo yourself. You should have talked to us."

You might have said no, Roland thought. It was childish, and he was ashamed of himself for thinking it, but there was just something about Lord Ludlow's type that brought out the worst in him. *Or you might have said the wrong thing to the wrong person and warned the enemy of what we had in mind.*

He leaned forward. "There is clear proof the rebels have agents within the government and military," he said. He was sure of *that*, even though few—if any—agents had been identified by the local counterintelligence officers. "I dared not let them know what was coming, even in vague terms. It would have been easy for them to set up an ambush or simply evacuate the camp, if they believed they couldn't hold it. My fist would have closed, pardon the expression, on empty air. At best, we would have looked like fools; at worst, we would have stumbled into a bloody disaster that put the program back years."

"The council is above suspicion," Lord Ludlow snapped. "Do you think we'd call the rebels to inform them you were about to land on their heads?"

"There are thousands of people who come in and out of Government House, and the rest of the district, every day," Roland countered. "Are they all above suspicion? Can you be sure that none of them will talk, after hours? Can you be sure that none of them are spying on you, reporting your activities to the local rebels? All it would take, sir, is a single spy in the wrong place to hear a rumour of the impending assault. The rebels would take action and the operation, like I said, would fail."

He took a breath. "I made the call, in line with the authority granted me, to tell as few people as possible what I intended to do. And it worked. The rebels didn't have the slightest idea we were coming until the first missile struck home, at which point it was too late. We smashed the camp, destroyed their supplies, killed a bunch of rebels and even took a handful of prisoners. I think we can reasonably count it as a clear victory. We took the war into enemy territory and proved, to them as well as us, that we could operate there."

His eyes lingered on the PM. Sandra's father hadn't said anything so far, which meant...what? Roland had no idea if any discussions had been held before he'd arrived at Government House. The PM might support him, on the grounds he'd won a victory, or he might be under intense pressure to slap Roland's wrist for commandeering the helicopters and taking them into combat. Roland suspected that wouldn't be easy—the written authority was as extensive as he'd suggested—but his peers wouldn't care. It wouldn't be easy to walk a tightrope between winning the war and keeping his allies onside without tumbling off and falling to the rocks far below. The PM was trapped between two fires.

Lord Ludlow snorted. "Is that your argument? All's well that ends well?"

"Yes, sir," Roland said. "We came, we saw, we kicked their butts. I count that as a victory. I count it as proof the new army can take the field and win. And, right now, the rebels are shaking in their shoes. How many other camps are we going to strike?"

"We don't know where the others are," General Falk said. "Not yet."

"Not yet," Roland echoed. "But they don't know it, do they?"

The PM cleared his throat. "I think we can agree that the entire operation worked out for the best," he said. "Captain Windsor may or may not have exceeded the authority we thought we were granting him, but he didn't exceed the authority we *did* grant him. A legal committee will be formed to consider the question, with the intention of determining if the treaties and agreements should be revised. Until then, the issue will be shelved."

So you sent the matter to die in committee, Roland thought, wryly. It was an old trick. The government would look like it was doing something, without doing much of anything. The PM was playing for time, waiting to see what happened. *And as long as I don't screw up, you'll make sure the question doesn't go any further.*

"We congratulate you on your success," the PM continued. "It might be best, for the moment, if you concentrated on raising and training more troops."

Roland looked back at him, evenly. "We also need to capitalise on our success," he said, carefully. "There will be other enemy camps. We need to take them out as quickly as possible."

"You don't know where those camps are," General Falk pointed out, for the second time. "Or do you intend to launch bombing raids at random?"

"No," Roland said. "But we can deploy troops to islands with high levels of rebel activity and start putting patrols through the front lines.

They can either come out to fight, in which case we'll have them in our sights, or fall back, allowing us to establish dominance. We can—and we will—start probing the outback, searching for enemy positions. The rebels would have to react to us, for a change. We'd have a chance to blow the hell out of them."

"If you found an enemy base," the PM said. "What are the odds of success?"

"Incalculable," Roland said. "The idea is not to gamble everything on finding a needle in a haystack, sir, but to force the enemy to react to us."

And take advantage of the pause to push for a political solution, he added, silently. He doubted he had enough clout to make the suggestion, not to them. *Unless you make reforms quickly, all the troops in the world aren't going to save you from yourselves.*

"You can lay your plans," the PM said. "You will, of course, discuss them with us before putting them into action. They will not go any further."

You don't want any more surprises, Roland thought, coldly. *What will you say if it does turn into a complete disaster?*

"I understand," he said, recognising the unspoken implication. He was grounded, at least for the moment. *That* would slow things down for a few weeks, at least until he convinced them to let him return to the front lines. "I'll keep you informed, at least in general terms."

The PM nodded, choosing not to push the issue any further. "Good."

"That leads neatly to the second issue," Lord Ludlow said. "The prisoners. They are to be handed over to us. Immediately."

Roland bit down on his first—savage—response. "The prisoners will be held in our custody until the end of the war," he said, silently thanking his lucky stars that he'd arranged to have them held at the spaceport. "I doubt they can tell us anything useful. We seem to have killed most of the rebel leaders, at least of that particular cell...."

"That isn't the issue," Lord Ludlow said. "Five of the captured prisoners are runaway indents who must be returned to the plantations. Two more are wanted criminals, who fled to avoid arrest. The remainder are little better. They must be shipped to a penal island to pay their debt to society."

"They are prisoners of war," Roland said. "They have, in line with both the Protocols of War and the Imperial Code of Military Justice, certain rights."

"Such rights depend on reciprocity," Lord Ludlow snarled. "I put the issue to my family's lawyers. They concluded, and I will forward their notes if you wish, that the captured rebels willingly stepped outside the laws of war and therefore forfeited the right to protection under them. Furthermore, even if that wasn't true, they owe money to their owners and have an obligation to repay it. They must be handed over, immediately."

Roland took a moment to compose his answer. He'd been forced to study the Protocols of War during Boot Camp, although—as his instructors had pointed out, rather ruefully—they might be a dead letter after Earthfall. The empire hadn't always enforced the protocols evenly when the empire had been alive and well. Now...he shook his head, mentally, as he considered his next words. His superiors would not thank him for openly breaking the protocols, no matter the reason. He'd be lucky if he wasn't summarily discharged from the corps.

"The issue is a thorny one," he conceded. "And I am not an expert. However, they were taken prisoner during a military operation and therefore they have a right to be treated as POWs, regardless of their pre-rebel status. It is true that we have a legal right to shoot terrorists and their enablers on sight, as your lawyers no doubt argued, but we have no proof the POWs are actually terrorists. We do not know they committed atrocities that would put them outside the law's protection.

"Furthermore, on a more practical basis, we must avoid mistreating prisoners where possible. The rebels will fight harder if they feel they will be tortured and executed if they fall into our hands; they will torture and execute any of *our* people who fall into their hands, in retaliation for the mistreatment of their people. And, legally, they would be perfectly within their rights to do so. As you say, the protocols are based on reciprocity."

"They're indents who ran rather than pay their debts," Lord Ludlow snapped. "They belong to their plantations!"

Slaves, you mean. Roland had to fight to hide his distaste. He'd known things were grim on some colony worlds, but he hadn't really believed it. Not until now. *And do you think they're just going to go back to work?*

He decided it would be better not to ask. Instead, he looked at the PM. "We can keep them prisoner, nicely isolated, until we bring the war to an end. There is no need to deal with them immediately, let alone sentence them to death or do something that would cause them to retaliate against us. There is nothing to be gained by abusing them."

"They were in a rebel base," Lord Ludlow said. "What next? Will you spare a man in your underage daughter's bedroom because he just *happened* to have clambered over the fence, slipped up the wall, climbed through the window and is now staring at your sleeping daughter, on the grounds it *might* be a wild coincidence?"

"No." Roland put firm controls on his temper. "I take your point. It is a good one. Being caught in a rebel base is a pretty good sign that the prisoner is a rebel. However, we don't know why they were in the rebel base, we don't know what—if anything—they've done for the rebels and we don't have any reason to think they pose an actual threat to us. Not now. And if we mistreat them, they will mistreat our people!"

"They've been mistreating our people all along," Lord Ludlow insisted. "Do you know what they did to an overseer who turned his back at the wrong time?"

"We don't know that our POWs were personally responsible," Roland said. There was no way to know if the POWs had been anywhere near that particular disaster. "That said, the point is moot. We have an obligation to treat them reasonably well, under the circumstances, and I intend to do so. If you wish to complain about this, you can do so to my superiors."

The PM held up a hand before Lord Ludlow could explode. "Very well," he said. "You will, of course, be responsible for ensuring they don't have a chance to hurt anyone. If they do, we will have to take steps."

"Understood," Roland said.

The PM nodded. "We look forward to reading your full report," he said. His lips twisted into a faint smile that looked fake. "However, we do expect you to keep us informed of your future plans."

"I understand," Roland said. He had absolutely no intention of telling them anything more than the bare minimum. It would be a good way to get people killed. He'd bet what little remained of his inheritance that Lord Ludlow would be fuming to anyone who'd listen within ten minutes. "I'll do my best."

On that note, he was dismissed.

CHAPTER TWENTY-FIVE

NEW DONCASTER SPACEPORT, NEW DONCASTER

"YOU KNOW, I THINK I WANT TO SWIM NEXT TIME," Private Chan Hosing said, as the aircraft rattled through the air. "It has *got* to be safer."

Private Bryce Ambrose nodded in agreement. The boat trip to Ivanovo had been a nightmare; the aircraft flight back to Kingstown was almost worse. The aircraft was a rickety old thing that looked to predate the first wave of colonists, perhaps even the empire itself; the airframe had creaked and moaned so often that he'd found himself half-convinced the aircraft was on the verge of breaking up and falling out of the sky. It was enough to make him wonder if the Marines had figured out he was a spy, that they'd put him on the aircraft as punishment rather than arresting him. Cold logic told him it was a stupid thought; the constant shaking made it impossible to entirely dismiss it.

He felt another pang of guilt as he eyed the prisoners. They'd been placed on hard metal seats and cuffed firmly to the airframe, making it nearly impossible for them to move. The escorts—a platoon of soldiers—had been ordered to leave them there, just in case they did something dangerous. Bryce was unsure if it was designed to harm or humiliate the prisoners—they were going to be sitting in their own wastes soon, if they weren't already—or if it was just a reasonable degree of paranoia. The airframe was so weak it was easy to believe a single punch would shatter the metal and send them all plunging to their deaths.

The intercom bleeped. "Take your seats," the pilot's voice said. "Prepare for landing."

Bryce glanced at the prisoners, then did as he was told. He'd tried to come up with a plan to get them out, but nothing had come to mind. He didn't want to shoot the rest of his platoon and, even if he did, getting into the cockpit would be tricky. The best he could do, if everything went his way, was kill everyone by firing through the hatch, hitting the pilot and sending the aircraft crashing into the sea. It burnt at him, leaving him feeling like a traitor—and a useless traitor at that—as he eyed the poor bastards. They were going to spend the rest of the war in a POW camp, if they were lucky. The cynic in him was sure they'd be sent to a penal island and worked to death instead.

The aircraft descended rapidly. Bryce winced in pain as his ears popped, his stomach twisting as if an invisible force had wrenched it. He heard someone being noisily sick behind him as the aircraft hit the ground with a crash, the sound of the impact so loud he thought they had crashed. The aircraft roared down the runway, veering madly from side to side before finally slowing to a more reasonable pace. He allowed himself a moment of relief. It wasn't the fall that killed you, one of his instructors had cracked, but the landing. Bryce was starting to understand just how true the old joke was.

He gritted his teeth, forcing himself to unbuckle and stand as the sergeant barked orders and the aircraft came to a stop. His legs felt wobbly, but...he kept going, somehow, as the hatches were opened and the warm air rolled in. Bryce peered out—they were back at the spaceport, with the Marines already waiting—and then helped the others to unlock the prisoners and get them stumbling towards the hatch. He felt yet another stab of pity as he half-carried a young woman into the bright sunlight. God alone knew what fate awaited her, in the not-too-distant future. The Marines might be taking them into custody now, but who knew if they'd *keep* them.

"Twenty-seven rebel prisoners, all cuffed," the sergeant said. "Where do you want them?"

"We'll take them from here," the Marine officer said. "You take your men through the gates. There's a bus already waiting to take you to the camp."

Bryce remembered himself and started to look around, trying to gather useful intelligence for when he next saw his contact. The spaceport didn't look *that* different, although there were a pair of new-looking shuttles resting on landing pads and a handful of tilt-rotor aircraft being fussed around by Marines and spaceport crew. A pallet of deadly-looking missiles were being wheeled towards one of the latter, the crew treating the weapons as if a single bump would be enough to trigger an explosion. He hoped that wasn't true. His instructors had told him, time and time again, that safety came first. It was always better to assume a gun was loaded until proven otherwise, rather than risk a deadly accident.

He kept his eyes open as they were marched through the gates, then up to a dirty bus. It felt surreal, as if they hadn't been away at all. They'd only left the camp three days ago. He wondered, numbly, if they were real soldiers now; he tried not to think of what his superiors might say, when he reported he'd been part of the raid. By now, they had to know what had happened...right? The media was untrustworthy—everyone knew it only told the world what the government wanted it to hear—but this time it would be telling the truth. The raid wouldn't remain a secret, not when the government *needed* a victory. Besides, too many people had seen the explosions and watched the helicopters go out and come back. His superiors would know something had happened, even if they didn't know precisely *what*.

I'll just have to tell them the truth, he thought, as the bus rumbled into life. He was sure he wasn't the only rebel spy in the ranks. There might be an entire *company* of spies within the ranks. *And hope they don't kill me on the spot.*

...

Susan *ached*.

It was hard, so hard, not to scream as she was freed from the hard metal chair and half-pushed, half-carried, into the bright sunlight. She had spent the last two days in a makeshift cell, cuffed to the wall; it had been unpleasant, a grim reminder of how she'd been treated since she'd been arrested on Earth, but heaven itself compared to the flight. The pilot was either insane or a complete incompetent. Even the guards, who hadn't been cuffed to the chairs, had looked fearful. Susan hadn't blamed them in the slightest.

The light was so bright it burned her eyes. She gritted her teeth, trying to look away as strong arms grabbed her and pushed her towards a dark building. It was very difficult, to walk with her legs in shackles. It seemed like pointless sadism. They'd searched her repeatedly, leaving no inch of her body untouched. They *knew* she didn't have a weapon, certainly nothing she could use with her hands in cuffs and her feet in shackles. If they were trying to keep her in her place, they were succeeding. The only upside, as far as she could tell, was that they'd been flown away from the island. She wasn't going straight back to the plantation.

She breathed a sigh of relief as she was pushed into a dark building. Her vision rapidly cleared, revealing a giant warehouse-like structure. The man holding her was tall and muscular, wearing a green uniform with a pair of gold tabs on his shoulders. He had no visible weapons, but she had the feeling he could break her in half with one hand tied behind his back. She swallowed hard as she was pushed into a chair and cuffed into place. The flight had been bad, but what awaited her could be worse. She knew what happened to young women who fell into enemy hands. They were often lucky if they were *just* shot out of hand.

"Hello," her captor said. His voice was oddly accented, neither the tones of Earth nor New Doncaster. "Would you like some water? A ration bar?"

Susan tried not to show her desperation. Her throat was parched. Her stomach was reminding her how long it had been since she'd eaten. And yet…she tried to remember what she'd been told about interrogation techniques. She'd been cautioned to say nothing as long as possible, to give away as little as she could. It would buy time for the free prisoners to make their escape, before she finally broke. She'd thought she could handle it. She was starting to think she couldn't.

She nodded, shortly. Her captor pressed a bottle against her lips. Susan sipped gratefully, realising—too late—that they could have put *anything* in the liquid. She'd heard all sorts of horror stories, from urine to alcohol and truth drugs. She wanted to spit it out, but it was too late. The water tasted a little *too* pure. She guessed it had been run through a purifier before it was poured into the canteen.

"My name is Amado," her captor said. "What's yours?"

Susan shook her head, not daring to speak. She didn't want to form any connection with Amado, if that was his real name. She didn't want to let herself be lulled into surrender, into giving away what little she knew. Her heart twisted. It wouldn't be long before he started hurting or drugging her, if she couldn't be convinced to talk of her own free will. The pain would break her, perhaps, but at least she would have held out for a while. Who knew? It might have a slight—a very slight—impact on the war.

Amado didn't seem put out by her silence. "You were taken prisoner during an operation directed by the Terran Marine Corps," he said. "Accordingly, you will remain in our custody—either here or within a dedicated POW camp—until the current unpleasantness is over. You have certain rights as a POW, which we will honour to the best of our ability; you also have certain responsibilities, which—should you fail to honour them—may result in you being moved into solitary confinement, physically restrained or, as a final resort, executed. We will make no attempt to interrogate you, or force you to work in any capacity, but if you attempt to contact your people or escape, we will do whatever we have to do, up to and including the use of lethal force, to stop you."

He paused. "If you have committed acts that put you outside the protection of the protocols, you have an obligation to declare them now. Should such acts come into the light after today, you will be stripped of legal protections and treated as a terrorist."

Susan swallowed. "Does escaping a plantation count?"

"No," Amado said. "If you decide to cooperate, you will be rewarded. If not, you will remain in the camp until the end of the war, unless we manage to trade you for someone in your side's custody."

"Oh." Susan shook her head. "No, thank you."

She was too tired and sore to smile at his reaction, but it didn't matter. She'd already thought about it. New Doncaster had treated her like...like a slave. No, worse than a slave. The rebels, by contrast, had taken her in, taught her how to shoot and treated her as one of their own. She knew she wasn't brave enough to keep her mouth shut, if she was tortured, but if they weren't going to torture her...she shook her head, again. She didn't trust the government to keep its promises. No one in their right mind would expect the government to do anything it promised. The landowners would sooner burn their plantations to the ground than pay a fair wage....

"If you change your mind, let us know," Amado said. "Until then"—he affected an even odder accent—"for you, the war is over."

...

Bryce wasn't sure what he'd expected, when they'd returned to the training camp. Their old barracks had been handed down to the next class of recruits, while the newer barracks for trained soldiers passing through the camp were still under construction. No one seemed to have a solid explanation as to why, but—reading between the lines—it seemed likely none of the folks who'd stayed on Kingstown had expected the troops to return so soon. They'd all been told they'd be away for weeks, if not months. He was still rolling his eyes at the absurdity of the situation—Captain Windsor's lies had struck his men in the back—when the sergeant told them that two days of leave had been authorised. Bryce almost wished he'd been told to stay with the prisoners. It would have given him more time to decide what to tell his superiors.

The city was buzzing, he noted, as he walked to the brothel. The news was out and spreading. Townies were babbling endlessly about vast numbers of rebels being slaughtered; debtors and indents seemed much less enthusiastic, exchanging grim looks whenever they thought their superiors weren't looking. Bryce hated to admit it, but some of the looks his former peers were sending at him weren't exactly friendly. They thought he was just another soldier, a sell-out who'd taken the government's money and set out to hunt his own people. The thought made him sick, even though he knew he could hardly wear a rebel shirt in the middle of the city. The police weren't *that* incompetent.

A chill ran through him. *If they start attacking lone soldiers…who knows where* that *will end?*

He put the thought aside as he walked into the brothel. It was oddly quiet, to the point he was tempted to see if he could meet a real whore before his contact. He wanted to, but he knew it would be a bad idea. His contact would not be amused. And besides, he had to give his report while the details were fresh in his mind. He allowed himself to be shown into the hidden staircase and up the stairs into the room, then waited. It was nearly twenty minutes before his contact arrived.

"Welcome back," she said. She dressed like a whore, but her voice was cold and hard and made it absolutely clear she was a person of authority. "What happened?"

Bryce took a breath, then ran through the entire story. The sudden call to barracks—and then the lockdown. The voyage to Ivanovo. The helicopter assault on the rebel camp. The victory. The prisoners. The return to Kingstown. And, finally, his one chance to get out and make a report.

"Interesting," his contact said. Her eyes bored into his. "You had no chance whatsoever to make contact with us?"

"No," Bryce said. "I didn't know what was going to happen until we were already marching to the helicopters. It was too late to send a warning even if I'd had a way to do it."

"Right." His contact said nothing for a long cold moment. "Who got taken prisoner and how are they being treated?"

"I don't have a list of names," Bryce said. "I have the impression none of them were particularly important, but that could easily be wrong. They were treated relatively well, once we got them back to the airport. They were fed and watered; no attempt was made to interrogate them. The Marines might try to do it themselves, of course, but…I just don't know. They are supposed to have ways of making people talk."

"Quite," his contact agreed. She sounded like someone trying desperately to find a droplet of good news in a lake of bad, although it was hard to be sure. "But whatever they knew is already outdated—and getting all the more outdated all the time."

"I think so, yes," Bryce said. "I heard nothing to suggest they were interrogated, at least until we got them back to the spaceport. Their intelligence will be at least three days out of date."

His contact looked pensive. "We'll hope for the best," she said. "Getting them out of captivity might prove difficult, if not impossible. "

She shook her head. "Tell me about Captain Windsor?"

Bryce blinked at the sudden change in tone. "I haven't seen him that often," he said. "He gave us a brief speech when we took the oath, and supervised some aspects of our training, but he spent most of his time with the officers. I heard rumours that he told some of them off for incompetence, although I don't know how many of them are true. And…he was in command of the operation, but he wasn't actually in the front lines. I didn't see him until the dust had settled."

"Interesting," his contact said. "A prudent man, or a coward?"

"I don't know," Bryce said. "He *did* come up with the plan to use helicopters and missiles for the assault. And it worked."

"A skilled planner could still be a coward," his contact mused. "How does he get on with the government?"

"I don't know," Bryce said. "I have never seen him interacting with the government."

"No." His contact smiled. It dawned on Bryce, suddenly, that the question had been a test of sorts. "I want you to embed yourself as deeply as possible, for the moment. Carry out your orders, whatever they are. And don't get caught. I will have a use for you, later on."

Bryce allowed himself a moment of relief. "If I get sent out on another mission…."

"I'll understand," his contact said. "Try not to get blown away by your own side."

CHAPTER TWENTY-SIX

KINGSTOWN TRAINING BASE, NEW DONCASTER

RICHARD HADN'T BEEN QUITE SURE what to expect, when he'd passed through the makeshift POW camp on his way back to the training base. A nightmarish maze of barbed wire, perhaps, or a row of POWs tied to stakes and left in the sun to roast. Instead, it had been almost strikingly civilised. The POWs had been put in an abandoned barracks, fed and watered and generally treated like human beings instead of monsters or criminals waiting for the hangman. Richard wasn't quite sure what to make of that, either. He understood the importance of accepting surrenders and treating prisoners decently, but—at the same time—he hadn't forgiven or forgotten the rebels for killing men under his command. The thought tormented him as he clambered into the official car and allowed the driver to take him back to the training base. If they were wrong....

If we make it clear we'll treat prisoners decently, we'll find it easier to convince enemy troops to surrender, he thought, again. *But, at the same time, we have to deal with enemy fighters who don't treat our people decently.*

He scowled as he leaned back in his seat, taking a moment to catch his breath. He'd spent a week as *de facto* military commander on Ivanovo—somewhat to his surprise, the local militia officers hadn't tried to assert themselves—and it had been exhausting. His men had run patrols through the plantations, trying to get a feel for the area before the rebels regrouped and resumed the offensive; he'd pushed them to set up checkpoints, search worker barracks and generally do everything in their power to convince the world they were in charge. It was hard to say what, if any, effect they'd had. They'd almost certainly made a whole new bunch of enemies.

And the rebels themselves have been ominously silent, Richard reminded himself. *They're plotting something.*

The thought worried him. He knew from grim experience that the rebellion would be very hard to eradicate. Even if they *had* wiped out every last rebel on Ivanovo—and he would bet his entire salary they hadn't—they hadn't done anything to the rebels on other, larger, islands. One glorious victory—the media made it sound as if they'd won the war in a single brief engagement—wasn't going to be enough to convince the rebels to give up. They couldn't. There was no way they could just walk away and leave the war behind. And...Richard suspected it was just a matter of time before the rebels launched a major strike of their own, in retaliation for the destruction of their base. They needed to make it clear they weren't a spent force before their supporters started backing away or launched strikes of their own.

He raised an eyebrow as he saw the line of men waiting outside the base. He'd heard recruitment efforts had continued, but he hadn't really understood what it meant. Now...there were hundreds, perhaps thousands, of men hoping to join the army. Richard hoped they were loyal, and that the government would give them a *reason* to be loyal. It was one thing to forget a handful of debts, but hundreds? Thousands? It was all too easy to imagine the landowners finding an excuse not to keep their word....

The car parked outside a new building, an HQ that had been hastily thrown up by the carpenters now the new army had proved its value. The sentries outside were within the base's perimeter, well inside the fence, but they were alert. Roland and his staff would have pitched a fit, Richard was sure, if the guards didn't remain alert at all times. The risk of a rebel agent joining the line of waiting men and slipping through the gates was just too high.

Rachel met him as he clambered out of the car. "Sir," she said. "The captain is waiting in the ops room."

Richard nodded, allowing her to lead him past the guards—they checked his identity before standing aside—and into the building. Rachel, by all accounts, had accompanied Roland when he'd walked into enemy territory…clear proof, if any were necessary, that she was more than *just* an assistant. Richard had no doubt of it. Rachel simply didn't *act* like the assistants he'd met, from the brainless bimbos hired by insecure landowners to formidable older women who ruled their offices with rods of iron. He'd marched through the outback himself. He knew how hard it could be, even if there wasn't a rebel base within shouting distance. It wasn't something he'd expect from a *normal* assistant.

"Richard." Roland stood in the centre of the room, peering down at a large paper map. "Welcome back!"

Richard smiled, feeling a twinge of warmth. He didn't understand Roland—the younger man was a bizarre mix of traits that simply didn't add up—but there was no denying his competence, or his nerve. Richard hadn't met many officers who'd put together a plan, then place all the pieces where they were needed without bothering to share his concept with his superiors. He still shivered, whenever he thought how badly things could have gone. They'd caught the rebels by surprise. Next time, it wouldn't be so easy.

"It's good to be back," he said. He saluted Roland, then nodded to Wimer. "There were no encounters with the enemy since you left, not even a shooting."

"We hurt them," Roland said. "Right now, they're probably trying to decide how best to respond."

He tapped the map. Richard studied it thoughtfully. Roland had printed out a detailed chart of every island within a thousand miles of Kingstown, although—unsurprisingly—the details of some of the more distant islands were frighteningly vague. Richard frowned. He'd served on a number of islands and passed through others, from Baraka itself to the tiny relay airfield on an island no one had bothered to name. He had no idea why they hadn't established the airfield on a bigger island. The average visitor landed at the airfield, then took a boat or a helicopter to the main settlements. It had never made sense to him.

"There have been a handful of tiny incidents over the last week," Roland said, "but it's hard to tell how many of them were responses to our operation, rather than either planned in advance or simply random attacks of opportunity. The rebel cell structure appears to be very loose, unsurprisingly. Their command network has very limited influence and a number of strikes, credited to the rebels, appear to have been carried out—instead—by lone wolves. I don't think any of the attacks were *really* intended as a response to us."

Richard's eyes narrowed. "You interrogated the prisoners?"

"A couple talked, after we treated them well," Roland said. "They didn't know any specifics—it seems we killed the rebel commanders during the raid—but they could and did talk about the rebel network in general terms. I don't think there's anything to be gained by pushing them a little harder, not now. They can't tell us what they don't know."

"No, sir," Richard said. He'd known officers who'd never understood that. "You think we'll be attacked, shortly?"

"Yes." Roland allowed his finger to draw a line on the map. "They have a problem. They need a guaranteed victory, because they'll look like losers if we kick their asses a second time, but they also need a *spectacular* victory. They'll want to regain the momentum they lost when we took out their base…ideally, they'll want the victory on Ivanovo to prove they're not a spent force, but that might not be possible. Our prisoners suggested there was one major rebel base on the island and we killed it."

"Assuming they're telling the truth," Richard pointed out. "Ivanovo isn't exactly a *small* island. There's plenty of room for another camp or two."

Roland didn't dispute it. "They also need to manage expectations," he added. "If they launch a spectacular attack, then fail to follow it up with *another*, they'll look as if they've shot their bolt. It's hard to say what they'll do, but I have a theory. I think they'll try to cut off and destroy an army patrol, perhaps even a full-sized garrison."

"They might also target the militia," Richard said. "There's a bunch of blockhouses and suchlike that would make ideal targets, as far as they are concerned."

"Yeah." Roland didn't sound convinced. "Problem is, they've hammered the militia in the past. There's nothing spectacular about *that*. They need to kick our asses instead—and quickly."

He shook his head. "We have other problems," he said, after a moment. "The government has approved expansion of the training program, but they've also…asked…us to train newer and better drill instructors. They want to integrate our training into the regular army training program, which may cause problems in the long run. New Doncaster simply doesn't have the manpower to make it work, not without issues that could bring the entire program crashing down. We may find ourselves clearing up the mess at some point."

Richard snorted. "Why don't they just run everyone through the training camp here?"

"Too small," Wimer said. The Drill Instructor sounded tired. "The regulars never pushed this camp to its limits. We *have*. They need to expand the camp here, but also set up other ones elsewhere. The rebels will hit us, sooner rather than later. They'll *have* to discourage the locals from joining the army."

"There are thousands of people who'd join, if it meant having their debts cancelled," Richard said. "Sir, you have *got* to make sure the government keeps its word."

"I'll do my best," Roland said. "Right now, the government has insisted I remain here and supervise the expanded training program."

Richard smiled. "They think you'll surprise them again?"

"Yep," Roland said. They shared a grin. "Right now, of course, I don't have a target in mind. In some ways, we have the same problem as the rebels. Our raid was a spectacular success. If the next one isn't so spectacular, we'll start looking like losers, too. It'll just take a single defeat to wash away a hundred victories—and we haven't *had* a hundred victories. Not yet, anyway."

He tapped the map. "There's been some minor reorganisation," he said. "I'm going to deploy two companies, a mixture of seasoned and unseasoned men, to Baraka. You'll go along as overall commander—you'll be wearing two hats, as both a company commander and overall deployment commander. I'm sending some experienced officers along with you, in hopes of making the deployment a little easier, but...."

Richard nodded. The command structure had been a mess for years. Roland could hardly make it worse. The thought of overall command awed and scared him. He'd wanted to have his own command, once upon a time, but he knew he could expect no mercy if he screwed up. He simply didn't have the connections to survive even a tiny mishap. And yet, was that still true? Roland wasn't the sort of person to blame an officer for losing a battle he couldn't possibly win.

A thought struck him. "Do I get a promotion?"

"Apparently, I can only give brevet promotions." Roland grimaced. "General Falk was kind enough to inform me of that, when I told him what I wanted to do. You'll be a captain for the duration of the deployment, with pay to match, but I can't make it permanent. I wish I could."

Richard nodded, then frowned. "The general just agreed to let you run the war as you see fit?"

"No." Roland shook his head. "He expects to be kept informed—and consulted on all major issues—and I have agreed. That said, he doesn't want the details and we will...*stall*...when it comes to informing him of certain plans. I don't think he'll leak willingly, Richard, but his office is full of unvetted staff. It'll just take one or two rebel spies to ruin our day."

"Crap." Richard shook his head. "How did he ever get the job?"

Rachel stepped forward. Richard tried not to jump. He'd nearly forgotten she was there.

"It's very simple," she said. "The military establishment is divorced from the realities of the war. The officers who get promoted, therefore, are the ones who can and do play the political game. They suck up to their superiors, rather than actually doing their jobs; this forces them to support their master's whims, to the point they submerge their own judgement—what little they have—and do as they're told. General Falk is a good example of the breed. He comes from a decent bloodline, as the people here reckon things, but he is caught between several different political masters, any of whom can destroy him if he outlives his usefulness. He is all too aware of it, hence a desire to make a show of keeping us on a leash without *actually* doing anything that might cause him problems later."

She looked, just for a second, as if she was lost in memory. "He lacks the self-awareness, let alone the self-sacrifice, to stand between his political masters and the men under his command. A strong man in his position, or at least someone dedicated to the interests of the military, could have accomplished much, by selecting the right subordinates and backing them to the hilt. Instead, he allows himself to be blown hither and yon by the political winds, which make it impossible to stabilise the situation, yet alone purge unsuitable or untrustworthy officers. Does that answer your question?"

Roland blinked. "How did you work *that* out?"

"I have a superpower called *listening*." Rachel smiled, thinly. "While you were consulting with the general, I was listening to his staff and noting very carefully what they didn't say. Half of them were only given posts because of their connections and he couldn't get rid of them if he wanted to; the other half, the ones who do all the work, are often ignored when they try to point out inconvenient things called *facts*. Hell, the sad truth is that he's probably saving lives by keeping incompetents on his staff. It prevents them from trying to lead troops into combat."

"Ah…thank you," Roland said. "It's just like home, isn't it?"

Richard had to smile. "Is there anything we can do about it?"

"There are ways to keep staff officers from getting disconnected from the realities of combat," Rachel said. "The corps rotates officers in and out of staff positions to keep them from getting lazy and losing their edge, but I don't know if it would be workable here. There are just too many people with an interest in keeping things the way they are."

Roland cleared his throat. "Richard, take a day of leave and then report to the spaceport for the flight to Baraka. Take up position along the front lines and try to lure the enemy into combat, then kill them. I leave the precise tactical deployments up to you. I'll pass through myself in a week or two, whenever I can convince the government to let me take my eyes off the training program and get back to the front. Don't push your luck too far. The enemy needs a victory."

"Yes, sir," Richard said. He couldn't help feeling proud, even though he knew he'd get the blame if something went wrong. At least Roland was letting him make his own tactical deployments. He wouldn't have to carry the can for a senior officer who hadn't even bothered to look at a map before issuing impossible orders. "I'll bear it in mind."

Roland grinned. "Good luck," he said. "Try and keep the militia from fucking things up."

Richard saluted, then left the room. A day of leave…it wasn't much, but it was long enough to meet his father and compare notes. Perhaps, just perhaps, they could push for political reform. The landowners had to realise—now—that they could no longer keep the world in stasis. They needed an army that might easily turn on them, if they broke their word. There was a window of opportunity, Richard thought, to establish lasting change. But if it didn't work….

Rachel followed him, moving so quietly he barely heard her coming up behind him. "A word of advice," she said. Her voice was very calm. "Don't wear your uniform in the city."

"Why?" Richard was astonished. There were thousands of uniformed men in the city, from soldiers to policemen and emergency first responders. "It's perfectly legal...."

"A couple of soldiers on leave got attacked," Rachel said. "It's possible it was just a random mugging, that they were just targets of opportunity, but thugs generally don't go after people who might be able to defend themselves. A soldier in uniform might not be carrying a gun, yet...."

She frowned. "There have been insurgencies, in the past, where the bad guys have targeted soldiers and their families in a bid to destroy morale. Sometimes, it worked; sometimes, it pushed the government into launching more and more repressive programs that often destroyed the planet they were trying to save. I think the rebels are targeting isolated soldiers and you could be targeted, too."

Richard scowled. He hadn't considered the possibility. But Rachel was right.

"I'll take care of myself," he said. He briefly considered inviting her to join him for a drink, then dismissed the thought a second later. He didn't want her—or anyone—knowing he was visiting his father. "And thank you."

CHAPTER TWENTY-SEVEN

KINGSTOWN TRAINING BASE, NEW DONCASTER

ROLAND WAS BORED.

The government had made it clear he was not to go to the front lines. Not without permission. And yet, he wasn't particularly useful in the training base. Wimer and his comrades knew their stuff and there was very little he could do, apart from helping to demonstrate a handful of basic skills, to make their lives easier. Wimer had been characteristically blunt when he'd told Roland to find something else to do and let them get on with it. Roland had been offended, at first, but he knew Wimer was right. He wasn't a drill instructor and all he could really do, if he tried, was get in the way.

He paced his office, feeling trapped. There was relatively little bureaucracy in the new army and he had no intention of creating more, even if it gave him something to do. He'd already inspected the armoured cars, tanks and aircraft coming off the production lines, then directed crews to start preparing to take them into combat. There was little else to do, beyond visiting Government House or consulting with General Falk and he refused to do either. It was something of a surprise, a week after he'd waved goodbye to Richard, when Sandra walked into his office.

"You didn't call me," Sandra said. "Should I be upset?"

Roland stared at her. The guards shouldn't have allowed her through the gates, let alone into the HQ itself. They should have asked her to wait and called him...he wondered, suddenly, if they'd even thought to *search* her before allowing her into the building. Sandra didn't look particularly dangerous, not compared to any of the guards, but Roland knew that was meaningless. Belinda hadn't looked particularly dangerous either and he'd watched her tear through grown men as though they were made of paper. For all he knew, she could have a small pistol concealed in her purse.

"I've been very busy," he said, making a mental note to lecture the guards later. They could have blamed everything on him, if she'd threatened to have them dishonourably discharged for denying her entry. He would have happily taken the blame. "What can I do for you?"

"Father informs me you're not leaving Kingstown for a few weeks," Sandra said. "Would you like to come on a cruise with me?"

Roland blinked. "A cruise?"

"I have a boat," Sandra said. "I was planning to sail to the island, perhaps sail around several other islands before heading home. I thought you might like to come with me. Dad's already given his permission."

"I have work to do here," Roland said. He was torn between the desire to go with her, to do something—anything—other than sitting in his office feeling sorry for himself, and the grim awareness it wouldn't amuse his superiors. "There is a war on, you know."

Sandra gave him a sweet smile. "And you think being here will make a difference?"

"Probably not," Roland conceded. There was next to nothing he could *do* on Kingstown. "I'll have to stay in touch with my subordinates, but...."

He stood, brushing down his uniform. It was something to do. A cruise with a pretty girl was not to be sniffed at...and besides, it would give him time to get a feel for the islands without people shooting at him. Wimer would alert him if something went wrong. And Richard, if his deployment came under heavy fire. Roland was rather surprised the force hadn't been attacked. The rebels were either much weaker than anyone thought, or they were planning something. General Falk and Lord Ludlow insisted it was the former. Roland feared it was the latter.

"I'll meet you outside," he said. "I just have to speak to my subordinates."

Rachel was not amused, when he told her his plans. "With all due respect, sir, are you out of your mind?"

Roland felt a twinge of guilt. He repressed it, firmly, as he changed into civilian clothes and shoved a handful of shirts, trousers and underwear into a knapsack. "Is there anything, anything at all, that demands my presence here?"

"That isn't the issue." Rachel sounded as if she wanted to pick him up and shake him. "You are going on a boat, alone, with no one to watch your back or cover you if you run into trouble. You will be in deep shit if you do. And even if you don't, what'll happen if something goes wrong elsewhere? You'll look like you abandoned your post in the middle of a war!"

"I'll take a communicator with me," Roland said. He straightened, brushing down his shirt and trousers. "And you'll be here. You can contact me if something happens that demands my immediate attention."

Rachel looked as if she wanted to say something cutting, but bit down on the impulse before it was too late. Roland didn't blame her, although it was unlikely he could do anything to salvage the situation if something went badly. Richard and the other forward-deployed commanders knew what to do, if the shit hit the fan. Roland could stay on the base and, as far as they were concerned, he might as well be on the other side of the star system. By the time he did something—anything—it might be too late. Any reasonable court-martial board would agree.

And they tend not to be reasonable, Roland reminded himself. Boards of Inquiry were often more interested in looking for scapegoats, rather than sorting out what happened and making sure it didn't happen again. Or so he'd been told. *But if I stay here, I'll go mad.*

"I'm going," he said. "You hold the fort here."

Rachel shook her head. "I'm coming with you, if I can't talk you out of it."

"No, you're staying here," Roland said. He liked Rachel, but he didn't want her with him *all* the time. It felt far too much like the cloying presence of his minders back in the Summer Palace. "When I get back, you can go on leave yourself."

"I urge you to reconsider," Rachel said. "It isn't a safe world out there."

Roland felt his temper threaten to snap. "I am going," he said. "And you are going to stay here."

He turned and headed out of the room, leaving her alone. He had no qualms about bringing her to a political meeting, or yet another planning session that turned into unsubtle suggestions he should put lads of good family on his staff, but neither he nor Sandra needed a chaperone. They were going on a pleasure cruise, not *working*. He doubted her invitation was entirely selfless—she'd clearly gone to some trouble to convince her father to authorise it, which suggested her father felt it was in his interests too—but Roland didn't care. It was something to do.

Sandra was already in her car when he stepped into the bright sunlight. He opened the door and clambered inside. "Didn't the guards ask you any questions?"

"I just told them who I was and who I was going to see." Sandra smiled, brightly. "And they let me through without a fight."

Roland groaned, inwardly, as she drove through the gates and onto the main road. They'd cleared more trees, creating space for more barracks and training grounds, but…it was useless, perhaps worse than useless, if the guards didn't do their bloody jobs. Sandra could have been a terrorist in disguise, relying on her smile and low-cut blouse to get through the checkpoint without being searched; hell, someone could have stuck a bomb under her car, turning her into an unwitting suicide bomber. The rebels hadn't adopted such techniques, not yet, but it was just a matter of time. Roland had read Captain Allen's assessment of just how easily the rebels could produce improvised explosives, given time and knowledge. It had made grim reading. The sniffers deployed around the base weren't perfect. They could be fooled.

Sandra kept up a steady stream of chatter as they kept going, circumventing First Landing and heading south to Kingsport. There were more checkpoints on the motorway, but the majority of the traffic seemed to be waved through without a search. Roland grimaced in disgust. He understood the importance of transporting food into the city—First Landing would start to starve very quickly, if the city was cut off from the countryside—but there were limits. The trucks carrying food into the city could also carry rebels and their supplies. He wouldn't be surprised to discover there were hundreds of fighters and their weapons already within the city.

He couldn't relax as they headed into Kingsport, driving through the richer parts of the city before heading into the port itself. Kingsport looked darker than First Landing, he noted, although he couldn't have put the feeling into words. Too many jobless people on the streets, perhaps; too many policemen marching up and down, eyes betraying a certain nervousness as they tried to keep the peace. Roland had been told that spaceports were always rough and ready places and it seemed that was also true of water ports. The marina, crammed with fancy boats that practically shone under the sunlight, was barely guarded. Roland was surprised the expensive craft hadn't been stolen a long time ago.

"Welcome to *Penelope*," Sandra said, as they parked outside a large boat. "What do you think?"

Roland clambered out of the car and studied the boat. She was larger than he'd expected, easily big enough to carry an entire company of Marines. There were three decks—perhaps four—lined with windows that were designed to prevent people from looking into the interior and dying of envy. Sandra produced a remote controller from her pocket and keyed a switch. The hatch opened, a gangplank extending down to the dock. There didn't seem to be anyone inside.

"I can operate her alone," Sandra said, when he asked. "I don't *need* a crew."

"Alone?" Roland was genuinely impressed. His experience with small boats—and shuttles and starships—was very limited, but he knew enough to think he didn't want to operate them alone. "You don't even have a cook?"

"No." Sandra led the way up the gangplank, leaving the car behind. "There's just me."

Roland followed, shaking his head in disbelief. He was used to a degree of luxury most people flatly refused to believe existed, a world where he could have practically anything he wanted for the asking, and yet the yacht impressed him. The level of automation was astonishing. *Penelope* had to be an import, something that would have probably added a few extra zeros to the price tag. Sandra's family was rich, and her father the Prime Minister, but the boat wouldn't be cheap even for her. And yet, she showed no hint of guilt as she retracted the gangplank and closed the hatch. She might not even realise just how lucky she was to own a boat worth millions of credits.

And why should she? Roland scowled at the thought. *You never realised how lucky you were.*

He followed her up the ladder and onto the bridge. Sandra pressed her hand against a scanner, bringing the control network online, then powered up the engines. Roland studied the consoles as they blinked to life, silently assessing what the boat could do. She might not be able to cope with a tempest, if she sailed right into a storm, but she could handle most other problems. Her automatics were designed to help her avoid weather conditions that might pose a threat to life and limb. The designers hadn't skimped on anything. He couldn't help being a little impressed.

"I like taking her out myself," Sandra said, as she steered the boat away from the jetty. It was hard to be sure—the automatics were an order of magnitude more capable than anything Roland had seen in the military—but she seemed to know what she was doing. "We'll put the autopilot on when we hit the deep blue sea."

Roland nodded, watching the boats heading in and out of the dock. Kingsport was supposed to be the busiest harbour on the planet and, looking at the traffic, he could believe it. Freighters and tankers jostled for space with fishing boats and clipper ships, the latter surprisingly primitive and yet easy to repair. He wondered, morbidly, how many of the crewmen were rebels. He'd be surprised if most of them weren't at least a little sympathetic to the rebel forces. They had the freedom of the seas, but government regulations were an ever-growing nightmare.

Sandra grinned at him. "What do you think?"

"I think you have a beautiful home," Roland said. It was true. Kingstown looked pretty in the bright sunlight. He couldn't make out more than a handful of human constructions on the shoreline. "I could get to like it."

"Really?" Sandra sounded innocent, but there was a hint of mirth in her voice. "You're planning to stay?"

Roland shrugged. "The corps will send me where it wishes," he said. He would be astonished if the corps wanted him to stay on New Doncaster for the rest of his life. "I might be reassigned tomorrow or next week or next month or...."

"Would you stay, if you could?" Sandra turned her eyes back to the sea. "Or would you be happy to leave?"

"I don't know," Roland said. New Doncaster had potential—there was no doubt of *that*—but the planet also had too many problems. And they had to be solved. The army could fight and win battles, but if the government failed to follow up with a political solution...he shook his head. "It depends on how things go."

Sandra nodded. "You would be welcome, if you wanted to stay."

And you might change your mind very quickly, Roland thought, silently. *If I wind up stuck here, I'm going to force the planet to reform whether you like it or not.*

He kept the thought to himself as the boat picked up speed, heading into deeper waters. The waves were a beautiful blue, schools of fish clearly visible just under the waves. They showed no fear of humanity, even though it would have been easy to put down a net and catch hundreds of fish in a single sweep. Roland reminded himself, as he saw a pod of dolphins swimming past the boat, that not everything on New Doncaster was safe to eat. The planet's native wildlife seemed to co-exist with the immigrants from

Earth. It was possible the fish weren't scared because they knew humans wouldn't catch and eat them.

Sandra grinned as she keyed the autopilot, then turned to him. "The boat can operate itself now, really."

Roland gave the console a dubious look. "And what if it encounters something it can't handle?"

"I tested it very carefully," Sandra assured him. She winked. "Right now, we're off the major shipping lanes and in deep waters. The sonar will ping an alarm if it picks up a rock that was missed, when they charted the waters; the radar will keep watch for other boats and sound the alert if they come too close. The autopilot is a very good one. It's programmed to be safe, rather than sorry,"

"I'll take your word for it," Roland said. Starships maintained a constant watch, even in phase space, but perhaps it was different for civilian craft. "And you're right, it is relaxing."

Sandra smiled, then took his hand and led him onto the deck. The air was cooler, away from the land, although nowhere near cool enough to make him shiver. Roland took a seat on the prow and stared into the distance. There were a handful of small islands, barely worth noticing, within visual range, but the remainder of the horizon was empty. He remembered the map and felt a sudden flicker of envy. Kids—and adults—could happily spend the rest of their lives exploring the world, sailing from island to island...never stopping in one place for more than a day or two. Sandra must have been tempted to board her boat and simply sail away, leaving her troubles and cares behind. Roland knew he'd have felt the same way too.

Except you never tried to leave the palace, his thoughts reminded him. *It wasn't until you met Belinda that you thought there might be a world beyond the walls.*

He leaned against her, the tension slowly seeping out of his body. Sandra was right. He did need the break. He felt another twinge of guilt at leaving his comrades to handle their duties while he took a cruise, but...what good would it have done for him to stay there? He promised himself he'd make sure Rachel got a few days leave of her own, when he returned. It wasn't as though he *needed* an assistant. He barely had enough paperwork to keep him busy for more than an hour a day.

Sandra lifted her lips to his. They kissed, slowly and lingeringly. Roland pulled her to him as the kisses deepened, his heart starting to race. His fingers fumbled with her shirt, pulling it free. Her hand pressed against his back, slipping into his trousers as he pulled her shorts down before pushing her gently to the deck. She smiled, brightly, as his hand stroked her breasts. Roland felt a surge of passion. It was suddenly very hard to get his clothes off without tearing something.

He wondered, just for a moment, if he was making a mistake. Sandra was more than just a pretty face. But his body was reminding him that it had been a *long* time since he'd lain with anyone…he put the thought out of his mind as he slid into her, as he felt her draw him deeper and deeper. She wanted him and that was all that mattered.

And I'll worry about the rest later, he told himself. *Right now, I just want her.*

CHAPTER TWENTY-EIGHT

PENELOPE, NEW DONCASTER

THE CRUISE, ROLAND DECIDED, felt like a dream he wanted never to end.

He was no stranger to mindless hedonism. He'd lost his virginity very early on, to a maid—he realised now—who simply could *not* say no, and had slept with so many women since then that he'd lost count. He cringed, in guilt and shame, when he reflected on just how far he'd gone as a young man. Some of his partners had wanted to use him, as surely as he'd wanted to use them; some had...not been entirely consensual. He didn't want to think about it, not really, but he might have crossed the line. No, the line hadn't existed. Not for him. It hadn't been until Belinda had made it clear there *were* limits that he'd come to see there'd been something wrong with him. And then the planet had collapsed and it had been too late to make amends for his behaviour. His partners, willing or not, were dead. He'd dedicated himself to the corps....

...And yet, the cruise felt almost like a holiday.

They sailed from island to island, sometimes dropping anchors in bright blue lagoons, sometimes swimming ashore to make love on sandy beaches. Sandra flatly refused to talk politics, kissing him whenever he tried; Roland objected, at first, then decided it was something best left for another time. He kept checking his wristcom, half-expecting an emergency message summoning him back to the camp, but there was nothing. The local news broadcasts were bland and boring, even when they talked about his victory. It was hard to believe anyone could outdo the Grand Senate when it came to sheer bare-faced manipulation of the news, but the landowners managed. Their news bulletins claimed the rebels had been brutally slaughtered, cut down in their thousands as they fled in terror. Roland hoped no one believed the nonsensical claims. The last thing he needed was for his men to go into battle overconfident, expecting a guaranteed victory. That was practically *asking* for a crushing defeat.

He felt himself smile as he lay on the mattress, studying Sandra as she slept. She was stunning, blonde hair framing a heart-shaped face and spilling down amongst perfectly toned shoulders. She was fit and healthy, even though she lacked the muscles of the average Marine. It was easy to look at her and feel his breath being snatched away, all the more so because he knew she was *real*. Some of his old partners had had cosmetic surgery every month, changing everything from hair colour to breast size in tune with the dictates of fashion. Sandra wasn't that vain. She'd spent her days walking and riding, when she wasn't learning how to be a good landowner wife. Roland wondered, suddenly, if Sandra had her own motives for getting close to him. She might find the idea of marrying another landowner, and becoming his helpmeet, distinctly unpleasant. Who knew? She might find the idea of marrying a Marine officer far superior....

His heart stopped beating, just for a second. Something had happened. No, something had *changed*. Roland knew it, even though he couldn't have put it into words. There'd been something, right on the edge of his awareness...a sound so low that even his enhanced ears could barely pick it up. He stayed very still, listening with instincts that had been honed by endless training exercises. The boat was anchored near an island...an empty island? Roland had thought so—he'd certainly seen no hint that anyone visited the island, certainly not regularly enough to leave signs of their presence—but it wasn't as if the shipping lanes were completely empty. Someone could have caught up with them...ice ran through his veins. He was used to thinking of himself as the biggest target around, yet one protected by anonymity. It had, quite simply, never occurred to him that *Sandra* could be the target.

The boat quivered, just slightly. They were not alone. Roland kicked himself, mentally, for being so fucking careless. They were naked, his wristcom and pistol where he'd left them...he stood, trying to think of a plan. If he woke Sandra, she might cry out; if he tried to move her while she slept, she might wake...he cursed under his breath as he forced himself to stand, as silently as possible. There was no easy way out, not unless he pushed the window right open and dived into the waters below. It might work, but they couldn't hide in the darkness...the intruders could use the boat's floodlights to pick them out, if they didn't have floodlights of their own. And then...he heard a brief conversation, too low for normal ears to hear even in the silence. There were at least three people on the boat, perhaps more. He inched back to the window. Perhaps he could scramble up the side and get to the radio—or his wristcom—before it was too late.

There was a crash as the door opened, violently. Roland barely had a second to register the orb flying into the room before it detonated, pulsing out a brilliant white light. He gasped, his body collapsing under its own weight as the nerve jangler did its work and hit the floor hard enough to hurt. Sandra screamed, her body convulsing as she was yanked from sleep. Roland wanted to go to her, but he couldn't move. He'd been jangled before, as part of his training. He doubted she'd ever experienced anything like it. She might not have the slightest idea what was going on.

He struggled to move, but he could barely twitch. His vision had blurred, his ears ringing loudly. Not a modern jangler, part of his mind noted. The rest of him was too busy trying to galvanise his body into working again, before it was too late. Pins and needles ran up and down his body, as he heard footsteps walking towards him. He cursed his own nakedness as strong arms gripped his wrists, pulling them behind his back and securing them in place with a plastic tie. If he'd been wearing something that covered most of his body, the effect wouldn't have been so bad.

"Well," a voice said. "I guess we don't have to search them."

"I'd like to search her," another voice said. "She might be hiding something in her crack."

Roland tried not to wince. He couldn't see very clearly, not from his position, but Sandra was probably tied and helpless too. His ears were still sore, yet...the accent sounded very much like someone from the lower reaches of society. A debtor, if not an indent; someone with a grudge against the landowners and a determination to extract revenge, whatever the cost. And Sandra was at his mercy. He could rape her, then sell whatever was left back to her father....

"A bitch like that, I wouldn't be surprised," the first voice said. "She wouldn't open her legs for anyone unless he had a million or two in the bank. And when she gets his money...."

"That will do, you two," a third voice said. It was more composed. "Go search the boat from top to bottom, then take control of the autopilot. We'll meet the rest of the gang at Point Blank."

"But I'm sure she needs to be searched," the second voice said. "She could have an entire arsenal up her twat...."

"Do as I tell you," the third voice ordered. "We don't have much time."

More than you think, Roland said. He'd made a habit of checking in, but...it would be hours, at best, before someone realised they were in trouble. He didn't *think* the boat carried an automatic beacon. Even if it did... they hadn't filed a travel plan. The local traffic control wouldn't notice anything was wrong until it was far too late. *This isn't going to end well.*

He lay still, trying not to react as he was pulled back into the centre of the room. The boss—he certainly appeared to be in charge—was wearing a black mask and an outfit that covered him from head to toe, concealing his features. Roland heard Sandra groan in pain as she started to regain control of her body; he kept quiet, hoping to convince the intruders that he was still helpless. It wasn't too far from the truth. His body was recovering rapidly, but—even at his peak—he wasn't strong enough to snap the tie and break his bonds. Belinda had done it, he recalled, yet...she'd been enhanced. He knew he wasn't anything like that strong.

Think, he told himself. He knew what would happen if he allowed himself to be moved to a rebel base. Captain Allen—and Richard—would do everything in their power to find him, but they didn't have the manpower to search *all* the possible hiding places. The planet's habitable zone might be small, compared to the immensity of the entire world, yet it was still huge by human standards. *There has to be a way out of here.*

The boat quivered, again, as the engines came online. Roland heard banging and crashing in the distance, followed by a splash. The boss cursed and hurried out of the room. Roland gritted his teeth and rolled over, staggering to his feet. He'd done the dreaded Escape and Evasion course, as well as the far worse Conduct after Capture course, but this promised to be worse. He could tell them who he was and they'd laugh in his face. He supposed in their place, he wouldn't have believed it either.

His legs hurt as he forced open a drawer and pressed the tie against a steak knife, sawing desperately at the plastic. He cursed as he cut himself, but kept going. He couldn't think of any other way to break free, not in time. He might be able to use his teeth to free Sandra, but...he allowed himself a moment of relief as the tie broke, freeing his hands. He rubbed away the blood—he'd worry about the wound later, if he survived the next few hours—and hurried back to Sandra. It was a great deal easier to free her, now he could see what he was doing.

"Keep your head down," he hissed. Someone was shouting in the distance. He couldn't make out the words. "If they kept heading away from the island, get into the water and swim to the shore."

Sandra nodded, wordlessly. Roland resisted the urge to give her a kiss as he hurried to the half-open window and clambered onto the side of the boat. It was picking up speed, dark water churning below the hull as the hijackers pointed them towards the wide ocean. Roland gritted his teeth as he forced himself to scramble up the side, all too aware he was dripping blood into the water below. New Doncaster had a sizable population of sharks, as well as dolphins and whales. They'd make life difficult if Roland and Sandra had to swim for their lives.

And even if we get onto the island, we might not be safe, he thought. *How the hell did they even find us?*

He put the thought aside as he reached the top and peered into the bridge. A man—wearing the same black outfit as the others—was standing by the wheel, steering with practiced ease. Roland braced himself, then leapt into the bridge and lunged straight at the man. His victim spun around, his eyes going wide an instant before Roland slammed a punch into his jaw. He stumbled back, too dazed to keep Roland from kicking him in the groin. His body fell, his head banging against the wheel before hitting the deck. Roland yanked the mask off and frowned. The man was a complete stranger. It had been stupid of him to feel as though he should *know* the bastard.

Maybe not that stupid, he thought, as he keyed the console and sent an emergency signal to the Marines. The local SAR teams were a mixed bag, from what he'd been told, but Captain Allen would have his QRF team on the way within seconds of the signal. *If someone on the base, or in the PM's office, ratted us out, they might have accompanied the kidnappers to be sure the job was done properly.*

He found his pistol, strapped the wristcom on his wrist and started to make his way down into the hull. Four kidnappers, one stunned or dead. That left three. They'd known what they were doing, he reflected. They'd come prepared, with zip-cuffs as well as jangle grenades and outfits that would leave nothing behind for investigators to find. They had probably planned to sink the boat, he thought, after transferring their prisoners into another vessel. The autopilot could carry her into uncharted waters, perhaps into the uninhabitable zone. No one would ever find a trace of her, once she was gone.

Three bastards to find, he thought. He kept moving, staying as quiet as possible as he slipped down the deck. *Find, then capture or kill.*

A shape moved ahead of him. He fired, instinctively. A black-clad figure hit the deck. The boss, Roland thought. He was as anonymous as his subordinates, but it wasn't so easy to hide his build. He pulled back the mask—another stranger—then removed a spare jangle grenade from his belt. It might come in handy. And yet....

He saw a body lying on the deck, resting at the bottom of the stairs. Roland frowned, inching forward in confusion. The man was dead, his neck snapped...Roland looked up, unsure what had happened. The stairs were pretty steep—they were really a fixed ladder, rather than a proper staircase—and it was possible the man had slipped and fallen, but...it didn't seem quite right. Roland was no WarCAT expert, no forensic specialist capable of telling how a man had died, yet...surely there should be more blood. It looked more like someone had come up behind the dead man and snapped his neck. Effortlessly.

Roland tensed. Three dead men...one left. Had the boss killed his own man? It wasn't impossible—the rape threats would have damaged their hostage, if they'd been allowed to put them into practice—but unlikely. Roland wouldn't have stayed with a boss who killed his own subordinates, even if they deserved it. Even Grand Senators didn't have their subordinates killed on a whim. It made no sense.

He heard someone above him and spun around, darting out of sight an instant before the bullet cracked through the air. The fourth man was above him...Roland glanced at the ladder, silently calculating his chances of getting up before he could be shot, then decided it was impractical. He opened his voice, intending to offer to accept surrender, but he heard another gunshot before he could say a word. It made no sense. Was the idiot hoping to ricochet a bullet into him? Or shoot through the deck? Or....

Roland scrambled up the ladder, moving as fast as he could. The final kidnapper was standing on the deck, gun pointed into the shadows. Roland hadn't *heard* the Marines arrive, but it was possible they'd sneaked up on the boat. And yet, how could even *they* have deployed so fast? It was simply impossible.

The kidnapper spun around, gun raised. Roland shot him through the head. He crumpled and hit the deck. Roland breathed a sigh of relief, even though he was still puzzled. Had someone else come to their aid? Or... he glanced up as he heard a Raptor flying towards them, clearly visible in the moonlight. The Marines were already rappelling down lines, ready to drop to the boat. He lowered the pistol, then placed it on the deck. The last thing he needed, after everything else, was to be accidentally shot by his own side.

"Sir," the lead Marine said. "Please keep your hands in sight."

"There's a young woman below decks," Roland said, quickly. He wasn't too put out by the automatic suspicion. It was a great deal safer, when launching hostage rescue missions, to treat everyone within the building as a suspected terrorist until the mission was over and the innocent sorted from the guilty. "She's not an enemy combatant."

The Marines nodded, but took nothing for granted. Roland watched as they swarmed the boat, finding Sandra and escorting her topside before searching the entire ship from top to bottom and dragging the bodies out for later recovery. The kidnapper he'd knocked out was alive, for better or worse. Roland didn't envy the man. It would be hard to convince the locals not to torture him, if he refused to talk. He didn't really want to try.

"The boat is secure," the leader reported. There was something in his voice Roland didn't like, although he wasn't sure what. A hint of suspicion, perhaps a belief that Roland and Sandra had planned their own attempted kidnapping. Or, more charitably, that they'd done something to draw the enemy to them. "We have orders to take you back to the spaceport."

"Let us get some clothes on first," Roland said. "And then we can start the investigation."

His mind raced. Orders? Orders from whom? Captain Allen? Or whoever was on command duty at the spaceport? It made sense. He had to admit there was *something* odd about the whole affair. There shouldn't have been *anyone* capable of tipping off the kidnappers. There hadn't been anyone who knew where they were going. Unless...had his own check-in messages been used to track him?

He frowned. No matter how he looked at it, there was something about the whole affair that simply didn't add up. And he needed to know why before it bit him again.

CHAPTER TWENTY-NINE

FIRST LANDING, NEW DONCASTER

"MY DAUGHTER WAS ALMOST KIDNAPPED," the PM said. The anger in his voice was shocking in its intensity. "I want to know what happened."

Roland stood in front of him, his mind racing. There had been no time to go back to the camp to grab a change of clothes, let alone organise a force to search the nearby islands for a rebel base. Assuming, of course, there *was* a rebel base somewhere in the area. A smart bunch of rebels would make damn sure *not* to carry out a kidnapping—attempted kidnapping—anywhere near their base. They'd certainly *planned* to take the ship into deep waters, transfer Roland and Sandra to another ship and leave all evidence buried deep below the waves. If they'd known who they were kidnapping, they'd certainly have planned....

"I asked you a question, Captain," the PM said, breaking into Roland's thoughts. "What happened?"

"Someone in your office must have leaked our itinerary," Roland said. It wasn't precisely accurate—Sandra and he hadn't really *had* an itinerary—but close enough. The rebels must have had a rough idea of their course, one gleaned from Sandra making brief contact with Kingstown every day. "And then they just lay in wait until we came into view."

The PM looked unimpressed. Roland winced, inwardly. Captain Allen had had a few sharp things to say about his decision to leave the camp in the middle of a war, even though there'd been nothing for him to do, but the PM was a different matter. He might have pointed his daughter at Roland, he might have laid the groundwork—inadvertently—for the kidnapping, yet…Roland wouldn't really blame the PM if he wanted Roland *gone*. The kidnap attempt might have been unsuccessful, but it had succeeded in one respect. It had made it much harder for Roland to work closely with the PM.

"And my daughter was nearly taken," the PM said. "Why didn't you take a bodyguard or two along?"

Because Sandra wanted us to be alone, Roland thought, grimly. He hadn't thought to question it. He'd spent so long in a goldfish bowl himself that he'd learnt to treasure what little privacy he'd been allowed to have. *And it didn't occur to either of us that we could be found and kidnapped.*

He kicked himself, mentally. It had been a mistake. He'd grown too used to thinking of Roland Windsor as just another Marine recruit, with no more importance than the thousands of others who passed through Boot Camp every year. There were few, if any, people on the planet who knew who he really was, but what did that matter? Roland Windsor, CO of the training program, was an important target in his own right. And Sandra too…daughter of the PM, probable bride to an important landowner later on…Roland shook his head. Sandra was an important target, too.

"I made the wrong call," he said. They'd gotten lucky. If the kidnappers had slit their throats at once, rather than try to take them into deep waters, they'd be dead. He wasn't *quite* sure what had happened on the boats, and the cynic in him wanted to look a gift horse in the mouth, but it didn't matter. They really *had* gotten lucky. "And I didn't realise the mistake until it was far too late."

"Quite." The PM scowled at him. "And you think the leak came from my office?"

"I believe so," Roland said. He wasn't fooled by the sudden shift in topic. The PM was still furious. And with good reason. "Sandra called back, every day. Her messages gave your people a rough idea of her location. That information was passed to the rebels and they mounted an attack. You have to find the enemy spy and get rid of him."

The PM's eyes narrowed. Roland half-expected him to insist, again, that every last member of his staff was above suspicion. It wasn't true and the PM had to know it. There were so *many* people on his staff that it would only take one or two enemy spies to collect the information and pass it on to their masters. Roland had studied incidents within the imperial bureaucracy, incidents that had bedevilled the corps before Earthfall. It wasn't *always* a high-ranking person in need of money or power. Sometimes, a lowly clerk in a tiny cubicle could do more damage than an admiral or general with an axe to grind. And why not? They had to save for their retirements too.

And it might not even be someone on the PM's staff, he thought. *A lone man in the coast guard or the ATC—even the militia—could have figured out our location and broadcast it to the bad guys.*

"My staff will look into the issue," the PM said, finally. "We'll find the person and snatch him."

"If you do, don't arrest him at once," Roland said. "We might be able to make use of him."

"Maybe." The PM met his eyes. "Did you get anything from the prisoner?"

"Not as yet," Roland said. "Captain Allen's men are interrogating him now."

The PM looked pleased. Roland kept his thoughts to himself. The prisoner *might* know something, but Roland would bet his heritage the bastard knew absolutely nothing of real value. The rebels hadn't survived so long without being very careful. They'd have ensured the kidnapping team knew as little as possible, just in case they were taken alive. The interrogation would be far from gentle—the kidnappers had crossed the line—but the prisoner couldn't tell what he didn't know. It might turn into an exercise in pointlessness.

"We'll see," the PM said. "For the moment, I believe matters are heating up on Baraka. I think it would be better if you went there, for a while. The troops there need you to lead them to victory."

Roland kept his face impassive, somehow. The PM wasn't *precisely* giving an order, but only a fool would consider it something else. He wondered, grimly, just what had happened to Sandra. The PM's staff and bodyguards had whisked her away, the moment they landed at the spaceport. He wasn't sure how he should feel about it. The coldly cynical part of his mind figured Sandra would be back, once her father got over the shock; the more empathetic part of him wondered if Sandra wouldn't ever want to see him again, not because of his actions but because of what had happened the last time they'd been alone. Sandra was young and unformed, certainly untrained. She might want to please her father—and prove her value to the family—but she'd had one hell of a shock.

"I intended to make an inspection tour when I returned anyway," Roland said. It wasn't entirely true, but it would suffice. Richard's last message had confirmed that his troops were starting to feel the heat. The rebels were testing them, sniping from a distance to feel out their reactions in preparation for a major offensive. "Rachel and I will travel there shortly."

"Very good." The PM stood, ending the discussion. "I'll see you when you return."

Roland saluted, then walked outside. Rachel was waiting, sitting on a chair and looking as frumpy as ever. Roland nodded to her as she stood, then led the way down to the official car. They'd go back to the base, get some sleep and then catch a flight to Baraka. It would hopefully give the PM a chance to calm down, before they met again.

"So," Rachel said, once they were on the road. "How badly did he spank you?"

"He wasn't pleased." Roland remembered Belinda suddenly and flinched. She'd told him his life was important, to others if not to himself. "I fucked up."

"Yes. You did." Rachel gave him a sharp look. "Captain Allen should have told you this already, but just in case…going out alone was fucking stupid. You should have taken me or a couple of bodyguards or… fuck, sir, even not checking in every day would have been smarter than what you did."

Roland frowned. *That* was oddly out of character for Rachel. "I wanted to.…"

"It doesn't matter what you wanted, sir, when you screw up so badly," Rachel said. "What'll happen if the PM asks the corps to send a replacement, then reassign you somewhere less dangerous? Like an asteroid mining camp in the middle of nowhere, light years from anywhere *important*?"

"I know I screwed up." Roland felt a hot flash of exasperation. It had been his mistake and he owned it, but…he was already sick of people pointing it out, time and time again. The PM was Sandra's father and Captain Allen was his superior…Rachel was his aide, not his boss. She wasn't Belinda. He'd have listened to *Belinda* even if she'd gone on and on and on about it. "But we survived. We escaped. We even took a prisoner."

"Through sheer dumb luck," Rachel said. "Don't count on it happening again."

Roland nodded, curtly, then turned his attention to his terminal as it linked into the Marine communications network. A single report rested in his inbox, waiting for him. The prisoner had been interrogated, but he'd known little of interest. He'd been part of a cell that had been kept isolated, probably because the rebel leadership regarded them as expendable. Roland frowned as he realised why. The cell wasn't composed of debtors or former indents, but townies.

I'll have to discuss it with Richard, he thought, as the car glided through the checkpoint and into the base. *But I think that bodes ill for the future.*

• • •

"The operation failed," Sidney said. "And that leaves us with a problem."

Sarah nodded, silently assessing all the ways in and out of the district.

She'd made a point of walking around, when she'd first arrived, until she knew the maze of streets and alleyways like the back of her hand. Get out of the room, hop down the fire escape, rip off the outer layer of clothes and vanish into the side streets. Or run down the red-light district, pick up a horny sailor and let him take her into the harbour barracks. The police might not look too closely if she was clearly a whore, particularly one who already had a client. They might just assume that a sailor could get them in real trouble.

And they'd probably be wrong, Sarah thought. A number of sailors were genuinely important, or had close ties to those who were, but they were a drop in the ocean. *But as long as they hesitated, it wouldn't matter.*

She calmed herself with an effort. They didn't know *precisely* what had happened—the government had managed to impose a near-complete information blackout—but what they'd heard suggested the operation had completely failed. The Marines had deployed a pair of aircraft in the right general direction...only two. They'd have made a much bigger effort, and dragged the coast guard and militia into the mess, if they knew their commander had been kidnapped. Sarah wanted to believe the Marines loathed their commanding officer, that they would do as little as possible to save the bastard's life, but she knew better. Even if they did, the daughter of the PM was *important*. They'd have pulled out all the stops to find her before it was too late. The entire island chain would have been flooded with troops. Every ship in the vicinity would have been stopped and searched. And then....

"They might have taken a prisoner or two," Sidney said. "We just don't know."

"No." Sarah frowned. "Send a runner to their contact. Tell him to go underground for a few weeks. He can take ship to a distant island and drop out completely."

Sidney looked surprised—she was effectively ordering the contact to abandon the rebels—but hurried to obey. Sarah sighed, inwardly. The cell had been kept carefully isolated. No one had been entirely sure if townies could be trusted. There had been a chance—small, but impossible to ignore—that they'd been spies, enemy agents trying to weave their way into the rebel structure so they could take it apart from the inside. Sarah had no doubt the enemy would have tried, if they thought they could get away with it. It was what she would have done.

Their leader only ever knew one of us, she told herself. *And yet, if they catch him before he can run, they can do a hell of a lot of damage.*

She cursed under her breath. She'd hoped the kidnapping would divert the enemy as she put the final pieces in place. She'd calculated she couldn't possibly lose. If the targets were kidnapped, the enemy would waste time and resources looking for them; if the targets were killed, the enemy would be disrupted, perhaps even disheartened. It pained her to realise she'd plotted the death of a young woman, someone not too different from herself, but Sandra was no innocent. She was very much an upholder of the system that had condemned Sarah and countless others to endless servitude, then discarded them when they were no longer useful. Her capture or death would have served a useful purpose. Sarah was sure the PM wouldn't surrender in exchange for his daughter's life—and if he tried, he'd be rapidly removed from office—but her death would have distracted him. Sarah told herself it would have been worthwhile, if the plan had succeeded.

It didn't, she told herself, sharply. *And we have to deal with it.*

She stared at the blank wall. The planned distraction had failed. There was a reasonable chance no one would realise that it had been, at least in part, a distraction, but…it wasn't going to distract anyone. The information blackout was worrying. She was sure the enemy knew there were spies within their ranks—it wasn't as if they'd done much of anything to guarantee loyalty—but if they were taking the threat more seriously now… she shook her head. It could become a major headache. Even tightening up internal security risked uncovering cells that had no direct links to the would-be kidnappers. There was no choice. They'd have to arrange another distraction and quickly.

Sidney returned, looking grim. "I sent the message."

"Good." Sarah rubbed her forehead. If the contact absented himself before the prisoners talked—assuming there were prisoners—the remainder of the cell structure should remain intact and uncovered. She briefly considered killing the contact, just to make absolutely sure he couldn't be made to talk, then discarded the thought before she could put it into words. It would have made logical sense, but hardly anyone would have seen it that way. "Is the ship ready to return to Baraka?"

"Yes," Sidney said. "She's due to leave tomorrow."

"Get another runner—a driver, this time," Sarah said. She'd have to go back to Kingsport herself soon. That might not be easy, if the enemy tightened everything up. Her papers would survive a brief inspection, but if they got suspicious and insisted on holding her while they checked them out…it didn't bear thinking about. "I'll have a message for him shortly."

"Got it." Sidney shot her a jaunty salute. "We could move now, couldn't we?"

Sarah shook her head. There were plans within plans and wheels within wheels and not all of them were ready to move. They had to get everything ready, to ensure they won the war in a single blow…or, if that failed, to make certain they were ready and able to *continue* the war if the plan went off the rails. She'd spent years laying the groundwork, drawing disparate groups together…all too aware that some of them regarded her as timid and others just wanted to hit back, lashing out in a manner that would unite the landowners and townies against the rebels. Sarah understood, better than she cared to admit. She wanted to hurt—to kill—the people who'd enslaved her. But she had to make damn sure her first stroke was effective enough to cripple, if not kill. They'd be committed the moment she blew the whistle. The enemy would be in no doubt of what they'd intended to do.

"We wait," she said. "We'll give the enemy another distraction, something to keep them busy while we put the final pieces in place. And then we'll strike."

She reached for a notepad and pen, then took a moment to compose a message. Paper didn't last long in the local environment, not outside air-conditioned rooms, but it had one great advantage over datanet messages. A hacker would have to actually take physical possession of the message, if he wanted to read it; he'd have problems *beginning* to decipher the message, even if he realised it *was* a coded message. Sarah's lips quirked as she penned a message conveying her undying love, a note that would be embarrassing to anyone who held it. It was quite possible the enemy would take it at face value, if they saw it. They'd certainly understand why someone might want to hide it.

And even if they think there's a hidden meaning, they won't be able to figure it out without help, she thought. *If they get that far, we're screwed anyway.*

"Get the message to the ship," she said. The sailing times weren't set in stone, thankfully, but they didn't want to risk an inspector asking awkward questions. A ship sitting in harbour any longer than it took to unload and reload was a ship that was losing money. Someone would ask why, sooner or later. *That* would be disastrous. "And then they can be on their way as planned."

"Got it," Sidney said.

CHAPTER THIRTY

BARAKA ISLAND, NEW DONCASTER

IT WAS NOT A GOOD SIGN, Richard reflected grimly, that the owner of the farming compound had only agreed to rent the small complex to the troops on the condition they made it absolutely clear they were giving him no choice. Richard had complied—he'd made a public show of giving the landlord money at gunpoint, then arranged for the man and his family to be housed in the city to the north—all too aware it meant the rebels were watching. His men had searched the compound from top to bottom, then shipped hundreds of sangars into the district to turn the cluster of farmhouses and barns into a makeshift fortress before setting up machine guns and mortars to give anyone who attacked a very bad time. Richard had ordered the men to clear fields of fire, too, but he was uncomfortably aware the local landowners had ensured they couldn't cut down too many of their crops. The enemy could get far too close before they came into view.

He scowled as he lifted his eyes towards the distant mountains, hidden under miles upon miles of foliage. Baraka was an odd island, a combination of an industrial powerhouse—they'd already started to churn out thousands of sangars as well as everything else the militia needed—and a series of plantations that covered the lowlands and pressed against the edge of the outback. Richard had been told the land grew increasingly unsuitable for cultivation, the further one went from the sea, although he wasn't sure that was true. The rebels certainly didn't have a problem feeding themselves. But then, they probably extorted food from the plantations. The smaller farmers, the ones who didn't spend half their lives on Kingstown, didn't have much choice but to give the rebels whatever they wanted. It wasn't worth their lives to resist.

Richard turned as he heard engines roaring along the road—more of a dirt track than a proper road—and smiled, despite himself, as the armoured cars came into view. The handful of visible locals didn't seem anything like so impressed. Richard had told his men to be careful not to go charging through the fields, particularly as some of the fields were swampy enough to drown an armoured car, but it wasn't easy to avoid damaging crops. He felt a twinge of sympathy for the locals. They were caught in the middle, between soldiers fighting for a government that was—at best—uncaring and rebels who wouldn't hesitate to kill anyone who showed even the slightest hint of collaboration. And the latter were making their presence felt. The sniping had started almost as soon as they'd arrived and refused to let up.

He signed, grimly, as the gates were opened long enough to allow the armoured cars to enter the complex and then closed again. The plan had urged employing local manpower to do everything from cooking and cleaning to scouting, but...he snorted in irritation. No locals had volunteered and, even if they had, he wouldn't have allowed them into the compound. They would have been spies or worse...it would be all too easy, he'd been cautioned, for an enemy agent to poison his men or spread disharmony or something, anything, that would make his job harder. And who knew what would happen then?

We might lose the war, he thought, as a man hurried up to him. *Or, at the very least, have to abandon this island and make our stand elsewhere.*

"Sir." Corporal Chang lacked in military polish, but he'd done well enough during basic training and the first engagement to earn a brevet promotion. "We completed our sweep, as planned. There were no contacts."

Richard nodded, keeping his face under tight control. The landscape was ideal for the rebels. They could slip through the plantations and wildlands beyond without being seen, popping up long enough to fire a handful of shots before vanishing into the countryside and heading to the next firing position. So far, no one had been killed, but everyone was jumpy and all too aware it was just a matter of time before that changed. He was surprised, really, that the enemy wasn't pushing even harder. They could have made life a great deal harder for him just by harassing his troops every time they drove out of the complex.

And they know what we're planning, he thought. *They have to realise they can't let us simply get on with it.*

He sighed. The overall plan had been discussed at so many levels, on Kingstown and Baraka and everywhere else, that he'd be surprised if the rebels *didn't* know. Hell, Richard would be surprised if the entire world and his wife didn't know. Roland had been right to keep *his* plan a secret. Someone would have talked and then the mission would have turned into a bloody disaster.

Get a network of interlocking fortresses in place to control the countryside, he reflected. The plan had probably seemed simple when General Falk and his staff had been putting it together, but in war the simplest things were often the hardest. *Force the rebels to fight us on our terms, when we have the advantage, or concede control of large swathes of the island to us. The rebels know what we're doing. They have to stop us or lose everything.*

He cleared his throat. "Did you speak to the locals?"

"Yes, sir," Chang said. "They were polite, but very distant. They kept their women inside."

Richard grimaced. The militia was known for harassing plantation women—and, although he hated to admit it, the regulars weren't much better. The debtor and indent women were powerless. No one was going to come to their rescue if they were attacked; no one was going to punish their rapists...his eyes hardened. Roland and his sergeants had made it clear there would be punishment, if anyone harassed the locals, but Richard feared it was too little too late. It would take a long time, perhaps too long, before the locals came to see his men as trustworthy. Who could blame them for thinking his men were just another bunch of thieves, rapists and reckless shooters?

"They'll warm up to us eventually," he said, although he wasn't sure it was true. "Tell your men to get a nap. They'll be going out again shortly."

Chang saluted, then hurried off. Richard turned back to the countryside. Baraka was a tropical paradise in so many ways and yet the people… landowners refused to consider even minor improvements, while workers did as little as possible even when they didn't run into the outback and join the rebels. There were so many little things that could be done to improve the island, to make things better for the discontented…but none of them would be done, simply because the people with the money and power saw no need. Who cared if the indentured workers were discontented? Their opinions didn't matter.

His wristcom bleeped. "Sir, we just had a message from Kingstown," the radio operator said. "Captain Roland is coming on an inspection tour."

"Good," Richard said. It was true. There were officers he'd rather stayed a long way from the front lines, or anywhere under Richard's command, but Roland wasn't one of them. He had to admit the younger man impressed and irritated him in equal measure. "We'll be ready for him."

...

Private Bryce Ambrose had thought, in all honesty, that he was used to deprivation. He'd grown up in the slums, all too aware that he'd inherited his father's debts as well as earned more of his own. His mother had worked herself to death for Bryce and his siblings and it simply hadn't been enough. Bryce had grown into an angry young man, who wanted revenge on the system that had crushed his parents and forced two of his sisters into prostitution. And yet….

He found it hard, as the four armoured cars drove through the fields, to grasp just how poor the locals truly were. The farms were huge and clearly prosperous, but the workers were in rags, grubbing in the dirt for roots and what little else they could find. The workers' barracks had been worse than the *army's* barracks, in such poor condition that he couldn't help thinking it was just a matter of time before they collapsed; the shacks and shanty towns were worse, somehow, than the slums of First Landing. He'd heard stories—yes, he'd heard stories—but the reality was worse.

Eyes—fearful, hostile eyes—followed them as they drove on. Bryce shivered as he saw young men, backs bowed by a lifetime in the fields, staring with cold, helpless fury. There were few women in evidence, most too young or too old to be interesting...he told himself, sharply, not to even *think* about it. He was on their side. He was a rebel...they didn't know it, of course. How could they? He shivered, again, as he saw a young girl work the fields. Her face was a mutilated mess. He knew, although he wasn't sure how, that she wouldn't last much longer. And yet, she could have been saved if she had proper medical treatment. Bryce wasn't a doctor, but he'd seen what army medics could do. It wasn't *right* that the girl, and countless others like her, were left to die in agony.

It wasn't right.

They barely spoke as they crossed a stone bridge over a fast-flowing river, moving from one plantation to the next. Bryce hoped some of his comrades were wondering, deep inside, if they were on the wrong side, although he didn't dare try to steer the conversation in that direction. The Marines had been quick to prove the government had kept its word by cancelling the debts of the dead soldiers. Bryce had asked a handful of pointed questions afterwards, in hopes of preventing his comrades from accepting their words uncritically, but it had been difficult to make headway. They wanted to believe the Marines. And who could blame them?

The road grew smoother and wider, revealing a large mansion at the heart of the plantation. It was small, compared to some of the buildings in First Landing, but so much larger and fancier than the worker barracks that there was just no comparison. A pair of women sat on a balcony, wearing fancy clothes as they peered down at the armoured cars. Bryce felt a surge of pure hatred, an urge to just lift his rifle and shoot them both before they could run. They were landowner brats, living in luxury while the indents worked the lands. Didn't they know how unfair that was? Didn't they know....?

He swallowed, hard, as they left the mansion behind. The road grew narrow again, the trees closing in. Bryce wasn't *that* experienced, not yet, but even *he* could tell it was the perfect place for an ambush. He kept his rifle at the ready, bracing himself to return fire. He might be a rebel, but none of the rebels on the island knew it. They'd kill him and never realise what they'd done. His contact back on Kingstown would probably decide it had been a terrible accident and leave it at that.

Sweat trickled down his back as the road narrowed even further. He knew eyes watched them, and he was sure their weapons were aimed at them...his eyes swept the undergrowth, calculating where the rebels might have concealed an IED. They'd given the militia a hard time with a number of roadside bombs. Why not do the same to the regulars? The rebels certainly had the expertise to hit them time and time again.

It was a surprise when the road widened again, revealing the base. It looked flimsy, but he'd helped assemble the defences. They were tough enough to stand off anything short of a major assault, with tanks and heavy guns. Or a bombing raid. He breathed a sigh of relief, then frowned as he heard a helicopter in the distance. It might not be good news. There just weren't enough helicopters on the planet, from what he'd heard. If one was here, it wasn't good news at all.

"We made it," Private Tully cheered, as they passed through the gates. "A successful mission!"

"We never saw the enemy," Bryce pointed out, more tartly than he would have liked. He wasn't sure that was true. The workers they'd seen could easily have been rebel fighters, just biding their time. "They probably saw us."

Tully slapped his back. "Yep. And they didn't come out to play. What does that tell you?"

That they have working brains, Bryce thought. *And that they're up to something.*

• • •

Roland's heart sank as the helicopter flew over the landscape and headed straight for the FOB. The land was beautiful, but so overgrown that he was starting to think there was little hope of clearing out the rebels long enough to impose the government's authority. Baraka looked small on the map, but—in reality—the island was large enough to support millions of people. Roland suspected the FOBs were islands themselves, islands in a sea of rebel activity. The plan might need to be revised.

The helicopter came to a hover over the landing pad. Roland unstrapped himself, stood and rappelled down the line to the ground. Rachel followed, landing neatly beside him. The helicopter turned and headed out, trying to get back to the airport before she ran out of fuel or encountered an enemy SAM team. The rebels hadn't made use of anti-aircraft weapons, according to the locals, but that was going to change. They knew how Roland had landed an entire strike force on their heads. They'd be doing everything in their power to obtain MANPADs and put them into service before Roland could build up his airborne forces and win the war.

Richard saluted, his face tired but happy. "Sir," he said. "Welcome to Fort Forward."

Roland returned the salute. "It's good to be here," he said. He'd read the reports, but he wanted to hear the facts from Richard directly. "How's it been?"

If Richard was taken aback by the informality, he didn't show it. "No direct enemy contact," he said, as he showed Roland and Rachel around the base. Roland was relieved Richard hadn't put on a welcoming ceremony. "They have sniped at us from a distance, sir, but otherwise they haven't shown themselves. I think they're waiting for us to get complacent."

"Or they might have realised that attacking the FOB is pointless," Roland said. "They may just go around it until we establish enough of them to start blocking the routes in and out of the outback."

"If we can," Richard said. "I had some pressure to start distributing my men in penny packets—a platoon or two, perhaps—across the countryside. The local landowners want a show of force, rather than *actual* force."

Roland grimaced. "Spreading our men thinly would be a good way to get them all killed," he said, curtly. "It would shorten the war."

"Yes." Richard frowned as he led the way into his makeshift office. "I told them my authority didn't go that far and that they needed to address their concerns to General Falk."

"Which isn't quite true," Roland said, as he sat on a stool. "But probably for the best,"

He accepted a cup of coffee and a ration bar. "I won't be here for more than a week," he said. "I have to accompany a patrol, to get a feel for the landscape, then move to the next FOB so I know what's happening there, too."

"You also need to check out the militia blockhouses," Richard warned. "And try to get them under your command, as a neutral outsider."

Roland made a face. He'd seen the militia during the exercises. A handful of units had been relatively good, or had skills that made up for their weaknesses, but the remainder had been decidedly amateurish. Maybe it was hypocritical—Rachel had tartly pointed out that going on a cruise, alone, had outdone any idiotic greenie lieutenant when it came to sheer fucking stupidity—yet it was true. The militia should probably be broken up, the men allowed to go back to their homes if they didn't want to be retrained. But he knew it would be politically impossible.

"I can try," he said. "But it might be better to keep them out of the way."

Richard snorted, then unfurled a map. "We are here," he said, tapping a crossroads. "I've been running patrols in circles around the base, partly to gain local awareness and partly to remind the rebels they can't ignore us. The longer we stay here, the weaker they look. I think it's just a matter of time before they come calling."

"Agreed," Roland said. "You think they'll come here?"

"I don't know," Richard said. "We have heavy defences. We're also very careful about what we let into the walls. They may see us as a target they have to destroy, to prove they're still the masters of the countryside, or they may see us as too strong to tackle directly. In that case, they'll go somewhere else. I don't know where, but...."

"We'll find out soon," Roland said. He felt a thrill, even though he knew he shouldn't. "And then we'll wish we hadn't."

CHAPTER THIRTY-ONE

BARAKA ISLAND, NEW DONCASTER

"MY LADY?"

Angeline Porter stood on the balcony, staring over the landscape. The plantation—her *father's* plantation—stretched as far as the eye could see, rows upon rows of crops worked by men and women who'd been lucky enough to get off Earth before Earthfall. They complained a lot, Lord Porter had said, and needed heavy discipline to ensure they paid their debts, but they were the lucky ones. Unlucky indents went straight to the mines. Angeline ran her hand through her blonde hair, trying not to shiver. The mines, from what she'd been told, were practically a death sentence.

And people only go there when they don't know their place, she thought. Her father had said so, time and time again. *They don't have the wisdom to realise what they were offered until it was too late.*

She turned. Sofia—her maid—was standing behind her, eyes modestly downcast. The maid was an indent herself, a girl who'd been exiled from Earth along with her parents and purchased—hired—by Angeline's father to keep her from going into the fields. She'd been with Angeline from birth, a maid and personal assistant and whatever else Angeline and her family required. She was grateful for her salvation. She'd told Angeline so, the sole time Angeline had asked. She barely remembered her life on the now-dead homeworld. And then Lord Porter had rebuked Angeline for asking.

"Yes?" Angeline didn't bother to keep the annoyance out of her voice. "What is it?"

"Your mother wishes me to inform you that your suitor is on his way," Sofia said, keeping her eyes lowered. "She wishes you to be presentable for his arrival."

Angeline stamped her foot. She was nineteen, old enough to marry and yet too young to have any real say in the matter. Gareth Royston was supposed to be a great catch for a young lady like herself, heir to a plantation on the other side of the island, but...he was local and therefore boring. Angeline wanted to travel, to visit Kingsport and be presented at the Annual Landing Ball before she even considered getting married. She doubted Gareth would take her anywhere further than a resort island, no matter how she pleaded or begged. He'd be expected to stay on the plantation, managing the family affairs, while she raised their children. She glared at Sofia, who showed no reaction. Angeline swallowed the harsh words that came to mind. She had shouted and screamed at the maid in the past, for carrying out the lady of the mansion's orders, but she was honest enough to admit—at least to herself—that she was only lashing out at Sofia because she didn't dare lash out at her mother. Her father would not be amused. And she really didn't want to make her father angry.

She forced herself to think as she returned to her bedroom, showered and allowed the maid to lay out her clothes. There had to be something she could do...perhaps she could rub raw or rotten fish on her teeth, to make her breath stink, or drop hints she'd been unchaste, or...or something, anything, that might discourage Gareth Royston from giving her so much as a peck on the cheek. She couldn't say no, but *he* could. Perhaps she could make the thought of marrying her so awful he'd defy her father—and his father—and marry someone else. Perhaps....

She was still trying to think of something, an hour later, when they descended the stairs into the lobby. The doors stood open, revealing that the skies were darkening rapidly. Gareth Royston was standing there, shaking hands with her father. He was handsome enough, she supposed, but she didn't know him. She'd never been alone with him. She never would, not until they were married. And then it would be too late.

"My Lady," Gareth Royston said. He bowed, politely. "Rumours of your beauty have travelled far and wide, but they scarcely do you justice."

Angeline nodded, trying not to cringe. It sounded so *fake*. Her suitor didn't *have* to woo her. He already had her father's approval and that was all that mattered....

The ground heaved. Angeline saw something flare brightly through the doors, an instant before the mansion shook violently. Something smashed in the distance...her father's hand dropped to the pistol on his belt, an instant before the inner doors burst open. A trio of manservants, wearing the family's livery, crashed into the lobby. Angeline barely had a second to register the pistols in their hands, the pistols no servant was permitted to carry on pain of death, before they opened fire. Her father, a hard man with a hard heart and harder hand, collapsed, blood pouring from his chest and staining his white shirt. Gareth fell a second later, his head exploding. Angeline nearly fainted in shock as brains splashed to the floor. She'd never seen violence, real violence, in her life. It just didn't happen.

Someone struck her in the back. She fell, hitting the floor hard enough to knock the wind from her. Strong hands grabbed her wrists, pulling them behind her. She realised, through a haze of pain, that it was *Sofia* who was holding her down. Angeline tried to struggle and discovered it was impossible. The maid, the maid who'd taken her slaps without complaint, was holding her effortlessly. And her grip was tightening...Angeline screamed, helplessly, as her wrists were twisted painfully, then taped behind her back. She went limp, her vision blurring as her former servant pressed down hard. It was all she could do not to fall into the darkness.

"Dumb bitch," a voice said. It was Sofia and yet it was *not* Sofia. It was a Sofia consumed with hatred and rage. "Useless, too."

"The rest of the plantation is ours," another voice said. She didn't recognise it. "The overseers are already dead."

Angeline whimpered. Sofia rolled her over. Angeline found herself looking into the maid's face, a face that was both familiar and very alien. This wasn't the submissive maid, but...Angeline shuddered, feeling the world turning upside down. The workers were rebelling? The servants were rebelling? Why? Didn't they know how lucky they were? Didn't they know....? She thought she smelled burning. Had they set the mansion on fire?

"Leave her," a man said. "Or cut her throat."

"She nearly got me fired," another man said. "Let us have some fun first."

Sofia put her lips close to Angeline's ear. Her voice was cold and hard and yet tinged with a wicked glee. "You know what your father did to me? They're going to do it to you."

Angeline felt sick as the maid walked away, leaving the men to surround her. She opened her mouth, to try to argue, to try to convince them she was worth more alive and unharmed, but knew—somehow—that it would be futile. Workers who rebelled were hunted down and executed. Her father had said so often enough. The men who'd betrayed their master, who were already undoing their trousers, were doomed. They'd be hanged the moment they were caught. What did they have to lose? She closed her eyes as they tore at her clothes, trying to convince herself it would be over soon.

It wasn't.

...

"They say there are aliens living here," Private Willis said, as the patrol made its way down the road. "In the dark, they come out and eat people."

Bryce snorted, rudely. The idea was insane. There were no aliens, certainly no *intelligent* aliens, in the known universe. The largest non-Earth animal anyone had ever discovered, according to his schoolteacher, had been roughly the same size as a large dog. Interesting, true, but hardly a friend or foe to humanity. The concept of alien races was about as real as the bogeyman.

And yet, looking at the countryside, he was starting to believe there could be *something* out there. First Landing was the city that never slept. The streetlights were bright, even in the darkest parts of the city; the bars and brothels and even supermarkets were open at all hours, to those who could afford to pay. The countryside, by contrast, was dark, yet surprisingly loud. Small rodents and snakes moved through the undergrowth, never quite coming into the light; owls and other, stranger, birds drifted through the night sky, watching and waiting for a mouse to reveal itself. The locals themselves were nowhere to be seen. The landowners had made it clear that anyone caught outside after curfew would be shot, on suspicion of being a rebel. Bryce hoped they wouldn't take a shot at *him*.

The sky lit up. A brilliant flash of light, followed by a fireball climbing into infinity...he froze, then ducked as thunder rumbled in the distance. A missile strike...or...or what? He forced himself to think, recalling the maps he'd seen. The explosion—and the fires—looked to have come from the mansion they'd passed a couple of days ago. He heard Willis calling the FOB, passing on the warning as the armoured cars picked up speed. The rebels had finally shown their hand. They hadn't gone for the FOB itself, but the mansion nearby.

Good, he thought, grimly. *Whatever else happens, they'll have given the landowners a nasty shock.*

His mind raced as his eyes swept the landscape. The fires were clearly visible, tinged with an unnatural colour that nagged at his mind. The plantation was huge, easily the size of First Landing if not bigger, and yet it was burning...but why? Did crops burn, despite resting in swampy paddies? Or had someone drenched them in oil or gasoline and lit a match? He cursed under his breath as they crashed through a wooden gate, approaching the mansion from the north. The building was caught in a roaring blaze, flames licking through the windows and kissing the stone walls. The balcony he'd seen earlier—and the girls—was gone, lost in the fires. He wondered, numbly, if they'd been asleep when the building was attacked and set on fire. Had they made it out? Or had they been burnt to death—or suffocated—before they ever woke up?

"The QRA is beefing up now," Willis said, as they dismounted. "They'll be here shortly."

"Forget them," Bryce said. "Where are the rebels?"

His heart pounded as he looked around. The worker barracks, hidden behind a copse of trees were on fire, the wind whipping the flames across the fields and fences. There was no sign of anyone or anything, not even the sheep, cows and chickens in the small fields. The workers had either fled or been burnt to death or....

A low roar split the air. He turned, just in time to see the mansion collapse into a pile of burning rubble. Anyone unlucky enough to remain inside would be dead now, if they hadn't died well before the fire was set. It wasn't a natural fire, part of his mind insisted. It had spread too far, with everyone inside either killed or rendered helpless or...or helped to turn the entire building into a towering inferno. Part of him rejoiced at what he'd seen, the hated oppressors finally getting a dose of their own medicine; part of him feared what the landowners would do, when they found out what happened. This was no minor skirmish, no shooting or bombing or isolated incident that could be safely ignored. There had been an entire family of landowners in the mansion. They were dead now, dead or wishing they were.

"There was no sign of life," Willis said. "Not here, not anywhere."

Bryce nodded as he looked back at the remains of the plantation. The fires were dying now, darkness advancing in pools as the flames ran out of fuel and were quenched by the water. The barns and barracks were gone, little more now than piles of ashes; he saw a water tower, the supporting structure weakened beyond bearing, collapse and dump its contents onto the ground. The remainder of the flames died quickly, plunging the scene into near-complete darkness. He snapped his NVGs into place as he continued to sweep the environment. The plantation workers appeared to have deserted. He didn't blame them.

"Fuck," he said, numbly. "I...."

A bullet cracked through the air. He hit the ground automatically, crawling for cover as more and more shots rang out. There were flashes of light in the distance, enemy fighters pouring fire into their position. He levelled his rifle and fired back twice, more in a desperate bid to force the enemy to duck than anything else. It didn't seem to work. Steve brought the machine gun around and fired a long burst towards the enemy positions, but it was hard to tell if he'd hit anything. The enemy kept firing, pinning them down.

"Call it in," Bryce shouted. "Tell them we have contact!"

A mortar shell dropped from the sky and exploded next to one of the armoured cars, picking it up and throwing it. Bryce hoped the crew had made it out as he sought more cover, hiding in a water ditch as he tried to pick out enemy targets. Something exploded, far too close to him for comfort; he realised, numbly that the enemy really did have them pinned. The ground heaved, suggesting...suggesting what? He looked back, just in time to see another fireball in the distance. It dawned on him, suddenly, that the plantation might not be the only place under attack. The rebels knew they were committed now. They'd throw everything they had into the fight.

And I'm on the wrong bloody side, he thought. He snapped off a shot at a dark figure, which vanished. He told himself he'd probably hit the bastard, but it was hard to be sure. *What the fuck do I do?*

He cursed under his breath. He didn't want to shoot his comrades in the back. Even if he did, he ran the risk of being shot by rebels...rebels who had no idea he was on their side. And yet, if he stayed where he was... he was fucked. His mind churned as he forced himself to consider their options. There weren't many. If they tried to run, they'd be shot down; if they tried to use the armoured cars to escape, they'd be taken out by the mortars; if they stayed where they were, they'd remain pinned down until they ran out of ammunition and then be blown to hell.

Willis caught his eye. "The QRA is coming," he said. "We have to hold out until then."

Bryce nodded, curtly. "Good."

• • •

Richard had been in the military long enough to snap awake automatically, the moment he heard the alarms. He rolled out of his blanket—he'd made a point of not using the farmer's bed, sharing his men's privations as much as possible—and grabbed his pistol and jacket with one hand while running into the operations room. It wasn't much—it had been the farmer's living room before he'd made a show of bullying the man into leaving—but it would suffice.

"Report," he snapped.

"Multiple incident reports," Lieutenant Glover said. Her voice was grim. "The Porter and Rayland Plantations have been attacked. The patrol near the Porter Plantation is reporting that it is taking heavy incoming fire. The QRA is arming now, ready to go."

Richard nodded, studying the map as his staff rapidly updated it. The Rayland Plantation would have to wait, at least until he got his patrol out of harm's way. If the enemy kept it pinned down, the soldiers would eventually run out of ammunition and get captured or killed. The landowners would scream bloody murder about the plantations being left to fend for themselves, but Richard's loyalty was to his men first. Besides, the Rayland Plantation was too far for his troops to get there before the enemy completed their mission and withdrew. The best they could hope for, when they got there, was for the rebels to be gone and the workers swearing blind they hadn't seen anything and they knew nothing, for fear the rebels would come back and finish the job.

Roland stepped into the room, looking disgustingly fresh. "It's started, then?"

"Two major attacks and a handful of minor ones," Richard said. He didn't bother to point out that there might have been other attacks, strikes that hadn't been reported yet...strikes that had been so successful they hadn't left anyone behind to scream for help. "And a pinned down patrol. I'm dispatching the QRF to extract them."

"I'll take command of the mission," Roland said. His voice made it clear he wouldn't tolerate an argument. "I've already contacted Captain Allen and told him to put his men on alert."

Richard hesitated, then nodded. There weren't many men with experience in using the new armoured cars and infantry fighting vehicles in combat. Roland had as much as anyone, perhaps more. He'd certainly been through a more intensive training course than Richard or anyone else on the base. And besides, Roland had more leeway for mistakes. If half the story about Sandra Oakley was true, a native officer would be lucky *just* to be busted all the way down to recruit before being dishonourably discharged.

"Get there, get them out, get back," Richard said. "Don't push your luck too far."

"Understood," Roland said. He shot a jaunty salute. "We'll be back."

CHAPTER THIRTY-TWO

BARAKA ISLAND, NEW DONCASTER

"KEEP YOUR HEAD DOWN," Rachel muttered, as the convoy started to make its way through the gates. "And keep your eyes open."

Roland nodded curtly—it was very basic advice—as he swept his head from side to side. His eyes were enhanced, and he was wearing a pair of NVGs, but the surrounding landscape was still dark and gloomy, save for the flames rising in the distance. The enemy could be lurking in the treeline, on the verge of the cleared zone, and he wouldn't have a clue until they opened fire. The convoy was armed to the teeth, spearheaded by a pair of armoured cars, yet... he swallowed hard, sweat prickling down his back. It might not be the first time he'd gone into danger, but it was the first time he'd led men into combat.

"Launch the drone," he ordered. "And keep me informed."

Rachel took the drone from the case, held it up and threw it into the air. Roland hoped—prayed—the enemy didn't have the sensors to spot the drone, nor the weapons to bring it down. The tiny craft was no bigger than his arm. A single rifle shot would be enough to blow it out of the sky, if the enemy shooter scored a direct hit. He would have preferred a high-altitude drone, but there were none on New Doncaster. The atmosphere was so weird that even the most advanced drone would have trouble remaining in flight long enough to be useful.

He tensed as the convoy reached the edge of the cleared zone and kept going, the undergrowth converging on them like darkened waves. One of the local militia officers had suggested coating the entire island in defoliant, an idea so insane—even by local standards—that he'd been hastily reassigned somewhere he couldn't do any harm, but Roland was starting to see his point. The foliage, the strange combination of terrestrial and alien plants, provided all the cover the rebels could possibly want. He made a mental note to start clearing the roads, cutting back the undergrowth as much as possible. The landowners would make a fuss if their workers were pressed into service, and paid in *real* money, but Roland couldn't bring himself to care. He could *feel* unseen eyes watching from the gloom.

"The patrol is still pinned down," Rachel reported. "The enemy seems reluctant to press the attack or let them go."

Roland frowned. Insurgents rarely cared for fights on equal terms. They might well prefer to merely pin the patrol down, rather than try to destroy it. And yet, it didn't quite make sense. They could have rained mortar shells on the patrol from a safe distance...he wondered, suddenly, just how many shells the rebels *had*. There was so much corruption within the local militia that it was quite possible a commander had let his entire armoury be looted or sold his entire arsenal to the rebels. And the rebels had been bringing in arms from off-world. Roland grimaced at the thought. They could have everything from common or garden assault rifles and RPGs, the kind of weapons a skilled gunsmith could put together effortlessly, to modern HVMs and antitank plasma cannons. The armoured cars were good, and the IFVs designed to take bullets and RPGs without damage, but Roland had no illusions about how well their armour would stand up to modern weapons. They'd go through the metal like a hot knife through butter.

"Tell them we're on the way," Roland said. He couldn't abandon the patrol, not now. The local soldiers would take note and know, beyond a shadow of a doubt, that neither Roland nor the rest of their commanding officers had their backs. Morale would fall faster than a KEW dropped from high orbit. The rebels would have no trouble convincing the soldiers to put down their weapons or simply switch sides. "And make sure they keep us informed."

He scowled as the convoy picked up speed. The undergrowth seemed silent and yet he was sure the enemy knew they were on the way. A lone man with a simple pair of binoculars, technology so primitive there was no hope of detecting it, could be watching from a safe distance...hell, a couple of men could be positioned right on the edge of the cleared zone, safely hidden under gillie suits. They might even be *in* the cleared zone. It was the sort of nervy trick a forward-thinking rebel might try. The corps had certainly done the same, more than once. Their enemies had *known* the cleared zone was clear.

There was no chatter amongst the men. Roland glanced back, feeling a mixture of pride and guilt. Last time, he'd thrown them into an assault he'd planned carefully; this time, they were charging straight into the unknown. They didn't understand, not really, that he had less experience than many of the militia officers, no matter how intensely he'd trained at Boot Camp. They thought he was a capable officer, not someone making it up as he went along.

Someone daft enough to go on a cruise with a high-value target, Roland thought. *And someone daft enough to think he isn't a high-value target himself.*

The convoy rattled across the bridge, the struts shaking under the wheels. Roland wished for a brace of tanks, or even a handful of corps ATVs. The rivers weren't very wide, as rivers went, but the armoured cars would still have trouble driving across the riverbed. The locals had gone to some trouble to reshape the rivers, altering their courses to direct water to the plantations and mark the edge of their territories. It had, inadvertently, made it harder for the militia to move from place to place before it was too late.

His ears picked up as he heard shots in the distance. The rebels were continuing their assault, but not pressing it any harder than strictly necessary. It might make sense—the rebels could afford to wait until the trapped men ran out of ammunition, then walk forward and kill them all—yet Roland couldn't help feeling he was missing something. The longer the rebels waited, the greater the chance Roland's force could stick a knife in their rear. They might be unsure what to do, they might not even believe he was on the way...no. He shook his head. They knew he was coming. They should either be upping the tempo of their assault, in hopes of crushing the patrol before Roland arrived, or simply breaking contact. What were they doing?

"The drone picked up a radio pulse," Rachel reported. "No content, just a pulse."

Roland frowned. The rebels had to know that using radio would bring long-range fire down on their heads. The merest signal would be enough to draw fire. They didn't have time to have a proper chat, or even speak a single sentence...the man who'd sent the pulse was probably running for his life, convinced—wrongly—that a hail of shells was already dropping towards his position. And that meant the pulse itself was the signal. Someone hiding in the darkness was waiting...waiting for what?

He looked forward as the second bridge came into view, an instant before it exploded with a flash of light. The lead armoured cars came to a halt, skidding to a stop bare seconds before they went over the edge and plummeted into the waters below. It wasn't deep enough to cover the vehicle, Roland thought, but there was a very good chance the drivers would have drowned even if they hadn't been injured by the crash. The remainder of the convoy slammed on the brakes, an IFV crashing into the back of one of the armoured cars and nearly shoving it into the river. The ground heaved, again. Roland glanced back to see another fireball rising behind them. He didn't need to check with Rachel to know the first bridge had also been destroyed.

"Dismount," he snapped. "Dismount!"

A hiss ran through the air. Droplets of water splattered against his helmet. Roland jumped to the ground, unsure what was happening. The skies were clear. It wasn't raining...he peered into the gloom and saw an irrigation system, twisted so it showered water towards the piled-up convoy. He frowned, puzzled, then looked down. The ground below his feet was turning to mud, too quickly to be natural. He cursed under his breath as he realised his mistake. The rebels had prepared their trap well. Even if he wanted to retreat, leaving the patrol to its fate, he couldn't get the vehicles over the destroyed bridge. And if he abandoned them, he risked letting the rebels search them for anything important before they blew them up.

Rachel landed beside him, holding the drone terminal in one hand. "The sensors are picking up movement towards us," she said. "They're coming."

Roland glanced at the terminal. It was hard to be sure—the foliage played merry hell with the drone's sensors—but it looked as if a sizable blocking force was establishing itself between the FOB and the trapped convoy. They'd caught him in a nasty bind. If he abandoned the vehicles and fled to the FOB, he'd leave the patrol to die; if he stayed where he was, his men would die, too. Hell, the enemy might even have overplayed their hand a little. Or they might not have realised the drone was watching. They might hope he'd turn and flee, running straight into their trap.

Or call for more support from the FOB, Roland thought. *And that runs the risk of leaving the base undermanned and effectively defenceless.*

"Shit." Rachel closed the terminal and slipped it onto her belt. "They just killed the drone."

Roland opened his mouth to reply, then hit the ground as the landscape seemed to explode with flashes of light. He heard mortar shells falling through the air, coming down in and around the convoy. An armoured car exploded, pieces of metal flying in all directions; two more opened fire, spraying bullets towards the enemy positions. Roland didn't notice the enemy fire starting to slacken, although it was hard to be sure. The rebel fire was devastatingly accurate. They'd had more than enough time to get their mortars into position, zeroed on their targets. They were shooting fish in a barrel.

He opened his mouth, barking orders. They had to move in the one direction the enemy wouldn't expect, *away* from the FOB. Roland couldn't think of anything better. The enemy only had a handful of troops in that direction, the ones pinning the patrol against the ruins of the mansion. If they were lucky, they might just wipe out a small enemy force and reinforce the patrol, then hold in place until sunrise. He doubted the rebels would stick around after dawn. The local militia would dispatch strike aircraft to chase the rebels back into the outback.

"Cover us," he snapped. "Set the guns on automatic, then head south."

The shooting grew louder as the machine guns started to swing from side to side. Roland had no idea if the bullets were going *anywhere* near the enemy position, but the sheer randomness of the fire would—hopefully—discourage the enemy from pressing their advantage. It was possible the enemy might even think Roland was panicking, spraying and praying in the wrong fucking direction, his finger stuck on the trigger until he was clicking empty. Roland hoped that was true, although there was no way to be sure. The rebels might be wary even if they thought he was panicking under fire. They couldn't afford a major defeat either.

They can afford more than us, Roland thought, as he splashed through the river and scrambled up the far side. *As long as their formations remain intact, they're winning.*

He gritted his teeth as the soldiers picked up speed, flitting from tree to tree as they advanced through the countryside. The soil below their feet was sodden, water boiling up every time they stopped for more than a second. Visibility was down to almost nothing...Roland kept his eyes open but saw very little. The distant fires were dimming, suggesting the plantation had been reduced to a pile of ash and bodies. Roland wondered, idly, what would happen to the remaining workers, if they hadn't already fled. The rebels might have taken them or...he shook his head as the shooting behind tailed off and stopped. A handful of explosions rent the air as the convoy vehicles died, then nothing. Silence fell, like a thunderclap. It was suddenly hard to hear the shooting in the distance. The patrol was still pinned down.

And the enemy will be coming right after us, the moment they realise what we've done, he told himself. *They won't assume we committed suicide when we saw them coming.*

Water pooled around his feet as they kept moving towards the distant fires. The plantation felt strange, almost *alien*. Long rows of weird plants—not bushes, not trees; he couldn't help mentally comparing them to seaweed—were broken by concrete structures and walls that separated one section from the next. Some looked as though they'd been knocked down by an angry god; some looked completely untouched, as if they could be harvested once the sun rose again. He stumbled across a dead body, lying in a ditch, and shuddered helplessly. The body's throat had been cut. A supervisor? Or just someone who'd refused to go with the rebels when they'd attacked the plantation?

The foliage widened suddenly, revealing a handful of rebels firing constantly towards the trapped patrol. They were so focused on their mission they didn't hear the troops behind them until it was too late. Roland would have liked to take prisoners, but his men were firing before he could give the order. The rebels were wiped out before they could run or fight. Roland breathed a sigh of relief as the shooting slackened, although it didn't die completely. The rebels had taken up a *bunch* of firing positions.

Rachel leaned forward. "They're coming after us."

Roland didn't doubt it. They didn't have long until the dawn. The rebels needed to press their advantage now or back off…practically, part of his mind noted, they could back off and declare victory and they'd probably be right. They'd wrecked at least two plantations and given Roland and his men a bloody nose; they could quit while they were ahead. But they also had a chance to score an even bigger victory by wiping out both the patrol and its reinforcements. Roland doubted he could pass up the chance to win, even though he was already ahead. War wasn't a game of football. The score didn't matter. All that mattered was beating the other side into a bloody pulp.

"We'll link up with the patrol, then take up defensive positions," Roland said. "Captain Allen?"

"They may not get here in time," Rachel said. "They're coming all the way from Kingstown."

Roland nodded as he strode forward, holding up his hands as he reached the remains of the mansion. The patrol's three vehicles were burnt-out wrecks, but most of them had survived and held their ground... partly, Roland realised grimly, because they'd been the bait in a trap. The enemy had nearly caught them...he cursed under his breath as the shooting started again, the rebel forces advancing to the point they could pour fire into his positions from a safe distance. His eyes swept the treeline, spotting a handful of dark figures. He shot at them and had the satisfaction of seeing one fall.

His earpiece bleeped. "Sir," Richard said. "The FOB is under heavy attack."

"Hold the line until morning," Roland ordered. They'd taken a beating, and there was no point in trying to deny it, but as long as they didn't lose the FOB it wouldn't be a total disaster. "Don't make any attempt to come to us. That's an order."

"Aye, sir," Richard said.

Roland sucked in his breath as the shooting intensified. His world had shrunk, rapidly, to the ruined plantation. There was no way to know what was happening outside the district, what the rebels might have done to press the advantage or keep the militia from mobilising and launching a counterattack. They'd probably planted IEDs along the roads, if they hadn't attacked the militia bases and airstrips directly. The militia would have trouble getting anywhere in a hurry. Hell, perhaps the entire island was exploding into revolution. If *all* the plantation workers rebelled at once...

He snapped off two more shots, reminding himself to conserve ammunition. He'd taught his men to carry as much as possible and to hell with barmy bureaucrats who insisted on each and every rifle round being accounted for, but there was no hope of resupply. His communicator crackled, bringing more and more bad news. The enemy were raining a seemingly endless series of shells on the FOB, as well as sniping at anyone foolish enough to show themselves. Richard was pinned down as much as the rest of them. His only advantage was that he had solid defences and enough ammunition to fight a minor war on his own.

"If we get out of this, remind me to insist on having the roads cleared," Roland said. The noose was tightening. He could practically *feel* something squeezing his neck. His mind raced, trying to figure out how to escape. They could break free of the trap, but there would be no hope of getting back to the FOB. "And on having more and better tanks shipped up here."

Rachel nodded. "Will do."

Roland gritted his teeth. The enemy were pressing closer, no longer deterred. If they ran…he shook his head. They'd moved from the frying pan into the fire. Surrender wasn't an option. He'd heard too much about what the rebels did to prisoners.

He raised his voice. "Fix bayonets!"

CHAPTER THIRTY-THREE

BARAKA ISLAND, NEW DONCASTER

STEVE MANDRELS SMILED COLDLY as he watched the engagement from a safe distance. It hadn't been easy to lay the groundwork for a running battle that pitted his men against the best the government could provide, not without tipping the bastards off ahead of time, but he'd made it. It helped that the local plantation owners could be relied upon to make a horrible fuss if the army didn't send troops the moment the plantations came under attack. Steve's plan had been simple enough. Attack the plantations, use them as bait for a small force; trap that force and use it as bait for a *larger* force. He'd studied the enemy patterns over the last two weeks and determined, roughly, how they'd react. And he'd been right.

His smile grew wider. He hadn't expected the soldiers to beat feet towards the plantation, instead of slipping into the undergrowth or trying to break through his lines and back to the FOB before it was too late. It might have worked, too, if he hadn't been bringing more men up from the north with the intention of throwing them at the FOB. The enemy troops were now pinned down, unable to escape or even hold out indefinitely. Steve glanced at his watch and grinned, nastily, as the shooting intensified. He'd been right. Sarah was a skilled diplomat—he was happy to admit that—but she was no fighter. She'd kept him from launching the kind of offensive he'd wanted, back before the Marine training officers had arrived. And now, her caution was exposed for the mistake it was. Steve didn't hate her—he rather admired her sheer determination—but he wasn't going to let her call the shots any longer. The time had come to strike, to take the islands for themselves and strike the landowners down.

A runner hurried up to him, gasping for breath. "Sir," he said. "The enemy troops are running out of ammunition."

Steve nodded. He wished he was down there himself. He wanted to be the one who led the assault in person. He was unpleasantly aware there'd be rumblings about cowardice from men who hadn't been there—even *Sarah* had gone into the lion's den, when she'd sailed to Kingstown to link up with the rebels there—and his record would count for nothing if the rumblings took shape and form. The plan had been his, but he wasn't the one on the front lines. He almost wished Sarah had returned, in time to take the lead herself. But then, she would never have consented to the plan.

"Tell them to push the offensive," he ordered, firmly. It didn't matter *who* got the credit for firing the final shot. People would remember it had been *his* plan, even if he hadn't charged the enemy positions in person. He glanced at the sky, long experience telling him it was only an hour or so before dawn. "We have to end this and fall back before the skies lighten."

"Yes, sir."

...

Bryce gritted his teeth as more and more bullets snapped through the air. The rebel plan had been a good one, made easier—he saw now—by the fact the patrolling troops had fallen into bad habits, habits the enemy had used to punch them in the nose. The reinforcements had reached the ruined mansion, somehow, but they were now pinned down and just as trapped as the remnants of the patrol. Bryce had tried to think of a plan, a way to escape and make contact with the rebels...perhaps even to lead his men into surrender. But nothing had come to mind.

He glanced at Captain Roland Windsor, who was organising the last-ditch defence. The young man seemed absurdly young, a strange combination of experience and inexperience that made absolutely no sense. Bryce had to admit Captain Windsor had come to their aid, even though he must have been tempted—very tempted—to abandon the patrol to its fate. He'd been told by the DIs that the Marines never left anyone behind and it seemed it was true. His heart clenched at the thought. If things had been different, if he hadn't been a rebel agent well before the Marines had arrived, who knew what he would have been? A loyal soldier? Or dead?

A green flare exploded in the sky. An eerie light swept over the scene. The rebels were about to begin their final assault, to destroy the patrol and the reinforcements before sunlight drove them back to their caves. Bryce lifted his rifle, checking his remaining ammunition. Did he dare aim to miss? Did he dare…he swallowed hard, caught between a number of different and contradictory impulses. He wanted to live and yet he didn't want to kill his own people and yet he knew they didn't know he was on their side….

"Stand ready!" Captain Windsor's voice echoed through the air. "And…."

He broke off, suddenly. "Get down! Get the fuck down!"

Bryce dropped, unsure what was happening. An instant later, the world turned white.

• • •

Steve barely saw the aircraft, moving silently through the night sky, before they swept over the front lines and opened fire. A stream of tracer bullets and antipersonnel rockets hammered his positions, followed by plasma bombs that blasted waves of white-hot fire through the trenches. He stared in horror as the aircraft kept going, ignoring a handful of shots aimed at them from the ground. Their weapons tore through the plantation's crops, ripping them to shreds with ease. The dark side of his mind noted the landowners were going to be pissed, when they realised just how badly their land had been hammered, perhaps even burnt to the ground. He swore as he saw more explosions surrounding the FOB. The forces laying siege to the base had been scattered, if they hadn't been destroyed.

A missile stabbed up from one of his rear positions. The aircraft avoided it—somehow—and fired back, hammering bullets into the anti-aircraft position until the crew had been practically disintegrated. Steve cursed, again. They'd been given MANPADs, but the sellers had warned them they weren't always effective against modern countermeasures. Steve watched, helplessly, as the aircraft swept back, emptying their guns into the remains of his positions and obliterating anyone who hadn't run. The plantation was on fire. Again.

He reached for a flare gun, pointed it into the sky and pulled the trigger. A red flare exploded above the battlefield, signalling the retreat. There was no point in trying to continue the offensive, not now that his lines had been broken. The newcomers—they had to be the Marines; he knew for a fact the militia and regular troops had *nothing* comparable to their aircraft—had won. Barely. Steve heard bullets whipping through the air behind him as he turned and ran. The enemy had cheated, but he'd still given them a bloody nose. They'd certainly be a hell of a lot more careful the next time they went on patrol.

And the landowners will whine and moan about the shattered plantations, he thought, with a flicker of gallows humour. *The Marines might wind up wishing they'd just let us kill them instead.*

He sobered as he ran, joining the headlong retreat. Sarah was *not* going to be pleased. Nor were the other cell leaders. He would have been forgiven much, if he'd produced victory, but he'd lost. There was no point in disputing the simple fact his failure had put the timetable back a few weeks, perhaps too *far* back. The enemy troops had handled themselves well. Who knew what would happen when there were more of them?

Sunlight glimmered in the distance. There was no pursuit. Steve shook his head in rueful annoyance. He wanted to claim it had been a victory, and he had hurt the enemy, but it wasn't true. He owed it to his people to be honest, to make it clear what had gone wrong and why. And if they demanded he paid for his mistakes with his life....

They won't kill me, he thought, morbidly. *They'll just send me on a suicide mission instead.*

• • •

Roland breathed a sigh of relief as the Raptors swept overhead, their weapons pounding the enemy positions into scrap. The enemy fire slackened, then abruptly cut off. He peered forwards as he saw more explosions surrounding the FOB, clearing away the enemy troops that had laid siege to the base. They were probably regretting, right now, coming into the open. They'd made themselves targets for a well-aimed airstrike.

"Sir." Rachel caught his attention. "Captain Allen requests you finish up here, then return to the FOB for debriefing."

Requests, Roland thought. It was an order, however phrased. *He wants to have a few words with me. Again.*

He pushed the thought aside as his men swept the remains of the mansion and the plantation beyond. There were only a handful of bodies, some in terrible state, which surprised him until he realised the majority of the former servants and workers had probably joined the rebels. A young woman, still alive despite horrible injuries, was found on the edge of the garden. Roland wasn't sure why she'd been left alive—perhaps the bastards who'd beaten her bloody and then raped her had assumed her injuries would finish her off—but he told himself it didn't matter. She could be taken back to the FOB and treated, then…he felt a twinge of sympathy. It was never easy to come face to face with the fact the world wasn't a safe place. He'd found it hard to understand this himself, and no one had raped *him*.

They would have turned me into their puppet, he reflected, as they started the walk back to the FOB. *But it wouldn't have been quite the same.*

They passed the remains of their vehicles as they walked, giving them a wide berth for fear of booby traps. Roland knew how to rig a vehicle himself and he dared not assume the rebels were any different. They hadn't had time to get the vehicles out themselves…he put it on the list of things to worry about later, after they made it back to the FOB. The Raptors circled overhead, providing top cover. Their presence was a grim reminder that the local forces—*his* forces—had been unable to carry out their mission without help. Their inexperience—his, as well as others—had let them be lured into a trap. Roland wasn't sure what he could have done differently—he couldn't have abandoned the patrol—but who knew?

He braced himself as the FOB came into view. The sangars were scorched and pitted, the scars bearing mute testament to the fight that had just ended. He was relieved to see they'd held, although the bodies lying just inside the base—under cloth—were a grim reminder the victory hadn't come without a cost. It wasn't a victory, although he was sure the government would make it out to be one. The plantations had been destroyed, their inhabitants either slaughtered or lost to the rebels, a number of vehicles had been abandoned and at least thirty men had been killed in action. And the rebels had come very close to winning.

And now they know they can give us a hard time, he thought. *They won't hesitate to resume the offensive as soon as the Raptors are gone.*

Richard met him as they reached the old farmhouse. "Captain Allen is in my office."

Waiting for you, Roland finished silently. He heard the words, even though Richard didn't say them. *And he isn't going to be pleased.*

"I'll see you afterwards," he said, to both Richard and Rachel. "Start drawing up plans to resume the patrol schedule as quickly as possible."

He barely heard their answers as he turned and walked down the corridor. He'd never really been punished, not for anything, until Belinda had walked into his life. The instructors at Boot Camp had drilled him in everything from military discipline and tactics, pointing out his mistakes in often excruciating detail, but…there, on the exercise field, it was hard to get someone killed. The dead would get up, after the exercise was completed; they weren't really dead. The thirty men who'd died under his command…he swallowed, hard. Captain Allen was about to tear him a new asshole. He probably deserved it.

There's no probably about it, he told himself. He knocked on the door, hard. *I fucked up.*

"Come," Captain Allen said.

Roland pushed the door open. Captain Allen sat behind a desk, looking grim. Roland entered, closed the door and saluted. There was no offer of coffee, let alone a seat. His heart sank further. He was definitely in trouble.

"So." Captain Allen's eyes bored into Roland's. "What went wrong?"

"We let ourselves be lured into a trap," Roland said. His thoughts ran in circles. He could have avoided the trap by simply leaving the patrol to die, but the effects of *that* would have been incalculable. "And then we were forced to abandon our vehicles and pinned down."

"Correct." Captain Allen showed no mercy. "Why did you let it happen?"

"I couldn't leave the patrol to die," Roland said. He wracked his brains, trying to think of something—anything—he could have done instead. Even with the advantage of hindsight, there hadn't been many options. "If I'd abandoned them, it would have destroyed morale beyond repair."

"True." Captain Allen, thankfully, was no armchair general. He'd know the obvious—in hindsight—was rarely so obvious at the time. "But you also followed a predictable route to the destroyed plantation."

"Yes, sir," Roland said. "But there were no other direct routes."

"No," Captain Allen agreed. "And yet, you didn't think to check the bridges before you charged through?"

Roland felt a flash of hot anger. "With all due respect, sir, there wasn't time."

"No." Captain Allen studied him for a long cold moment. "I can see your thinking. I can also understand that you made a serious mistake. The rebels could easily have done a great deal worse."

"Yes, sir," Roland said. He wanted to argue, but he knew better. "We got lucky."

"For a given value of *luck*," Captain Allen said. "The engagement was inconclusive. We gave them a taste of our firepower, and they broke, but it won't last. We probably won you and your new army some time, Windsor...."—the words hung in the air for a moment—"yet they'll resume the offensive as soon as they can. They won't make the same mistakes twice."

Roland nodded. His understanding of insurgencies was largely theoretical—and there was no point in pretending he'd gained years of practical experience in a few months—but they tended to follow similar patterns. The insurgents stayed in the shadows, building up their forces, before trying to take political power at gunpoint. It had been alarmingly clear that New Doncaster was inching steadily towards that point, with islands like Ivanovo and Baraka clearly on the verge of falling into rebel hands. They'd taught the rebels a sharp lesson—they hadn't been ready for the Raptors—but they'd just sneak back into the shadows. Time was simply not on the government's side.

Captain Allen met his eyes. "You made mistakes. So did they, to be fair, but your mistakes came very close to getting you killed. You got very lucky. If we hadn't been able to get the Raptors to you in time, you would have been fucked. The entire district would have either fallen into rebel hands, with the FOB captured or under siege, or simply collapsed into chaos. You need to learn from your mistakes—and *fast*."

"Yes, sir," Roland said.

"You also need to push the government into organising reforms," Captain Allen added. His face was completely expressionless, his voice devoid of emotion. "This entire planet is dangerously unstable."

Roland nodded, remembering the brutalised girl. Young woman, really. No one could inflict those injuries, and then leave the victim to die in agony, if there hadn't been some degree of hatred and resentment involved. He remembered Richard's words and cursed under his breath. There was so much resentment, at practically all levels of society, that draining the poison might prove impossible. Even slight reforms might lead directly to chaos.

"Yes, sir," he said. "I was planning to stay here two more days, then return to Kingstown. I'll speak to the PM then."

"If he's forgiven you," Captain Allen said. "You might want to come with us. The news is already halfway to Kingstown and that means the PM and his enemies will be putting their own spin on it. They might want you to do the impossible, or simply blame you for the disaster."

Roland hesitated—it felt as if he were abandoning Richard and his men, once again—then nodded. "Yes, sir."

Captain Allen stood. "Roland, keep your eyes on the goal at all times. This planet needs to be stabilised—and fast—before it falls into chaos or outside powers get involved. And that will be the end."

Yeah, Roland thought. He had no doubt the captain was right. The PM would have his hands full with demands that the remaining plantations would be protected, even though that was impossible. His political enemies, who didn't have to deal with the crisis themselves, would have fun making him squirm for *not* doing the impossible. *And would an outside invader really be a bad thing?*

CHAPTER THIRTY-FOUR

FIRST LANDING, NEW DONCASTER

"IF THIS REPORT IS TRUE," Sarah said to herself, "we may have a problem."

She studied the handful of papers thoughtfully. The PM had managed to lock most of the rebel agents in Government House out of everything important, practically keeping them prisoner when they weren't at their desks, but her agents in Lord Ludlow's offices still had access to reports as they came in from Baraka. Lord Ludlow had numerous investments in the islands and he insisted on being kept informed, even though she had a feeling he rarely bothered to read the reports. The agents had certainly made it clear they were almost never accessed by their superiors.

That'll have changed, she thought, morbidly. *The island has suddenly become a real battleground.*

She kept her thoughts to herself as she read the report from cover to cover. Steve had been ordered to probe the defences, to test the government's mettle without crossing the line between *nuisance* and *serious threat*. She cursed inwardly as she realised he'd exceeded orders to the point he hadn't just crossed the line, but burnt the bridge behind him. Two plantations destroyed, several more damaged; the enemy troops lured into an ambush that had come very close to destroying them before the Marines had pulled their fat out of the fire. It wouldn't have been so bad, if the Marines hadn't ended the fight. If they'd smashed an entire company of soldiers....

And I can't even dispose of Steve, she thought. The hothead had his uses, but his desire to simply lash out at his tormentors had turned him into a liability. *Too many people think he's a hero.*

Her heart sank as she forced herself to consider the implications. Steve never had. He thought in terms of winning battles, not wars. He didn't realise—to be fair, neither had Sarah until she'd studied military history—that one could win every battle and still lose the war. Steve's engagement had been a draw, at best, but it had given the rebels a taste of Marine firepower and damaged their formations beyond immediate repair. Steve would claim tactical victory, of course; strategically, it had been a defeat. The new troops had performed well. They wouldn't make the same mistakes twice. And the government would just keep training and deploying new soldiers until they buried the islands in uniformed manpower. The war was within shouting distance of being lost.

She clenched her fists, wishing—not for the first time—that she could simply put a gun to Steve's head and pull the trigger. Perhaps she should, even though it would probably cost her everything. His allies would kill her in retaliation and, even if they didn't, the alliance would die with him. She'd worked hard to put all the pieces in place, laying everything to ensure that—even if she lost some engagements—she'd still come out ahead. It might have been a mistake, she conceded ruefully, to think she could run an insurgency like clockwork. But, at the same time, a handful of isolated incidents would do nothing more than sting the government. They wouldn't be enough to destroy it, root and branch.

I should have him assassinated, she thought, *and blame his death on the government.*

Sarah put the thought out of her head and forced herself to think. The government and the Marines might not know it—she dared not assume their ignorance—but they'd done a hell of a lot of damage. They'd won themselves time. The formations would be rebuilt, of course, but with the damage to the cell structures it would be tricky to get everything back into place before the government started mounting its own offensives. And that meant she needed to stake everything on one final roll of the die. It would be risky—her plan to win the war in a single blow would have to be discarded—and yet, if it worked, she'd be very close to winning the war. She would certainly have made up for the damage the Marines had inflicted on her men.

She winced. She'd left the Marines at the spaceport alone because she didn't want to provoke trouble from off-world. She'd even told herself they'd surrender the spaceport once the government had been destroyed, then replaced. New Doncaster needed interstellar trade, at least until newer—and more modern—factories and industrial nodes could be set up. And yet, the Marines had shown their willingness to intervene. They'd become a threat. They had to be removed and yet, the price would be high. She understood, suddenly, why Steve never thought beyond the next battle. It was easy, so easy, to over-think until one was paralysed by the thought of everything that could go wrong. It was easy to convince herself to do nothing....

But there's no more time, she told herself. She stood, brushing down her dress. There were arrangements to make, before she headed back to Kingsport. The plans already existed, so did the agents. She just had to put them on alert, waiting for the signal. *And if we don't move now, we won't be able to move at all.*

• • •

"It's good to see you again," Sandra said. She gave Roland a long hug, despite Rachel's sour disposition. "My father told me to drive you to Government House."

"How...*nice* of him," Rachel said, sarcastically. "I trust you recovered from your ordeal?"

Roland shot her a sharp look.

Sandra seemed unbothered. "I have rested and recuperated and now I am fit to return to my father's side," she said. "He doesn't have many people he can trust."

"No," Rachel agreed. "It's a common problem in undemocratic states."

Sandra didn't rise to the bait as she drove them into the city. There were fewer cars and trucks on the streets, Roland noted, and militiamen and soldiers were everywhere. It was hard to be sure—it was early afternoon—but it looked as if there were fewer debtors and indents too. The news broadcasts had been hysterical, switching between glowing praise of the soldiers who'd kicked rebel ass without taking a single casualty and howling in outrage about thousands of men, women and children being raped and murdered by the rebels, neither of which was particularly true. Roland scowled as they passed through a pair of checkpoints, noting the protest march outside Government House. The protesters wanted immediate action against the rebels, apparently. Their signs promised a bloody end for any rebel who fell into their hands.

"An organised rent-a-protest," Rachel commented. "I can see the signs."

Roland glanced at her. "Are you sure?"

"Yes." Rachel was studying the crowd, worriedly. "It's an old tactic. You rustle up a crowd and pay them a few hundred credits each to take your signs and protest somewhere you cannot be easily ignored. The protest is often so loud it sucks in others—and, by astonishing coincidence, there's plenty of signs for the newcomers. The organisers probably paid the cops to stay well back too, just to make sure the protest went off without a hitch. It's only the unplanned protests that get met with violent repression."

Roland frowned. "So who's funding this protest?"

"I don't know," Rachel said. "But we should find out."

"They think my father's too soft," Sandra volunteered, as they parked in the underground garage. "They want to use more extreme methods to bring the rebels to heel."

"Really?" Rachel's tone was almost agonisingly polite. "And what methods do they have in mind?"

Roland shot her another glance as they clambered out of the car and headed for the elevator. A pair of guards searched them, removing both their weapons and wristcoms before allowing them to enter the elevator. They even searched Sandra, somewhat to Roland's surprise. The PM's daughter had enough clout to get a guard in trouble, if he put his hand somewhere she didn't like. But then, they were now taking security a little more seriously. Sandra had probably been told, after she'd nearly been kidnapped, to put up or stay out. Roland was impressed she hadn't gone back to the family island, after they'd made their escape, and stayed there. There were depths to Sandra he was only just starting to realise existed.

The PM was sitting in his office, looking tired and harassed. Lord Ludlow and General Falk sat in front of his desk, the latter reading a report on a terminal. Roland remembered hearing something about the Ludlow Family owning a bunch of plantations on Baraka and winced inwardly. Even if Lord Ludlow had been a reasonable man—or realised, in the privacy of his own mind, that he didn't want to have the responsibility of sorting out the mess himself—his family would be beating down his door, demanding he make the PM do something about the fighting on their island. Roland was almost sorry for the older man. If he did what his family wanted, he'd find himself in an even worse position and his relatives probably wouldn't give a damn.

"Captain," the PM said. He didn't acknowledge either Rachel or Sandra. "We've heard a number of reports that have clearly been exaggerated, if not made out of whole cloth. What really happened?"

Roland took a breath—Captain Allen had been right, it seemed—then went through the whole story. He made no attempt to hide his own mistakes, or the sophistication of the enemy action, or the simple fact he'd come very close to disaster. The troops had performed well—Roland was proud of them—but it hadn't been enough. They could have been wiped out, if the Marines hadn't saved their lives.

"Are you saying," Lord Ludlow said when he'd finished, "that our new army is useless?"

"No, sir," Roland said. "The men performed well. There is no doubt of *that*. However, the flat truth is that they don't have the experience, or numbers, to make a big difference. Yet. It will come."

"The flat truth is that we—the owners—have lost millions of credits they invested in the two destroyed plantations," Lord Ludlow said. "You were supposed to protect them. Their owners said they asked you to deploy a handful of men to cover the plantations. That would have made a difference."

"Yes," Roland agreed, flatly. "It would have added an extra ten men to the casualty list."

Lord Ludlow glared. "That isn't funny."

"It wasn't meant to be," Roland said. He'd never seen the point of gallows humour—or joking about someone's death. "If we had done as they suggested, our entire force would have been wiped out in short order. The rebels would have crushed us. Instead, we tested their mettle—and ours—and hurt them badly."

"After you walked into a trap," General Falk said. "It was *obviously* a trap."

Roland sighed. "General, with all due respect, the only other option was leaving the patrol to die. What would you have me do?"

The PM cleared his throat. "We'll put the issue of guilt and blame aside for the moment," he said, directing a sharp look at the general. "How do you propose we proceed?"

Roland took his map from his pocket and unfurled it. "The rebels gave us a fright and there's no point in denying it," he said. "However, we also gave them a thrashing. We have a window of opportunity to take the fight to them. I propose a two-prong strategy. First, we continue to recruit and train troops while expanding the network of FOBs and blockhouses until we have fairly tight control over the region. We'll clear the roads and ram patrols right up to the outback, forcing them to engage on our terms or let us move freely. We'll also put more close-support aircraft and helicopters into production, allowing us to deploy mobile firepower to back up the groundpounders."

He allowed himself a moment of relief. Rachel had advised him, during the flight back to the spaceport, to draw up a plan to take control of the situation. The vague plan he'd pencilled on the map would take months, if not years, to turn into a reality, but it was more optimistic than merely sitting on his ass waiting to be hit. Or fired. The local government had plenty of reason to be annoyed with him.

"Second, we need a political offensive alongside the military one," he added. "The current situation is unsustainable. The rebels go to the debtors and indents and tell them there is no hope of ever getting out of debt, that their children and grandchildren will inherit the debt and the interest on it until the entire banking system collapses under its own weight. You insist they're not slaves...."

"They're not," Lord Ludlow interrupted.

"...But, to all intents and purposes, they *are*." Roland met his eyes. "They are forbidden to leave the plantations and seek jobs elsewhere; they are paid in scrip and generally treated like slaves. Worse than slaves really, because a smart slaveowner might just realise that working his slaves to death means he won't have them anymore. They have no hope. They work all day for a fucking pittance, while your sons and daughters look down on them and make their lives miserable. They are not animals! They are perfectly capable of realising how badly they're screwed and wanting a little revenge!"

He dug into his belt and removed a datachip. "This is the results of a medical examination carried out on Angeline Porter, the sole survivor of Porter Plantation. You may wish to read it in the toilet. You'll throw up at least once."

"Do you think," Lord Ludlow snarled, "that we have the slightest interest in extending an olive branch to people who do *that*?"

"No," Roland said. "If we catch them, we'll shoot them. But you need to tackle the resentment before it boils over and scalds you, *kills* you."

"We built this planet," Lord Ludlow said. "We're the ones who paid their fines; we're the ones who bought out their contracts. Why should we just...just let them off?"

"People will work hard if they think they'll benefit in some way," Roland said. "You have created a world in which, no matter how hard your debtors and indents work, they're not going to get off the plantations. They have no hope. And so, their hatred and resentment builds up and up until you get workers running off to join the rebels or lashing out at their masters or just waiting for something to happen that'll give them a chance to get their own back. Most of them didn't even *agree* to be sold into *de facto* slavery. Do you expect them to be happy?"

"And if we were to cancel their debts," Lord Ludlow said, "do you know what will happen? The plantations will collapse. Off-world income will vanish completely. Hundreds of thousands of people will starve, because they won't be getting paid or being fed or *anything*."

"You could always pay them a fair wage," Roland said. "Look, you inherited this mess and I don't blame you for being annoyed at the charge you're responsible for creating it. But you have an obligation, for your own good if nothing else, to try to make it better before it blows up in your face. The clock is ticking. The bomb is about to explode. You are about to run out of time."

The PM cleared his throat. "We will take your concerns under advertisement," he said, calmly. "For the moment, please concentrate your attention on raising new troops and readying them for battle."

Which is political-speak for we're not going to listen to you, Roland said. He wasn't a practiced politician, by any measure, but he knew how the game was played. A protest could be disarmed by a show of interest, even if the interest was about as real as the smile on the politician's face. Pretending to take someone seriously was surprisingly good at keeping them from making a protest that couldn't be ignored. *And even if we win the coming war, you're just going to find yourself refighting it again and again until they win, or you wise up.*

"As you wish," he said. He'd have to do something, but what? All the solutions that came to mind were, at best, so far in excess of his orders that he doubted the corps would let him get away with it. His court martial would be the shortest formality on record. "With your permission, sir, we'll return to the base and resume training operations."

The PM nodded. "Draw up a plan to deploy additional troops to Baraka and the surrounding islands," he said. "We need to win the war as quickly as possible."

"And you will refrain from any further political suggestions," Lord Ludlow added, curtly. "You do not live here. This is our world and we will make the decisions in such matters."

Roland shrugged and walked out, Sandra and Rachel following. It wasn't polite, but it was better than what he'd *wanted* to say. The Marines could hold the spaceport long enough to evacuate, if the shit hit the fan. The locals—the PM, Lord Ludlow, even Richard and his fellows—would remain, to face the wrath of the rebels. Roland didn't envy them. It wouldn't be a pleasant end.

"I'm sorry about my father," Sandra said, as they returned to the car. "He's just under a lot of stress right now."

"He'll be under more if he loses the war," Roland said. "At least, until he dies."

Sandra shrugged. "On a different note, would you like to attend a party with me next week?"

Roland blinked. "Are you insane?"

"No." Sandra smiled at him, but there was something hard and desperate in her eyes. "I just think we need to enjoy ourselves before time runs out for good."

CHAPTER THIRTY-FIVE

KINGSTOWN TRAINING BASE/ SPACEPORT, NEW DONCASTER

ROLAND SMILED AS RICHARD was shown into the office. "Help yourself to coffee," he said, waving a hand towards the coffee pot. "Long day?"

"Yeah." Richard had been recalled to assist in preparing the newer companies, a difficult task when even their most experienced men had only a month or two of combat under their belts. The older men had been promoted and reassigned to serve as team leaders, but they didn't have the weight of experience—or the time—they needed to make an impression. "Does it get any easier?"

Roland shrugged. "I keep being told the only easy day was yesterday," he said. "I thought the instructor only spoke in clichés, until I realised he was right."

Richard poured himself coffee and sat, studying the younger man thoughtfully. Roland looked as if he were being run ragged, even though he'd spent the last month on the base rather than in the field. There were just too many things that needed his personal attention, things that—in a more normal army—would be left to the staff. Richard understood why Roland didn't want to borrow General Falk's staff officers—half of them were aristocratic landowners and the other half might well be rebel spies—but he thought it was time Roland built a staff of his own. There were just too many matters that needed his undivided attention.

"The latest reports from Baraka are grim," Roland said. He sounded like a man desperately looking for a silver lining in a dark cloud. "Or are they exaggerated?"

"Understated, if anything," Richard said. "We need more men."

Roland grimaced. Richard knew what he was thinking. The rebels hadn't risked another major attack, but they'd kept up the sniping, bombing and intimidation until morale had hit rock bottom. Again. There were soldiers—and not just militiamen—who'd been reluctant to go beyond the wire, let alone patrol towards the outback. Richard understood, all too well. The FOBs and blockhouses were islands of government control in a sea of rebels. There was no *need* for the rebels to mount a second major attack. They were winning just by not losing.

"It may be a while before we get them," Roland cautioned. "The government isn't quite taking the matter seriously."

"They're not?" Richard raised an eyebrow. "With the plantations themselves coming under constant attack?"

"It's politics," Roland said. There was a hint of weary cynicism in his voice. "The landowners want the rebels defeated, but they're unwilling to make the concessions they *need* to get more people to fight for them. They're reluctant to extend the debt relief program—they even barred a number of debtors from signing up—and they're even hinting the program might be cancelled if the war isn't won quickly. And *that* will blow the whole planet sky high."

He shook his head. "The planet is a pressure cooker," he said. "They need to let off some of the pressure. But even *trying* risks blowing the lid off completely."

"I know." Richard had told Roland—it felt like years ago—pretty much the same. "They don't even listen to you?"

Roland laughed. "In the last two weeks, I attended nine parties. I was told there would be"—he held up his hands to form quotation marks—"*discussions*. What was discussed? Hunting, fishing, a handful of young girls who are shortly to be presented to their peers as potential wives...to hear them talk, you'd think there wasn't a war on. They spent more time talking about how sad it was"—he made a show of rolling his eyes—"that some girl wore the same dress as another girl than talking about the war. It's *just* like Earth, before Earthfall."

"Like Earth?" Richard had always thought Roland was an Earther—he had the accent—but his file had been more than a little vague on his life before joining the corps. "You were there before Earthfall?"

Roland looked into the distance.

Richard wondered what he was saw.

"It was crazy," Roland said. "The Grand Senators were playing petty power games, scrabbling over scraps of power that were growing increasingly worthless; the sons and daughters of the aristocracy were holding party after party, each one striving to outdo the last in indecency; the middle classes were struggling desperately for some kind of financial security; the lower classes were trying to survive....

"I was told that most people didn't know the wolf was at the door. But I think they did know. They just didn't want to admit it. They lost themselves in mindless hedonism because it saved them from having to admit, if only to themselves, that the sky was falling. The news reports were bland and boring, without a single admission that things were going wrong until it was too late, but everyone knew anyway. They partied like mad until the world fell to pieces. Enjoy the decline, I suppose; the crash is going to be lethal."

Richard shivered. "What were you doing, at the time?"

"Being a bloody fool." Roland sounded, just for a second, as though he'd hated the young man he'd been. "I didn't know what was happening. I didn't realise...not until Belinda and then it was too late. The fall was too advanced to be stopped by anyone. All I could do was run and seek safety, as the skies fell and the planet died. Belinda was nearly killed getting me out."

"Belinda?"

Roland said nothing for a long moment. "My...my bodyguard," he said. "She never put up with my nonsense."

Richard had the odd feeling there was more to the story than that, but he chose not to pry. Roland had earned a degree of trust. Richard could wait to hear the rest, if Roland ever wanted to tell it. Besides, Roland wasn't that young fool any longer.

"I guess I didn't have a chance," Roland mused, more to himself than to anyone else. "I never had to deal with reality until it was too late."

Richard frowned. "Is that why you understand the landowners?"

"Yeah." Roland looked up. "And why we have to find a way to make them see sense before it's too late."

"It might already be too late," Richard said.

There was no humour in Roland's smile. "You took the words right out of my mouth."

Richard grimaced. There was a bit of him, he admitted sourly, that wanted to see the landowners get their comeuppance. Maybe not the looting, raping and burning that had swept over the plantations like a plague, but permanent exile to a penal island while the townies turned the planet into something worth having. And yet, he was all too aware of what would happen if—when—the rebels won. They saw the townies as complicit in landowner crimes. Richard—his father, his mother, his siblings—would be put against the wall and shot if the rebels took First Landing. There was no way they could surrender.

"Keep pushing," he said. "Who knows? Maybe the horse will learn to sing."

Roland snorted. "Yeah. And maybe the king will die."

• • •

Elizabeth Shaw was sure, as she passed through the checkpoint outside the spaceport, that her nerves were visible to the Marines manning the gates. They were more civilised than the militiamen and police she'd met—they certainly didn't grope her under the guise of patting her down—but she knew from experience that they were far more capable, and perceptive, than their local counterparts. They'd seen Elizabeth come and go time and time again, yet they never seemed to relax. At first, she'd feared they were onto her. Later, she'd realised they gave the same treatment to everyone.

She nodded politely to the Marine who waved her though, then headed straight for the spaceport terminal. It hadn't been easy to get a post in the spaceport, let alone climb all the way to management level. Elizabeth knew she wouldn't have advanced beyond cleaner if she hadn't been the daughter of a minor landowner, one who'd died long ago. It galled and amused her in equal measure that her relationships made her trustworthy, in the eyes of the planetary government. The government had never stopped to think how she might feel about them.

The thought mocked her as she walked through the empty terminal. It had been so long, between her recruitment and the call to action, that she'd fallen into the habit of thinking it was never going to happen. She'd spent hours devising other ways to hit back at the government, from simply redirecting shipping to ensure the planet was lumbered with heavy fines to messing with the ATC and causing a shuttle to crash into the spaceport. The plans hadn't got off the ground by the time the Marines had arrived, somewhat to her relief. They'd been polite, but very thorough. And they would have asked a lot of hard questions if they hadn't liked what they'd found when they'd searched the spaceport.

She shivered as she reached the elevator and fumbled in her pocket for the keycard. She'd gone to some trouble to ensure her keycard granted her access to everywhere in the terminal, authorised or not. She was mildly disappointed—and relieved—the Marines hadn't thought to question it, if they'd even noticed. They gave their officers so much authority, from what she'd heard, that they might not have realised there was something odd about her having the keycard. She could see their point. Under normal circumstances, she had to wait for her superiors if she wanted to step outside the authorised zone.

The elevator was cool but sweat prickled on her back as she pushed the button and crossed the line. She'd have no excuse now if she was caught. Her heart pounded in her chest as the elevator descended, into the secure zone. It stopped, doors hissing open. Cold air brushed against her skin as she made her way into the fuel storage bunkers, the great tanks buried beneath the spaceport. She thought she tasted kerosene in the air, although it was probably just her imagination. The sensors would have sounded the alert if the tanks had started to leak.

Probably, she thought, with a flicker of dark amusement. *The bastards always skimped on the really important stuff.*

She slowed as she approached a computer console that looked like something out of the Dark Ages. The systems within the storage bunkers were completely separate from the remainder of the planetary datanet, mainly to keep hackers out. Her lips quirked as she pressed her fingers against the controls, bringing the system online. It wasn't very smart. The designers, from what she'd heard, had reasoned that anyone who gained physical access to the system would have a perfect right to be there. Under normal circumstances, Elizabeth supposed they would be right. They hadn't expected a landowner to turn on them.

A low rumble echoed through the complex as she started to open the tanks, allowing the different fuels to intermingle and destabilise. She was no chemist, and she didn't pretend to understand the science, but she'd been assured that mixing the chemicals would result in utter disaster. Her smile grew colder as alarms started to howl, too late. The system was so dumb it couldn't even shut down automatically. She'd seen more safety precautions on handmade rowing boats.

She heard the communicator bleep, but ignored it. There was nothing to be gained in speaking to the Marines. Or anyone. She wanted to taunt the government and landowners, to punish them for turning a blind eye to what their militia had done, but no one would listen, let alone understand. They might never know why she'd turned on them…she shook her head as the bleeping grew louder, her head spinning as she breathed the poisonous fumes. It would be enough to know that her parents and sisters had been avenged....

The world went white, then black.

...

"And they want me to go to another party," Roland said. "It won't be fun."

He snorted. Sandra was a fun companion—and far more perceptive and insightful than she let on, as well as great in bed—but the endless parties were just blurring together into a mass of boredom. Perhaps he was more jaded than he'd thought. The landowners liked to think of themselves as edgy, particularly the younger ones; they liked to think they were pushing the limits of good taste about as far as they'd go. They had no idea that, compared to Earth, their parties were so vanilla they might as well invite their elderly relatives. Roland wasn't sure if he should laugh or envy them. Towards the end, back on Earth, simple human decency and informed consent had been nothing more than meaningless words. It wasn't a real party until....

The ground heaved. Roland threw himself to the floor, drawing his pistol as he hit the ground and rolled over. Were they under attack? He was sure the rebels were planning to attack the training base, to make it clear there was nowhere safe from them...the door burst open, Rachel crashing into the room. Roland levelled his pistol, then lowered it. He could hear shooting outside.

"We're under attack." Rachel snapped. She moved with a cool professionalism that was very unlike her. Or was it? "The spaceport has been hit!"

Roland blanched as the ground heaved again. The spaceport? Captain Allen and most—if not all—of his men and machines had been there. He'd convinced the captain to keep a QRF ready and raring to go at all times, but if they'd been sitting on the ground...he glanced at Richard, seeing the same realisation cross his face. The Marines might already be dead or badly wounded.

He hefted his pistol as he led the way out of the room, Rachel pushing past him as soon as they were in the corridor. Roland's eyes narrowed—he'd never done close-protection duty, but it was clear Rachel *had*—before he put the thought aside. The ground heaved again, the shooting growing louder. The training base was under heavy attack.

"Report," he barked, as he strode into the command centre. The operators were running around like headless chickens, half of them clearly on the verge of panic. There weren't many reports flowing in...he told himself, sharply, that his subordinates were too busy to send reports. "What's going on?"

An operator swallowed hard. "A fuel tanker arrived at the gates and exploded, sir," he said, between gasps. "Armed men followed it in and opened fire."

Roland cursed under his breath. Half the men on post were unarmed. The remainder...the local military frowned on soldiers carrying loaded weapons when they weren't in a combat zone. Roland had countermanded the orders, but he wasn't sure they'd stuck. The locals liked to think Kingstown was safe. Idiots. It had been just a matter of time before the rebels did something a little more daring than kidnapping a Marine advisor and the PM's daughter.

"Richard, go to the front and take command," Roland ordered, quietly. He wanted to take command himself, but Rachel would never let him. "Rachel, try and get me a link to Government House."

"Yes, sir," Rachel said. She cursed a moment later. "Sir, the main communications network is down."

"Try the Marine datanet," Roland ordered, although he suspected it no longer existed. "And then the military or emergency services network."

Rachel worked her console for a long moment. "The Marine net is down too," she said. Her tone suggested she also thought it had been destroyed. "The emergency network is reporting bombings and shootings in First Landing, as well as incidents in Kingsport before contact was lost. Government House is apparently under attack."

Roland stared at the map. The rebels wouldn't have risked such an attack unless it was for all the marbles. Hell, a failed offensive might galvanise the government into breaking the logjam and making the concessions it needed to win. No, the rebels intended to decapitate the government and secure most of the island before resistance could be organised. There was no way to be *sure* there weren't other attacks taking place, but he'd bet his remaining salary that there were attacks scattered over the entire island. He'd *thought* the rebels were being suspiciously quiet.

He forced himself to think as more and more reports flooded in from his staff. The training base had survived, barely. The rebel timing hadn't been perfect and yet…it would have worked if he'd disarmed his men. He breathed a sigh of relief, then cursed under his breath as it dawned on him that *he* was now the ranking officer on New Doncaster. Captain Allen was dead or out of contact, along with the rest of his company. There was no such thing as overkill when it came to dealing with Marines, he'd been told. The report suggested the spaceport had been nuked.

Which is worrying, because a nuke would have to have come from off-world, he thought. *And whoever gave it to the rebels is playing for all the marbles, too.*

He put the thought aside and considered his options. There weren't many. He could sit on his ass and do nothing, but that would mean conceding the planet to the rebels and their backers. Or he could take advantage of the opportunity and hit the rebels before they had a chance to consolidate their gains. It would be risky, but the alternative was worse. If they took out the government, they'd either win by default or the planet would slip into chaos.

"Assemble the troops," he ordered. "Get them mounted up. We're going to First Landing."

CHAPTER THIRTY-SIX

KINGSPORT, NEW DONCASTER

GENERAL TOBIAS FALK HAD ONCE HEARD A JOKE, years ago, about a highborn admiral who'd somehow managed to climb all the way to the top of the navy without so much as setting *foot* on a starship. The joke had been funny at the time, but it had become rather less amusing when he'd realised he wasn't much different. His military education had been very limited and his experience practically non-existent. He knew which end of a gun fired the bullet, he conceded privately, but little else. He'd never thought he needed to know as he climbed the ladder to the top, eventually becoming the senior uniformed officer on the planet. His career had been assured by a combination of family connections and a simple willingness to kiss the ass of anyone who could help him, if only it got him what he wanted.

He winced, inwardly, as he sat in the mayor's office and listened to the mayor and local magnates ranting. He had no illusions about what his juniors thought of him—or his seniors, come to think of it. They didn't like him or trust him...they certainly didn't *respect* him. And why should they? He couldn't even protect them from landowner brats who thought a fancy uniform made them hot stuff on the battlefield, or politicians who thought the soldiers were just another workforce they could exploit.

Tobias had to admit they were right. The war was growing hotter and the army needed experienced officers, not men who knew which fork to use at a dinner party. He was a liability and knew it and there was nothing he could do about it. His replacement would almost certainly be worse.

"And we have a right to their services," a magnate was babbling. Tobias couldn't remember the man's name. "They can't *all* join the army."

Tobias tried not to rub his forehead in despair as the rest of the group started talking, their words blurring until they gave him a headache. The fishing magnates were used to their workers being dependent on them, not going off to join the army in hopes of having their debts cancelled. He sighed inwardly, wondering why they hadn't figured out they needed to pay higher wages or simply cancel the debts ahead of time. Tobias wasn't stupid. He wasn't unaware that it was literally *impossible* to repay most of the debts. But he couldn't figure out a way to forgive the debts without causing a banking crash and massive chaos....

"You must reject them," the magnate snapped. He glared at Tobias, as if he expected the general to snap to attention and do as he was bid. "We need them back. Now."

"They were accepted as soldiers," Tobias said, as calmly as he could. "There is no way they can be returned to you...."

"Then you must refuse to take any more," the magnate said. "Do you know what this'll mean for me?"

Do you know what this'll mean for me? Tobias managed, somehow, to keep from saying it aloud. *You'll bitch and moan to your MPs and they'll bitch and moan to the party leaders and they'll go to me and tell me to do the impossible and....*

There was a flash of light, followed by a loud bang. The building shook. Tobias looked through the window, just in time to see another explosion in the distance. He knew the port well enough to tell the blast had gone off very near, if not inside, a police station. He heard someone gasp behind him as bursts of shooting echoed over the city, men and women screaming as bullets zipped through the air. The government complex was under attack.

The door burst open. Tobias spun, just in time to see three people charging into the room, weapons raised. "Hands up! Hands up!"

"Indi?" The mayor sounded stunned. "What are you doing?"

"Hands up," the young woman snapped. She jabbed a rifle into the mayor's face. "Hands in the air."

Tobias swallowed hard and did as he was told, forcing himself to think as he was shoved against the wall, roughly searched and then had his hands tied behind his back. A magnate started to protest, only to have a rifle butt smashed into his jaw. The rebels—Tobias realised, grimly, that the building was already in rebel hands—kicked and beat the magnate who'd complained, then finished securing the prisoners before searching the office. Tobias gritted his teeth as he heard some of the older men whimpering. It wasn't hard to tell why. They were unlikely to survive the next few hours, let alone the rest of the day. Best case, the army stormed the building and they were killed in the crossfire; worst case, the rebels already ruled the city and they would be executed within hours. Tobias had no illusions. The rebels hated the mayor and the magnates and with good reason. They probably hated him, too.

The mayor was yanked to his feet. "Unlock the terminal," Indi growled, as her former boss was shoved towards his desk. "Now."

"I...."

"Now," Indi repeated. "Or we start killing your family."

"Please," the mayor whimpered. "Please...."

"Do it," Indi said. The hatred in her voice was striking. "Or your daughter will be the first to die."

The mayor broke. Tobias watched, unsurprised, as the rebels started to work, sending out orders onto the datanet. Surrender orders, probably; they'd be addressed to the soldiers, militiamen and policemen who'd survived the first harrowing moments of the fighting. He hoped they'd have the sense to withdraw, rather than surrender or simply wait in place to be killed. They'd never gamed out what they'd do if the city fell into enemy hands. The possibility had never been considered. In hindsight—he shivered as he remembered how many debtors and indents lived in the portside city—that might have been a serious mistake.

"Good," Indi mocked. "Thank you for your service."

Tobias tried to think of a plan, of a way to escape. But nothing came to mind. He was trapped.

. . .

Sarah allowed herself a moment of relief as she stepped out of the shadows and strode towards the town hall, accompanied by a trio of bodyguards. A dozen bodies lay on the steps before the building, police and militiamen who'd been knifed in the back by their comrades or the mayor's personal staff. The checkpoint outside the building had been destroyed beyond repair. The police and militiamen outside the centre of town had been wiped out, when their stations had been blown to hell, or were currently fighting their own hopeless battles. The people had risen, tearing apart the handful of police on the streets before taking the rest of the city. She'd already deployed a number of her people to the richest part of the town, in hopes of taking prisoners and seizing records before the mob tore the district and its inhabitants apart. Sarah had no sympathy for them—the prisoners would be executed, after a show trial—but she wanted the records. She needed to know what the enemy knew.

The air smelt of blood and power as she walked into the town hall. Her people were everywhere, covering the doors and windows. A handful of prisoners—staff who had never been recruited by the rebels—lay on the floor, their hands and feet bound with plastic ties. The fear on their faces made her wince. She'd have their records checked, when she had a moment, and the innocent would be free to go. The remainder, the ones who'd abused their power, would be executed along with their masters.

Indi met her at the stairs. She was a dark-skinned young woman, hired—she'd admitted as much—for her looks rather than her brains. The mayor had never considered her anything other than an office ornament, treating her as a filthy whore and abusing her constantly. And yet, Indi had slipped armed men into the building and overwhelmed the defenders before they realised they were under attack. Sarah doubted the mayor would underestimate her any longer.

"They're in the office," Indi said. "We unlocked the datanet and sent the surrender orders."

"Good." Sarah doubted the orders would be obeyed—an enemy soldier would have to be blind to miss the explosions and fires—but it was worth a try. "Did you manage to make contact with First Landing?"

"No." Indi shook her head. "The datanet is down outside the city itself."

Sarah nodded, keeping her thoughts to herself as they walked up the stairs. The planetary datanet had been designed, right from the start, to be easy to monitor and abuse. It lacked the decentralisation necessary for free speech to flourish. Ironically, the centralisation had made it easier for the rebels to cripple the datanet themselves. She'd cut herself off from her people in First Landing—there was no point in pretending otherwise—but they knew what to do. She didn't need to micromanage from a distance.

She allowed herself a cold smile as she walked into the mayor's office. It was large, ornate and completely useless, just like its owner. The mayor had no taste whatsoever. He'd lined the walls with pornographic paintings—tame, compared to some of the crap she'd seen on Earth—and covered the floor with expensive carpeting that, Indi had told her, was surprisingly comfortable. Sarah suspected the mayor was congratulating himself on his foresight right now. He was lying face-down, hands bound behind his back. His eyes followed her as she entered. He didn't recognise her. Sarah wasn't surprised.

Her eyes widened, just slightly, as she recognised General Falk. They'd hadn't known he was visiting the city and yet…she considered, briefly, letting the general have a chance to escape. The man was believed to be useless, at least from what she'd been told. His replacement could hardly be more useless, which would be bad news for her. And yet…she told herself, firmly, that they had no time to be clever. The city was on fire. Her troops were already disembarking. Shortly, she'd known if her plan had succeeded or if it was time to fold some of her cards to preserve the others.

And we might want to take the general with us, when we go, she told herself. *He could probably tell us one hell of a lot.*

"Good afternoon," she said. Her eyes narrowed as she studied the magnates. "The city is ours. You have been sentenced to death. Do you want to say anything in your own defence before we hang you?"

The magnates stared at her. Sarah's nostrils twitched in disgust. One of the bastards had pooped on himself. She'd seen worse, but still...she shook her head in disbelief. These men—*these* men—were the tyrants who oppressed the masses, who kept the debtors and indents in slavery? These cowards, trembling as they faced her? But then, she supposed, it was always easy to be brave when one was sitting in an estate, surrounded by bodyguards. It was a great deal harder to be brave when one was facing certain death.

"I have money," one of the magnates said. "Whatever you want, I can give...."

The rest of the magnates chimed in, offering everything from money to power. Sarah snapped her fingers as the rest of the squad arrived, telling them to take the magnates to the computer terminals and try to transfer their money to the hidden bank accounts. There was a very good chance the scheme would fail and the transfers would be reversed, if the government survived and started pushing back, but even that would work in her favour. The government would find it harder to raise money if it proved accounts could be fiddled with at will....

And then we'll shoot them anyway, she thought, with a flicker of pleasure. *It isn't as if we need them after today.*

Sarah stared at the mayor, who fearfully looked back at her. He'd soiled himself, too. She rolled him over, put her foot on his throat and pushed down. Hard. He let out a gurgling sound as she crushed his throat, then died. Indi swallowed hard. Sarah understood. She'd seen enough horror, since she'd been exiled, to be numb to it. Indi might have worked for a drooling pervert, all too aware she could be sent to the brothels or plantations for the slightest mistake, but she wasn't so hard. Not yet.

"Strip the building of everything important or valuable, then set the charges," Sarah ordered, as two runners appeared. She'd considered turning the town hall into her base, but it was too obvious a target. The government would target it, if the government survived long enough to mount a counterattack. "Indi, you're with me."

She walked back out of the building and down the street. The shooting and explosions had come to an end, but the city was still in chaos. Homes and apartments were being searched, scores being settled as men and women were dragged out and hung by hastily organised lynch mobs. Landlords seemed to be particular targets. Sarah watched, coldly, as a bunch of landlords and their families were hacked to pieces, their blood pooling on the streets as the remains of their bodies were dropped in the gutter. She made a mental note to have them picked up later, if the city remained in their hands. She felt no sympathy for the landlords—they'd extracted every last credit from their tenants—but their bodies would start to decay and become a health risk. They had to be buried before it was too late.

"Sarah." Conrad Georgetown greeted her as she stepped into the rebel base, an anonymous building hidden amongst other anonymous buildings. "We got a brief message from an observer up north. The spaceport is gone, but the attack on the training base was apparently unsuccessful."

Sarah nodded in relief. The Marines were outsiders—and blowing them up ran the risk of inviting outside intervention—but they'd been too dangerous to leave alone. Their firepower would have tipped the balance, perhaps giving the government a chance to collect itself and counterattack before it was too late. She'd *had* to gamble everything on the offensive. She'd had no choice, but to sentence the Marines—and everyone on the spaceport—to death.

And to think we were concerned about Shaw's true loyalties, she thought. There might be townies who'd joined the rebels and fought alongside them, but *landowner* rebels were vanishingly rare. Shaw's story—her father killed by militiamen, her mother and her sisters and herself brutally raped—had been difficult to verify. The evidence had been very thin on the ground. *We'll put up a statue in her honour if we survive the next few weeks.*

"As expected," she said. She hadn't dared risk moving more men up north. There was too great a chance of being noticed. The enemy tactic of throwing up checkpoints at random had been alarmingly effective. "Where do we stand?"

Georgetown indicated the map. "We've secured the city. The police, militia, soldiers and civil servants are dead, captured or on the run. There's no further resistance. We have control of the local rebels and the handful of independents have been told to stay out of the way or else. They may cause trouble later, but right now they're busy looting the richer parts of town now we've taken what we wanted."

He drew a line on the map with his finger. "I've deployed our troops as planned, with half of them building barricades and the others collecting the people on the blue list; I've also deployed scouts to probe north, checking the way is clear to First Landing. We should be ready to go tomorrow morning, once the troops have been disembarked and the vehicles have been collected."

Sarah nodded. "And the rest of the island?"

"We've heard very little," Georgetown admitted. "Radio contact has been sporadic. A couple of bombings, a handful of shootings...not much beyond that, for all the planning we did. We may not hear more for several days."

"No," Sarah agreed.

She studied the map for a long moment, half-wishing Steve had accompanied her to Kingstown. He would have been an ideal commander for the next stage of the operation, the thrust north to First Landing. If the plan worked, they'd walk straight into a battered city, take possession and declare victory. If not...they might have to fight for it. She grimaced in concern. They'd smuggled hundreds of weapons into Kingsport, and shipped some of them up to First Landing, but nowhere near enough.

The plan called for the capture of enemy arsenals, so the weapons and ammunition could be turned against their owners. If that had failed....

Sarah took a breath. "How do we stand for weapons and ammo?"

"We captured the city's arsenal and also recovered weapons from the various enemy installations," Georgetown said. "However, the fighters have a nasty habit of wasting ammunition. Our training was very basic and they simply don't know much more than point, shoot, reload."

"Yes." Sarah shook her head. They couldn't have fired weapons within the city or they'd certainly have attracted attention, even in the most deprived parts of town. The police would have investigated and the entire plan would have collapsed before it got anywhere near fruition. And yet... there was no point in fretting about it. They'd done better than they'd had a right to expect. "We'll give them what training we can before we head north."

"Of course," Georgetown said.

"And start evacuating everyone on the blue list as soon as possible," Sarah added. "We want them gone if the worst happens."

Georgetown blinked. "But we're winning!"

"Yes," Sarah agreed. Steve would have mocked her caution, but she'd learnt long ago that an ounce of prevention—and planning—was better than a pound of cure. "And that can change at any moment."

CHAPTER THIRTY-SEVEN

FIRST LANDING, NEW DONCASTER

BRYCE WAS UNSURE OF WHAT TO DO as the armoured troop advanced down the motorway towards the city. He'd barely had any time to make contact with the rebels before he'd been promoted and reassigned to training duties, a position that would have given him the perfect opportunity to cause trouble if he'd known it would be needed. Instead, he'd found himself defending his recruits from the rebels and then assigned to the convoy heading straight to the city. He had to give Captains Windsor and Collier credit. They could have sat on their hands and waited to see who came out ahead, particularly after the spaceport had been destroyed, but instead they'd launched an immediate counter-attack. Bryce liked to think the rebels were waiting for them, that they were about to charge right into another trap; privately, he wasn't so sure. The captains had not only called upon the new and better IFVs, but also tanks, aircraft and self-propelled guns that had been earmarked for training duties too.

He frowned as the city slowly came into view, smoke rising from a dozen separate places. First Landing's poor and dispossessed hated the landowners as much as the rest of the planet—Bryce himself was proof of that—but they'd never been as well organised as the rebels who'd given the army a bloody nose only a few short weeks ago. How could they be? The city was under constant surveillance, direct and indirect. Bryce had heard rumours that criminal gangs were allowed to roam free, preying on the poor and defenceless, in exchange for keeping rebels out of their territory. He believed it, too. It was the kind of lazy concept the landowners would think brilliant, keeping the population under control while—at the same time—letting them pretend their hands were clean. Bryce feared the worst. The first rebel offensive might not have succeeded, giving Captain Windsor a chance to tip the balance back in his favour.

And there's nothing I can do about it, he thought. *All hell is about to break loose.*

The convoy swept into the city and confronted a barricade, manned by armed men. Bryce ducked as bullets started zipping through the air, bouncing of the IFV's armour and pinging away in all directions. The armoured cars opened fire, machine guns tearing through the barricade and disintegrating the defenders. A handful of snipers on higher buildings opened fire, trying to snipe at the convoy's commanders, only to draw fire themselves. Bryce hoped some of them managed to get out as the convoy pressed on, leaving the outer districts for later. He listened, grimly, as orders snapped through the radio net. The follow-up forces would try to seal the city, to keep the rebels from escaping into the countryside, but they had strict orders not to enter the disputed districts. Bryce had to admit that was common sense. The men didn't have anything *like* the training they needed to clear a single apartment block, let alone a city.

A rocket shot through the air, narrowly missing an armoured car as it crashed through another barricade and plunged down. Bryce saw bodies dangling from lampposts—government officials, job centre bureaucrats, landlords—and smiled coldly. Win or lose, the government would never feel safe again. The rebels had burnt a police station to the ground, along with a bunch of job centres and other government officers. It wasn't pointless vandalism, Bryce told himself. It was a blow for freedom and self-determination, struck against a planet that simply didn't care. He hoped the banking systems were taken out, too. It would be impossible to demand the debtors and indents repay their debts when the records of who owed what were destroyed. He smirked, then sobered. If the government backed up any records, it would be those.

Another rocket struck the armoured car as they plunged into the government district, flipping the vehicle over and over until it crashed into a building and smashed to the ground. Bryce had no time for sympathy—or glee—as the IFV skidded to a halt, the hatches slamming open to allow the men to jump out. Bryce led the way, trying to ignore the sound of bullets cracking through the air. There were snipers in the nearby buildings, pouring fire down on the convoy. A missile—launched from one of the AFVs—hit one of the buildings and sent it to the ground. Bryce sucked in his breath as he saw the sniper plummet to his death. The bastard had been trying to kill him and yet....

He peered towards the core of the district. The rebels had dragged a bunch of cars into position, welding them in place to construct a makeshift barricade, then positioned their men to turn out covering fire. He heard Captain Collier barking orders, forming up the men to prepare for their advance. They could punch through the barricade in seconds...Bryce wondered, suddenly, if he should shoot Collier in the back. It might go unnoticed, in all the chaos, but...he looked at the men around him and felt a pang of guilt. They were traitors, men who'd sold their souls to the government, and yet he felt a certain responsibility towards them. He couldn't abandon them to the government. He couldn't let their lives be thrown away.

The shooting seemed to reduce, just for a few brief seconds. Bryce listened carefully. The briefing—if one counted a handful of shouted orders as a briefing—had stated Government House was still in friendly hands. Bryce doubted *that*, but...he shook his head, putting the snide humour aside for later. Had the rebels won? Taken the government ministers as hostages? He couldn't help smiling. The surviving government, such as it was, would be wiser to offer to pay the rebels to *keep* the hostages, rather than letting them go. It would certainly improve the government's general efficiency and do wonders for morale.

He saw a man moving on the far side of the barricade, weapon clearly visible, and fired once. The man fell. Bryce cursed under his breath, telling himself he'd shot a government official or a looter or someone—anyone—other than a legitimate rebel. He knew he had to do whatever it took to maintain his cover, yet there were limits. There *had* to be. The rebels wouldn't thank him if he ruined their plans....

A runner stopped beside him. "We go when the rockets are fired."

Bryce nodded. "Understood."

...

The irony, Richard decided as he surveyed the enemy position, was just sickening.

It was hard to be sure—the rebels had spent the last hour putting together a pretty good barricade—but it *looked* as though Government House's security officers were still holding the building against the rebels. The rebels could destroy the building at any moment, if they chose, yet they needed to take the PM alive to force him to order a surrender. Richard suspected they were nervous about trying to storm the building, even with light weapons. The risk of accidentally shooting the PM were just too high.

He ground his teeth in frustration. He didn't *like* the PM or the government. The only reason he hadn't switched sides—he admitted it to himself, if not to anyone else—was that the rebels were worse. He wouldn't shed a single tear if the PM and his people were assassinated...although he rather feared it would lead to Lord Ludlow or someone even worse taking the reins and making the war a hell of a lot worse. And yet, he had to spearhead the mission to save the government before it was too late. He'd heard, once, about a general who'd secretly been on the enemy side and deliberately delayed, maintaining plausible deniability until the battle was over. He understood how that long-dead general must have felt. The urge to just sit on his hands and do nothing was almost overwhelming.

But the rebels are worse, he told himself. He'd seen the bodies as they drove through the streets. They'd been hanging from lampposts and lying in gutters, their blood and guts spilling into the sewers...some of them had deserved it, he was sure, but others had merely had the misfortune to be related to the wrong person. *They have to be stopped.*

He studied the barricade for a long moment, then gave the order. "Fire!"

The antitank missile slammed into the pile of cars and detonated. The barricade exploded, debris flying everywhere. Richard lifted his rifle and charged, leading his men into the morass. The rebels turned, seemingly torn between maintaining the assault on Government House—now scorched and pitted by enemy fire—and turning to deal with the new threat. He was aware of men running behind him as he opened fire, cutting down a pair of rebel fighters before the remainder started shooting back. Richard hit the ground and kept moving forward, hurling grenades into the enemy positions. He felt a bullet snap past his ear, so close that a millimetre to the left would have killed him. There was no time to think as the first of the armoured cars plunged into the chaos and charged past him, machine guns hosing down rebel positions in a manner that offended his professional soul. He made a note to worry about it later as the enemy fire slackened and died, the last of the rebels turning and running only to be shot in the back. Richard shouted orders for his men to stop shooting, to accept surrenders, but their blood was up. They wanted—they needed—to kill the rebels before they were killed themselves.

"Take prisoners," he shouted, as he neared the building. "Take prisoners!"

He breathed a sigh of relief as the engagement came to an end, although he heard more shots in the distance. The armoured cars stopped outside the steps, machine guns traversing to cover the approaches to the building. Richard smiled, tiredly, as he realised the gardens—once the planet's pride and joy—had been reduced to a muddy nightmare by rebels and soldiers alike. The PM's wife would probably start bitching about it—he'd been forced to listen to a lecture from a snobby wife after he'd gotten lost on exercise and found himself crossing her lands—when the fighting was over, if she wasn't already dead. He wondered, suddenly, if the PM was even there. It would be...he chuckled, helplessly, as he directed his men to secure the perimeter. He didn't want to think they'd charged through the rebel-held streets for *nothing*.

Lieutenant Harris saluted. "We took two prisoners, sir," he said. "Both badly injured."

"Get them to the medics, under guard," Richard ordered. His men wouldn't be happy, but they'd just have to put up with it. "We'll see what they can tell us, when they're stable."

"Yes, sir."

・・・

Rachel fired, once.

Roland blinked as he saw a sniper fall from the rooftop, his body vanishing out of sight as it plummeted to the ground. He was an expert shot himself—he'd gone hunting as a young man and he'd been pretty good even before the corps had started to train him properly—and there was no way *he* could have made the shot with a *handgun*. The corps wasn't in the habit of issuing substandard weapons, but...handguns simply weren't that accurate at long range. And Rachel had pulled off the shot....

He tried not to think about the implications as the armoured car drove down the street and into the government complex. His men were holding the motorways and main roads, loudspeakers bellowing orders for the citizens to stay indoors and keep their heads down, but the remainder of the city was a mess. He couldn't tell which sections were ruled by criminal gangs, taking advantage of the chaos to loot everything that wasn't nailed down, and which sections were controlled by rebels and their allies. The attack on Government House itself might have failed—barely—but the rebels had done a hell of a lot of damage. He'd driven past a pile of ruined buildings, all targeted for destruction. He didn't know why—he didn't know the city that well—but he doubted he'd like the answer when he found out.

The car parked in the remains of the garden outside Government House. Roland stood, clambered out and headed up the steps, Rachel right behind. The security officers looked tired and worn; they glanced at the soldiers worriedly, as if they expected the army to turn on them at any moment. Roland understood. Many of the soldiers were debtors or indents and could hardly be relied upon to *like* the PM or Government House. They might even decide to finish the job for themselves.

And if the government doesn't learn from this, it is completely beyond salvation, Roland thought. The rebels had taken out the spaceport, killed nearly seventy Marines and laid siege to the government in its own lair. What else had they done? Roland's communications officers had picked up a brief message from Baraka, then nothing. *We'll have to take the government out in order to save the world.*

The PM looked edgy as Roland was shown into the situation room. A large map hung on the wall, covered with red splodges. Roland eyed it, hoping to hell the PM's staff had taken all the unconfirmed reports at face value. If the map was even remotely accurate, the island was doomed. They'd have to go into hiding or try to surrender for the best terms they could get and he was pretty sure the terms wouldn't guarantee their lives. Roland wondered what the hell *he'd* do, if the worst happened. There was a very good chance the rebels wanted him dead, too.

"Thank you," the PM said. "They nearly broke through our defences."

"You're welcome." Roland was tempted to point out that they needed a bigger army, but it wasn't the time. "Do you have an updated report?"

The PM didn't seem to hear him. "They would have broken through, if we hadn't tightened security up after Sandra was nearly kidnapped," he said. He sounded as though he was talking to himself. "We could have lost Government House. We could have lost everything."

Roland frowned—there was no *time* for the PM to have a breakdown—then glanced at the operators. "Do you have an updated report?"

"Yes, sir," the nearest operator said. "The rebels appear to have occupied Kingsport. I was able to speak briefly to an officer in the militia, who confirmed that the city was under heavy attack and the town hall had fallen before the line went dead. We picked up radio broadcasts from the mayor ordering the remaining defenders to surrender, but we don't know how many actually did. We don't have any solid reports from the city itself...not yet. I haven't even been able to establish contact with General Falk and his staff."

"And if we don't hear something from him quickly, we have to assume he's dead," Roland finished. He'd never thought highly of the general, but at least he'd had the sense not to try to micromanage Roland and his team. "The city is in enemy hands...."

He frowned, making a show of stroking his chin as he studied the map. The rebel plan appeared to be relatively straightforward. Take out the Marines, take out the training base, take control of First Landing and Kingsport and then take the remainder of the island and its industrial base. They'd failed to take out the training mission, or capture the capital, but they'd certainly taken Kingsport. Roland remembered the endless flow of ships moving in and out of the port and shuddered. The rebels could have moved a small army into the port and no one would even have noticed, particularly if the right palms were greased. And that meant....

If we let them get a secure lodgement, we're fucked, he thought. He'd studied amphibious assaults. The corps had a long and proud tradition of landing on enemy shores, dating back thousands of years. Once they secured the beachhead, victory was just a matter of the proper application of overwhelming force. *We have to push them back into the sea before it's too late.*

He looked at the PM. "Prime Minister, we have to act fast," he said. "I request emergency authority to do what must be done."

The PM didn't try to argue. "Do it," he said. "You have my full support."

You'll regret that later, Roland predicted, as he and Rachel headed back outside to join Richard. *But for the moment, it's the only thing that'll save your planet from certain destruction.*

THE PRINCE'S WAR

...

The briefing had been a little more detailed this time, Bryce conceded as he led the unit to their jump-off point. The rebels had taken Kingsport. The army intended to recover the city and drive the rebels back into the sea, quickly. Captain Windsor and his men were already bringing up aircraft, tanks and self-propelled guns. And he had the authority to use them inside the city. It was going to be a long and bloody fight and....

Bryce kept his thoughts to himself as he arranged to take first watch. His men needed their sleep. He felt oddly guilty for leaving them, even though he was fairly sure they'd be safe until the offensive actually began. They'd been warned about rebel snipers and kidnappers. Hopefully, they'd assume he'd been killed or simply chosen to desert before the fighting got any worse. If they worked out he'd been a spy...what could they do? They could hardly change their plans on a moment's notice.

He sighed as he waited for twilight to fall. He had no close family, no one who might be held accountable for his actions. And...he shook his head. The time had come to take action and to hell with everything else. He took one last look at his men, sleeping in the commandeered barn, then mounted the farmer's motorcycle and rode into the gloom. By the time they realised he was gone, it would be too late....

...And the rebels in the city ahead would know what was coming for them.

CHAPTER THIRTY-EIGHT

KINGSPORT, NEW DONCASTER

SARAH HADN'T SLEPT WELL.

It was odd, given that the die was well and truly cast. She had good reason to be pleased with herself, even if they hadn't heard much from the north. Kingsport was in rebel hands. The guilty were being purged, if they hadn't fled ahead of avenging armies; the innocent, particularly the ones with valuable skills, were being shipped overseas even as she brought more and more armed men into the front lines. Her people were rounding up street gangs and recruiting them into the rebel army, giving them what little training they could before the recruits had to fight. She knew she'd done well and yet....

She tossed and turned on the makeshift bed, uneasy and unsure of herself. The gamble had worked, at least in Kingsport, but hearing nothing from the north worried her more than she dared admit to her subordinates. There hadn't even been a brief radio signal, which suggested... what? Enemy jamming? Or an advance guard already wiped out? Sarah didn't know. She'd laid her plans on the assumption of failure and yet not *knowing* was almost worse than hearing the worst. She rubbed her forehead, wishing she'd dared take something to help her sleep. Or found someone to share her bed for the night.

The thought revolted her, even as her lips twitched in dark amusement. It would be a long time before she willingly shared her bed with anyone, after everything she'd endured. There were few people she trusted in any way and none she trusted enough to sleep beside her, not even amongst the rebels. It had been bad enough in the brothels, before she'd joined the rebels and started uniting the different factions. Now....

There was a knock on the door. Sarah sat up, rubbing the sleep from her eyes. "Come!"

The door opened, revealing Indi. "General, the advance units just captured a man on a motorbike," she said. "He claims to be a deep cover agent and gave us his recognition phrases, but...."

Sarah nodded as she stood. There were ways to make someone immune to interrogation, from simple torture to truth drugs and lie detectors, but none were available to her. A deep cover agent could have been uncovered and broken, his recognition phrases given to an enemy agent and used to work his way into her good graces. She gritted her teeth as she checked her pistol and spare magazines automatically, then followed Indi though the door and down the corridor. The enemy could be playing games, although...if they were, it was almost certain the assault on First Landing had failed. She didn't want to think about the implications, but she had no choice. The Marines might have survived, too, and who knew what would happen then?

They'll be gunning for us, Sarah thought. The simple fact the Marines *weren't* raining death on the rebel positions suggested, strongly, that they'd been crippled even if they hadn't been wiped out. *They won't be pretending to be neutral after we tried to blow them to hell.*

She tensed as she stepped into the makeshift interrogation room. A beefy man sat on a chair in the centre, hands cuffed behind his back and a large black bag covering his head. Two guards stood behind him, weapons at the ready; a third ran a scanner over his body. Sarah frowned. There didn't seem to be anything alarming, such as a transmitter hidden within the man's body—perhaps inserted without his knowledge—but it was hard to be sure. The Marines had access to technology that would daunt even the landowners, let alone her. And if they'd decided to be devious....

"He's clear," the tech said. "No traces of anything, as far as I can tell."

Which might be meaningless, Sarah thought. She'd been told that some transmitters were almost impossible to detect, as long as they were powered down. *If they sent him here to scout out our base....*

She glanced at the guards. "Remove the hood."

The deep cover agent took long breaths as his face came into view, his eyes widening as he looked at Sarah. Sarah allowed herself a smile of relief—she recognised him—before reminding herself to be careful. Bryce Ambrose could have been turned at any moment—he might even have been a spy before he joined the rebels, let alone allowed himself to be recruited into the landowner's army—and she couldn't afford to take anything for granted. And yet....

He stared at her, confused. Of course. He'd thought she was a contact, just a messenger girl. He'd never realised she was actually in command... Sarah put the thought aside. She'd needed to be sure the reports didn't get garbled in transit, even if it meant putting her life at risk. And the fact he'd broken cover to come to her meant...what? She had the feeling she didn't want to know, but she *needed* to.

"Report," she said, calmly. "What happened?"

Bryce Ambrose started to speak. Sarah listened, as her heart sank. The Marines were gone—she breathed a silent prayer of thanks—but the assault on First Landing had failed and the new army was readying itself for an counterattack on Kingsport. She cursed under her breath as the agent—the spy—told her about tanks and aircraft as well as men who wanted a little payback after the attack on their base. The irony would have made her laugh, if it wasn't about to get a lot of her people killed. She'd captured General Falk—now on his way to Baraka for long-term imprisonment—and, in doing so, she'd done the government a big favour. Captain Windsor was clearly a hell of a lot more competent than the local-born landowner general.

And we cleared all the dead wood out of the way for him, she thought, as she checked her watch. There were only three hours until dawn. *Whoops.*

"I knew you had to be warned," Bryce Ambrose finished. "And so I deserted and came here."

Sarah nodded, then looked at the guards. "Take him to the ships," she ordered. "I want him on his way before dawn."

She turned away, forcing herself to think. The first and second parts of the gambit had effectively failed. She had no illusions about what would happen if her forces encountered the enemy in a running battle. Captain Windsor and his men would chew them to pieces without so much as slowing down. She might be able to hold the line at Kingsport...she shook her head a moment later, dismissing the idea. Given a couple of weeks to prepare, she might have been able to make an assault more costly than the landowners were willing to bear, but...she had a few hours at most. Come sunlight, the attack would begin.

We can't let them score a victory, not now, she thought. The rest of the plan had worked. Large swathes of the islands—their plantations, their factories—had fallen into rebel hands. The war would take longer than she'd hoped, and there would be much more fighting, but it was far from lost. *It's time to cut our losses.*

She summoned the messengers as she walked into the planning room. "Tell the commanders on the alpha and beta lists that they are to start withdrawing to the ships, effective immediately," she ordered. "The commanders on the remaining lists are to ask for volunteers to stay behind and man the defences, while we pull the rest of the army out."

Her eyes lingered on the map as she continued to issue orders. The enemy was going to be *mad* when they discovered the rebels had stolen every ship in port, from fancy pleasure boats to dingy freighters, but it didn't matter. By the time they realised the retreat was under way, it would be too late. They'd lose most of their shipping to the rebels and it would take months, if not years, to replace it. They'd certainly have problems mounting an invasion of the rebel-held islands.

We might have lost this round, she conceded, as her people started to pack up and leave the command post. *But we did enough to ensure we'd still win the war.*

...

"The advance scouts are reporting in," Rachel said. "The enemy has thrown up a barricade around the city, but otherwise appears to be falling back into the city."

Roland nodded, trying not to yawn. He'd barely had any sleep since he'd led his troops into First Landing, then started to establish lines to seal off Kingsport from the remainder of Kingstown. The units were more than a little scattered and the communications network was a mess—and he was starting to fear that the coming engagement would turn into a thoroughly nasty brawl. He'd studied urban combat in Boot Camp. The only upside, he told himself firmly, was that the enemy simply hadn't had *time* to turn the city into a meatgrinder.

"Good," he said. "And the refugees?"

"They were told to keep moving," Rachel said. "The outflow appears to have slowed to a trickle."

Roland cursed under his breath. There were no solid figures for the population of Kingsport—the harbour city had people coming and going all the time, many of whom wanted to remain unnoticed and untaxed—but Richard had estimated it to be over two hundred thousand. It might well be a great deal higher. Roland hadn't managed to get a solid count on how many people had escaped into the countryside, when the rebels took the city, but he was sure upwards of a hundred thousand remained within the city. Many would be rebels, or at least sympathisers...he shook his head. Hopefully, most of the civilians would have the sense to keep their heads down and stay off the streets. There was no way he could delay the offensive long enough to evacuate the city, even if the rebels wanted to play ball.

They could ship an entire army into the city and make it impregnable, he thought. They'd received a brief radio message from an FOB on Baraka, reporting that the base was under heavy attack, then nothing. *We can't afford a prolonged battle to retake the city or all-out war across the countryside.*

He sucked in his breath. Captain Allen should have survived. Captain Allen should have taken command. Roland felt...inadequate. It was hardly the first time a Marine—or an auxiliary—had wielded authority far in excess of his formal title, but he still feared he wasn't up to the task. Captain Allen would have done a far better job, he was sure. Captain Allen...his heart clenched. Captain Allen was dead. And there was no point in trying to find someone else to take command. He was the man on the spot.

The sunlight glimmered in the distance. Dawn was coming.

"Signal the gunners," he ordered. "They are to open fire as planned."

"Aye, sir."

Roland nodded, stiffly, as the distant guns began to boom. They weren't *that* accurate, certainly not compared to the smart weapons the corps deployed as a matter of course, but they'd hit the right general area. The enemy would be scattered, unable to mount a concentrated defence... he hoped. The advancing army should be able to punch into the city, taking control of the roads and harbour itself. It wasn't ideal—the rebels would have plenty of time to finish the purge and set up defences—but there weren't many other options. He didn't have the manpower for an advance across a wide front.

We will, he promised himself.

He glanced at Rachel, a question on his lips. He wanted to ask...he hesitated, then put it aside for later as bangs and crashes echoed across the land. The shells were coming down, striking their targets....

"Signal the lead forces," he ordered. "They are to advance under cover of the guns."

"Aye, sir."

...

Sarah hit the ground as she heard the first incoming shells, bracing herself for the impact. It was suddenly very easy to believe she'd been personally targeted. If the enemy knew where the CP was, they'd take it out first in hopes of scattering her forces...she rolled over as the ground heaved beneath, trying to spot where the shells had come down. It looked as though the enemy was shelling the barricades, the ones that had been recently abandoned...she allowed herself a tight smile as the guns boomed again and again. They wanted to waste their ammunition...she shook her head. She had no intention of trying to stop them.

She picked herself up and kept walking. It was hardly the first time she'd been under fire, let alone in mortal danger, although she had to admit there was something oddly impersonal about the shelling that made it worse. The men hurling high explosives into the city weren't trying to hit her personally—they didn't even *know* her—but if a shell came down in the wrong place she'd be dead before she even knew what had hit her. The ground heaved again as another shell came down to the south, the sound of the explosion echoing over the city. She saw pale faces in the windows, rapidly hidden. The civilians—those who hadn't been earmarked for death or impressment—would hopefully stay inside and wait until the fighting came to an end. The streets were very far from safe.

A messenger ran up to her. "They hit the Town Hall!"

Sarah had to smile. "How badly?"

"They destroyed it," the messenger said. "It's just a pile of rubble."

Sarah felt her smile grow wider. "Good thing no one was there," she said. Her people had searched the building from top to bottom, then abandoned it. There was nothing to be gained, she'd thought, from trying to use it herself. She'd planned to destroy it. The enemy had saved her the trouble. "Hopefully, they'll think they hit something vital."

She dismissed the messenger as they kept moving, flitting from cover to cover as the enemy shells rained down. It was clear they weren't *intentionally* targeting the harbour, or the residential blocks, but their shells were so inaccurate they couldn't help hitting the wrong places and killing dozens, perhaps hundreds, of innocent civilians. Sarah saw a tower block crumble and prayed the inhabitants had made it out before she'd taken control of the city and trapped them within her defences. If anyone had remained in there, they were likely dead. There was no time to search for survivors.

The noise grew louder, the shells falling more and more to the north. The defences—what remained of them—were getting pasted, smashed flat without any way to retaliate against their distant tormentors. Sarah winced, promising herself she'd remember the dead as she joined the throng flowing down to the harbour. Her people were already working hard, loading the evacuees onto the boats and sending them into deeper waters. She felt an odd little pang of guilt as she, and her command staff, were urged onto a pleasure yacht. The sailors had already bypassed the security systems, ready to take them to safety. And yet, she knew she was leaving hundreds behind.

You planned for every contingency, her thought reminded her. *You knew there might come a time when you'd have to concede the battle, in order to win the war.*

The thought tormented her as the engine came to life, thrusting the yacht onto the waters and through the harbour mouth. The seas were alive, hundreds of ships making their escape and heading towards rebel territory. Sarah wanted to cheer, knowing just how many ships and experienced sailors would be denied to the enemy, and yet she knew it wasn't a real victory. She'd hoped to win the war in a single blow. Instead...she'd committed herself to a far longer war, one that would tear the planet to pieces even if they won.

You had no choice, her thoughts reminded her. *And they know it, too.*

She stood on the deck, heedless of the risk as she stared at the burning city. She was no stranger to horror and yet...there was something chilling about the pillars of flame and smoke rising into the skies. She tried to tell herself that the landowners had committed atrocities, that they deserved a taste of their own medicine, yet...she knew hundreds of innocents had been caught in the flames. The townies would hate her and her people as much as the landowners did, when they took stock of the aftermath. And the war would get worse.

Another line of explosions blasted out, shockwaves shaking the deck. Her people were destroying everything they couldn't steal, ensuring the harbour facilities were denied to the enemy. It wouldn't keep them from rebuilding, if the projections were correct, but it would win the rebels more time. And time was what they needed. And yet....

She shook her head as the flames grew worse, refusing to turn away. She owed it to herself to watch, even though she felt as though she was staring into hell. She wanted—needed—to bear witness. And to remind herself, as if she'd forgotten, that it was now a total war.

As if there was ever any doubt, she thought, grimly. *Everything we did, in the last day, was nothing more than a pale shadow of their crimes.*

But, somehow, the thought didn't make her feel any better.

CHAPTER THIRTY-NINE

KINGSPORT, NEW DONCASTER

"SIR," LIEUTENANT WIGGIN SAID. "We have orders to move in two minutes."

Richard nodded, checking his rifle. He'd insisted on leading the attack personally—or, rather, one small section of the attack—even though both Roland and Rachel had had doubts about the wisdom of putting him in danger. Richard understood their concerns—there were only a handful of experienced local-born officers—yet he needed to make a name for himself to make it impossible to demote him again, when the planetary establishment reasserted itself. General Falk might be dead—the last report had placed him in Kingsport, which was now under enemy control—but there were plenty more uniformed politicians waiting in the wings, ready to take his place. Roland was a good officer, if unformed, yet...he wasn't *local*. It was just a matter of time before the planetary government tried to sideline Roland and everyone under his command. Richard intended to be ready.

He peered into the distance as the seconds ticked away, gritting his teeth as shells crashed amidst the enemy defences. Kingsport had never been pretty—ugly apartment blocks, even uglier factories and warehouses on the edge of the ring road—but he couldn't help thinking the city was about to become a great deal worse. The skyline was rent with flames and smoke, started by the shellfire or—worse—by the rebels themselves. He tried not to think of the number of times he'd passed through the city, of the people he'd met during his brief visits. How many of them were dead now? How many had fled? Kingsport had never kept close track of its population either. The final death toll might be much higher than anyone thought.

And a bunch of people might take advantage of the chaos to change their names and vanish, Richard thought. He'd spoken to a bunch of refugees. They'd cautioned him that the rebels had taken the government buildings largely intact. *There's no way we'd be able to track them down in time.*

He glanced back, watching as the armoured cars and tanks moved into position. They wouldn't be spearheading the assault—no one knew what kind of antitank weapons the rebels might have, waiting for them—but they'd be ready when the infantry needed them. Richard caught sight of their commanders, peering towards the city, and inwardly winced. The tanks looked solid, and brutally intimidating, but they'd never been tested in combat. Their crews might not have realised, not yet, that their vehicles could easily turn into death traps. The rebels might have obtained modern antitank weapons from their mysterious off-world allies. Richard had the feeling they were about to find out.

"Ten seconds," the sergeant said.

Richard nodded. The rebels had turned the warehouses ahead of them into a barricade, weaving cars and trucks together to form a crude but effective barrier. The shelling had blown the vehicles to hell, scattering metal everywhere, yet there was still plenty of cover for enemy fighters. Richard braced for combat, even as he tried to convince himself the shelling had wiped the enemy out and all they had to do was walk into the city and repossess it. He knew better. He'd seen enemy fighters survive far worse bombardments. A trench would be enough to protect them unless the shells came right down on their heads…

The whistle blew. Richard ran forward, keeping his head down. He didn't look back to see if his men followed. It was important not to show the slightest hint of doubt that they would. Richard heard them running and smiled, sweeping his eyes from side to side. The mangled remains of the cars, still smoking, would give the enemy far too much cover. The scouts had reported hundreds of rebels manning the barricade. It was too much to hope for them all to be dead.

Nothing moved as he peered through the debris, then led the way into a warehouse. It looked as through a bomb had detonated inside, the shelves blasted to rubble and their contents—what hadn't been looted—on the ground. He kept his eyes open as his men spread out behind him, muttering into his throatmike as they reached the far end of the warehouse. There was still no sign of the enemy, not even bodies. His sense of unease deepened as the communications net crackled, updating him. None of the advancing forces had contacted the enemy....

He saw someone moving ahead of him and yanked up his rifle, taking aim. The figure swung around, lifting a rifle of his own. Richard shot him without hesitation, then ran forward as he heard more shots in the distance. The enemy fighter lay on the ground, dead. Richard checked his pulse, just to be sure, then frowned as he took in the young man's clothing and tattoos. Gang colours...practically uniforms in their own right. The rebels were sending gangs against them?

They probably see the gangsters as expendable, Richard thought, as his men cleared out the remaining defenders. They'd been slowed, but they'd hardly been stopped. *It isn't as if the rebels would have any more use for the gangsters than us. They probably hoped the bastards would die at our hands....*

He pressed forward, hearing shooting and mortars in the distance. A rocket whooshed over his position and exploded somewhere behind him. The firing seemed erratic, as if the rebels were trying to slow them down rather than stop them in their tracks. He kept moving, ducking from side to side as he spotted another enemy strongpoint. They hadn't had time to make it *really* strong, but...he unhooked a grenade from his belt and hurled it neatly through the oversized window, then led his men inside as it detonated. The enemy would have been wiser, part of his mind noted coolly, to seal the windows and cut new murder holes in the walls. The windows had made it far too easy for him to counterattack.

The fighting ground on, an endless series of tiny skirmishes that wore him and his men down even as more and more reinforcements entered the fray. The enemy rarely counterattacked, for which he was grateful, but they held the lines surprisingly well. They grew more diverse, too—many of the defenders were clearly male indents and debtors, but some were women who fought as hard as the men—and even though they hadn't had time to turn the city into a death trap they'd certainly managed to set a handful of traps. A soldier died when he put his foot in the wrong place and triggered a bomb; another was horribly burnt when he made the mistake of firing his rifle in the midst of a gas cloud. Richard found himself unmoved, even when they stumbled over a pile of bodies. They hadn't been killed by the shellfire, he noted grimly. They'd been garrotted, then their bodies had been left to rot. He wondered, numbly, who they'd been.

They took cover inside an abandoned house and waited, allowing the reinforcements to take the lead. Richard unhooked his canteen and took a drink, tasting strangely unpleasant electrolytes in the water. The REMFs swore blind it was good for the men, and Richard hadn't noticed any ill-effects, but it still tasted odd. His teeth tingled as he returned the canteen to his belt, then checked the communicator. The command network was a mess—half the units had fallen out of contact, as expected—but there seemed to be no reason to panic. The enemy were holding each defence point for a few short seconds, then falling back. Richard wondered, suddenly, where the hell they thought they'd go? Kingsport was a harbour. They were going to be shoved right into the sea....

Or they'll take ship and run, he thought, suddenly. *Shit.*

• • •

Roland frowned as he studied the reports. Rachel had forbidden him to go any closer to the front lines, pointing out that he had to remain in overall command of the operation, but...it was clear something wasn't right. The enemy should have put up a nastier fight. He doubted the shelling had knocked the stuffing out of them. And yet...they were just holding the line, delaying his men for a few brief moments and then retreating further into the city. They were wise not to let the army pin them down—Roland had no qualms about dropping shells or bombs on enemy strongpoints, taking them out without endangering his men—but...they were going to run out of city.

His intercom bleeped. "Sir," Richard said. His voice was grim. "They're planning to take ship and abandon the city."

Roland said nothing for a long moment, swallowing curses as the pieces fell into place. He should have seen it at once. Sandra had taken him through the harbour, when they'd started their ill-fated cruise. There were enough ships to evacuate most of the city's population, if they managed to get organised in time. Perhaps they had. Kingsport was more than *just* a harbour. The rebels could have press-ganged—kidnapped—everyone with useful skills and taken them away before the counterattack got under way...a contingency plan, perhaps, designed to go into operation even if the main thrust of the offensive succeeded. He wondered, idly, who was in command on the other side. Local intelligence hadn't identified anyone, beyond a handful of codenames that could easily have been designed as red herrings.

Whoever is in command, they did very well, he thought. *They even managed to come up with a plan to take advantage of their own defeat.*

He looked at Rachel. "Change of plan," he said. "The lead units are to advance towards the harbour and take possession as quickly as possible."

Rachel grimaced. Roland had no trouble guessing what she was thinking. Charging straight into the teeth of enemy fire would get a lot of people killed, perhaps for nothing. The rebels wouldn't hesitate to hold the harbour, if they were evacuating their own fighters as well as the useful townspeople. There'd be one hell of a fight and a lot of civilians would get killed in the crossfire...but he dared not let them pull out. They'd simply wind up facing the rebels again on a different battlefield.

His mind raced. The guns could rain shells on the harbour...he shook his head before he could even *start* giving the order. They might just sink most of the boats—he smiled at the thought of how Sandra would react if her yacht was sunk—but they'd kill most of the kidnapped people in the process. If he was right...he scowled. He *knew* he was right. The rebels hadn't hesitated to recruit, sometimes at gunpoint, from the plantations. Why would they hesitate to do it here?

"And then send in the tanks," he added. It was a risk—they'd seen the enemy use a handful of antitank rockets, although there'd been no hint of plasma guns—but one that would have to be borne. "We need to close the escape route as quickly as possible."

...

Danial Drake knew he was going to die.

He felt oddly calm as he waited, rifle in hand, and watched the street from his hidden vantage point. He'd stepped forward at once when they'd asked for volunteers and remained in line, even when they'd told him there was a very good chance he was going to die. They'd *tried* to suggest that the volunteers *might* manage to break contact and escape into the untouched parts of the city, then flee into the countryside, but it struck him as wishful thinking. There was no hope of getting out alive. He knew it and he'd accepted it. It was why he'd asked for the mission in the first place.

His lips twisted in disgust as the sound of shooting grew louder. The advancing army, composed of traitors to their class, was picking up speed. He wondered, not for the first time, what could induce men to betray their own interests so openly. Did they think there would *really* be debt-forgiveness? Daniel's father had worked himself to death on the farm, only to lose everything he'd built on a teeny, little technicality. He'd hung himself that night. Daniel had found the body and sworn revenge.

And now he had his chance.

The detonator beside him seemed to glow with heat. He touched it lightly. The glow was his imagination, but...who cared? All that mattered was what he could do...he tensed as he saw the remaining fighters running to the next strongpoint, well behind *his* position. It was time. The next people who came down the street would be the people he needed to kill. He leaned forward, one hand on the detonator. The soldiers were coming forward, a handful rushing to the next place of concealment while the remainder covered them before leapfrogging forward themselves. They were definitely trying to move faster. Their speed was taking them right into the blast zone.

"For you, Dad," Daniel said.

He closed his eyes and pushed the detonator. The ground exploded. His ears popped. His eyes snapped open. He saw a smouldering crater in the street...no, the street itself was gone, the buildings on each side collapsing into rubble. They'd told him the IED was big, but...he smiled as he spotted a handful of soldiers, probing into the blast zone. He lifted his rifle and opened fire. Two fell; the remainder ducked for cover. Daniel allowed himself a smirk as he kept firing, the rifle jerking in his hand as he sprayed bullets towards his targets. He'd already wiped out an entire platoon and more of enemy soldiers. Maybe he'd get out of it alive after all....

Something flashed towards him. The air went white.

...

Richard cursed under his breath as the rocket struck home. The sniper had been very well placed, damn him, although Richard had no idea how he'd intended to make his escape. The soldiers had orders to take prisoners, where possible, but the command net had noted a number of snipers had been shot trying to escape. It was hard to blame the men for taking revenge—snipers were nasty—even though he knew he'd have to stop them if they tried it under his command. They had to accept surrenders, or the enemy wouldn't accept them either.

He summoned a pair of medics as they resumed the advance. Roland's orders had been clear. They had to get to the harbour as quickly as possible to block the enemy's escape, even if it meant taking additional risks.

Richard suspected they were already too late—the enemy had had a day to ship thousands of people out of the city—but orders were orders. And besides, they had permission to call for supporting fire if they needed it.

The ground heaved as shells landed within the former red-light district, destroying bars, brothels and expensive shops with grim abandon. Richard prayed they'd been abandoned, the owners and workers ordered to leave...they would have been sent away, he told himself, although he wasn't entirely sure. The red-light district was just a little *too* close to the harbour for the enemy's peace of mind. Evacuating it would make it easier to defend the harbour for a few minutes longer....

He gritted his teeth as they punched through and saw, for the first time since Kingsport had been settled, an empty harbour. A couple of boats rested near repair yards, clearly beyond immediate use, but the remainder had been stolen and sent out to sea. He lifted his eyes, watching helplessly as the massive fleet sailed into the distance. Gunshots were still echoing through the city, the last of the rebel forces fighting desperately to buy time...Richard shook his head. They'd won the battle, but the rebels had salvaged most of their forces and their allies in the city. The war was far from over.

"Secure the harbour," he ordered. Now the main body was gone, the remanding rebels might surrender. They'd completed their mission. He hated to admit it, but it was true. They'd die for nothing if they kept fighting. "And then we'll deal with the stragglers."

He keyed his communicator and made a brief report to Roland. He'd have to report back to the PM...Richard didn't envy him. The government had probably already recovered its usual arrogance. Roland would be blamed for not winning an unwinnable battle. They could try to spin the battle into a victory—they *had* recovered Kingsport, before it could be turned into a base for an attack on First Landing—but somehow he doubted the government would be impressed. They were fond of spinning stalemates and defeats into victories. They'd recognise Roland was doing the same.

The shooting slowly died away as the soldiers took possession of the city. None of the rebels surrendered, some even blowing themselves up when they were wounded. Richard feared a number had simply hidden their weapons, then slid back into the local population. It would take time, time they didn't have, to find the bastards…he felt a surge of sudden loathing and hatred as he walked past the piles of bodies. The rebels had killed the landlords and other parasites, then turned their attention to shop owners and merchants whose only crime had been having more than them. Richard understood, but….

It's not over, he told himself. *It's only going to get worse.*

CHAPTER FORTY

FIRST LANDING, NEW DONCASTER

ROLAND SHOOK HIS HEAD, wiping the sweat from his brow, as Rachel drove the car through the checkpoint and into the underground garage. They'd spent the last few hours trying to consolidate their victory—he admitted, privately, that the engagement had been more of a draw—before the PM had summoned them back to Government House and, in truth, he wasn't looking forward to the coming conversation. He'd pushed his authority much further than anyone, including the PM, had expected it to go and there would be consequences. A clear victory would have made it harder for anyone to call him out, but....

He sighed, cursing under his breath. The spaceport was a burnt-out ruin. Captain Allen and his men were dead. Their equipment and supplies were gone. He didn't know—yet—how many of his own men had died in the last two days, but the figure was, at the very least, well over five hundred. The outposts on Baraka and a dozen other islands were gone, their defenders seemingly wiped from existence. He dreaded to think how many civilians—and even rebels—had been killed. And the rebels had managed to extract most of their forces from Kingsport before it fell.

"Chin up," Rachel said. "The war isn't over yet."

Roland studied her thoughtfully, then threw caution to the wind.

"You're not what you seem, are you?"

Rachel shrugged. "Neither are you."

"No." Roland felt himself flush. "You're like Belinda, aren't you? A Pathfinder."

Rachel's face shifted, just for a second. Roland stared. The effect was minimal and yet...the frumpy assistant was gone, perhaps for good. In her place, a trained soldier looked at him. Roland tried not to cringe. An assistant...no, an undercover bodyguard, one so good at maintaining the illusion that she was harmless that he'd had problems believing she was anything other than what she seemed. And yet...he kicked himself, mentally. He'd thought he'd been allowed to train as a proper Marine, but *of course* they wouldn't have sent him out alone. They'd wanted to make sure nothing happened to him....

He clenched his fists. "Didn't they think I could take care of myself?"

Rachel quirked an eyebrow. Roland flushed. He knew he'd made mistakes...in hindsight, he was sure, now, that Rachel had secretly accompanied Sandra and him to the yacht. If she was anything like Belinda, she could have taken out some of the kidnappers while leaving him none the wiser. He felt a sudden stab of regret she *wasn't* Belinda, mingled with the grim awareness he would have *deferred* to Belinda. He wouldn't have had a chance to show what he could do.

"Fuck." Roland shook his head. "Why didn't you tell me?"

"The idea was to let you take the lead," Rachel said. "And to see what you did with yourself."

Roland snorted. "What now?"

"We go meet the PM, as ordered, and see what he has to say," Rachel said. "You continue with the mission. I remain as your loyal bodyguard, assistant and general dogsbody. Does that answer your question?"

"No," Roland said. "Will you tell me if I fuck up? Again?"

"Yes," Rachel said, flatly. "Everyone fucks up. I've fucked up. The trick is to recover from your fuck ups, before they fuck you. You've done well enough at that, I think."

She opened the car and stepped outside before Roland could come up with an answer, moving with an easy grace that awed him. Roland followed, studying her carefully now he knew what she was hiding. Her ill-tailored uniform seemed designed to hide a paunch, but actually hid her muscles; her unkempt hair gave her a scatterbrained appearance that made it hard to take her seriously. His eyes dropped to her rear, noting how her uniform hinted at one thing while concealing others. He looked away, hurriedly. Belinda hadn't been pleased when he'd ogled her. Rachel would be no different.

He opened his mouth to ask if she knew what had happened to Belinda, then closed it again—without speaking—as they entered the elevator and allowed it to carry them upstairs. She might not know anything, not beyond the basic story he'd already heard. And yet...had they trained together? Served together? Were they friends? Or rivals? Or...or what? He promised himself, silently, that when he got back he'd demand answers from his superiors. If they insisted on treating him differently from the other recruits, they could damn well give him answers to his questions. He owed it to Belinda to find out what had happened to her.

Sandra met them at the door, looking tired and wan. She shot Roland a slight smile—he was morbidly sure she was wearing a mask, too—and then led them into the office. The PM, Lord Ludlow and a man who looked oddly familiar were standing around a table, studying an updated map. Roland frowned, then snapped a salute. The PM smiled back at him, looking as tired as his daughter. It had only been a few short hours since his world had turned upside down.

Good, Roland thought. He knew it was wrong of him, but...*the planetary government needed a solid kick in the backside. At least something good came out of the shitstorm.*

"Captain Windsor," the PM said. He indicated the stranger. "Please allow me to introduce Daniel Collier, MP for First Landing, Secretary of the Town League, and the third member of the Emergency Committee."

Roland nodded, thoughtfully. Richard's father? The man looked like an older version of his son, although his face was a little harder...Richard guessed the man had been worn down by his years of trying to save *something* for the townies. The landowners hadn't so much pummelled him as simply ignored him. Richard wondered, as they shook hands, if being ignored hadn't been worse.

"I've heard good things about you," Collier said. "And about your approach to the problems facing our world."

The PM cleared his throat. "The situation is grim," he said. "The rebels may have been driven off Kingstown, for the moment, but they have seized control of Baraka and a number of other islands. As far as we can determine, they were successful in taking control of the industrial plants as well as the plantations themselves. They have since proclaimed a rival government and announced their intention of uniting the planet under their banner. Their first proclamation was complete and total debt forgiveness, effective immediately."

"As if they could," Lord Ludlow snapped.

"Their power, legal or practical, is not the issue here," Collier pointed out, smoothly. "The point is that thousands upon thousands of debtors will choose to recognise them as the government because the rebels are giving them what they want. Their next proclamation will have an even more drastic effect."

They ended slavery, Roland guessed.

"They have declared a formal end to indenture," the PM said, as if he knew what Roland had been thinking. "Practically, it will be difficult for them to actually enforce it outside their territory, but it will serve as a rallying cry to indents still on our side of the line. There have already been...*incidents*. It will get worse."

"Yes," Roland agreed.

"The government has decided to tackle the issue directly," the PM said. He nodded to Collier. "We have put together a compromise that allows the townies a greater say in political affairs, and greater local autonomy, while maintaining the core of the planetary government. It will not be perfect, but we think it will help calm some of the tensions pervading our society. Furthermore, we will put a moratorium on debt interest and—as before—forgive all debts owed by those who join the army. Again, it will give tensions a chance to calm down while not immediately upending planetary society."

"And spur demands for more and more concessions," Lord Ludlow growled. "What will we give them next?"

Roland kept his thoughts to himself. It wasn't perfect, but it was a start. Who knew? Clear and steady progress towards reform might just be enough to save the planet from itself. And yet…it didn't go fast enough. The rebels lost nothing by proclaiming an end to debt slavery and indenture and gained much. It wouldn't be *their* fault if the planetary government refused to do as it was told.

"You have no choice," Collier said, flatly. "Either you bend in the wind, or you break."

The PM nodded. "It will work," he said. "It must."

He looked at Roland. "And we have a request for you," he said. "Will you take command of the army?"

Roland blinked. "Me?"

"General Falk is missing, believed dead," the PM said. His voice was grim. He'd worked closely with Falk for years. They hadn't found a body, not yet, but that was meaningless. A large number of bodies had simply been dumped in the water, before the rebels had abandoned Kingstown. "The next three officers in line were killed yesterday, when the rebels blew up their HQ. Beyond them…there would be a great deal of political scrabbling over who gets promoted into the empty slots. We'd like to cut the knot by asking you to take command."

Roland forced himself to think. His orders were to train an army and stabilise the planet before it collapsed into chaos. If he took command directly, at their request, he'd be working towards that goal. And yet…he suspected it wasn't *quite* what his superiors had had in mind, when they'd drawn up his orders. They'd certainly hoped the planet could be stabilised on the cheap. New Doncaster simply wasn't that important, in the grand scheme of things. Captain Allen would have had more troops under his command if the planet had been too important to simply abandon. He wanted to look at Rachel, to silently ask for her advice, but he couldn't. It would draw too much attention to her.

"I could do it." Roland was tempted to point out he had very little experience, but most of the officers on the planet had a great deal *less*. And a bunch of them were so incompetent they made normal incompetents look like great generals. "How much authority would I have?"

"Considerable," the PM said. "You would be in charge of running the war."

"But subject to oversight," Lord Ludlow added. "We cannot surrender power to you."

"No," Roland agreed, coolly. He took a moment to choose his next words carefully. "I want the authority to wage war, to order the supplies I need and recruit and promote the soldiers and officers I want, without checking with you all the time. I understand that you'll set the political direction of the war, and decide on our war aims, but beyond that I want complete control. There is no point in trying to run a war if you keep trying to micromanage me."

"You will keep us informed, of course," the PM said. He shot a sharp look at Lord Ludlow, who looked ready to object. "But otherwise, we will allow you near-complete authority."

Roland's eyes narrowed. They'd agreed a little *too* quickly. Either they were desperate, which was possible, or they were up to something. If so, what? His mind raced. He could see their logic in appointing him, avoiding a polarising struggle over selecting and then perhaps replacing a local officer, yet...yet what? Did they want him to win the war for them? Did they think they could steal the credit? Or...or was he simply overthinking the matter? They'd come far too close to defeat. Surely, it should have concentrated a few minds.

"Very well," he said. He'd promote Richard, of course. And a few others.

It would serve as a good test of his authority. "And what *are* our war aims?"

"Complete victory," Lord Ludlow said, harshly. "We want you to win."

Roland considered it for a long, cold moment. There were possibilities...there were *always* possibilities. They'd lost most of their shipping, but not all of it. And they could churn out more. And they already had an edge in tanks and aircraft...yes, it could be done. They could beat the rebels in the field, then bring them to the table. If...*if*...the government was prepared to pay the price.

"We can do it," he said. He hoped, desperately, that he was right. "It will be bloody, and you will have to be prepared to make concessions, but it can be done."

...

END OF BOOK ONE

Roland will return in:
The Prince's Gambit
COMING SOON

AFTERWORD

"When Adam delved and Eve span, Who was then the gentleman? From the beginning all men by nature were created alike, and our bondage or servitude came in by the unjust oppression of naughty men. For if God would have had any bondmen from the beginning, he would have appointed who should be bond, and who free. And therefore I exhort you to consider that now the time is come, appointed to us by God, in which ye may (if ye will) cast off the yoke of bondage, and recover liberty."
—JOHN BALL

SOMEONE—I FORGOT WHO—once complained that science-fiction writers could only imagine monarchies, that numerous stories set in the far future included monarchies that wouldn't have been unrecognisable to our ancestors from the distant past. Their complaint, if I recall correctly, was that there were other possibilities—direct democracy, for example, or actually workable communism—and monarchies were just plain lazy. Leaving aside the simple observation that monarchies tend to make for better stories, even if you wouldn't want to live in those worlds personally, the simple truth is that the human race has been governed by monarchies for thousands of years. Large-scale constitutional democracy is actually, on a historical scale, a fairly new invention. Indeed, monarchy appears so often that one is tempted to wonder if there is something in humanity that adores a monarch.

The historical record seems to suggest that democracies have a short shelf life. The democracy of Athens, which operated on a very limited franchise, was brought low by its own internal quarrels and weaknesses and eventually gave way to outside rule. The Roman Republic effectively suffocated under the weight of its own empire, eventually leading to civil war and the *de facto* creation of a monarchy. Peasant revolts against the European aristocracies often ended with the peasants choosing not to land the killing blow, only to be slaughtered when the aristocrats regained their nerve; the downfalls of King Charles I and Louis XVI were rapidly followed by political chaos, the rise of rulers with monarchical powers (Cromwell, Napoleon) and, eventually, the restoration of the monarchy. Even the modern-day United States has not been immune to this trend. President Bush43 was the son of President Bush41, while Hillary Clinton was the wife of President Clinton42; there are, as of this writing, suggestions that the wives or daughters of Presidents Obama44 and Trump45 will enter politics. If they do, their connections will both help and hinder them.

Monarchy, a system of hereditary rule, is in fact near-universal throughout human history. So are the problems it brings in its wake. A king who remains in power too long will grow set in his ways, unable to change with the times. Strong and capable kings give way to sons who are far less capable and therefore weaken—and sometimes lose—the throne. And, of course, there is not even the pretence of democracy. Kings claimed to be the protectors of their people—smart rulers worked hard to create the illusion all the *bad* stuff was done by evil counsellors, who could be sacrificed if necessary—but the idea of commoners having a say in their own affairs was effectively blasphemy.

Why did this happen?

The first king, it is often said, was a lucky bandit. This isn't entirely true—no one can call Augustus Caesar a bandit—but there is a degree of truth in it. The first kings (however termed) were men who reshaped society to support their primacy, creating a network of supporters who upheld the king's position because to do otherwise would weaken their own position. This pattern was followed by every successful king, but also powerful figures as diverse as Hitler, Stalin and Saddam Hussein. The reshaping gave the aristocrats, however defined, a stake in society; it also carved out a logical and understandable chain of command and line of succession that provided a certain governmental stability. There could not be—in theory—any struggle over the succession, once a king died. His firstborn son would take the throne. In practice, it was often a little more complex. It was not until the institution of monarchy became predominant within Western Europe that the line of succession was clearly laid down and unhappy heirs still posed potential threats to newly crowned monarchs (and usurpers, such as Napoleon, found it hard to gain any real legitimacy.)

This structure went further than you might think. It co-opted religious institutions, merchants and, right at the bottom, commoners, serfs and *de facto* slaves. It was incredibly difficult for them to rise in the world, but there was—again, in theory—certain limits on how badly they could be abused. They knew their place in the world, yet they also knew how far their lords could go. The Poll Tax of 1381 England, for example, was sparked by the government demanding more and more taxes, taxes that were beyond the commonly accepted levels and collected with a previously known fervour. The monarch's representatives had broken the rules, as far as his subjects were concerned, and therefore waging war on them— to teach them a lesson, rather than destroy them—was perfectly legal. Naturally, the aristocracy disagreed.

There were, at least in theory, advantages to this structure. The king was a known figure, a person who could reasonably expect to be on the throne for decades and therefore show a degree of long-term planning; the imperative to sire an heir and a spare was a clear commitment to securing the future of his holdings. The king would have a bird's eye view of the kingdom, as well as experience in administration and warfare, and could therefore make decisions that benefited the entire kingdom. On paper, monarchy may seem to be amongst the better forms of human government.

The problems of monarchical rule, however, are manifold. No human ever born can hope to absorb and process an entire country's worth of information, even when that information reaches the monarch without being altered by his servants. Kings therefore make poor decisions because they don't know what's really going on. Second, kings are often the prisoners of their own throne. A king cannot easily rule against his great lords, the ones who are abusing the commoners, for fear of turning them against him permanently and therefore being deposed when a new challenger arrives. Third, a king's sons are rarely as capable as their father because they haven't struggled and suffered in quite the same way. The great kings of England—Henry II, Edward I, Henry V, James VI and I, Charles II—were often followed by sons and grandsons who lacked their father's insight. Indeed, an heir's failings may become apparent very early on—Henry the Young King, for example—but because of the nature of monarchy it was very difficult to remove them from the line of succession.

And, when they become kings in their own right, they were very hard to remove. Richard II was deposed by his own cousin, Henry VI became a pawn in the original game of thrones, Charles I had his head lopped off after a civil war and James II was replaced by his sister and brother-in-law. The price of monarchy, in short, is periods of instability caused by kings who were not up to the task or lacked a power base of their own (Mary of Scotland) and ambitious aristocrats manoeuvring for power.

At its core, the problem of monarchy is that it puts the primacy of the monarch and his aristocrats ahead of the interests of the entire kingdom. The king practices—he *must*—a form of nepotism. He *must* put forward men who are loyal to him personally, rather than the kingdom itself; he *must* use his sons and daughters as pawns on the diplomatic chess board, rather than let them marry for love (or bring new blood into the monarchy). He must raise his sons to take his place, all too aware that refusing to grant them real power will lead to resentment, hatred and (perhaps) civil war when—if—the heir's courtiers start pushing him to grant favours he simply doesn't have the wealth or power to give. The kingdom therefore becomes a collection of scorpions in a bottle, the monarchy unwilling to make any compromises for fear of where they will lead, let alone allow people to question his power, and the aristocracy unwilling to put aside its prerogatives for the greater good. This is a recipe for chaos and revolution. And revolution can often lead to a tyranny worse than the now-gone monarchy.

...

Why, then, are monarchies so popular?

There's one argument that suggests the myth—and yes, it is a myth—of the 'Father Tsar' is actually quite appealing, that one can find comfort in it as one might find comfort in spiritualism and religion. There's another that suggests a person bred and trained for power will do a better job than someone elected to their position, although both the historical record and simple common sense suggests otherwise. And there's a third that says we look at the fancy outfits and romantic lives and don't recognise the downsides. And there's a fourth that hints we all want to surrender our autonomy, to unite behind a single divinely anointed leader and follow him wherever he leads, rather than questioning him too closely for fear of what we might find. Personality cults are growing increasingly common these days and those who ask if the emperor has no clothes often come to regret it.

Personally, I think the blunt truth is that very few of us have any real idea of what it is like to live under an absolute monarchy. The few remaining Western monarchies are jokes, compared to their predecessors. It is easy to watch *Bridgerton* and debate whether or not Daphne raped Simon; it is harder to understand why a real-life Daphne might feel driven to such an action, or the consequences if she'd taken any other course. The fancy costumes we love hide a grim reality, one better left in the past. As the joke goes....

"My girlfriend wanted me to treat her like a princess. So I married her off to a man old enough to be her father, a man she'd never met, to secure an alliance with France."

There is a temptation in monarchy. There is an entirely understandable sense that uniting behind a single man is best, particularly if that man has divine right, and if you do that man will fight for you. But no one can be trusted with such power. They would, eventually, be corrupted or be replaced by those who became corrupted themselves. Those people do not fight for you. They fight for themselves.

And now you've read this far, I have a request to make.

It's growing harder to make a living through self-published writing these days. If you liked this book, please leave a review where you found it, share the link, let your friends know (etc., etc.). Every little bit helps (particularly reviews).

Thank you.
Christopher G. Nuttall
Edinburgh, 2021

APPENDIX

NEW DONCASTER

DESPITE BEING RELATIVELY NEAR TO THE CORE WORLDS, New Doncaster was only settled roughly 500 years prior to Earthfall. The system itself was regarded as a prize, and settlement rights were claimed by an exploratory consortium—the New Doncaster Development Corporation—but settlement itself was slow. When it did, it rapidly took on a deeply poisonous form that threatened the future of the entire planet.

New Doncaster is extremely unusual amongst Earth-type worlds in that only a relatively small percentage of its surface area is suitable for settlement. The planet orbits its star far too close for comfort, ensuring tropical weather and weekly thunderstorms within even the habitable zone. The atmosphere is rough, even when relatively tranquil; high-altitude energy distortions and near-permanent hurricanes make it impossible to settle permanently outside the habitable zone and very few people choose to leave even for short periods. The weather is dangerously unpredictable, severely limiting the amount of aircraft and shuttles that can be operated within the atmosphere. The terrain is arguably worse. The star's gravitational pull—and that of two moons—has ensured that, even within the habitable zone, the landscape is comprised of islands rather than continents. The largest landmass on New Doncaster is roughly the size of Cuba. Many are much smaller.

This has given birth to an unusual ecosystem that is the planet's core attraction. New Doncaster is one of the few worlds where plants and animals from Earth co-exist with the native ecosystem without displacing it. The islands can and do host terrestrial food crops—the native flora is highly poisonous—and attempts to introduce fish and wild game into the environment were successful, but the majority of islands have preserved, intentionally or not, a considerable amount of the original ecosystem. This deterred settlers for quite some time, as clearing the land for settlement was a difficult job. It was not until the local biosphere turned out to be a valuable source of off-world income that the New Doncaster Development Corporation was able to obtain the investment it needed to swing into high gear and begin a large-scale settlement program. However, owning to other political issues, it rapidly became clear that the NDDC was storing up problems for the future.

It was unfortunately true that the vast majority of people who were willing to invest- and even move to the planet as its newborn aristocracy—were unwilling to do the hard work of clearing the islands, establishing and maintaining plantations and, eventually, turning the world into a power base for future expansion. The NDDC was forced to resort to buying up debt, in order to force the debtors to work on New Doncaster for a pittance, and then to start effectively purchasing indents from Earth's penal system. While this was not uncommon on Earth—the homeworld was so overpopulated that deportation was the penalty for just about everything from jaywalking to rape and murder—the vast majority of colony worlds were unwilling to accept more than a handful of indentured workers (indents). New Doncaster took all it could get, trying to select for males who could work in the field and females who could support them and bear their children, who would grow up to take their own place in the system. This was, of course, a flagrant breach of imperial law—it was *de facto* slavery—but the NDDC used a complicated system of legal trickery to ensure any investigators were forced to conclude it didn't *quite* cross the line. The handful of indents who complained were sent to mining camps, brothels or simply executed.

Officially, New Doncaster—generally shortened to Doncaster—is a representative democracy, with a parliament composed of elected MPs. Practically, voting rights are highly restricted and based largely—almost completely—on land ownership. The original investors—the Landowners—own roughly 70% of the planet's land surface (as well as the moons, asteroid belts and gas giants) and generally run the planet to suit themselves. They have endless privileges, written into the constitution by the first legal settlers; the majority of government jobs are reserved for them. Naturally, the parliament is little more than a rubber stamp. Decisions are taken in private, by the dominant landowners, and then effortlessly passed through parliament. The handful of MPs from townie factions are unable to do anything about it.

This is bitterly resented by two of the other factions: the townies (who form a growing business/middle class) and the debtors/indents (who are effectively serfs, working to pay off impossible debts). The economic slowdown that came with Earthfall has hit the planet hard, ensuring that the debts are even more unserviceable. The townies want more say in planetary affairs—in effect, an end to the landholding scheme—and are prepared to agitate to get it; the debtors want an end to debt and a more fair sharing of planetary resources. The more perceptive landowners realise that they'll have to make some concessions, sooner or later, but they're blocked by their fellows, who feel that any concessions will come back to bite them.

The remaining two factions—the sailors and the spacers—try to have as little to do with the other factions as possible. However, that may not be able to endure indefinitely.

There is a surprising amount of ethnic diversity amongst the population, but the planet is resolutely monocultural. The price of settlement—as a townie or a debtor—was abandoning one's former culture, if it was believed to be incompatible. Racism is thankfully rare—classism is considerably more prevalent—and it isn't unknown for a particularly competent debtor or townie to climb the ladders. However, this is uncommon. There are very few slots for newcomers, no matter how talented they may be.

The planet's military is more of a glorified police force. The landowners disliked the idea of a standing army—particularly one drawn largely from the lower classes—and kept it as low as possible. They preferred the idea of a volunteer force drawn from the higher classes, who were the only ones allowed to bear arms. Accordingly, the army consists of little more than 5000 infantry, with a handful of supporting aircraft and boats, backed up by volunteer militia. Logistics are minimal. Training is very much a mixed bag, as officers are almost exclusively drawn from the landowners. Some are strikingly competent; some are practically useless.

The planet is orbited by a small halo of asteroid settlements and industrial nodes, with varying levels of ties to the planetary government. Some are owned directly by the landowners; some owe formal fealty to the government but pay as little attention to it as possible. Smuggling is big business. Doncaster's government will never admit it, but the planet sells a considerable amount of advanced technology on the black market. There is a formal planetary defence network, but no one is really sure how capable it is. The handful of outdated gunboats patrolling the system are completely inadequate.

Outside the high orbitals, there are small settlements on the rocky worlds, cloudscoops orbiting the gas giants (both owned by the landowners) and an ever-increasing union of settled asteroids (some independent).

The planet's major exports are food, rare chemicals (harvested from the plantations) and a small—but growing—trade in advanced technology and starship components.

Unsurprisingly, Doncaster has been heading steadily towards disaster. Earthfall has ensured that the planetary government can no longer call on the Imperial Navy for help. Worse, the steady economic collapse across the sector has brought pirates, (more) smugglers and independence activists to Doncaster. The Secessionist League, in particular, has been trying to supply the debtors—and some of the townies—with advanced weapons, hoping the rebels can take the planetary surface and industrial nodes. The government has reacted poorly, as it remains unwilling to make any substantial concessions to either the townies or the debtors. Instead, it has tried to crack down—unsuccessfully—on subversion. Its heavy-handed tactics have only made things worse, ensuring more resentment and more recruits for the rebel factions.

It is only a matter of time until the planet explodes.

HOW TO FOLLOW

Basic Mailing List—http://orion.crucis.net/mailman/listinfo/chrishanger-list
Nothing, but announcements of new books.

Newsletter—https://gmail.us1.list-manage.com/subscribe?u=c8f9f7391e5bfa369a9b1e76c&id=55fc83a213
New books releases, new audio releases, maybe a handful of other things of interest.

Blog—https://chrishanger.wordpress.com/
Everything from new books to reviews, commentary on things that interest me, etc.

Facebook Fan Page—https://www.facebook.com/ChristopherGNuttall
New books releases, new audio releases, maybe a handful of other things of interest.

Website—http://chrishanger.net/
New books releases, new audio releases, free samples (plus some older books free to anyone who wants a quick read)

Forums—https://authornuttall.com
Book discussions—new, but I hope to expand.

Amazon Author Page—https://www.amazon.com/Christopher-G-Nuttall/e/B008L9Q4ES
My books on Amazon.

Books2Read—https://books2read.com/author/christopher-g-nuttall/subscribe/19723/
Notifications of new books (normally on Amazon too, but not included in B2R notifications.

Twitter—@chrisgnuttall
New books releases, new audio releases—definitely nothing beyond (no politics or culture war stuff).

Printed in Great Britain
by Amazon